The Magic Flute

Alan Spence

BLACK SWAN

THE MAGIC FLUTE
A BLACK SWAN BOOK 0 552 99456 1

Originally published in Great Britain by Canongate Publishing Ltd

PRINTING HISTORY
Canongate edition published 1990
Black Swan edition published 1991

This book is set in 11/12pt Melior by
County Typesetters, Margate, Kent

Black Swan Books are published by Transworld Publishers Ltd.,
61–63 Uxbridge Road, Ealing, London W5 5SA, in Australia
by Transworld Publishers (Australia) Pty. Ltd., 15–23 Helles
Avenue, Moorebank, NSW 2170, and in New Zealand by
Transworld Publishers (N.Z.) Ltd., Cnr. Moselle and
Waipareira Avenues, Henderson, Auckland.

Made and printed in Great Britain by
Cox & Wyman Ltd., Reading, Berks.

Alan Spence was born in Glasgow in 1947. He lives in Edinburgh where he and his wife run the Sri Chinmoy Meditation Centre. His published work includes a collection of short stories – *Its Colours They Are Fine*, two books of poetry – *Ah!* and *Glasgow Zen*, and three playscripts – *Sailmaker, Space Invaders* and *Changed Days*. He has also written for television and radio. He has been Writer-in-Residence at the Universities of Glasgow and Edinburgh, and has held similar posts at the Traverse Theatre and with Edinburgh District Council. *Its Colours They Are Fine*, published by Corgi Books, is regarded as a classic, and Allan Massie has hailed it as 'the finest piece of Scottish fiction of the Seventies' (*Independent*). *The Magic Flute* is his first novel. It was published in 1990 to wide critical acclaim, and won a Scottish Arts Council Book Award.

Author photograph by Graham Clark

Also by Alan Spence

ITS COLOURS THEY ARE FINE

and published by Corgi Books

TO
C.K.G.

Contents

The Old Orange Flute

1

Through the noise of passing traffic, there could just be heard the high shrill note of a flute, the staccato batter of a snaredrum. The sounds came from the school, the Catholic primary for the area. The two-storey building sat, squat, between a dark factory on one side, closed down for the night, and a row of tenements on the other. Its ground-floor windows were patches of bright light, shining out on the empty playground.

Four boys, nudging and shoving, came in at the gate, crossed to the main door and pushed it open. Inside, the janitor showed them into a classroom and told them to wait. The Bandmaster would be in to see them. Shortly. When the door was closed behind them, the boys looked about, and at each other, sniffed and laughed and grinned reassurance.

It was Tam that had first heard about the Band, from a friend of his father's. Tam had told Brian, who had told Eddie and George. That was a month ago, and now they were all here, waiting.

'Funny, intit,' said Tam.

'Weird,' said Brian.

'Imagine it being a Catholic school but!' said Eddie.

George said nothing, but sat down at one of the small desks.

They all felt the strangeness of being there; the emptiness of the place, the school at night, the alien trappings, Catholic images on the classroom walls. And strangest of all was to see those images – the crucifix, the Sacred Heart, a plaster Madonna on the windowledge – and hear at the same time from faraway rooms the flutes playing fragments of Orange songs, the tripping military rhythm of the drums. Christ on the cross. No Surrender. The Virgin Mary. The Protestant Boys.

Brian felt a kind of awe towards the pictures and statues, especially the figure of Our Lady. He looked at it with something like reverence, caught by the simple grace, the painted face and hair, the plaster folds of the blue robes.

Tam stood at the window, looking out across the playground.

George lifted the lid of the desk and peered inside.

Eddie padded about the room, restless, whistled bits of the songs he could hear. He picked up the Madonna, sneering at it. 'She must be a Rangers supporter on the fly,' he said. 'She's wearing the right colour!' He tipped the statue upside down, and, digging out a stub of pencil from his pocket, wrote RANGERS on the chalky base. Then he put it back in its place, but turned it away to face the wall.

From the innards of the desk, George fished out the shrivelled brown stump of a rotting apple core. He sniffed at it, screwing up his face in distaste, and threw it back in. From the underside of the desk-lid he picked off a pink clot of bubble-gum that had hardened, stuck there. He sniffed at this too, then threw it across at the bin in the corner, pleased at the noise it made as it hit the tin rim.

Behind Eddie's back, Brian turned the Madonna the right way round, facing out.

'Wish the guy would hurry up,' said Eddie, kicking at George's desk.

The classroom door opened and in came the Bandmaster, a big man, middleaged, in a dark suit and tie.

'Right boys!' he said, and they turned, attentive, feeling as if they'd been caught.

'So yis want to learn the flute, eh?' He took the teacher's chair from behind its desk, turned it round and straddled it, the way detectives did in films, leaning his elbows on the backrest. 'Well, yis could do a lot worse.'

And carefully, with just the suggestion of a flourish, he took from his inside pocket the separate sections of a short wooden flute, piecing it together as he spoke.

'So what's your names then?'

'Eddie Logan.'

'George Wilson sir.'

'Brian Ritchie.'

'Tam Rae.'

'Eddie / George / Brian / Tam. Fine. And you're all, what, twelve?'

'That's right,' said Tam.

'All born in 1950 then?'

They nodded.

'Always was good at arithmetic. Not just a pretty face!'

None of them laughed.

'So, yous are what they call the Baby Boom,' he said. 'God help us!'

They were beginning to feel uncomfortable.

'Anyway,' said the man. 'I'm Mr Bennett.' He held up the flute.

'Great wee instrument,' he said, and he blew one soft sustained note. 'See music. It's magic. I'm telling you boys, this is a great opportunity yis are getting. A wee bit work and you'd be amazed at what you can play on this.'

He raised the flute to his lips and played a slow Irish air.

'Anybody know that?' he said, when he'd finished.

'Lark in the Clear Air,' said Brian.

'Good!' said the Bandmaster. 'Thank God they still teach you something! Here, do any of you play an instrument?'

'I know a couple of tunes on my da's moothie,' said Eddie. 'The Sash and that.'

'Well,' said the man. 'That's better than nothing, eh? Better than a poke in the eye wi a sharp stick!'

He wiped the drops of spittle from the mouthpiece

11

and began to play again, this time a jig. On his right hand he wore a Mason's ring that glinted as his fingers moved, fingers that were stubby and brown with nicotine. But the fingers danced, had a grace, in the playing. The touch was light and sure, a ripple and flurry of notes, so quick, but each note separate, sharp and clear. Without stopping, he changed the tempo again, moved, easy, into *The Cry Was No Surrender*.

And this was it, what they wanted to hear, what they had come to learn. It was theirs, the music they knew. They felt it deep and familiar, sung in their guts. The Cry. The master was playing on *them*. They moved to the rhythm, the rap of fingers on wooden desks. Eddie stamped and pranced, jabbed his fists in the air, brandished an imaginary banner. The bandmaster rounded off the song with a high flying trill, and he laughed.

'Thought that would get you going!' He held out the flute, ceremoniously, towards them. 'Who wants to try it then?'

They crowded forward and Eddie made a grab at it.

'Me sir!'

'Me!'

'Me!'

The man drew the flute back, held it out of reach above his head.

'Wait a minute!' he said, pushing them back with just the tone of his voice. 'Just hold your horses, right?' He looked at Eddie. 'You. You're making plenty noise. See if you can get a noise out of this.'

He showed Eddie how to hold the flute. 'Never mind the fingers. Just try and get a note. Same way you blow across the neck of a bottle.'

Eddie blew into the hole, made a dry breathy sound. He blew harder, but only made a louder harsher noise.

'Not down into it,' said the Bandmaster. 'More *across* it.'

Eddie tried again, getting impatient, spitting spray.

'Take it easy,' said the man. 'Here, let somebody else try it.'

Eddie shoved the flute into George's hands.

'I said *easy* son!' There was a sharpness in his tone. 'It's not just a dod of wood! Right you are, George. See what you can do.'

George was suddenly awkward. He raised the flute and blew only a shaky whisper.

'Tighter,' said the man. 'Your lip's too slack. Has to be just right. Here, I'll show you.'

He took the flute and blew one note.

'See the position of the mouth. It's like a wee half smile. The fancy name for it's *embouchure*.' He handed the flute back to George. 'So, if I tell you to tighten your embouchure, that means less of your lip!'

George blew again, harder, still made no sound but the shoosh of his breath.

'That's a bit better anyway,' said the man. 'Least it's got a bit more body to it. Let Tam have a go.'

Tam blew more softly, made a sound that was fuller, but still not a note.

'Keep going,' said the man.

Tam blew again and it almost came, a faint sharp whistle in a rush of air.

'We're getting there,' said the man. 'Pity is we've only the one flute. You'll just have to take turns each. Give Brian a shot now.'

Brian made the same sound as Tam.

'Good,' said the man. 'Softer now.'

Brian tried to shape his mouth. Just the way. Getting the embouchure right. A wee half smile. He breathed deep and blew across the mouthpiece, slow and even. At first there was nothing. Then it came, clear.

'That's it!' said the Bandmaster. 'Again!'

He blew once more and the sound had a resonance. A full round note.

'Perfect!' said the Bandmaster.

'Magic!' said Brian, grinning.

The idea was that they could borrow the flute, take it in

13

turn, a week at a time. It was given first to Brian, and he hurried through the grey streets with it clutched tight, wrapped in brown paper.

Home, he placed it on the kitchen table, unwrapped it, careful and reverent, pieced it together and blew his one note.

'That's great!' said his father. 'It's terrific that they let you bring it home.'

'It's because I was the best at blowing it,' he said, proud.

'There you are,' said his father. 'What did I tell you hen! Natural talent. Takes after his father!'

Brian's mother said nothing, clattered dishes into the sink. He could tell she was annoyed. The way she turned the tap to gush water into the kettle. The way she banged it down on the gas.

'What can you play then?' asked his father.

'He showed me the fingering for four notes,' said Brian. 'G, A, B and C.'

'Let us hear them well.'

He covered the holes with the fingers of his left hand, raising them one at a time as he blew.

G A B C

'Great!' said his father.

C B A G

'Brilliant!'

G A B C B A G

'I've had enough of this!' said his mother, turning. 'I'm sorry, Brian, you'll just have to take the flute back. I'm not having you playing in that band.'

'Aw come on!' said his father. 'We've been through all this already. It's a chance for the boy to learn an instrument.'

'A chance for him to be in that stupid Orange band,' she said. 'And march in that stupid parade wi all these headcases.'

'Playing in a band's the greatest,' said his father. 'When I was in the Sally Army I used to love it.'

He had played the trumpet as a boy, in the Salvation

14

Army band. Brian had heard the story before, but it didn't matter.

'Course it was all bare feet in those days. As if it wasnae bad enough playing the tune and keeping in step, you had to watch your feet on the horses' keech in the road!'

'Salvation Army's one thing,' said his mother. 'Orange Walk's another.'

'There was nothing to beat it,' said his father. 'I was really sorry I had to give it up.'

Brian played his four notes.

G A B C.

'It was the Bandmaster,' went on his father. 'Torn-faced auld bugger. See me and some of the boys had a wee jazz band. Nothing fancy. A banjo and a couple of mouthorgans. Washboards and spoons and that. And me wi the trumpet.'

C B A G.

'Anyway, we were practising up in my house. A wee jam session. Bye Bye Blackbird it was. I remember it well. We were wiring right into it. Giving it big licks. And suddenly there's a knock at the door, and there's the Bandmaster standing, face like grim death. He comes in and starts ranting and raving. The music of Satan he called it. Said I was a disgrace to my uniform. You know, General Booth, him that founded the Sally Army, he said why should the devil have all the best tunes! But auld sourface stopped short at Bye Bye Blackbird. So that was it. He took the trumpet off me. Made me clean it up and put it in its case, then he took it away. I chucked it after that. Left the Army. Never went back.'

G A B C B A G.

'All this is beside the point,' said Brian's mother.

'Och but . . .'

'As far as I'm concerned there's no more arguing. It's finished.'

The music of Satan. Pack up all my care and woe. Here I go.

15

'Finished.'

The kettle came to the boil, its whistle rising to a shrill insistent pitch.

George's father seemed disappointed.

'How come you didn't get to bring the flute home?'

'They only had the one for practising,' he said. 'Brian was the best. So he got first shot.'

'You would think they'd have more than one,' said his mother.

'And the teacher was definitely Mr Bennett?'

'Aye.'

'He's in our Lodge. I'll have a word with him. See what I can do.'

He wore a tie-pin with the same Masonic emblem as the Bandmaster's ring, the crossed compasses and square.

George's older brother Malcolm muffled a laugh. 'It's amazing what a wee handshake can do!' He was in his last year at school, would soon be moving on to University.

'Don't you be so cheeky!' said his mother.

'Cynical,' said his father. 'Cynical.'

'Yes folks, it's the kitchen cynic!' said Malcolm. 'How about this one? Wee guy goes up to this factory. *Got a job?* he says.' Malcolm crossed himself as he asked the question. Then he rolled up his left trouser-leg and made as if playing a flute. '*Naw!* says the boss.'

'Oh very funny,' said his father. 'Very funny.'

'Just roll up your breeks and I'll follow you any-where!' said Malcolm.

'That's enough,' said his father. 'Don't you listen to him George. He's just ignorant. Oh, he might be clever, but he's ignorant.'

Malcolm was on his way out of the room. 'Runs in the family then!' he called back.

His father shook his head. 'He just doesn't under-stand. Anyway. I'll see what I can do about getting you the flute next week. Learning music's a great opportunity son. I mean, who knows what doors it might open up, later on. Oh aye. A great thing music.'

Tam asked his mother what the chances were of getting a flute for his birthday.

'Oh I don't know,' she said. 'You'll have to ask your father.'

'He'll just say they're awful dear,' said Tam, but he asked his father anyway.

'They're awful dear,' he said.

'But Moira got a recordplayer,' said Tam. Moira was his older sister.

'That was secondhand.'

'You could get a secondhand flute well,' said Tam.

'You wouldn't know where it had been,' said his mother. 'Whose mouth it had been in.'

'You didn't know where the recordplayer had been either.'

'Frankie's pawnshop,' said his father. 'Anyway, it's not the same. You don't put a recordplayer in your mouth!'

'You don't put a flute in your mouth either,' said Tam. 'You blow across it. Just touches your bottom lip.'

His father laughed. 'You're keen then!'

'Oh aye. It's great. A wee bit more practice and I would've got it.'

'I had a mate learned the flute,' said his father. 'Same sort of thing. Learned it in one of these bands. Then when he was a bit older he got a bigger flute, you know the concert ones. Then later on he got a saxophone. Had to practise in the cupboard, it was that loud! But he wound up in a dance band. Used to get jobs on these cruises. Travelled all over the world.'

Just a note of longing in his voice. Cruises. The world.

'Can I get a wee flute then?'

'We'll see,' said his father. 'No promises mind. Depends on the money.'

17

No promises, but it was hope, was enough.

'Can I finish that ginger?' he said, pointing at a cola bottle, almost empty, on the sideboard.

'Just enough to wet your whistle,' said his father. 'Sure. Go ahead.'

Tam drained it, sucked the dregs, and took the bottle through to his room. It was only a boxroom between the kitchen, where his parents slept, and Moira's room at the back. But it was his own space. Through the walls he could hear his mother and father talking, Moira singing along with Elvis Presley's *Wooden Heart*, scratched and tinny on her secondhand birthday recordplayer.

Squatted on the bed, he unscrewed the cap from the bottle and blew across the neck, one deep note.

Eddie's big brother Davie opened the door to him, grabbed him by the lapels and hauled him into the lobby.

'Any fags on you?'

'Leave us you!' said Eddie, struggling clear. But Davie was stronger, grabbed him in a bear-hug, jammed him against the wall and rifled his jacket pockets; found a penknife, a beermat, a bit of chalk, a book of matches, and at last what he was looking for, a Woodbine fivepack; flicked it open, counted two whole cigarettes and a half-smoked stub. He shoved open the door into the kitchen, held out the packet to his mother.

'Told you he'd have some,' he said. 'Two fags and a dout.'

'Thank Christ,' she said. 'I'm gasping.'

Eddie slunk in, still raging, blinking in the sudden light, harsh after the dark of the lobby.

'Shouldnae be smoking at your age anyway!' said Davie.

His mother lit up, took a deep drag, coughed and relaxed. She passed the packet back to Davie. 'Take the other one,' she said. 'And let him keep the dout.'

'Right enough,' said Davie, taking out the other

cigarette and tossing the packet back at Eddie. 'Who wants to smoke it if it's been in *his* mouth!'

Eddie sat, sullen, stared at the TV in the corner. On the screen, a talking head, ignored, was mouthing away, the voice an electronic drone. *Houses and Jobs* said the head. *Building for the Future.*

'Where have ye been anyway?' asked his mother.

'Oot,' said Eddie. 'Where's my Da?'

'Oot,' said his mother, just as curt back. She smoked only half of the cigarette, nipped it and kept half for later. Just in case.

But it wasn't long till they heard the heavy footstep on the stairs, heard the key fumble in the lock. Eddie's father stood, swayed a bit in the doorway, peered at them, grinning.

'What a miserable-looking bunch!' he said.

'It's all right for you,' said his wife. 'Oot gallivanting. I've been stuck here and no even a bloody fag in the hoose.'

'Just say the word,' he said, digging into his coat pocket and handing her a packet of twenty Regal, unopened. 'Got a wee snifter as well.' He brought out a half-bottle of whisky.

'Did you screw a bank or something?' she asked, pouring herself a cupful.

'Knocked it off at the bookies,' he said. 'Three doubles, a treble, an accumulator.' He punched the air. 'Ya beauty!'

His eyes focused on Davie and he made as if to square up to him, jabbing, mock-sparring. 'Youse boys been sitting here all night as well? When I was your age I was never in.'

'Havenae changed much, have ye?' said his wife.

He dropped his guard, about to spit back a reply, but Davie took advantage, hit him with a left to the guts. Winded, he swiped at Davie's head, but missed as the boy ducked and bobbed away.

'Sleekit wee bastard!' he said, and eased himself down into his chair.

'I was oot the night,' said Eddie.

'Where?'

'Band practice. Learning the flute.'

'That's the stuff.'

'Don't really fancy it but. I only got a wee shot.'

'Canny expect it all to come at once.'

'Think I might try the drums next week. Should be better.'

'Where's my moothie?' said his father. 'Get my moothie and I'll give ye a tune.'

'Christ!' said Davie.

'What's that?'

'Nothing!'

Eddie rummaged in the sideboard drawer, raked aside old buttons and bobbins and hanks of wool, playing cards and boxes of pills, snapshots, envelopes, broken pencils. And right at the back of the drawer, in a fankle of unravelled string, he found the mouthorgan in its bashed cardboard box. His father took the instrument, breathed on its shiny metal and gave it a quick wipe on his sleeve to polish it. Peering at it, he saw for a moment his own bleary eyes, reflected.

'What's that pish on the telly?' he asked, becoming aware of the droning voice, the talking head.

'Party political broadcast,' said Davie.

'Who for?'

'Don't know.'

'What's on the other side?'

'Same thing.'

'Put it off well.'

'There's a murder picture coming on,' said his wife.

'Murder polis,' he said. 'Somebody should murder that lot. Never had it so good, eh? Never mind. I'll give you a tune till the picture starts.'

He played *The Sash My Father Wore* and *The Black Hills of Dakota, I Love To Go A-Wandering* and *Que Sera Sera*.

'Doris Day sung that,' he said to Eddie. And he started to sing it, his voice crooning and flat.

'When I was just a little boy
I asked my mother, what will I be?
Will I be handsome? Will I be rich?
Here's what she said to me . . .'

'Give us a break,' said his wife. 'The picture's starting.'

'Que sera sera
Whatever will be will be
The future's not ours to see
Que sera sera.'

'I used to think your mother looked like Doris Day,' he said, still talking to Eddie. 'The blonde hair and that.'

His wife leaned forward and turned up the volume on the TV. Murder music blared over a hazy dockland backdrop.

'I canny be bothered watching this,' he said. 'I'm away to my bed.' He picked up the half-bottle.

'Suit yourself,' said his wife.

He banged the door behind him, started singing again, through in the other room. Whatever will be will be.

Eddie picked up the mouthorgan, blew into it.

'Don't *you* start!' said his mother.

He polished the instrument on his sleeve, the way his father had done. It glinted, and he turned it, catching the light and reflecting it onto the far wall. He guided the faint patch of light, wobbled it up the wall till it faded and disappeared.

He held the mouthorgan up to his eye, saw the room reflected, his mother and brother at the television. He put it back in its box and settled to watch the film.

2

Only Tam and George went back to the flute class the next week. Brian had given the instrument to Tam, with a note for the Bandmaster to say sorry, he wouldn't be back. Eddie had decided to take up the drums.

Tam and George struggled again with the lip and the blowing and getting it just right. By the end of the session they could both play a note and had the fingering for half a scale. Tam had the knack now. The note he blew was sweet. But George's father had spoken to the Bandmaster, and George it was who took the flute home. Tam was annoyed at that, but he knew his turn would come.

Eddie, in another room, learned the basics of drumming – how to hold the sticks, two beats with the left hand, *mammy*, two with the right, *daddy*, alternate, *mammy/daddy*, faster and faster, blurring towards a roll, *mammydaddymammydaddy*.

That was where it broke down, for his left hand wasn't quick enough, stuttered and lost the beat. That made him rage, and he felt like battering, breaking the sticks. But the drum tutor told him he had potential, could be good, if he worked at it.

The three boys met up again on their way home.

'Rangers are playing away on Saturday,' said Eddie. 'Fancy going to the Barras? Or Paddy's Market?'

'Sounds good,' said Tam.

'Suppose so,' said George.

'You after something special?' said Tam.

'Pair of drumsticks,' said Eddie. 'On the cheap.'

'Barras is better than Paddy's,' said Tam. 'More stuff.'

'You're right,' said Eddie. 'You never know, you might even get an auld flute for ten bob or something.'

'Never know!' said Tam.

Saturday at the Barrows, the place was crammed, the markets, the passageways, the streets, packed tight with people. Brian had come along and the four of them elbowed and shoved their way through the crowds. It was a whole other world, had scents and smells of its own – women's perfumes, heady and sweet,

22

smoke and chipfat and hamburgers frying. The Top 20 blared and crackled through loudspeakers and through tinny transistors, going cheap. And over it all came the singsong litany of the marketeers, the chancers, the patter merchants, their wares laid out, enticing, in the open backs of vans, caves filled to brimming with bright treasure.

And I'm not asking two pound.

I'm not even asking thirty bob.

Not even twenty-five bob.

To you darling, a quid.

A lousy nicker (!).

I'm giving it away.

Cutting my own throat.

Three quid along in Argyle Street.

I kid you not.

Yes darling?

Sold!

The boys sniggered at a turbaned swami selling little green bottles of snake oil, a miracle potion, guaranteed to cure all ills.

'Swami Bammy!' said Eddie.

Tam sang through his nose. 'He's a hindoo howdoo hoodoo yoodoo man!'

The swami brandished a bottle of snake oil at them, fixed them with the evil eye. But they just laughed at him as they moved away.

On a patch of wasteground they gawped at a midget, bending iron bars round his chest. He gathered a crowd, but most of them moved on when he passed round the hat.

The boys kept their money for bags of chips, for Danny's Delicious Doughnuts, deepfried in oil, wiped in sugar and gobbled down still hot.

They were looking too for the great find, the incredible bargain – the cheap pair of drumsticks or the flute-for-ten-bob.

But they found nothing, no drumsticks at all and only a solitary flute, that was going for four pounds.

'No worth that,' said Eddie. 'Looks pretty scabby to me.'

Scabby or not, Tam couldn't afford it, and, disappointed, he put it back among the other junk on the stall – an accordion, a television, a few old pairs of spectacles, a fiddle with no strings.

'Don't handle the merchandise,' said the man behind the stall. 'Unless you're gonnae buy.'

'Away ye go!' said Eddie. 'Your stuff's no worth tuppence!'

'You'll no be worth tuppence if I get my hands on ye!' said the man.

Further along was a stall that sold secondhand records on one side and comics on the other, and the boys crowded round it, jostled for space.

The afternoon was passing. They would have to buy soon or the day would be empty. Home on the subway with nothing.

George and Brian went for the comics, Tam and Eddie for the boxes of records.

'Didnae know you had a recordplayer,' said Eddie.

'I can use Moira's, if she's in a good mood,' said Tam.

'Looking for anything special?'

'Shadows,' said Tam. 'They're brilliant.'

'Here's *Frightened City*,' said Eddie, passing it to him.

'I've got *Wonderful Land* here as well,' said Tam.

'*Frightened City*'s better,' said Eddie. '*Wonderful Land*'s sort of slushy.'

'I like it,' said Tam.

'Suit yourself.'

Tam turned his attention to the LPs, found one called *Mozart's Greatest Hits*.

'What ye looking at that for?' asked Eddie.

'Sometimes this sort of stuff's great. My da bought some when Moira got the recordplayer. Dead cheap as well. Ten bob and that. He got *Tchaikovsky's Greatest*

Hits, and *Ravel's Bolero*. You'd like that. It's got terrific drumming.'

'Lot of pish,' said Eddie.

Tam read the list of tracks on the sleeve of the record.

'It's got a couple of tracks from *The Magic Flute*,' he said, and he was decided. He didn't know the music, but it had flutes in it, and that was enough. He put the Shadows back in the box and bought the LP. The picture on the cover showed a clearing in a green forest and what looked like the entrance to a temple.

'I don't know!' said Eddie.

Brian had found a bundle of *Classics Illustrated*, had bought *Ivanhoe, Kidnapped, The Black Tulip* and *Oliver Twist*.

'You're as bad as Tam,' said Eddie. 'Him wi his classical records and you wi yer classical comics. Right pair of snobs.'

George had bought American imports – *Superman* and *Green Lantern, GI Combat* and *Sergeant Rock*.

'That's better,' said Eddie. 'I'll get some as well and we can swap.'

'I'm no swapping but,' said George.

'How no?'

'I like to save them up,' said George. 'Keep them good.'

'Keep them nice and new looking,' said Eddie, scornful. 'Nice and glossy and mind you don't get a mark on them!'

He looked at the three of them. 'What a fuckin bunch!' And he shoved past them into the crowd.

The others looked at each other, shrugged and went after him.

'What's up wi him?' said Brian.

'Just in a bad mood,' said Tam. 'Maybe cause he hasnae bought anything.'

Eddie had a good start, and by the time they caught up with him, he was along at Trongate, looking in a shop window.

'Look at this!' he said, turning to them, brighter again.

The window was cluttered with musical instruments – flutes and drums, guitars, trumpets, saxophones.

'Could go in and look at their flutes.'

The doorbell tinkled as they went in, and the old man behind the counter looked them up and down, suspicious.

'Yes, *boys*?'

'Ask him!' said Eddie, shoving Tam forward.

'Can I see your flutes mister?' said Tam.

'Are you buying one?' asked the man.

'My da's getting me one for my birthday,' said Tam. 'And I just wanted a wee look.'

'Well. You come back wi your father and I'll let you see the whole range.'

'Aw mister . . .'

'I'm not about to try to serve you *and* keep an eye on your friends here.'

'Och!'

'And will you leave those instruments *alone*!'

George plunked a banjo-string. Brian rattled maracas.

'Come on now. On your way!'

'Mingey auld bastard,' said Eddie, outside again.

'You got something up your jook?' said George.

'Show ye in a minute!' said Eddie.

Further along the road, away from the shop, he brought out from under his jersey a brand new pair of drumsticks. Light wood, shiny varnished, red at the end.

'Where d'ye get them?' said Brian.

'How?' said George.

'Knocked them when the auld guy was talking to Tam. They were in a rack behind the door. Beauties, eh?'

'Mental bastard,' said Tam. 'Could've got the lot of us nicked.'

'Ach!' said Eddie. 'Bunch of crappers!'

Outside a TV rental shop, a huddle of men watched for the football results coming up. The boys edged their way close to the window, just in time for the Scottish scores.

Rangers had won 2–1 at Aberdeen. Celtic had drawn with Hearts.

'Hullo!'

The boys pummelled each other, even George, who didn't care much about football.

The mood that took them was infectious. They caught it from Eddie, a swagger, bravado in the walk. Rattling out the beat on an invisible sidedrum, Eddie started whistling *The Old Orange Flute*. Then he belted out the words, the others joining in the bits they knew.

'I married a fenian, her name was McGuire
She picked up my flute and she flung it in the fire
But as it was burning she heard a strange noise
Twas the Old Orange Flute playing The Protestant
  Boys.'

And they raised their voices, defiant.

'Tooraloo . . . Tooraloo . . .
Twas the Old Orange Flute playing The Protestant
  Boys.'

'Ea-sy the Protestant Boys!' shouted Eddie, enjoying the looks thrown at them. He would almost have welcomed a challenge, was ready for it, but none came. He sang again, the same tune but the words a mad parody.

'Old Mother Riley was lying one night
And all of a sudden she needed a shite
Up wi the windae and oot wi her bum
And doon came a mixture of apple and plum.

Now under that windae a polis did stand
And on to his helmet the mixture did land

27

Oh Mother Riley it just is not right
A polisman's helmet's no place for a shite!'

On the last line, they swung round into St Enoch's Square. They saw a policeman across at the subway and the laughter brimmed out of them.

'Wonder if he heard us?' said Eddie.

'If he did,' said Tam, 'maybe he'll be more careful about standing under windows!'

The bright mood was still on them as they trundled home on the subway. Brian and George flicked through their comics. Tam re-read, again, the sleeve notes on his record. Eddie with his stolen drumsticks beat *mammydaddy* on the back of the seat. The day had come good.

3

The boys were in the same class at school, last term at Primary. Along with their report cards they were given letters for their parents about the move up to Secondary.

Their teacher, Mrs Kirk, had a word with each of them. Brian and Tam were down for the local Senior Secondary, but would also be sitting a bursary exam for a High School in the city centre. Eddie and George would be moving to the Junior Secondary, just across the road.

'Well now Thomas, Brian. I'm sure I don't have to impress on you the importance of this examination. You're already down for the Senior Secondary of course. That goes without saying. And you *can* take your Highers there and go on to the University. But the bursary would make things so much easier for you boys. So much less of an uphill struggle. It is a *very* prestigious school. And for boys from your background, it is a *tremendous* opportunity to make your way in the world. The first step is passing this exam,

28

next week. It is entirely up to you to do yourselves justice, I can only wish you the best of luck.'

'Now then George. I expect you're disappointed at not going to the Senior Secondary. But your last exam result wasn't really up to scratch, was it? And it's not as if the Junior Secondary is inferior. It just offers a different *kind* of education. It will prepare you for learning a trade, something sound and practical. It is up to you to make the most of it George. I wish you the best of luck.'

'Well Edward, I'm afraid your record speaks for itself. Some of your behaviour over the last two or three years has been just deplorable. All I can say is you should think yourself lucky you're still at a *normal* school at all. I know you probably can't get out of school soon enough Edward. But for your own sake, try to get something out of it. Try to do something *with* yourself. And the best of luck.'

'She's an auld cow,' said Eddie, as they crossed a stretch of wasteground on their way home. He took out the letter from the school, crumpled it into a ball and played keepy-uppy with it, kept it up for a count of three.

'She's no bad,' said Brian.

'It's all right for youse two,' said Eddie. 'Wee brainboxes. You get the special treatment and that. But the likes of me and George here, she doesnae give a fuck.'

He kept his paper ball in the air for a count of four.

'All I'm saying is,' said Brian, 'she's OK if you just get on wi your work and don't give her any bother.'

'And all I'm saying is,' said Eddie, 'it's fuckin all right for some!'

He flicked up the crumpled paper again, kept it up for a last count of five, kicked it into a puddle and left it.

The boys split up, went their separate ways home.

Brian's father was pleased. 'I told you he was clever,' he said to his wife. 'Runs in the family!' He grinned at Brian. 'You get stuck in son. Pass this bursary exam and you're on your way. Go to University. Get yourself a decent job.'

'Never have to take your jacket off,' said his mother.

Eddie's mother skimmed over his report card. 'Just like yer faither,' she said. 'No brains.'

'It's a disgrace,' said George's father. 'Sending you to that Junior Secondary with all these scruffs and hooligans. Just because you let yourself down in one miserable exam.'

'It's not as if he's done badly all the way through,' said his mother.

'Well I'm not going to stand for it,' said his father. 'I want a word with that teacher. *And* the headmaster. It just won't do at all.'

'If I pass the exam,' said Tam, 'will you get me a flute for my birthday?'

'You pass the exam,' said his father. 'Then we'll see what's what.'

The morning of the exam, Tam and Brian were stiff and awkward, dickied up in suits and ties, shiny polished shoes. Moira worked in an office in the city centre, and was taking them in to the High School.

'You don't have to bother,' said Tam, half annoyed at being escorted.

'Just making sure you don't get lost,' said Moira. 'And anyway, it's on the way to my work.'

Brian was glad she was with them. He had no sisters of his own, and being near her was a wonder to him. He loved her smile and her soft scent, loved her pertness, her cheek and backchat to Tam.

On the bus, sitting behind her, he almost forgot his terror at the coming exam. But as they walked towards the school, his stomach started churning again, and he wished he had something to bite, to ease the tingling in his teeth.

Moira said goodbye at the gate, wished them luck. She made to kiss Tam but he turned away.

'OK!' she laughed. She touched Brian's cheek. Warm soft hand. 'All the best,' she said, and was gone.

They passed through the gate into the playground where hundreds of other boys were milling around, boys from all over the city, some in groups, loud and confident, some on their own looking lost, overwhelmed.

'I always yawn when I'm nervous,' said Brian, yawning.

'That's funny.' Tam yawned. 'So do I!'

A bell rang, and numbed, in a dream, they followed the crowd into the building. They had been issued with numbers, in alphabetical order, assigned to the same classroom. Rae and Ritchie. Brian sat at the back. Tam, two rows in front, turned and gave him the thumbs up. Brian yawned.

The teacher was a fierce-looking greyhaired man in a dusty black gown. He looked at his watch. This was it. It was real, was actually happening.

'You may turn over your papers and begin *now*.'

The first paper was English – Grammar, Vocabulary, Composition, and they calmed down, felt easier, as soon as they started writing.

> *Give the meaning of each of the following words and use it in a sentence: temporary; unpredictable; frustration; abhor.*
> *Analyse the following:*
> *We started off and we had not gone far before the men began to sing loudly.*

For Composition they had a choice of subjects. *A Busy Day; A Journey; My Hobby.* They both chose *My*

31

Hobby, though neither of them had ever thought of anything they did as a hobby. The word was cosy and English, a word they would read in a book but never use.

Brian wrote about collecting football programmes. He invented his hobby, discovered it in the writing.

When I leaf through my colourful collection of programmes I vividly remember the games I have been to. (Crossed out, rewritten *games to which I have been.) Foreign programmes from European Cup games are the most exciting of all as I can imagine the atmosphere of stadiums in far off places like Amsterdam or Madrid . . .*

It wasn't that he was making it up, just looking at it new.

Tam wrote about playing the flute, made sure he used the word *embouchure*, to impress.

Soon I hope to have a flute of my own and then I will be able to improve my playing. If I am good enough I will play in a flute band and I also want to learn classical tunes by famous composers such as Mozart . . .

They were still scribbling when the teacher looked at his watch.

'You will stop writing *now*.'

Between papers they had a half-hour break.

'No too bad so far,' said Brian.

'A skoosh!' said Tam.

Above the doorway was carved the school crest, a coat of arms emblazoned with instruments for drawing and measuring – sets of compasses and a square – under it the school motto, *Scientia*.

'Must mean *science*,' said Brian.

'The design looks familiar,' said Tam.

'Masons,' said Brian. 'They've got something like that on their badges.'

Tam remembered where he'd seen something similar before. The ring on the finger of Mr Bennett the flute teacher.

Eddie had brought his drumsticks to school, carried them tucked in his belt, the way bandits in films carried pistols or knives.

At the morning interval he held court in the playground, showed off his tricks for a few boys gathered round, rattled and pattered with his sticks on the wall, ended with a quick one-two on George's head, for a laugh.

But George didn't laugh. The raps had been just that bit too hard.

'Give it a chuck,' he said.

'What if I don't?' said Eddie. And George had no answer, said nothing.

'Can you do a roll?' asked a younger boy.

'Sure,' said Eddie. 'Easy.' He flexed his wrists and the sticks blurred, a burst of rapid fire against the stone wall. Not perfect, but getting better. He had worked at it.

'I'll be in the band soon,' he said.

'So will I,' said George.

'That's no what I heard,' said Eddie. George was getting on his nerves. 'I heard Tam was much better and he'd be getting the flute for a while.'

'So?'

'So Tam'll get in the band. That'll be you scrubbed.'

'Maybe I'll get a flute of my own.'

'Oh aye. Daddy'll buy one!'

'Well if I do get one it'll be bought and paid for.'

'What's that supposed to mean?' said Eddie, shoving him. 'Wee shitebag.'

George was mad now, said what he shouldn't. 'It means my da's no a pauper and I don't have to knock things.'

Eddie slammed him against the wall, smacked him a backhander with the drumsticks across the face.

George slumped, no fight in him, his nose streaming blood.

*

Paper Two was Arithmetic, began with easy questions but quickly became more difficult. They were on shakier ground now, too many tricks they didn't know, techniques they hadn't been taught.

By selling a piano for £32 a dealer lost one ninth of the cost price. What would he have gained if he had sold it for £38?

Tam took each problem in turn, as it came, did what he could with it, muddled through.

Brian missed out the ones he couldn't do, left them till later, came back to try them again. And again.

Two pipes fill a bath in 7½ minutes and 10 minutes respectively, while a third pipe can empty it in 15 minutes. If the three pipes are opened together, in what time will the bath be half full?

Brian started to panic, saw his chances of passing drain away. He would fail and let everybody down.

Selling a piano. One ninth of the cost price. What would he have gained?

The boys around him had their heads down, looked concentrated, sure of what they were doing.

A contractor engaged to do a piece of work in 36 days and employed 52 men. After 20 days the work was only half done. How many additional men must he employ to finish the work in the given time?

The whole thing was stupid and meaningless. Who cared about the dealer and his stupid piano? Who cared about the contractor and his 52 men? He tried to picture them, 52 men. One for every week in the year. He saw them digging a hole. Navvies. Taking their jackets off. Stupid. And who would run water into a bath and out again at the same time? It was just as pointless as him sitting here trying to work it all out.

He thought of Eddie and George. For them it would just be an ordinary day.

'It's fucking all right for some.'

*

Eddie stood, hangdog, at Mrs Kirk's desk, shuffled from foot to foot while she ranted at him.

'You've really gone too far this time my lad. This time you've got yourself into serious trouble. Do you realize that George Wilson has been taken to hospital with a broken nose?'

Eddie looked at the dusty floorboards, his eyes focused on nothing, noticed, for no reason, where the grey wood was splintered here and there.

'And what was the fight about anyway?'

'Nothing.'

'Nothing! You break a boy's nose for nothing!'

She held up the drumsticks. 'Well Edward Logan, I'm confiscating these for a start. In your hands they are an offensive weapon, and I have no intention of letting you use them on anyone else. Further than that I'm not prepared to deal with you myself. I'm sending you to the headmaster, and he can do with you whatever he sees fit.'

The headmaster, Mr McNeil, said less. He gave Eddie eight of the belt, made him wait in the corridor while he phoned the police.

The time was almost up. The greyhaired teacher was looking at his watch. Like a football referee. Last minute.

The atmosphere of stadiums in far off places.

Playing away from home. Closing seconds. No extra time.

If he had sold the piano for £38.

The bath half full.

How many additional men?

Finish the work in the given time.

'You will stop writing and put down your pens *now*.'

That was it. The final whistle. Full time. Finished.

'That was harder, eh?' said Tam on the way out.

'Hellish,' said Brian.

They didn't talk much on the bus journey home, just

stared out the window at the traffic, the shops, the people passing.

They walked back from the bus stop through grey familiar streets, the same old streets they had walked through that morning, long ago. They passed their school.

'It doesnae really matter,' said Tam. 'If we fail, I mean.'

'Suppose so,' said Brian.

But home, on his own, he cried till he was dry-eyed. Then he changed into his old clothes and sandshoes.

Tam was already out, had brought a ball. And they spent the rest of the afternoon lost in the aimlessness, the pure freedom, of booting it around the back court.

4

They had braced themselves against failure, the disappointment dulled to an ache, but they were unprepared for what came.

We have pleasure in informing you . . .

There were 50 places. Tam was 32nd, Brian 38th.

They met on the way to school, raved and laughed and slapped each other on the back. Unable to contain it, they raced each other down the road.

Mrs Kirk was quick to pass the Good News round the school, and she led the boys in triumph to the headmaster.

'I'm proud of you,' he said. 'You're a credit to the school.' He made a speech to them about making their way in the world. He solemnly shook hands with them and wished them well.

Going back to the classroom was drab after that, a descent. But they carried the glory of it deep inside them, a quiet flame that burned bright. And Mrs Kirk fanned it with a look, a word, a smile.

Eddie and George were not there to share it. George was still off, nursing his hurt face. Eddie had been suspended from school, was seeing a social worker, for report.

Tam and Brian passed him on their way home. He was hanging about the corner with three or four other boys, older than him and out of work.

'How's the wee brainboxes then?' asked Eddie.

Tam told him they'd passed the exam.

'Very nice for ye. Can mix wi all the other wee snobs.'

One of the boys behind him laughed, sneering.

'See you, Eddie,' said Tam, as they moved away.

'Aye,' said Eddie. 'Maybe.'

Tam's father was late back from work, but his mother was unconcerned.

'He's away a message,' she said. 'Into town.'

Tam thought no more about it till his father, home, called him into the kitchen. They were all there, his mother, father, Moira. Conspirators, grinning.

His father handed him a small brown parcel. 'This is just a wee something.'

'A wee reward,' said his mother.

Tam tore at the paper, fumbling. He knew what it might be, but he couldn't, didn't dare believe it. The shape was right, and the feel. It was padded around in tissue paper. Eager, he peeled it away, uncovered the gift.

A flute.

'Didn't seem any point in waiting till your birthday,' said his mother. 'When you could be getting the use of it now.'

'It's secondhand of course,' said his father. 'But the man says it's in good nick.'

A real flute. His own.

'We chipped in,' said his father. 'Moira put a good bit towards it.'

It was suddenly too much, the goodness of it. He felt the stupid tears about to start. But Moira saved him, made him laugh.

'So that's you for the next two birthdays,' she said.

'And don't go expecting a Christmas present either!'

The way was clear now for George to have the practice flute to himself. But he didn't want to go on with it.

'Don't fancy it any more,' he said.

'Is it because of that Eddie Logan?' said his father. 'Because if it is, I'll just see Mr Bennett again. Get him put out on his ear.'

'It's no that,' said George. 'It's just . . .'

'The boy's a menace,' said his father. 'Should be locked up.'

'It's just that I'm not all that good. I find it hard.'

'But if you work at it.'

'I just . . . don't think I'm very musical.'

'You're sure it's not just that Logan character you're worried about?'

'No,' said George. 'No. Honest.'

'I'm going to see that headmaster of yours on Monday,' said his father. 'About this Junior Secondary business. I mean, the place'll be full of thugs like this Logan. I'm just not about to put you at risk. And that's all there is to it.'

The social worker was young and earnest. He opened his briefcase, brought out Eddie's drumsticks, handed them to him with great seriousness.

'I managed to persuade Mrs Kirk to give me them.'

Eddie's mother stuck her head round the door. 'Ye gonnae be much longer? I want him to go a couple of messages.'

'Just a few more minutes Mrs Logan.'

She disappeared into the kitchen. Eddie took the drumsticks, said nothing.

'I'm sticking out my neck for you Eddie, getting these back. But I'm doing it because I trust you. And because I know how much these mean to you.'

Eddie held the sticks, balanced, in his open palm.

'They're real beauties,' said the social worker. 'Where did you get them?'

'The Barras,' said Eddie. 'Secondhand.'

'They look very new.'

Eddie tightened his grip on the sticks, drummed on the arm of the chair.

'George Wilson says you stole them.'

'He's a liar,' said Eddie. 'That's how I gubbed him.'

'Yes. Well.'

Eddie's mother came in again, bustling.

'I'll be going,' said the social worker. 'Same time next week Mrs Logan.'

'Aye. Right. Fine.'

'Cheerio then Eddie.'

'Cheerio. And thanks for getting my sticks back.'

When the man had gone, Eddie brought out his practice pad, a rubber mat his father had brought from the pub. ('They'll never miss it' he'd said.) *McEwan's* it read, with a picture of a Cavalier. He laid the mat on the table, tried a roll. His wrists and fingers were stiff, but he knew he would pick it up again, quickly.

'Never mind that the now,' said his mother. 'Away and catch the corner shop before it shuts. Ask her for these.' She handed him a list. 'Tell her I'll pay at the weekend.'

He put away his sticks and his mat, annoyed. 'How come it's always me?'

'What ye moaning about this time?'

'Nothing,' said Eddie. 'Nothing Nothing Nothing!' He banged the door shut behind him.

George's father was shown into the headmaster's office.

'Ah yes, Mr Wilson.'

Mr McNeil reached across his desk and the two men shook hands, sounded each other out with the Masonic grip. It was formal, ritual, a questioning and the correct response, mutual recognition.

'So,' said Mr McNeil, relaxing. 'It's about your son George.'

But the important part of the conversation had

already taken place. It was there, unspoken, behind the words. Contact had been made. George's father knew he could expect co-operation, respect. The matter was well in hand.

Although Tam and Brian were friends, their fathers didn't know each other well. Aleck Ritchie and Willie Rae might nod to each other if they passed in the street, but not much more.

They met by chance at the bus-stop on their way to a parents' meeting at the High School, both dressed up in their best, the way the boys had been on the day of the exam.

They were glad of each other's company at the meeting. It was reassurance, bolstered up their sense of themselves in an atmosphere that was strange to them, and awesomely impressive.

The headmaster addressed them in the school's main hall – dark panelled wood, shields and crests on the walls, a roll of honour, trophies in a glass case. Centre-stage in his black academic gown, he held them attentive, told them what they had come to hear. He spoke of the school's history, used words like Heritage, Tradition. He boasted of its famous Old Boys, the contributions they had made in science and engineering, government and commerce. He lightened his rhetoric with jokes, anecdotes, well-rehearsed asides to his heads-of-department, seated behind him on the stage. The whole performance was a finely-judged piece of theatre, and he brought it to a close by invoking the school motto.

'Scientia,' he intoned, relishing the sound. 'As some of you will no doubt know, it is Latin for *Knowledge*. And I want to assure you that here we do not just mean knowledge in the abstract, knowledge for its own sake. The knowledge we are offering your sons is above all practical. It is up to them to use it, to go out into the world and build their future. We are here to give them that opportunity.'

He gathered up his notes and stepped back from the lectern, acknowledged the applause with a brisk nod of the head, made a dignified exit, stage right. The meeting was over, apart from a few formalities, announcements from department heads. The parents could choose which foreign language their sons would study, the only part of the curriculum that offered any free choice.

Aleck Ritchie put Brian down for Latin. 'It'll help him with his English,' he said. 'Meanings of words and that.'

Willie Rae chose German for Tam. 'Better wi something modern. Something he can speak if he goes abroad.'

On their way home, away from the school, the two men were easier. The meeting had confirmed them in their sense of achievement, their pride in their sons and in themselves. They had glimpsed another world that the boys were heir to. They were eager to keep talking, to bask in it.

'This is some place the boys are into now,' said Aleck.

'It is that,' said Willie.

'That headmaster's quite a character, eh?'

'No half. Bags of patter!'

'He'll be a stickler for discipline all the same.'

'You're right there. I bet there's no much goes past him.'

'I liked his stories about the excuses he got when folk came in late!'

'The wee fella that said the subway was held up cause there was a cow on the line!'

'You've got to laugh!'

'Ach aye.'

'Still. It's some chance the boys are getting. To get on.'

'More than we ever got!'

They had both left school at fourteen. Aleck was a storeman in the drawing office of an engineering works. Willie was a fitter in the yards. Their faith in education was absolute.

Almost home now, they stood at the corner, lingering. They talked round in circles, and off at tangents. They talked futures, opportunities, careers.

'The boys have done well for themselves,' said Aleck.

'They'll get out of this anyway,' said Willie. He took in the grey street and everything in it, his life there, his job, his world.

Across the road, the pub was spilling out its last few customers. The dregs of another Friday night.

Further along a gang of young boys had been thrown out of the chip shop for scuffling and yelling. Gathered on the pavement, they pressed their faces to the window, leered and grimaced at the customers.

'I wouldnae eat they chips if I was you mister.'

'Give ye the dry boke.'

'Make ye spew yer ring.'

'Ye want to see what he puts in his pies.'

'Turn yer stomach.'

'See that black pudding missis. A darkie's walloper, that's what it is.'

Most of the people inside found it funny, but old Gino behind the counter was getting more and more upset. He scowled at the gargoyle faces, flatnosed against the glass.

'No more now,' he said. 'You go now or I call the polis.'

'Anybody ever tell you you've got a Roman nose?'

Three of them chorused. 'Roamin all over yer face!'

'Ya greasy wee papish I-tie bastard ye!'

'OK,' said Gino, banging down a basket into deep fat. 'Is enough!' And he stamped through to the back shop, where the phone was.

The boys still jeered after him, behind the glass, but they started to move away, in their own time.

Eddie, in amongst them and buoyed up by his new friends, decided he would come back later, chuck a half-brick through Gino's window. He noticed vaguely, across at the corner, Tam's father and Brian's father solemnly shaking hands. The mood he was in, they looked funny. Eddie laughed, spat.

The two men parted, went on their way. The boys moved on, reluctant to break up and go home. But the word went round that Gino had phoned the police, and they separated, disappeared through closes and across back courts.

The other loiterers too began to drift away from the street, the winemoppers, the last stragglers from the pub.

By the time the two young policemen came by, on their beat, the place was quiet again, empty.

Blowing in the Wind

1

Time at school was grey time, weeks and months and years of it, brightened only by a moment here and there, a glimmer, a spark. Brian and Tam had been assigned to different form classes in first year, because of the choices their fathers had made for them. 1L for Latin, 1G for German. At first they had still met up in the mornings, travelled in together by bus and back again at the end of the day. They had looked out for each other in the playground at morning break, in the canteen queue at dinnertime, compared notes on the regime and their different teachers – this Vicious Bastard / that Boring Turd.

They would try out jokes they had heard.

What's brown and smelly and sounds like a bell?

Dung!

They would get each other to 'speak in tongues'.

'Tell me something in German.'

'*Es geht mir gut.*'

'What does that mean?'

'Means I'm fine.'

'Oh aye?'

'So tell me something in Latin.'

'*Poeta deam semper laudat.* Means the poet always praises the goddess.'

'Handy thing to be able to say!'

After a few weeks they had made other friends. Tam had taken to walking with some of them down through town, coming home on the subway. Brian still preferred the bus. Tam started taking the subway in the mornings as well. They saw each other less and less.

'*Salve et valete.*'

'*Auf Wiedersehen.*'

What kept Tam going was music. The school had an orchestra, and there were tutors who came in to give lessons. Tam had signed up for the flute class, every Wednesday after school, along with half a dozen other boys. It was the flute-band scenario all over again, with only one flute to go round. The tutor said he would have to whittle the numbers down. His name was Mr McKenna and he was old, in his eighties.

He'd passed round the head of the flute, let each of them try blowing a note. Only Tam was able to do it, and the old man asked him if he'd played before. He told him about the band and the old man nodded, said, 'Never mind!' He gave Tam the flute to take home.

It came, dismantled, in a hard black case like a jewellery box, with a soft brush for cleaning. It wasn't like the simple wooden fife he'd played in the band. It was a piece of precision machinery. All the way home on the subway he'd kept opening the box, held safe across his lap, to peer in, astonished, at the lovely shining thing inside.

Waiting for his lesson always felt strange, end of the day, the last bell gone and the whole school evacuated, corridors and classrooms left empty, the odd shout echoing, a door banged shut. He might have been the only person left in the whole place as he sat on a desk swinging his legs. Somehow there was a tiredness in the air, in the old paintwork and the grubby floorboards, chalkdust in the late afternoon light. The room was normally used for maths, and the board was covered with figures and diagrams, equations, theorems, proofs. He stared at it all as if he might understand, penetrate its mysteries, but for all the sense it made to him, it might as well have been hieroglyphics. It made him feel uneasy in the pit of his stomach.

The door opening made him jump to his feet, a

reflex. Mr McKenna chuckled at him. 'As you were son. Stand easy!'

Sometimes the old man made Tam feel squeamish. It wasn't just the black teeth, the occasional cough and howk and spit into a hanky. As well as all that it was the smell of him. He smoked a pipe and stank of tobacco, and behind that was a nameless, old man's smell, a staleness from always wearing the same clothes, an old tweed jacket, grey baggy trousers worn shiny with age. Today he was complaining, about his wheezing chest, and the stiffness in his joints, and his fingers no longer supple. 'Old age,' he said. 'Comes to us all.'

He made Tam go over the scales he had been practising, play them again and again, till he thought if he played them one more time he would scream, and he made him play them one more time then stop.

'Only way to do it,' he said. 'Play till it's second nature and you don't have to think about it.'

Then he made him play long notes, sustain them as long as he could. And he played the same notes himself, and for all his complaining and the wheezing cough he held them longer and the tone was full and strong.

'Terrible!' he said. 'Young lad like you. Got to learn to *breathe*!'

He took some sheet music from his old scuffed leather briefcase, propped it up on the music stand. It was handwritten, on new manuscript paper.

'You were telling me last week you liked Mozart. See how you get on with this.'

'What is it?'

'You do German, don't you? What does that say?'

Der Vögelfänger bin ich ja.

'The something am I yes.'

'Birdcatcher. It's Papageno's song from your *Magic Flute*. Here, I've simplified it for you.'

The first time through, Tam faltered a bit. He still had problems with sightreading. It didn't come naturally, was still three separate processes – recognize the note, remember the fingering, and play. It wasn't yet a continuous flow, was something he had to think through, especially on faster runs.

'It's just a matter of speeding it up so there's no thought in it and your fingers know what they're doing. Takes work!'

They tried again and it was better. It helped that Tam knew the tune, had heard it before. He began to feel confident, put a bit of expression into it. And Mr McKenna added a touch and a flourish here and there, embellishments like the little run that was Papageno's pipes.

'Good!' said the teacher. 'Good!'

And Tam became aware again of the grubby room and the fading light and he realized the music had carried him out, made him forget that sense of emptiness and mortality and the sad old smell of decay.

'I'm telling you,' said the old man, grinning. 'Mozart was an angel. No two ways about it!'

Brian's experience of music at school was different. They had one period a week, timetabled, and the teacher was one that he and Tam had categorized as Vicious Bastard. His name was McLeish, a small man, stubby, in a light blue suit too tight for him, his short hair oiled and flattened forward. With boys who played in the orchestra, or were learning instruments, or had signed up for the school choir, he was friendly, paternal, called them by their first names. The rest were dull scum, not worth his time. He would sit at the piano and hammer out traditional Scottish songs for them to sing, *Ye banks and braes, Speed bonny boat*. Occasionally he would try to teach them to sightread using *sol-fa*. One afternoon in a particularly bad mood he went round the whole class, one by one, made them read a song they hadn't done before. *Flow gently sweet Afton*. McLeish beat out the tempo with his leather strap, coiled tight like a spring. He dared them to make

47

the slightest mistake, and those who did were hauled out for two of the belt. When Brian's turn came his stomach was churning. He made it through two bars of the song then stumbled, read *doh* instead of *doh-oh*. He couldn't believe it was happening as he held out his hands, palms crossed, and the belt was uncurled, lashed down on him, twice.

He sat back down with his hands tucked under his armpits to try to ease the sting. Johnstone, the boy beside him, was doing the same. He had mistaken a *mi* for a *fa*.

'Great way to enhance your love of music!' he said.

'Right enough!' said Brian.

'Disturb not her dream . . . Skelp!'

'Don't you mean drea-eam!'

'Right you two. Out here!' McLeish had heard them talking, called them out and belted them again.

Tam had been pressganged by McLeish into joining the school orchestra. The previous flautist had been good, a virtuoso. He had left and gone on to Music School. Tam's excitement at being called up was tempered by the fear that they might be expecting too much of him. But there was a concert coming up. They needed a fluteplayer. So.

The first rehearsal was a nightmare. Tam felt nervous, tentative, as he eased open the door into the school hall. He had heard the noise from out in the corridor, but inside it engulfed him, the din of the instruments tuning up, blasting brass and whining strings.

Above it McLeish shouted across at him, indicated a space where he should sit, beside two older boys on oboe and clarinet.

'Welcome to the woodwind section!' said the oboist.

'Thanks.'

The clarinettist ignored him, blew a rasping bass note and fiddled, irritated, with his reed.

'OK!' shouted McLeish. 'Let's get in tune.'

He stubbed out an A on the piano, challenged the pitch of every instrument in turn.

'Flat,' he said, at Tam's hesitant approximation.

'As the proverbial pancake,' said the clarinettist before playing the note, perfectly, then pitching it up an octave for good measure. Tam hated him.

McLeish raised his voice again. 'All right, let's take it from the top. March from Scipio.'

Tam had practised that one with Mr McKenna. He just had to play the melody and that was straight-forward enough. He was able to play it loud and still be caught up in the swell of the other instruments, so if he did make any mistakes he would be drowned out.

He felt more exposed in the next set – three songs McLeish had strung together and called *Keltic Twilight – The Ash Grove, The Minstrel Boy, The Rowan Tree*. But he made it safely through. Then came selections from *Oklahoma*. The score was pages long, like nothing he had tackled before. He might play for two or three bars, a simple phrase, then be out again for a few bars more, then back in to play incidental notes, then out for an even longer rest. Sometimes he would be out for a whole page and his concentration began to drift. He found himself listening to the music instead of counting time. He became aware of a lull, and McLeish looking puzzled, glaring at the score.

'What's supposed to be happening here?'

The orchestra fizzled to a stop.

'Flute! You're supposed to be playing there! Solo!'

'So-lo you couldn't hear him,' said the clarinettist, not quite under his breath.

Tam panic-scanned the page in front of him, couldn't find the point where he should have come in. The oboist leaned across, turned two pages, showed Tam where they were.

'It's easy to lose the place,' he said.

'When you're quite ready!' shouted McLeish.

Tam was ready to give up after that, just out of sheer frustration and embarrassment. He didn't touch the flute for days, until it was time for his lesson with Mr McKenna. The old man wormed the story out of him and laughed.

'Happens to the best of us,' he said. 'No point in letting it get you down.' Then he told Tam to forget about his sightreading and fingering, go right back to basics and work on the quality of his tone, play only on the head of the flute.

'But.'

'No buts. Do it.'

Tam dismantled the instrument, raised the head to his lips. Mr McKenna put him through his paces for the best part of an hour, made him concentrate on breath control, on maintaining intensity and brightness in the playing. And only then did he turn to the score for *Oklahoma*, take Tam through it page by page till he began to have a feel for the shape of it, for the timing of his entrances, for what he was to play.

'Good,' said the old man. 'You're getting there.'

Tam nodded, grateful.

'And do you know what you've learned today?'

Tam shook his head.

'You've learned the importance of two things.' He paused. 'Using the head and knowing the score!'

They were probably old jokes he had told a hundred times. But to Tam they were new and he gave an appreciative groan. The old man cackled, well pleased with himself. 'Using the head!' he said again, nodding, his old eyes twinkling. 'Knowing the score!'

2

Tam first met Bird when he was in third year and Bird was in sixth. His name was Gordon Baird, but he hated the Gordon, and when somebody butchered his surname to Bird, he liked it and held on to it.

'They call me Bird,' he said to Tam, introducing himself. 'Like Charlie Parker.' Tam had no idea who Charlie Parker was.

They were at a rehearsal for the school concert. Bird played electric guitar and had been called in to lead a version of *Blowing in the Wind* with the whole orchestra and choir.

Tam already knew him by sight and by reputation. His red hair was long but combed back so he could disguise its length if the headmaster, the Boss, should be on the rampage. His regulation uniform was always off-set by a bright jersey, or checked trousers, white socks or suede shoes. Once he had even stitched a velvet collar on to his blazer, covering it with a scarf if the Boss passed anywhere near. Tam admired his ability to get away with it. Any time he himself tried the slightest deviation he would encounter the Boss at his most ferocious, and the Boss would bark at him about the length of his hair, or the tightness of his trousers, or the pointed toes of his shoes, or whatever else was giving offence.

Right boy! Grey pullover. Decent trousers. Dark socks. Proper shoes. And get that hair cut boy!

Tam had once seen Bird, in a paisley-pattern waist-coat, take part in an interschools debate. The motion had been something to do with the permissive society. Tam couldn't remember a word that had been said, but he did remember being impressed with his style. The judges had commented on his triumphant use of the non-sequitur and had given him the points for the panache of his delivery.

Tam was surprised and a little bit flattered when Bird came up and spoke to him at the orchestra rehearsal. After the opening gambit about Charlie Parker, Bird asked him if he'd ever played jazz.

'Afraid not,' he said.

'Pity,' said Bird. He looked as if he might leave it at that, then he added, 'I've got this band you see, and we could use a flute player.'

'Oh.'

'Too bad, eh?'

'I could try.' Tam was anxious, now that a door was

open, not to see it slammed in his face.

'Suppose so,' said Bird. 'Obviously you can read music.'

'A bit, yeah.'

'Can you improvise?'

'Never really tried.'

'Oh well. I guess we can give it a go.'

So Tam found himself one Friday after school heading out with Bird on the bus to Bearsden. The house was big, stone-built, with a garden front and back. Tam had never been in a house like it. The hall they passed through was as long as Tam's whole house, just about as wide, and carpeted. Bird's mother sat by a little half-moon table, talking on the phone. Tam had never even been in a house with a phone.

'This is Tam,' said Bird. The woman nodded, gave a vague wave, acknowledging him. Bird dumped his briefcase, draped his blazer over the banister, led Tam straight through and out the back door. Right at the back of the garden, overhung by trees, was a big old shed, and Bird's parents had let him use it as rehearsal space.

'They're happier to have me making my racket out here,' he explained. 'Away from the house.'

Tam was amazed at it. The walls were soundproofed with egg-boxes, polystyrene tiles. In one corner was a whole drumkit, set up.

'That's Mike's,' said Bird. 'He should be here any minute. And so should Rob. Poor bugger's got to humph his double bass out here on the bus. But this is the best place for us to practise.'

Mike and Rob arrived together. And even if Rob hadn't been lugging his instrument, Tam would have known which of them was which. He wondered why bass players were always long and skinny. Mike was the opposite, small and stocky, muscular. He had been in Bird's year at school but had left at the end of the fifth, gone on to Art School. Tam hadn't known him, but he recognized his face though he'd grown a moustache, a chinstrap beard.

'Sorry I don't know your face, man,' said Mike. 'I never really got to know anybody outside my own year.'

'I did tell him he should use a deodorant!' said Bird.

Mike gave him the V-sign, turned back to Tam. 'So you're just going to sit in with us, see how it goes?'

Tam nodded. 'I'll just be listening today. I didn't bring my flute.'

He felt himself blush as he said it, and Bird noticed.

'Says he forgot it. Very Freudian don't you think?' He put on a German accent. 'Interestink.'

Tam knew it was true. Scared of making a fool of himself, he had forgotten his flute on purpose. Now he felt stupid. Bird laughed, said, 'At least you came. We asked that little shite of a clarinettist from the orchestra and he said the only jazz he liked was trad.'

'Fucking Acker Bilk!' said Mike.

Tam enjoyed the put-down, but he still felt foolish. He was glad when they turned their attention to setting up, getting in tune.

He hadn't known what to expect, but the first tune they played was something he recognized, the theme from *That was the week that was*. The bouncy upbeat energy of it, the sheer volume in the small space, made him laugh. Bird nodded across at him. 'Good, eh!'

After they had played through the melody a couple of times they played variations, began to improvise, and Tam felt less at ease with it. He sometimes heard music like this on the radio and it made him feel uncomfortable, had him reaching for the dial to find something classical or a blast of simple pop. But he said nothing. He didn't want to end up like the clarinettist, dismissed. And maybe if he worked at it.

The improvisation sputtered to a stop and they moved on to another piece.

'Square dance,' said Bird. 'Dave Brubeck. Only he plays it on the piano!'

Tam loved the rhythms of it, and Mike's drumming was good, his touch light. But they had to keep stopping, going over passages again because Bird didn't have the fingering up to speed. And that made Tam feel a little bit better, less apprehensive.

The last thing they played was completely free form. And although it seemed wild and unstructured, there were sections within it when they blended and it all fell into place. And Tam didn't really understand what was going on, but there was a fire in their playing, and moments too when it moved into pure melodic flow. And that opened up a door to him, just wide enough to offer a way in. Next time he would bring his flute.

Near the end of the third year, Brian's thoughts were taken up with the bursary exam. There shouldn't really be anything to worry about. There were fifteen places, and for the last two years he had been second in his class. That put him in the top half-dozen of his year. But still, the tightness of it worried him. What if he just had an off day, slipped up?

'I think it's disgusting,' said his mother. 'They take in, what, fifty of you to start with? They let you get used to the place, then bang! The year before your O-levels they cut it down to fifteen.'

'It is bad,' said his father.

'Mean,' said Brian.

'But the boy'll do it no bother. He's practically top of his class.'

'Second,' said Brian.

'I'm sure he'll manage fine,' said his mother. 'It's just the principle of it. I mean, what happens to the ones that don't pass?'

'Some of them leave,' said Brian. 'Some stay on as fee-payers.'

'You mean their parents have to find the money? Just ordinary folk like us?'

'And it's not just the fees,' said Brian. 'It's the money for books as well.'

'It's terrible,' said his mother. 'A damned disgrace.'

'Dead sneaky,' said Brian.

'We knew all this from the start,' said his father. 'We knew the set-up. And anyway, you've got nothing to worry about. You'll pass with flying colours, won't you?'

'Should do.'

He tried to sound confident, but that faint doubt still niggled. The one thing that made him feel better about it was comparing his situation with Tam's.

Tam shrugged it off, said he couldn't care less. They had met one day outside a music shop near the school. Tam, an LP under his arm, stood staring in at the gleaming display of instruments in the window, and didn't notice Brian till he spoke.

'Thinking of taking up the guitar?'

'Eh?' Tam turned. 'Oh, hiya! Naw, I'm looking at the saxes, wishing I could afford a soprano. They sound magic.'

'What's the record?'

Tam held it up, Brian read the title. 'At the Golden Circle.'

'Is that modern jazz?'

'That's right.'

'Don't know much about it.'

Tam shrugged. 'It's good once you get used to it. This one's really way out!'

'Weird is it?'

'Kind of. What about you? Still into the Beatles?'

They had both seen the Beatles at the Odeon a couple of years back, sharing top of the bill with Roy Orbison. It was something to boast about, seeing them before they were *really* big.

'I still like them,' said Brian. 'But I like the Stones as well. And the Who.'

'So I see,' said Tam, gesturing at Brian's bag, a canvas haversack with pop-art designs drawn on the flap in a felt-tip pen – a stylized fish, as if cut from a Union jack, a target beside the name of the Who.

Across the top, *Stones* was lettered roughly in red, and along the bottom like a streetsign it read *Desolation Row*.

'I see you're into Dylan as well.'

'He's brilliant,' said Brian.

'You know we're doing *Blowing in the Wind* at the school concert?'

'Is that right? Maybe I'll come along. It's right at the end of term, isn't it?'

'Last day.'

'So the bursary'll be out the way, over and done with.'

'Don't talk to me about that,' said Tam. 'After the exam I reckon it'll be *me* that's over and done with!'

'I'm a bit worried as well,' said Brian.

'You!' said Tam. 'Don't talk shite. You'll skoosh it.'

'I don't know.'

'Don't come it!' Tam was beginning to sound annoyed, so Brian didn't persist.

'So what'll you do if you don't pass?'

'No ifs about it,' said Tam. 'I haven't a chance in hell.' He stared again at the bright electric guitars in the shop window, the cymbals and drums, the shining saxophones. 'Anyway,' he said. 'Who the fuck cares?'

Only a week after the exam, the results were posted on a noticeboard in the main hall. Tam managed to shove his way through the boys crowding round, saw that Brian's name was in seventh place and his own was not on the list.

'I knew it,' he said.

He had told his parents what to expect, but still it came as a shock to them, the finality of it.

'It doesn't matter,' he said, convincing himself. 'I'll just leave.'

'Don't be stupid!' said his mother. 'What about your Highers?'

'I can get them down the road at the Senior Secondary,' he said. 'Just as easy.' But the Senior

Secondary didn't have an orchestra. There would be no more lessons with Mr McKenna. He would have to give back his flute.

'Your mother's right,' said his father. 'You can't go chopping and changing at this stage.'

'But how can you pay the fees and stuff?' Moira was engaged, would soon be married. That meant less money coming into the house.

'It'll be tight,' said his father. 'But we'll manage.'

'How?'

'There's plenty overtime going. I'll work an extra night, the odd Sunday.'

Tam was quiet, taking it in. He had resigned himself, now there was a reprieve.

'If you think it would work,' he said.

'You could help as well,' said his mother. 'I was talking to Mrs Wilson, and she says George has got a Saturday job in that new supermarket, and they're taking on more boys.'

'I'll go in and ask.'

'Fine,' said his father. 'That's it settled.'

'Thanks,' said Tam, awkward because the word was so much less than adequate. He wanted to say more but it wouldn't come out.

'Thanks,' he said, again.

The last weekend before the end of term, Bird threw a party to celebrate. Tam's memory of it afterwards was fragmented. He remembered turning up early, being handed a can of lager. He was wearing his good suit, a pair of Chelsea boots, a new denim shirt with a black knitted tie. He sat tapping his feet to the Beatles *Ticket to Ride*, felt lost among faces he didn't know. Then Mike was calling to him from the door, and Tam followed him out along the hall, outside and along the garden to Bird's shed.

Bird and Rob were already there.

'Musicians only!' said Bird, taking a drag from a roll-up cigarette and passing it over to Mike. The smell of it hung thick and sweet. Mike inhaled, held, breathed out with a sigh, and passed the roll-up to Tam.

'I don't smoke,' he heard himself say, feeling ridiculous.

'Well it's about time you learned!' said Bird.

'It's a deadly reefer!' said Rob. 'Guaranteed to blow your head off!'

Tam took it, excited but unsure. He put it to his lips, sucked in, choked and coughed as the hot smoke burned his throat.

'Christ!' said Mike. 'Don't waste it!'

'It's OK,' said Bird. 'Try again.'

And he did, he inhaled, and he managed to hold it down though his eyes watered and it made him feel sick.

Then they were back in the living room and he was slumped in a chair laughing at Bird who was standing up, quite ludicrously himself, sharply in focus, vividly threedimensional, announcing with high seriousness that a game of Stations was about to begin. All the girls left the room and the boys were numbered.

'Like the fucking Lifeboys!' said Tam. 'From the left, *Number*!'

He was given number seven, thought that might be lucky. Seven was outside right, on the wing. Stanley Matthews, Willie Henderson, Garrincha the Little Bird. A little bird on the wing! He was flying!

The girls came back in and number seven, a thin bony girl, came over and sat in his lap.

'Are you on the wing as well?' he asked.

'Eh?'

'You're my opposite number,' he said. 'It must be fated. It's in the stars!'

She looked at him as if he might be a dangerous maniac. The volume on the recordplayer was turned up loud and the Moody Blues' *Go Now* blared out. And he started to kiss her, because that was the game, but she stayed stiff and distant, going through the motions, and as soon as the record was finished she disentangled herself and moved on.

He must have changed partners three or four times, ended up on the floor with a young girl called Sandra – short blonde hair, eyes made up black, a shiny tight red dress. And by now Bird had turned the lights down and the music on the recordplayer was some cool jazz he didn't recognize, all tinkling piano and mellow sax, and Sandra's breath tasted faintly of toothpaste and cigarettes. Then the music had changed again, and Tam recognized the Ornette Coleman album he had borrowed from Bird. But he heard it now with a new clarity, as if for the first time. *The Golden Circle.* And it all made perfect sense. There was nothing to understand. It was all just play, and it made him laugh.

'What is it?' said Sandra.

'Nothing,' he said. 'Everything!' And he rolled over, kissed her again.

Tam was due to have one last lesson with Mr McKenna, the day before the concert. He sat again in the empty classroom, waiting. It was warm in the room, stale. The blackboard, as always, was covered with figures, calculations – an algebraic theorem, a geometric proof. He could recognize elements here and there, but most of it was still impenetrable. He sat at the teacher's desk, took off his jacket, loosened his tie. Then he spread out his music, pieced together the flute and ran through his part for *Blowing in the Wind.* He smiled at the thought of Bird strumming chords and singing along with the school choir backed up by the orchestra. He was sure he would jazz it up a bit on the night, throw in some interesting changes.

The door opened and he turned, still smiling, expecting to see old Mr McKenna. Instead he saw McLeish, looking grim. Without thinking, he stood up from the teacher's seat.

'It's OK,' said McLeish. 'You can sit down.'

McLeish looked at the blackboard, seemed just as

uncomprehending as Tam had been, but he continued to stare at the chalked figures as he spoke.

'You're waiting for your lesson.'

It wasn't a question, but Tam felt he should answer.

'That's right, sir.'

'Got a bit of bad news son.'

Tam had never heard him call anyone *son*, except as a threat. *Now listen son. I'm warning you.*

McLeish turned from the blackboard, looked at him.

'We just got a phone-call from Mr McKenna's daughter. I'm afraid you won't be seeing him again.'

'How do you mean?'

He knew what McLeish was saying, knew what he meant, but he went through this strange formality of pretending otherwise.

'The old fellow took a bad turn last night. His heart I think. He died in hospital this morning.'

Somebody shouted in the playground. 'I'll get ye!' Another voice replied, falsetto. 'I'll let ye!'

A high shriek of laughter, running feet.

McLeish looked at his watch. 'I'm in a bit of a rush,' he said. 'But I thought I'd better come and tell you myself.'

Tam nodded. 'Thanks.'

'Right,' said McLeish. 'Well. I better go.'

At the door he stopped and turned as if struggling for something to say. Then he shrugged. 'Comes to us all,' he said.

When he'd gone, Tam went to the window, looked out. He saw McLeish cross the playground to his parked car, chuck his briefcase in the back seat, drive off. Tam gathered up his music, dismantled his flute and packed it away. Comes to us all. The old man had used the same words, talking about old age. And he'd given him advice, made a joke about using the head, knowing the score. The sum total of all his wisdom. A lifetime. He felt his lip shake and suddenly there were tears in his eyes.

When it had passed he found himself staring again at

the blackboard, at a diagram – a circle containing a right-angle triangle. ABC. As easy as. QED. Brian could tell him what that stood for in Latin. The answer. Blowing in the wind. Voices in the playground. I'll get ye. Comes to us all.

He picked up a duster and wiped the board, rubbed out the diagram, the equations, calculations, the stupid problems and their useless solutions. He wiped it clear with great sweeping strokes, made shapes like waves, like clouds, and filled the air with chalkdust that danced as it settled through the streaks of sunlight filtering into the room.

'So who's this girl you're going out with then?'

Brian was annoyed at his father for asking, could feel himself blush.

'Nobody,' he said. 'Just a girl.'

'That's nice,' said his mother, sarcastic. 'That's very nice!'

'But I mean she's not, it's not.'

He wished he had never told them. But he had been full of himself when Cathy had agreed to come with him to the school dance. He'd been desperate to find somebody. Hendry the gym teacher, who organized the dance, had threatened them, said they had to come with a partner or else. But Brian didn't know anyone he could ask. That was the trouble with an all-boys school. And he'd long since lost touch with girls he'd known at primary.

His salvation was the Saturday job at the supermarket. He had heard about it from Tam, who was planning to go for a job himself, sometime. Brian had gone along one Friday after school, been told he could start right away, found himself the next day washing dishes in the snackbar. That was where he had met Cathy. She too was still at school, only worked Saturdays. On his first day she had showed him how to use the dishwasher. Then she had dumped a pile of greasy plates in the sink for him, told him he had to

61

scrub the egg off them before they went in the machine.

'Dead romantic!' he had said to Tam, telling him about it. But something in the way she had said it, and her smile, and the fact that she took the trouble, encouraged him. And after another three weeks of awkwardness, and hesitant attempts at conversation, and stacks of greasy dishes in the sink, he finally worked up the courage to ask her to the dance. He had tried to sound casual, was sure it had come out wrong, offhanded, as if he couldn't care less. But incredibly she said yes, fine, OK, she would come.

He had felt even more selfconscious meeting her, sitting next to her on the bus. But at the same time he was exhilarated, lightheaded. She looked really good and he was glad to be seen with her. At work her dark hair was always pinned up, tucked inside a cap. Now it hung, straight and shiny, to her shoulders, swung when she turned her head. He told her she looked like Cathy McGowan from *Ready Steady Go*. She said thanks. Brian had a picture of Cathy McGowan, cut from *Rave* magazine, tacked up on his wall alongside the Beatles, Marianne Faithfull, Bob Dylan, Dylan Thomas, Lenin, Van Gogh and Jim Baxter. He asked if she liked poetry, but she only knew what she'd read at school and that was boring. She hated football – her brothers drove her mad going on about it. How about music? She liked the Hollies, Wayne Fontana and the Mindbenders. Worse and worse. There was no point of contact. He was running out of things to say, to ask. He was floundering, treading water.

It was easier once they got to the dance. The music took over and they didn't have to talk. The school gym was tarted up, beams and wallbars hung with tinsel, streamers, balloons. Someone he didn't know from sixth year was disc jockey, played his own selection of singles on an old recordplayer, the volume up full blast and crackling. Hendry, his muscled bulk packed into a sports jacket, patrolled the hall, ordering anyone who was sitting it out to get up and dance, have a good time. For Brian that was no problem. He was lost, absorbed, in watching Cathy dance, in being with her. She really was beautiful. He realized he had never seen her out of the dull green overall she wore to work. Now in a white dress she spun and moved away from him with a lightness and grace that made him feel like crying – that turn of the head, the shimmer of her hair. His only regret was that Tam hadn't come to the dance, was busy rehearsing with this jazz group. Brian would have liked to show Cathy off to him.

At the interval he still had nothing much to say. He joked about the school, made smalltalk about the supermarket. She didn't seem to mind, seemed happy enough. When he saw her home they went into the back close. She stopped his hand when he tried to move inside her coat, but he was content just to be there, to be kissing, bodies hardly touching. On the way home he was beyond himself with sheer joy. He punched the air, kicked a tin can hard across the road. It startled a drunk in a doorway who yelled at him, swore. But it didn't matter. He didn't care.

Now Cathy had agreed to go out with him again and his parents were giving him a hard time.

'Do you think it's wise?' said his mother.

'Going to the pictures?'

'Having a girlfriend, at your age.'

'I'm fifteen!'

'Aye, well,' said his mother. 'All I'm saying is you shouldn't get too serious. Not now. You'll have plenty of time later on.'

He couldn't believe this. He put all his annoyance into slamming the door, hurried down the road to meet Cathy.

He had been waiting half an hour when he started to admit to himself that she wasn't going to turn up. He paced up and down outside the subway where they were to meet. He stood at the corner, looked this way and that. He looked again at the clock across the road.

He would give her ten more minutes. Bits of a song started going through his head. *Girl Don't Come.* Sandie Shaw. He could see her shuffling barefoot, singing it. *Some distant bell starts chiming nine.* Ten more minutes. He found himself staring in at the window of a café, became aware of the owner staring back at him, curious. *You wanna see her, oh yeah.* Round the corner opposite came a gang of mods, sharp suits, razorcut hair. They were crossing the road towards him. For a moment he felt threatened, thought about taking refuge in the café, but he saw Eddie Logan at the head of them, felt reassured, thought Eddie wouldn't go for him. Then he looked at Eddie's face, saw the hardness in it, and he wasn't so sure. He remembered Eddie breaking George Wilson's nose. He always called Brian brainbox, spat it out like venom. He stepped inside the café, was engulfed by the smoky warmth, the jukebox thumping out something by the Dave Clark Five. *Bits and Pieces.* Eddie's pack went past the door. He heard them whooping and rampaging down into the subway.

'You want something?' said the owner.

'Eh, no,' said Brian, pointing at his wrist, where a watch would be if he had one. 'It's later than I thought.'

Outside he went to the corner again. Five more minutes. *Still you wait.* Look up and down the street. *You wait and wait.* Check the clock. One more minute. And counting down. Rumble from the subway, the smell wafting up. Time up. Zero. *Girl don't come.* The bastard.

'Gave ye a dizzy did she?' asked his father when he came home early. 'Ach well. Never mind. Plenty more fish and all that, eh!'

'Maybe it's for the best,' said his mother. He said nothing.

On the Saturday, at the snackbar, Cathy was apologetic. She'd had a headache she said, hadn't felt well. There had been no way of getting in touch, she was sorry. That was all right he said, and he asked her to the end of term concert.

'I'm sorry,' she said, again. 'I don't want, it's just that.'

He didn't tell her he had already bought the tickets. And now she was saying no.

'I just don't want to go with anybody special,' she said. 'Not right now.'

'Fine,' he said. 'That's OK.'

The rest of the day she was friendly enough, but at night as he was leaving he saw her step into a car. The driver must have been at least eighteen. He leaned over and kissed her. He looked a bit like Wayne Fontana. Brian stepped back into the doorway so they wouldn't see him as they drove off. George came out behind him, asked him what was the matter.

'Eh?'

'You look miserable.'

'Do I?' He shrugged.

For a moment he thought about offering George the extra ticket, the one he had bought for Cathy. A shame to waste it. But he suddenly couldn't bear it, the thought of taking George *instead*. He just couldn't do it, would rather tear up the ticket and throw it away.

'I'm fine,' he said, moving away. 'Be seeing you.'

He thought then of tearing up both tickets, not going to the concert at all. But on the night he changed his mind, decided just to go on his own.

It didn't help that the first person he met, on his way into the hall, was Tam.

'On your own?' asked Tam. 'I thought you were bringing that wee bird you've been telling me about.'

'Och,' he said. 'That's finished.

'Finished? It hardly got started!'

'Och well. You know.'

He knew he shouldn't have come. It was more than he could take. But Tam seemed disinterested, distant, already looking about him, ready to move on.

'Anyway. Got to go backstage. Get warmed up and that.'

'Aye, right.'

'Aye. So. Be seeing you.'

'Sure.'

Brian sat at the back of the hall, felt fidgety and ill-at-ease. He was thinking about leaving when the Boss appeared on stage, started making a speech of welcome to the parents. Brian was hardly listening, let it wash over him. He didn't like the man. Like Tam he had run into trouble with him over variations in his school uniform, nothing more. But that was enough to make Brian afraid of him, nervous in his presence. Nobody ever argued with the Boss, not even the head teachers. He imposed his authority with ferocity and impatience, intolerant of any opposition. He was right, and he had the power.

Only once had Brian seen another side to him. On the Monday morning after President Kennedy's assassination, the Boss had called the whole school into this same hall and spoken about what had happened. His voice had been quieter than usual, even a little bit shaky, and had seemed on the point of breaking altogether as he told them, 'Take care in your own lives, lest you murder not men but principles.' Brian had always remembered that morning, the sense it had given him that what they were living through was a time, like any other, was history.

Now the Boss was talking about the Two Cultures, saying although the emphasis in the school was on science, the arts were not neglected, they were educating the whole man. And as evidence of that he was presenting the orchestra and choir under the able direction of Mr McLeish.

McLeish came on stage then, smiled and bowed. He looked sleek in a black suit. The orchestra tuned up and he led them into the opening medley, a selection from *Carmen*. Tam was at the end of the back row, the light glinting on his flute as he moved in time to the music. At some points Brian could hear him loud and clear, trilling high in the top octave. And it made him feel strangely empty and sad, a pang, wishing he had stuck with it, persevered with learning to play. He'd had the same chance.

Towards the end of the concert, Tam's friend Bird came out, carrying a red electric guitar. Brian had never taken to him, thought he was far too sure of himself. Brian wasn't sure of himself at all. He thought again of Cathy and the Wayne Fontana lookalike with the car. Bastard! He pushed the image away. As Bird leaned over to plug in to his amplifier, his long hair fell forward. He stood up, made a grand gesture of sweeping it back from his forehead. Then he fiddled with his tuning, with the volume, and when he was quite ready gave McLeish a nod and started to play, stepping up to a microphone at the front of the stage.

Brian recognized the chords right away. He knew every line from the Dylan album, inside out. He started tapping his feet, found himself singing along. *How many roads must a man walk down.* The choir came in on the chorus. *The answer is blowing in the wind.* And with every verse more of the orchestra came in, till everyone was playing and singing together, and McLeish was encouraging the audience to join in. And Brian was overwhelmed by a whole flood of emotion as the red guitar wailed and Tam's flute flashed light at him. He couldn't keep a girlfriend and he couldn't play music. All he was good at was getting through exams. Time was passing, he would grow old and die. He hadn't even begun to understand anything. He had no idea. He hadn't a clue. And the answer was blowing in the wind.

3

All George was good at was Technical Drawing. The arithmetic wasn't too difficult, or the geometry. It was neat and clean, straightforward, almost mechanical. A simple matter of projecting, plan and elevation, measure and mark out, use compasses and setsquare, fill in the shapes. The hard 2H pencils didn't smudge, made sharp clear lines. Only his lettering was weak – he had no eye for the spacing, spread words out then crushed them up. But at least for that they used a darker HB that was easier to rub out. There was nothing else that needed freehand skills, except for the occasional ellipse, and his father had bought him a set of French Curves to help with that.

His father was glad to see him doing well at something. Though he wasn't the best in his class, he was getting by. He said when George left school he would get him a start in the drawing office, maybe an apprenticeship. Malcolm gave him a hard time about that. 'The old handshake does it again, eh? Jobs for the boys. A nod's as good as a wink.' Then he gave George a lecture, told him there were firms run by Masons that just refused, flat, to employ Catholics. 'In this day and age,' he said. 'It's incredible. I mean we're talking about people's livelihoods here.' George switched off, as he always did when Malcolm started to rant. Malcolm was at university now, studying Politics. He had moved into a flat and rarely came home to visit. When he did he would end up arguing with everybody. 'Cause a fight in an empty house,' his father would say, and Malcolm would look at the ceiling, mouthing, 'Give me strength!'

He even had a go at George about his Saturday job, went on about multinationals and exploitation and American imperialism and Vietnam.

'But they employ Catholics,' George said, and Malcolm laughed.

'Oh I'm sure they do George. I'm sure they do!'

George gave up. There was nothing wrong with the supermarket, nothing wrong with Americans. Malcolm took everything far too seriously.

'Anyway,' said George. 'Brian works there. And Tam's just started as well.'

'What do they know?' said Malcolm.

Tam had been assigned, like George, to the check-outs,

packing customers' shopping into brownpaper bags and cardboard boxes, sometimes lugging them to the carpark on the roof. George was looking out for him, keeping him straight on his first day.

'I suppose you got the pep-talk from Butch,' he said.

'Sure did!' said Tam in an American drawl. 'Quite a spiel!'

Butch was the American manager of the place. He would be in his thirties, fat, with hornrimmed glasses and a crewcut cropped so short you could see his scalp shine pink under the striplights. His briefing to the Saturday boys was all about politeness, efficiency, neatness. They were in the front line, were often the last impression a customer had of the store. 'And remember,' he would say, 'last impressions are lasting impressions.' George had liked that, had thought it was very good.

'Did you get the training film as well?' he asked Tam.

'Yeah. How to chuck stuff into a paper bag. Really riveting!'

'Pretty straightforward really,' said George. 'Just a matter of keeping the heavy stuff to the bottom, your tin cans and that, then build it from there. Oh and don't forget to keep anything smelly, like your soappowder or onions away from stuff like butter that soaks up smells.'

Tam was yawning. 'I think I can manage it,' he said. 'But I'll tell you what's really hard.' He tugged at the elasticated black bow tie round his neck. 'Wearing this fucking dicky bow. Makes you feel like a right dooly!'

'Och, you get used to it,' said George, but Tam shook his head, said, 'I doubt it.'

George stayed with him for the first couple of customers, made sure he didn't pack the bags too full or top-heavy. Then he had to move to another checkout, leave him to it.

At lunchtime in the canteen George sat beside Tam and Brian. 'Just like old times,' he said.

'Just need Eddie Logan to make it immortal,' said Tam.

'Christ!' said Brian. 'Can you imagine Eddie working here!'

'First word out of Butch,' said Tam, 'Eddie would stick the head on him as quick as look at him!'

George couldn't understand the way they were talking, as if they admired Eddie. But he didn't say anything. They had a way of ganging up on him, talking down at him. They could make him feel small, the way Malcolm did, as if he knew nothing. That was what education did for them.

Like his father before him, George had joined the Boys Brigade. One Friday evening he was getting himself ready as usual to go out, polishing his black shoes, shining up his belt buckle and the numerals on his pillbox hat. It was a little ritual he enjoyed. The dark smell of the bootpolish, the metallic tang of Brasso, were comfort to him, and order. They made him feel warm in the pit of his stomach.

He put on his navy blue blazer, the white webbing band diagonally across it, over the left shoulder. He clipped the brownleather belt round his waist, holding the band in place. He positioned the hat, just so, at an angle, adjusted the chinstrap. There.

'You look smart,' said his mother.

'Great thing the BB,' said his father. 'Sure and Stedfast, eh!' And George braced himself, ready for a speech.

'Course you could get more involved.' Here it came. 'I mean when I was your age I was on my way to being a corporal.'

'I know, you've told me.'

'Ended up a sergeant.'

'Aye.'

'God I was fit. Could walk round the hall on my hands.'

George had tried. He took part in the tumbling,

gymnastics. He just wasn't particularly good at it. He was useless at football, hadn't even turned up for the trial. He had tried to learn the drums, to play in the marching band, but he had no sense of rhythm, no co-ordination.

'I just think sometimes you could put a bit more into it,' said his father.

'Och the boy tries,' said his mother. 'He does his best.'

'Time I was going,' he said.

He was halfway to the door when there was a knock. 'I'll get it,' he said, anxious to be out of the room.

He was surprised to see Malcolm standing there.

'Well hello there!' Malcolm grinned. 'How's the flower of young Christian manhood then?' His breath smelled of polo mints, so he had been drinking.

'Who is it?' called his father from the kitchen.

'It's Malcolm,' he shouted back. There was no response.

'The prodigal,' said Malcolm. 'The black sheep.'

'I'm just on my way out,' said George, stepping out and holding the door open.

'I'd never have guessed,' said Malcolm, then he stepped back and saluted. 'Sure and Stedfast!' He started to sing.

'Will your anchor hold in the storms of life
When the clouds unfold their wings of strife'

George pushed past him, and Malcolm sang again.

'Following in father's footsteps
Following your dear old dad'

His father appeared in the doorway, impatient.

'Are you coming in or what?'

'How kind of you to ask me, father!'

George ran on down the stairs and out into the street, glad to be away from the pair of them.

When he got to the hall he felt more relaxed,

71

comfortable. The musty smell of the place, the warmth, the brightness of the lights, were familiar, made him feel a glow. Mr Bell, the Captain, gave him a nod as he came in and he started helping to shift chairs, stack them at the back of the room.

'Clearing the decks,' said Mr Bell.

George enjoyed the marching and drill, the exercises, even the tumbling. And after all that they broke up into smaller groups for Bible Study. George's group were working through the Shorter Catechism, testing each other with the questions and the set answers.

> *What is man's chief end?*
> *To glorify God and enjoy Him forever.*

George wasn't so good when it came to discussion, had nothing much to say. But he knew the texts off pat, word perfect.

> *Into what estate did the fall bring mankind?*
> *The fall brought mankind into an estate of*
> *sin and misery.*

On his way home he saw Eddie Logan across the road. There was another boy with him and they were swaying about, laughing. Eddie shouted something after him, but George looked straight ahead, hurried on.

Malcolm was still there when he got home. He had come round to collect some books he'd left behind, had meant just to pick them up and go. But his mother had persuaded him to stay for a bite to eat.

'Didn't need much persuading,' said his father.

Now he was sitting watching *The Fugitive* on TV.

'Don't see much of this nowadays,' he said. 'We don't have a TV in the flat.'

'For somebody that doesn't like it,' said his father, 'you've certainly watched plenty tonight.'

'Just keeping in touch,' said Malcolm. 'Observing it as a sociological phenomenon. It's even more bizarre when you don't see it for a while.'

'Ach!' said his father, standing up. 'Havers! I'm away to bed. I suppose you'll be staying the night?'

'Could do,' said Malcolm. 'Or I could make the last subway if I rush. Otherwise I could walk it, through the Clyde Tunnel.'

'You'll do no such thing,' said his mother. 'I'll make up your bed.'

When their parents had both left the room, Malcolm stretched and yawned, seemed suddenly more at ease. He looked across at George who was still in his uniform.

'So how was the old BB tonight then?' he asked, and for once there was no sarcasm in it.

'Fine,' said George. 'OK.'

'You working at the supermarket tomorrow?'

'That's right.'

Malcolm turned down the volume on the TV but didn't switch it off. It still flickered its images at them.

'Listen,' said Malcolm. 'I've got this idea. And you can help me with it.'

George was beginning to wish he had never opened his mouth, never told Malcolm anything.

It was the end of the day, the supermarket was closed, and George had been given his usual job of sweeping out and mopping the back shop. Tam was helping him – he'd had the choice of doing that or using a machine to crush cardboard boxes into bales and tying them with wire.

'I've got my delicate musician's fingers to think about!' he'd said, opting to help George. 'And I've done enough heavy lifting for one day. Just about ruptured myself humphing one of these fifty-six pound bags of potatoes up to some bitch's car on the roof, and she turns round and hands me ninepence. Ninepence!'

George had almost finished sweeping. Tam took off his bow tie and stuffed it in his pocket, unbuttoned his shirt at the neck. 'That's better,' he said, and he slopped his mop in the bucket, squeezed out the excess water.

It was the smell of the place at this time of day that George had happened to mention to Malcolm. The sharp tang of disinfectant overlaid the faintly sweet stench that hung in the air, from old fruit and vegetables beginning to rot as it lay in bags and boxes, waiting to be thrown out. It was the smell that always stayed with him from the supermarket, the smell of decay, and he'd tried to describe it to Malcolm, said it made him feel a bit sick.

And Malcolm had actually shown an interest in what he was saying.

'So they throw a lot of stuff out do they?'

'Sacks of it,' George had said. 'If they think it won't keep till the Monday. And anyway, they're always getting fresh stuff in. Got to make room for it somehow.'

'So some of what they throw out isn't too bad.'

'Some of it stinks! But no, you're right. Some of it's just a bit bashed, or bruised.'

'Imperfect.'

'That's right.'

Malcolm had gone quiet then, thinking. He had said no more about it until last night when he'd asked George for help with his 'idea'.

George hadn't been keen, didn't want to do it. But Malcolm had persisted.

'I don't see the problem,' he'd said. 'You can even ask them for it. I mean it's going to be chucked out anyway. You'd just be taking it off their hands.'

'What would I say it was for?'

'For a soup kitchen. To feed the needy. How can they refuse?'

'Well . . .'

'Come on! Where's your Christian charity?'

'OK.'

'Good man! I knew you had a bit of gumption really.'

So George had asked Butch, who had said it was OK,

and he'd rummaged through the vegetables for anything that could be salvaged – potatoes beginning to sprout, carrots gone dry and shrivelled, onions turning moist and brown through the middle but firm on the outside. There was even a full-sized cauliflower with only a few flecks of black here and there on the surface, and a whole turnip that seemed to have nothing wrong with it at all except that by Monday it would have started to go soft. He had easily filled a sack, and when Danny the produce manager had heard what he was about, he had given him half a cabbage and a bag of bashed tomatoes, said, 'I hate to see waste myself.'

George had stashed his sack at the back door, to be picked up when he left. He peered in again when they had finished mopping the floor. 'Amazing,' he said, to Tam. 'And the thing is, I could have filled this a dozen times over.'

Butch came by then, doing his rounds, a last check of the premises.

'Finished back here?' he asked. They nodded.

'Is that the stuff you're taking?'

'That's right,' said George. 'Thanks.'

'No problem. It was going in the garbage anyway.' He looked at Tam. 'Lost your tie son?'

'It's in my pocket.' Tam pulled out the black bow, dangled it on its elastic.

'OK,' said Butch, smiling. 'Just as long as you wear it when the store's open, when you're dealing with the public.'

'Fine.'

'See you guys next week,' said Butch, turning away.

When he'd gone, George said, 'See! I told you he was all right.'

'You're kidding!' said Tam. 'Tightlipped wee bastard. He's worse than our fucking headmaster. And that's saying something!'

George shook his head, took another look at the contents of the sack.

Malcolm was well pleased with George's haul.

'It's brilliant,' he said. 'Can you believe this lot was going in the rubbish?' He shook the bag, poked around in it. 'We'll start the operation on Monday.'

The operation was called FEAST: FREEFOOD, and the aim was to make a big pot of soup every day, give it out free. Malcolm had managed to get the use of the kitchen at one of the student chaplaincies, borrow their pot. Someone else had laid hands on a supply of plastic cups, and they had set themselves up outside the University refectory.

'You've no idea how suspicious people were,' said Malcolm. He had come in to the supermarket to see George the following Saturday, collared him in his lunch-hour. 'I mean, they literally wouldn't take it. Thought there had to be a catch, you know. *How can it possibly be free?* Then I hit them with the philosophy of it. This is *waste*, and that's what our society's built on – mountains of grain held back to keep profits up, food deliberately destroyed while folk are starving. And all that's needed is fairer distribution, and that's what we're doing here. This free food is an example of how it works.'

'So it went down well?' said George.

'What, the ideology or the soup?'

'Both.'

'Well, let's say they're swallowing the soup, and I'm spicing it with the ideas!'

Malcolm looked pleased with himself at that.

'So!' He grinned at George.

'So this'll be a regular thing?'

'Absolutely. And there's no reason why it shouldn't spread. Multiply this by the number of supermarkets in the country. We're talking about *tons* of waste here, all just waiting to be redistributed.'

'And who's going to organize that?'

'The right people will come along.'

Butch came out through the door to the canteen. He

looked at his watch, looked at George, walked on. The tannoy was tinkling out *Wheels Cha Cha*.

'I better go,' said George.

Malcolm nodded. 'So you'll get me another sackful?'

'I'll see what I can do.'

'Good man!'

After a few weeks the routine was well established. Malcolm would turn up at closing time on Saturday and George would bring out the sack to him at the back door. One week he was driven up in a car, said it would make life easier. The girl driving it had long dark hair, tied back. She had an English accent and Malcolm introduced her as Angie.

'Your girlfriend?' asked George, when Malcolm came inside.

'Not exactly. We're not possessive in that kind of way.'

'Oh,' he said. 'I see.'

Malcolm laughed. 'Do you?'

'Listen,' said George. 'There's something I wanted to ask you.'

It seemed a good time to bring it up. The other night George had been rummaging in a cupboard in what had been Malcolm's room. His father had been out at a Lodge meeting, his mother stuck in front of the TV. George hadn't been looking for anything in particular, just snooping around out of boredom. He had pulled out a cardboard box, full of old papers of his father's – masonic journals, minutes of meetings. But right at the bottom he had found the magazines, three of them.

'And I think it was a pretty stupid place to hide them,' he said to Malcolm. 'If the old man finds them, it's just the kind of thing that'll make him blow his top. In amongst his masonic stuff too.'

Malcolm looked puzzled. 'What are you talking about? What magazines?'

'Come off it,' said George. 'These dirty magazines you stashed away in your room.'

77

Malcolm stared at him. 'Are you talking about *porno* magazines? Bums and tits sort of thing?'

'You know fine what I mean.'

Malcolm burst out laughing. 'I don't believe it!'

'What's so funny?' George was beginning to get annoyed.

'The dirty old bugger!' said Malcolm.

'Talk sense will you!'

'You don't think I'd buy crap like that do you?'

George's brain had seized. He didn't understand.

'They must be *his*,' said Malcolm. 'The old man's.'

George stared at him, blank.

'Can you believe it?' said Malcolm, laughing again. 'Buried away under all his masonic secrets! He must have planked them there when I moved out. Hey, maybe I'll chin him about it the next time I come round!'

'No!' George was anxious.

'Why not?'

'He'll think I've been looking through his things, on purpose.'

'So!' said Malcolm. 'Now I've got something on both of you!'

George tried to smile, tightened his face in a kind of grimace.

'Relax,' said Malcolm. 'It's OK. I won't say a word.' He paused. 'I'll keep it up my sleeve. Say no more.' He picked up the sack of vegetables. 'Just shows you, eh? Still, I suppose it means he's human!' He shook the sack to settle the vegetables towards the bottom, gathered the neck of it and hoisted it up, slung it over his shoulder.

'Same time next week?' he said.

'OK,' said George. 'Fine.'

When Malcolm had gone, he sat down, stared at nothing, tried not to think.

Tam jolted him out of it, clattered his bucket into the deep sink, turned on the tap.

'Come on George!' he shouted. 'No slacking there!'

He picked himself up, took his brush and started sweeping.

'Cheer up,' said Tam. 'It might never happen.'

George didn't respond, just carried on sweeping.

'Your face is tripping you,' said Tam. 'Big brother been annoying you?'

'No really,' said George. 'Och it's nothing. Just something he said.'

'Must be that sort of day,' said Tam. 'Did you see Brian?'

'Can't say I noticed.'

'Face like fizz. Looks like he's ready to chuck himself in the Clyde.'

'How, what's up?'

'Well, you know that wee bird he was going out with a while back, the one he met here?'

'Cathy?'

'That's right. She ditched him pretty quick.'

'I thought that, aye.'

'Started going out with some big guy. Anyway, apparently she stopped working here a few weeks ago. Said she wasn't well, some sort of gastric bug supposed to be.'

'Right enough, I haven't seen her.'

'Well guess what?'

'What?'

'She's expecting. Gastric bug my arse. She's in the club. Pregnant.'

'But she can't be any more than sixteen.'

'Old enough.'

'Is she getting married then?'

'Suppose so. Who knows?'

'So Brian's just heard about it?'

Tam nodded. 'I think he's really cut up because he never got it up her himself. Wishes he'd just got right in there.'

George supposed Tam was telling him this to make

him feel better. But somehow it didn't work, had the opposite effect, made things worse. Maybe if he could talk it out, tell somebody.

'Do you get on all right with your old man?' he asked.

'Suppose so,' said Tam.

'I mean, do you feel as if you know him?'

'I think so, yeah.' Tam looked puzzled. 'Mind you.'

'What?'

'Och, he's been a bit funny recently.'

'How do you mean?'

Tam hesitated. 'It's just, och, he's been betting a bit more than he used to. I heard him and my ma arguing about it. And I think he's bevvying more than usual. Nothing much you know. He's just not like himself.'

'Och well,' said George, not knowing what else to say.

'So what's your problem?' said Tam.

'It's really nothing,' said George. 'Nothing at all.'

'OK. Suit yourself.'

A potato had dropped from Malcolm's sack and George bent to pick it up. It had gone soft, was sprouting a cluster of white tubers, and it suddenly looked grotesque to him, made him feel sick. Something in the seething life of it made him physically recoil, and he dropped it, kicked it away from him, wiped his hand on his apron.

The swing doors behind them bashed open and Butch came through.

'You guys all done?'

'Just about,' said George.

Butch looked at Tam. 'Planning on joining the Beatles?' he asked.

'Sorry?'

'Your hair. It's getting kinda long.'

'That's the style,' said Tam.

'Well it's not the style in here. Get it cut.'

'I'll think about it,' said Tam.

'I'd think about it seriously. If you want to keep working here.'

Tam watched him go, spat out 'Bastard!' after him. Then he turned to George, said, 'See what I mean about it being one of those days!'

Malcolm had moved his operation to George Square.

'It's all very well feeding a bunch of students,' he said. 'But this is the real thing. Old winos and dossers from the hostels, guys that hang about the station. We're feeding folk that really need it.'

The first week it had gone well. They had made the soup in the afternoon, carried it down in the boot of Angie's car and dished it up in the evening. The atmosphere had been good – plenty of soup for anybody who wanted it, and a steady stream of passers-by for Malcolm to harangue.

'It was great!' he said. 'Just great!'

But the second week was a disaster.

'Word must have got round,' he said. 'So there was a queue of folk waiting by the time we got there. Next thing we're starting to run out of soup. And a couple of drunks start complaining, saying some folk had got two or three helpings and they hadn't had any. Before we knew what was happening they'd started a fight. Somebody cowped the table and spilled what was left of the soup. That was it. Developed into a total rammy. And of course the polis came in to break it up. Started coming on heavy as if it was our fault. So one word borrowed another. I ended up calling them a bunch of fascist bastards and they booked me.'

'Christ,' said George. 'What did they charge you with?'

'You name it,' said Malcolm. 'Breach of the peace, obstruction, resisting arrest, assaulting a police officer. Threw the fucking book at me.'

'Godalmighty!' said George. 'Does da know?'

'Not yet. So don't you go telling him. He'll find out soon enough.'

'I'll keep it up my sleeve,' said George. 'Say no more!'

The following Saturday Butch called George into his office. Somehow he had heard about Malcolm getting into trouble. The police had wanted to know where the soup had come from, how come it was free, where they had stolen the vegetables. Malcolm had explained it wasn't stolen, it was waste, excess to requirements, but wouldn't tell them where it had come from. That had made them even more suspicious, and an empty sack in Angie's car, with the supermarket's logo on it, had led them to phone Butch and check if he'd been missing any stock from his produce department.

'Seems this brother of yours is some kind of communist,' he said to George.

'Sort of.'

'I had no idea this was going on,' said Butch. 'Stirring up trouble.'

'He was just trying to do some good.' It sounded feeble, even to George's ears.

'That's what they all say, son. All the crazies, the extremists, the terrorists.'

This was Malcolm he was talking about. It was ridiculous.

'But.'

'He's an agitator. According to the police he was just using this whole business to get up on his soapbox and sound off. He's anti free enterprise, anti democracy, downright anti American. We give him this stuff for free and he uses it to criticize us for Godsake!'

'I'm sorry,' said George.

'I'm sure your involvement was in good faith,' said Butch, cooling down. 'You just got to be careful. That's all.'

George stood up to go.

'So that's it,' said Butch. 'No more creaming off stuff from the garbage. I guess it just proves the old saying. There *is* no free lunch.'

George had no idea what he was talking about.

82

'Tell your friend to come in now,' said Butch.

Outside Tam was waiting to go in. '*Another* one of those days!' he said.

George saw him later and he said Butch had bawled him out, fired him for refusing to cut his hair.

'But couldn't you just have cut it a wee bit?' said George. 'Just to keep the job?'

'Stuff the fucking job!' said Tam. 'It's the principle.'

That was the way Malcom talked. Principles. George didn't understand it. It was all madness. All he wanted was a quiet life.

'I must say I'm surprised at *you* George,' said his father. 'I'd have thought you would have had more sense. I mean if you had kept your mouth shut, if you hadn't got him those vegetables.'

'It wasn't George's fault,' said his mother. 'He didn't know.'

'Well he *should* have known. Getting mixed up with that waster.'

'He's my brother!'

'Country's gone to the devil,' said his father. 'Ever since bloody Wilson and his bloody Labour lot got voted in. No standards.'

George was sick of the whole business, couldn't wait to get away for a break at the weekend, to BB camp in Arran. He had been looking forward to it for weeks.

The short crossing on the ferry had made him feel queasy. Then there had been the foolishness of marching in formation through town, packs on their backs, to pitch camp in a field. It was late afternoon by the time they were settled, and all they'd had to eat was a bag lunch – crisps, a cold pie, a chocolate biscuit. George was sharing a four-man tent with three other boys his own age. He didn't know them well but they seemed to be friends – something in the way they joked with each other. Alan, Ronnie and John.

It had started to rain. The four of them lay on their

sleeping bags listening to the sound of it pattering on the tent roof. The canvas smelled of mildew and some kind of waterproofing.

'This is miserable,' said Ronnie.

'Dreich,' said John.

'Never mind,' said Alan. 'It can only get better.'

George wasn't so sure, thought it could easily get worse.

'I'm starving,' he said.

'We'll be going to the chippy later on,' said Alan.

'I thought there was food here,' said George.

'Gyuch!' said Alan.

'Boke!' said John.

The three of them made spewing noises.

'Slop,' said Alan. 'They call it stew.'

'More like spew,' said Ronnie.

'And God knows when they'll get a fire going in this rain,' said Alan. 'So it might end up being *cold* slop!'

'Maybe I will go with you right enough,' said George.

Alan nodded. 'You can chip in to the kitty if you like.'

'What for?'

'A carry-out. One of the older guys'll get it for us out the hotel.'

'I don't know.'

'What else is there in a dump like this? Fish suppers. A bevvy. And then.'

'Then what?'

'Find a couple of wee herries. You never know your luck.'

John groaned, in agony or ecstasy, rolled over groping himself.

'Well George?' said Alan. 'Are you in?'

The rain battered harder. Outside a bugle blared, calling them.

'OK,' he said.

The chip shop was packed, queued-out to the door. A few of the boys had had the same idea. And there were girls, in twos and threes, joining the line or hanging about outside the shop.

'Like flies round a toly,' said Alan. 'I told you!'

They had already collected their carry-out. An older boy had brought it out to them from the hotel, handed it over in a brownpaper bag. 'I kept the change,' he'd said. 'Commission.' There were a dozen cans, and at Alan's insistence, a quarter-bottle of whisky. George's share of it was more than he had drunk in his life, cost him most of the money he had brought.

They headed down to the shingle beach. George was so hungry he guzzled his food, wolfed it down, licked the salt and vinegar from his greasy fingers. It was dark now, but at least the rain had eased off. They stood staring out at the sea, a twinkle of lights on the far shore, the mainland. Alan opened the quarter-bottle, swigged from it, passed it round. George screwed up his face as the raw taste of the whisky hit his throat. But he swallowed it down, felt warmed by it. Alan used an attachment on his pen-knife to pierce a can for each of them, poke a couple of ragged holes they could drink from. The gassiness of it made George belch, came back up his nose. But he persevered. After the third can he was laughing out loud with the others, not at anything in particular, just at the stupid night and themselves standing there and their empty cans bobbing back to them on the waves. George felt buoyed up, exhilarated, and when he needed to empty his bladder, he sent an arc of piss steaming into the sea. And when the wind caught it and he dribbled down his trouser-leg, felt the warm seep of it, that too made him laugh. And by the time Alan said 'Right, come on and we'll find some talent,' he was ready for anything.

Back on the main street they met the girls – three of them coming towards them on the opposite side of the road. Alan elected himself as spokesman, crossed over and started chatting them up. The girls laughed at something he said, and he came back over, gave the thumbs up. 'I think we've knocked it off here,' he said.

'Only one problem George. There's three of them.'

'And three of us,' said John.

'Sorry Georgie boy,' said Ronnie. 'You're redundant. Surplus to requirements.'

'Ach,' said George, relieved and disappointed all at once. 'Who cares?'

'See you back at the tent,' called Alan as they moved off, leaving him.

'Later,' shouted Ronnie.

John laughed. 'Much later!'

He turned away, tried not to let it touch him. But the drink was wearing off, the night was ebbing away from him, leaving a bleakness, desolation. There was nothing else to do but head back to the camp.

'Damnation!' he said, then he saw her, standing in the dark doorway of a shop.

'Got a light?' she asked, stepping forward. She was younger than him, maybe only fourteen, wore a black pvc raincoat with the collar turned up. She had a stray-cat look about her, scrawny and thin, her short hair plastered flat by the rain. Normally he wouldn't have looked twice. Normally.

'Sorry,' he said. 'I don't smoke.'

She laughed. 'A good boy, eh?'

'Well . . .'

'No bad habits?'

'I wouldn't say that.'

He watched her, watching him.

'You here with the BB?'

'That's right.'

He wanted to say something smart, something funny. He could think of nothing.

'Is this your first time?' she asked.

Did she mean what he thought? Could she really be asking?

'First time you've been here?' she said.

'Oh. Aye. That's right.'

'Fancy a walk?'

He looked about him, nodded. 'OK.'

She led him back down the main road, across it and through a carpark, round behind a building out of the wind.

'This'll do fine,' she said, and her quick directness took him by surprise as her arms were round his neck and she kissed him, darting with her tongue, and writhed her whole body against him making him hard. And without really knowing what to do, he pressed her left breast through her jersey, awkwardly, amazed at how small it was and the way it flattened out under his hand. And a stupid pop song came into his head. Pardon me Miss. But I've never done this. With a real live girl. And quickly again she had him unzipped and flipped out and she was working on him, then she stopped.

'Don't stop!'

'Have you got an f.l.?'

He had only just recently found out what that meant. 'No.'

'Why the fuck not?'

'I don't know. I didn't expect.'

'I thought you lot were supposed to Be Prepared.'

'That's the Scouts.'

'What's your motto then?'

'Sure and Stedfast.'

She laughed. 'Sounds dead boring!'

He didn't want to lose it. He made a grope at her, clumsy, up under her skirt, felt the warmth.

'I suppose I better finish you off,' she said.

He bucked and spurted and it was over. He subsided, clinging to her, breathing in the smell of her cheap scent, her wet hair.

He walked her back round to the road. Her name was Marie. He knew nothing else about her.

'I go this way,' she said.

'I'll walk you home.'

'No,' she said. 'It's OK. You better not.'

He didn't ask why. It didn't matter.

Back at the camp a torch shone in his face, dazzled him.

'George?' It was Mr Bell, checking up on stragglers and latecomers. For one ridiculous moment George thought of his catechism, as if in readiness, as if the man was about to test him on it. Man's chief end is to glorify God and enjoy Him forever. The fall brought mankind into an estate of sin and misery. The drink must still be fuzzing his brain. He felt tired, and dirty, and sad.

'You all right?' asked the Captain.

'Just felt a wee bit sick. Went for a walk.'

'You haven't been drinking have you?'

'No!' George shielded his eyes from the torch-light.

'Thought I could smell it,' said the man, lowering the beam.

'Well,' said George, 'somebody gave me a wee sip of beer out a can.'

'That's how it starts son. Just a wee sip. At your age you want to be careful.'

George said nothing. The torch was switched off. They stood there in the dark.

'You better get some sleep George. It's an early start in the morning.' There were games planned. Football, an obstacle course, a hike. He wasn't looking forward to any of it.

'Yes sir,' he said. 'Good night sir.'

'Good night.'

George crawled into the tent and straight into his sleeping bag. He was exhausted but he couldn't sleep. The ground was hard and cold. After maybe an hour of it he heard a commotion outside and Mr Bell's voice, angry. Then the other three boys came bundling into the tent, bumping and stumbling over each other, laughing.

'Moaning faced auld sod,' said Ronnie.

'Read the fucking riot act,' said John.

'You all right Georgie boy?' said Alan. 'Did we wake you up?'

'I'm OK,' said George. 'I'm fine.'

'Sorry for ditching you. We just couldnae pass up a chance like that.'

'Three fucking scrubbers!' said Ronnie.

There were footsteps just outside the tent and the torchbeam shone in on them.

'That's the last warning for you lot. If you don't settle down you're on the first boat back in the morning. And that's final.'

The beam was cut. They lay down and tried to keep quiet, snorted from time to time as they giggled and stifled it. And after a while George could tell from their breathing they were all asleep, but he still lay awake, staring into the dark.

He couldn't solve it, couldn't work it out. It had seemed like a straightforward problem, the kind of thing he had dealt with dozens of times before. You were given the plan and part of the first elevation, asked to complete it, add the second elevation, then draw the three-dimensional view of the object in the top right corner of the page. But somehow he must have done something wrong. The finished shape refused to come clear. And it had to happen now, in the class test. Life was miserable. Things were getting on top of him.

There was the whole carry on with Malcolm. His case had come up in court and he'd been fined, and that had set his father off again. 'Damned disgrace!' he'd said, and he'd loaned him the money but said it was the last time, told him not to ask again, ever. Stew in his own juice. George had never seen his father so grim and moral. And he thought of the dirty magazines hidden under his masonic papers, and he felt disgusted, and for some reason he blamed Malcolm for that too, remembered him laughing about it.

And it was because of Malcolm that things had changed for him at the supermarket. Butch no longer trusted him, was brusque and wary when he spoke to him, forever pulling him up, telling him off. Over the last few weeks everything seemed to have changed. Nothing was the same. Even the BB was different after that weekend camp. It was unfair the way Mr Bell had lumped him together with the others for coming back late, and drinking, and causing a disturbance. He had given them a dressing down at assembly the next morning.

George hadn't told the others about the girl, Marie. That was his secret. The first girl he'd ever got off with, and she'd let him go so far, so quickly, would have let him go all the way if only. He tried to picture her face but he'd lost it. And in behind the guilty thrill of remembering what she'd done to him, the slightly shamefaced triumph that she'd fancied him enough to do it, there was something else, a sadness at the thought of her.

'Ten more minutes,' said his teacher, Mr McCann. 'You should just be finishing off.'

That was what the girl had said to him. Finish you off. She was so young. A stray cat. Scrawny. For a moment he saw her face, remembered it.

He looked at his drawing, ready to give up. He had printed the heading, as neatly as he could. Isometric Projection. But the space was blank, only smudged with rubbed-out guidelines that hadn't linked up. Ten more minutes. Then he looked again and he saw what he had missed. It was there. The basic shape was a cube with a pyramid on top. And he suddenly saw, in the way the dotted lines connected, that there was a kind of archway cut into one side and the centre of the cube was hollow, like a room with a doorway leading into it.

He couldn't believe he hadn't seen it before, and he worked quickly to finish the drawing. He barely had time to underline the lettering and rub out the guidelines, and as he stared at this shape that had emerged, solid and real with its clean sharp edges, it seemed so perfect and beautiful that it made him want to cry.

4

There was nothing to beat playing in the band.
Nothing. Eddie had worked hard at the drumming,
even though he hated practising. 'Too much like hard
work,' he would say. But gradually he had mastered
the tricks, the skills, could rattle off quickfire bursts,
sustain a beat, flick intricate syncopated patterns
across it. And although Mr Bennett the bandmaster
didn't like him, said he was a troublemaker, he had
drafted Eddie into the band.

The uniform was red, white and blue. Blue trousers
with a red stripe down the side. White shirt with red
epaulettes, a red tie. Blue peaked cap with a chinstrap,
the skip pulled down low over the eyes. Mean. Eddie
had strutted and turned in it, admired himself in the
wardrobe mirror, till he'd heard his mother come in at
the door and he'd whipped off the cap and the tie, sat
down in a chair, acted casual.

The first time he'd marched in the Walk he couldn't
believe how it made him feel. It was brilliant, it was
magic, it was real. It was triumph and glory. Hello
there! Ya beauty! The music caught him up and he
battered hell out of his drum.

Eddie had left school as soon as he could, a week
after his fifteenth birthday. They couldn't force him to
stay on after that, not even to the end of term. And
anyway, his teachers and headmaster were glad to see
the back of him.

By that time Eddie's father had already left his
mother, found a job in Corby and walked out.

'Good riddance to bad rubbish!' she had said.

His brother Davie had finished his apprenticeship
the year before, had emigrated to Australia. So now it
was only Eddie and his mother in the house. For a
while it hadn't been too bad, no constant niggling from
his mother, no black brooding moods from his father,
no stand-up screaming fights every weekend. But now

91

she had started on Eddie again, especially when she had a drink in her.

'As bad as yer faither,' she would say. 'Neither work nor want.'

He had tried to work – took a job as a baker's van-boy straight from school. But the pay had been terrible and he'd hated it – up at five in the morning for a six o'clock start, delivering trays of bread and rolls, cakes and pies. He'd been assigned to a driver by the name of Brennan who had made Eddie do all the lifting and carrying, never gave him any help. 'That's what you're gettin paid for,' he'd told him. 'All brawn and fuck all brains.'

Eddie had taken it, said nothing. Then one morning he had slept in, turned up late for his shift, and Brennan had had to load the van by himself. He'd been raging, called Eddie for everything.

'Ya shitefaced orange bastard ye! I've a good mind to get you your jotters for this!'

Eddie had turned on him. 'Suits me just fine pal. Cos I've had it up to here wi you and your shity fuckin job!' And he'd picked up a breadboard, tipped its load of rolls on to the ground. Then he'd slammed the board at Brennan, sent him staggering back against the van.

'That's it!' Brennan had screamed at him. 'You can pick up your cards. That's you finished!' But Eddie was on his way, out the door. He had been in the job three weeks.

'Oh that's brilliant,' said his mother. 'Absolutely brilliant! Three weeks dig money, a few lousy quid, and that's it, out the windae.'

She worked as a cleaner, didn't earn enough and drank half of it anyway.

'And no fuckin broo money because ye walked out.'

'I'll get money,' he said.

'How?'

'Never you mind.'

And she didn't mind at all, didn't care, as long as the money came in.

At first it had just meant hanging about together, moving around in a pack, causing a bit of bother, provoking aggravation. They had staked out their territory and any outsiders wandering into it were liable to be picked off. Rockers and students were legitimate targets, fair game. But best of all were other gangs, the Tongs, the Cumbie, the Fleet. Sometimes one of them would come over mobhanded, seek out Eddie's team and take them on, and there would be a running battle in the street or on some patch of wasteground, with blades and bricks and bottles, anything that came to hand.

It was one of these pitched battles that had established Eddie's reputation. They'd been warned that the Fleet were coming over to claim them, and they'd been ready. Eddie had armed himself with a cleaver, and during the fight he'd waded in, swung it about him like a madman. He had ended up leading his mob in a charge, chasing the Fleet halfway back to Maryhill. He had made his name.

'See that Eddie, man!'

'Mental!'

'Pure mad!'

'Aff his fuckin heid!'

Eddie had liked the sound of it. Mental. Pure mad. It was something to measure himself against, something to live up to. And in any fight it gave him an edge. Don't mess with Mental Eddie. Eddie's a headcase. Eddie kills.

'What about this money you were gonnae bring in?'

'I'll get it.'

'When?'

'You'll see.'

'When?'

'It's comin.'

'Aye, so's fuckin Christmas.'

One night at the dancing, Eddie was talking to Spasm.

Spasm had to raise his voice above the noise of the band, pounding away in the background, belting out *Down at the club*.

Friday night has finally come around . . .

Spasm's real name was Sam. As a child it had been distorted to Spam, then to Spasm. He had grown used to it, even come to like the sound of it, would spray-paint it on walls. Crazy Spasm. Spasm Rules.

'Anyway,' he said. 'This guy wants to talk to us.'

'And he asked for me?' said Eddie.

'He asked for somebody hard. And mental. But smart.'

'Mental but smart! Is this guy Irish?'

'Eh?'

'Forget it. And he never said what it was?'

'Just said it could be worth wur while.'

'He's no some kinda poof is he? An arse-bandit!'

'Away and fuck. He wants to see us later on the night.'

'Well,' said Eddie. 'Maybe. That depends.'

'Depends on what?'

'How we get on here.'

He nodded across to where two girls were dancing together, their handbags on the floor between them. He knew one of them, Sandra. She was small, her dark hair cut short, mod style. She had looked across towards Eddie, said something to her friend and they had laughed.

'Fancy her quite strongly do ye?' asked Spasm.

'Fuckin right I do,' said Eddie. 'Think you could get off wi her pal?'

'Could try.'

The band had moved into another Drifters number, *Take you where the music's playing*. Eddie stepped in between Sandra and her friend, went into the old *You dancin?* routine.

'You askin?'

'I'm askin.'

'I'm dancin.'

As she turned away with him she shrugged at her friend who didn't look too happy to be lumbered with Spasm.

The music was too loud for them to talk while they danced, and anyway they had nothing much to say. So they said their nothing much between songs. Eddie told her about playing the drums, about running mental with a cleaver. Then they let the music carry them as the band played *Get Ready* and *Uptight* and *Hold on I'm coming*. Sandra's friend had cut in at one point, said she was fed up and was going home.

'Suit yourself.'

'I will.'

Spasm was hanging about the edge of the floor, on his own.

'Looks like they never hit it off,' said Sandra.

'Who the fuck cares?'

They were still up dancing when the band played *Save the last dance for me*, a signal that the next song was the last.

> *Oh I know (yes I know)*
> *that the music's fine*
> *like sparkling wine*

The last dance was always a slow one, a moonie, something like Del Shannon's *Kelly*. Tonight it was *Please Stay*.

> *I loved you before I even learned your name*
> *And I wanted to give you my heart*

'I love that song,' she said, as Eddie held her close.

'Brilliant,' he said.

'Who was it used to sing it?'

'Crying Shames.'

'Never heard of them.'

'One-hit wonders.'

> *If I called out your name*
> *like a prayer . . .*

'Maybe I'll start a group,' he said. 'Play the drums.'

'You should.'

He kissed her neck, her ear.

Would this time be different?
Please stay, don't go.

He pressed against her and they moved together.

'See you hame?'

The music stopped.

'OK.'

As they made towards the exit, Spasm came after them.

'Hey Eddie.'

'What is it?'

'There's a coupla guys here that are in the Cumbie. We're gonnae claim them outside.'

'How many?'

'Three or four.'

'Christ, yis can handle that. There's about a dozen of our boys here!'

'Just thought you might have fancied it.'

'Aye, but that's no the only thing I fancy.'

'Fine. Just thought I'd tell you.'

'Sure.'

'What about later on? That guy.'

'I'll see. Wait for me at the corner.'

'Right.'

Outside, as they headed for the bus-stop, they heard a yelling behind them, turned and saw the claim. It was hard to tell what was happening, but one boy was already down and Spasm was going in with the boot.

From upstairs on the bus it all looked unreal in the harsh light from the dance-hall, red and green, flickering on and off. People spilling out of the hall crossed the road to avoid trouble, and the bouncers stood back in the doorway and watched. As long as it was out in the street, it wasn't their problem.

'Is that no terrible!' said a woman in the seat behind.

'So it is missis,' said Eddie, craning round to look back as the bus moved off. 'Terrible!'

In Sandra's back close they clung together up against the wall and his hand was down and stroking between her legs and inside her and she was rubbing him hard but she wouldn't let him get in, go all the way.

'Fucksake!' he said, breathing hard. 'How no?'

'I don't want to get a wean.'

'Jesus fuck!'

'Next time we'll be ready for it,' she said.

'I *am* ready for it!'

'You know what I mean.'

He knew what she meant.

Get ready cause here I come.

Ready for it.

Hold on I'm comin.

Next time.

Uptight out of sight.

'Shite!'

He jerked himself against her till he came.

Spasm was still at the corner, waiting for him.

'Well?'

'What?'

'D'ye get it up her?'

'What d'*you* think?'

'Lucky bastard!'

Spasm had a swollen nose, a cut above his eye.

'Gave ye a hard time did they?'

'Should see the other guy!'

'I did,' said Eddie. 'You had him down on the pavement.'

'Kicked his head in!' said Spasm, grinning.

'So. We're goin to see The Man?'

'Right.'

The man lived in a scheme, the Wine Alley. There was no name on the door. Spasm knocked three times, a signal. They knew they were being watched through a spy-hole, then a rattling of locks and bolts and the door was opened to them. The man was small, middle-aged. His hair was parted just above his left ear, spread across in thin strands to cover his baldness. He showed them into his kitchen, opened a can of lager for each of them.

'Cheers!' he said. 'Want a fag?'

They nodded. He opened a drawer, brought out ten Capstan, unbroken, passed them to Eddie, gave another whole packet to Spasm.

'Keep them,' he said.

'Thanks.'

'You must be Eddie. I've heard all about you.'

'Oh aye?'

'I'm Jimmy Anderson. Folk call me Andy.'

Eddie said nothing, took a drag at his cigarette, a swig of his beer.

'I thought yis weren't comin. Christ, Spas, you look like you've been in the wars!'

'Aye.'

'Should see the other guy, eh!'

'That's right.'

'So we're here,' said Eddie. 'What's the score?'

'Straight to the point,' said Andy. 'I like that.'

So he spent the next half hour telling them the score.

He said he was a businessman, had contacts, could shift any merchandise that came his way.

'Take the likes of booze and fags,' he said. 'Suppose you boys do a shop, right? If you're lucky you get a few quid out the till and whatever you can cart away – bevvy, smokes, sweeties, whatever.'

'I've never done a shop in my life,' said Eddie.

'I said *supposing*,' said Andy. 'We're talking about a business proposition here.'

'OK.'

'So you've got this stuff. What are you gonnae do wi it? Get bevvied for a week? Smoke yersels into an iron lung? Or else you try and flog it, some cunt shops you and that's it, you're inside.'

'So you're wanting us to knock stuff and you'll sell it.'

'Right first time! We'd be like business partners.'

'Equal splits?'

98

'Of course!'

'And how would we know what you sold the stuff for?'

'You'd just have to trust me, wouldn't you? But I'm telling you, it would be worth your while.'

'What d'you reckon Eddie?' said Spasm.

'Don't know.'

'Be like a steady job,' said Andy. 'Keep you off the streets!'

And it might shut his mother's moaning face. He shrugged. 'Could give it a try,' he said.

'Good!' said Andy. 'Shake hands on it.'

The thieving was easy, the pickings good. Andy checked the shops out beforehand, told them where there was a weak lock, an unbarred back window, an alarm system that was easy to break, an empty house above so they could come in through the ceiling. He watched the policemen on their beat, worked out when they would be furthest away. The boys would go in, stock up, get out again fast, escaping across back courts, through gaps in railings, over walls. If they thought there would be too much for them to carry, they would call in a couple of boys from their Young Team to help them lug it away. They paid them in cigarettes and told them to keep their mouths shut or they were dead. They stashed the stuff in an old bomb shelter in the middle of Andy's scheme, shifted it in relays across the backs to his house.

They always kept some back for themselves, just enough, and Eddie kept his mother supplied with cigarettes, the odd half bottle of *Bell's*. Sometimes he even brought her chocolates – her favourites were Cadbury's *Roses*. When Andy paid him his commission he gave her a share of it.

At first she wanted to know where he was getting it, but she wasn't really bothered.

'Ask no questions,' he said. 'You'll get told no lies.'

'Just as long as you don't get the jail,' she said.

99

'No chance.'

Andy was happy with the set-up. He said he might have more work for them, a different kind of job altogether.

'See, I do my moneylender on the side,' he explained. 'Maybe some bloke's behind wi his rent or his tick money, or he's lost a bit to the bookie. Well I'll help him out, lend him a few quid. And I don't get much out it mind you, just charge a wee bit interest. Every week. But some of these punters don't appreciate what I'm doing for them, and they're in no hurry to pay me back. That's where you boys come in.'

'You want us to lean on them,' said Eddie.

'That's it exactly. Just persuade them a wee bit. Make them see reason sort of thing.'

'And you'll pay us extra for this?'

'Commission on the payments you bring in.'

'Sounds OK.'

'Right you are then. It's a deal.'

They had a drink to celebrate and Andy gave them some pills, purple hearts he called them, and out in the street Eddie felt he was flying and he couldn't stop laughing at everything. Then his legs gave way and he sat down on the edge of the pavement. And across the road, walking in a hurry, he saw George Wilson in his Boys Brigade uniform and he thought he had never seen anything so ridiculous.

'How's the Georgie Porgie?' he shouted. 'How's the BB? The fuckin Bum Boys!'

George kept his head down, walked on even quicker. Eddie rolled over, lay flat on his back, still laughing.

Later he found himself at a party with no clear idea of how he had come to be there. Looking round the room, he could see a few boys from his Team, but no sign of Spasm. Then he just seemed to appear beside him, whispering into his ear. 'Wee Agnes is doin a line-up.' Agnes hung about the Team, was available to anybody who wanted her.

'Fuckin hacket features,' said Eddie.

'She's no that bad,' said Spasm. 'And you can always leave the light out. Put a bag over her head!'

It was that kind of night, everything was crazy, and here he was pushing his way to the front of the line and nobody arguing about it. Then the bedroom door was open and another boy, Jimbo, came out and Eddie was in. Agnes smiled at him from the bed. He hung his jacket over a chair, kicked off his shoes. This was actually happening. The only light was a bedside lamp. He switched it off, unzipped himself and climbed in on top of her. She held him and he shoved it in, came quick.

As he came out of the room he saw Sandra. She had just arrived at the party. She looked at Eddie, looked at the door.

'You're all the same,' she said. 'Fuckin animals!'

One night Eddie came home and found Andy waiting for him, sitting having a cup of tea with his mother. It made Eddie feel strange to see him there, in their kitchen. It was two separate parts of his life coming together, and he didn't like it.

'What is it?' he asked. 'What d'you want?'

'Eddie!' said his mother. She had a drink in her. 'That's no way to talk to Mr Anderson.'

'Aw please, call me Andy.'

Eddie felt sick. 'What are you here for?' he asked.

'Got a job for you,' said Andy. 'The business we were discussing.'

'When?'

'Themorra. Back of five. Come round to my place. Bring Spas.'

'Fine.'

'Eddie's doing his agent for me Mrs Logan. Collecting.'

'Maisie,' she said.

'See you themorra night then,' said Eddie, showing him to the door.

The three of them stood waiting, opposite the yard gates, Andy watching out for his customer, Eddie and Spas standing back in the closemouth.

'I know the cunt gets paid on a Thursday,' said Andy. 'Got to nail him before he gets to the boozers.'

The hooter had gone and hundreds of men poured out into the street, all of them in a hurry to be away.

'Look at them!' said Andy. 'Mugs! Slog their fuckin guts out. Week in week out. Two nights and a Sunday. And for what? Place'll be shuttin down soon, and then where'll they be?' He spat. 'Definitely a mug's game.'

'How d'you know you'll see this guy?' said Eddie.

'He always comes this way,' said Andy. 'I've watched him. In fact here he is.'

Eddie poked his head out, saw a man coming towards them wearing overalls and an old suit jacket. His cap was pulled down over his eyes, but as he looked up Eddie recognized him as Willie Rae, Tam's father.

'Fucksake,' said Eddie. 'I know the cunt.'

'All the better,' said Andy. 'He'll know what a hard man you are!' He stepped forward, blocking the man's path. 'A minute, pal. I'd like a word.'

'Listen . . .'

'No, *you* listen!'

Eddie and Spas stepped out behind him.

'What *is* this?'

'You owe me,' said Andy.

'You'll get paid.'

'Fuckin right I will.'

'Is that supposed to be a threat?'

'No, it's a promise. Is that no right boys?'

'That's right,' said Eddie.

Willie looked at him. 'Christ!' he said. 'I know you. You're the Logan boy. Were at school wi Tam.'

Eddie said nothing, shrugged.

'God's sake!' said Willie. 'You've been in my house!'

'Well that's nice,' said Andy. 'Means we can keep it friendly.'

'Look, I told you. I'll pay you the lot when I get back on my feet.'

'I need some right now. On account.'

'OK,' said Willie, opening the flap of his overall pocket, dipping into his pay-poke. 'I can give you five.'

Andy took it, shook his head. 'Fifteen.'

'Come on!' said Willie. 'That would leave me bugger all for the week!'

'You can always borrow it!' said Andy. 'Tap somebody else!' He laughed. 'No, I'll tell you what. I'll be reasonable. Make it ten and that'll do. For this week.'

'Bastard!' said Willie, handing him another five, pushing past.

Andy called after him. 'Same time next week then!' He took out his wallet, put the two crisp notes in it, handed two singles to Eddie and Spas.

'Talk about easy money,' he said. 'I told you. Mugs. The lot of them.'

A Saturday afternoon and the match with Hearts had ended in a 0–0 draw. Eddie and Spasm were bored, had twenty minutes to kill before the pubs were open, so they had gone into the supermarket, were wandering up and down the aisles.

'Imagine screwin this place!' said Spasm.

'Need a fuckin fleet of lorries to shift it!' said Eddie, imagining it.

'Hey, is that no that guy you know, him that's in the BB?'

Eddie looked across, saw George at a check-out, packing an old woman's shopping into a brownpaper bag. 'Christ, so it is! Look at the state of it! The wee bow tie and that! Make you sick so it would.'

Further along he saw Brian in the snackbar washing a sink-full of dirty dishes. 'No another one,' said Eddie. 'I don't know! And he's one of they ones that's supposed to have brains. I mean, imagine it, gettin dickied up like that, scrubbin dishes for half a dollar a fuckin hour.'

Brian caught his eye, gave him a nod. Eddie stared back, didn't smile.

'Come on,' he said. 'We'll get out of here before I throw up.'

Later, in the pub, Andy sought them out, ordered up a round.

'What is it this time?' said Eddie.

'It's your man again, that guy that works in the yards.'

'Rae?'

'That's him. He's back in arrears. Heavily.'

'So he needs persuaded again.'

'Right.'

'When?'

'The night. I know where he's drinking. He'll be there till closing time. I know his road hame. Goes through a quiet bit. I'll show you.'

So they found themselves standing in another close-mouth, waiting for the pubs to come out. Andy had shown them the best spot and left them to it, said he had other business to attend to. Eddie was restless, kept sticking his head out, looking up and down the road.

'Fuck this for a game of soldiers,' he said, then he saw their man come lurching round the corner, a bit unsteady on his feet.

'Look at it!' Eddie shook his head. 'Thing is, the boy's another one of they brainboxes. Makes you wonder.' He stepped back and they waited till Willie Rae was passing the close, then they grabbed him, bundled him in and flattened him against the wall.

'What the fuck?'

'Just a bit of business,' said Eddie. 'Anderson wants paid.'

'I've told him, he'll *get* paid.'

'Aye. Now!'

'I havenae got it.'

'That's too bad,' said Eddie. 'That's really too bad.'

'Christalmighty, son, I *know* you!'

'Check his pockets Spas.'

Spasm raised a hand and the man brushed him aside. Eddie jumped in and grabbed him by the lapels. He was about to put the head on him, butt him in the face, when another figure appeared in the closemouth.

'What the hell's this?'

Mr Bennett put a hand on Eddie's shoulder, spun him back.

'You,' he said. 'Logan. On your way.'

Eddie thought about it, weighed up the odds, backed off.

'You OK?' said Bennett, turning his attention to Willie Rae.

'Aye, sure. Fine.'

'I'll see you about this another time,' he said to Eddie, who spat back at him, 'Bastard! Think you're a fuckin big man.'

'Big enough for you son. Any day.'

When Eddie got back to the house, he heard a man's voice from the kitchen, heard his mother laughing. He pushed open the door, saw her sitting at the table and Andy standing behind her, an arm round her shoulder as he leaned over to pour her a drink.

'You here again?'

'Just a wee social call,' said Andy.

'I can see that.'

'Don't be like that, son. Nice to be nice, know what I mean?'

'Is this the other business you had to sort out? Meantime me and Spas are out doing your dirty work.'

'That's what you're paid for.'

'Coupla lousy quid!'

'Much did you collect?'

'Fuck all.'

'Eh?'

'That big bastard Bennett showed up, handered him out.'

'Christ!'

'I wasnae gonnae take *him* on. No for you anyway.'

Andy sat down, worried. 'He didnae say anything about reporting it to the polis or that, did he?'

'I wouldnae put it past him.'

Andy knocked back his drink, stood up. 'I better be going. Be seeing you Maisie.'

'Aye,' she said, her voice flat and dull.

When he'd gone, Eddie turned on his mother. 'What the fuck's he doin, hangin about here?'

'What's it to you?' she said. 'And what's the harm in it? Wee bit company. A wee drink. But you've got to fuckin spoil everything.'

Andy kept his distance after that, didn't get in touch, didn't come round to the house. Eddie and Spasm were running short of money, and Spasm did something stupid. He tried doing a shop on his own, going in through a back window. But somebody upstairs heard the noise, went out and phoned the police, and they were waiting when he came out. Then they took him back to his house, found a stash of cigarettes and chocolate under his bed. He was charged, summoned to appear in court.

He showed off the summons at the streetcorner, to Eddie and a few others from their Team, acted as if the whole thing was a laugh. The summons listed the things they had stolen, included three cakes of Highland Toffee, a box of Buttermilk Dainties and six Mars Bars. And there was something ridiculous about seeing it in black and white. But Eddie was serious. 'You'll no be saying anything about they other jobs now Spas? Mentioning any names or that?'

'Christ Eddie, I wouldnae do that!'

'That's all right well.'

Eddie met Anderson one day in the street, and he too was bothered about Spasm. 'Don't think he'd shop us do you?'

'I doubt it,' said Eddie. 'But you never know.'

'He'll likely get off wi a fine,' said Andy. 'And I can help him out wi that. Got to stick by each other, eh? We're all in it thegether!'

'Aye.'

'Tell your ma I'll be round to see her, sometime.'

'Aye, sure.'

But he never mentioned it to his mother, never said a word. Then one night there was a hammering at the door, and he said 'It might be your fancy-man.' But they looked at each other and knew it wasn't. The knock was too hard, too loud. Too official.

'More like the polis,' she said.

They thought about ignoring it, the way they always did with the tick-man, switching off the light, sitting quiet. But the knocking came again, ever harder.

Eddie answered it, saw not the police but Mr Bennett standing there. He had come to collect Eddie's uniform, said he didn't want him in the band any more.

'Not after that carry on the other week,' he said. 'I don't want your sort. That's you finished. Scrubbed.'

'Big deal,' said Eddie. 'I'm greetin my eyes out.'

He pushed the door closed, made the man wait out on the landing while he gathered together the uniform and stuffed it in a plastic bag.

'Who is it?' said his mother. 'What's the matter?'

'It's OK,' he said. 'It's nothing.' He opened the door again, shoved the bag at Bennett. 'Here.'

Bennett checked the contents. 'Right.' He opened his mouth, about to say something else, but Eddie slammed the door shut.

A few nights later there was another heavy knock at the door, late on.

'No again!' said his mother. 'I'm gettin sick of this.'

Again Eddie answered it. And this time it *was* the police, two of them, in uniform. His first thought was to dodge past them, make a run for it. But they were asking for his mother.

'Is Mrs Logan in?'

'Eh . . . aye.' He led them in and their bulk seemed to take up half the kitchen

'Mrs Logan?'

'Aye?'

The one doing the talking had taken off his hat, was referring to a notebook. 'Wife of Robert Logan?'

'That's right. But he doesn't live here now.'

'No.'

'What's he done?'

'I'm afraid there's been an accident Mrs Logan.'

She looked at him, not sure.

'Mr Logan's been knocked down by a car. I'm sorry. He's dead.'

Eddie couldn't take it in. The two black figures made the kitchen small. His mother in the chair was tiny and far away. The place was suddenly strange to him, but familiar as if he remembered it from another time. He stood staring at a milk bottle on the table, half empty, a hole poked in its tinfoil lid, and nothing made sense. They were saying his father had been killed half a mile away, crossing the road. It had taken the police a while to check, but it seemed he had been laid off work, had left his digs in Corby the day before.

'Looks like he was heading for here,' said the policeman. 'Coming home.'

After they had gone, his mother sat for a long time, saying nothing. They had asked if she could go to the mortuary in the morning to identify the body, and she had said yes, not thinking. Now she asked Eddie if he would go instead.

'I couldnae face it son.'

Her voice was strange, quiet.

'OK,' he said. He picked up his jacket.

'No the night,' she said. 'In the morning.'

'No. I'm just going out for a walk.'

She nodded. 'Aye.'

He walked down to where it had happened. The scene of the accident they had called it. That was what it had been like back in the kitchen. A scene. Like something in a TV play.

A yellow line had been chalked round the body and was still there, an outline. The shape of his father. The driver hadn't stopped. Hit and run. It was in a side street, off the main road. Eddie stood and stared at the chalkmarks, the figure. Now and again a car ran over it.

In the waiting room at the mortuary he remembered his father and mother yelling at each other, his father walking out for good. *Good riddance to bad rubbish.* Further back, his father in a good mood after winning at the dogs, a drink in him, money in his pocket, playing a tune on the mouth organ. *Que sera sera.* The attendant called his name, showed him into the room. There was a strong sharp smell he didn't recognize. The man guided him to the body, held him by the elbow, pulled back the sheet.

An old dead face, the skin smooth and waxy, mouth twisted as if in pain, the teeth removed, the cheeks clapped in. A mask. His father but not his father.

'Your father?'

He nodded, felt suddenly weak.

The face was covered up, the hand on his elbow guided him out. It was over, in and out, so quick.

'Just sign here son.' The man shoved a huge ledger at him, gave him a pen. 'These are your father's effects. You can take them now.' He handed Eddie an old suitcase fastened with a belt to hold it together. 'We just burned the clothes he was wearing. That's usual. They were marked.'

'Fine.'

'This is the contents of his pockets.' He gave him a brown envelope and Eddie looked inside. Three five pound notes, two singles, some change. A few scraps of paper, a bus-ticket, a betting-line, his last pay-slip.

Eddie put the money in his pocket, crumpled up the rest and threw it in the bin. He picked up the suitcase and stepped outside. The daylight was bright and hard.

He had already thought seriously about getting out. He had torn an advert from the paper – *Join the Professionals.* He could go in as a boy soldier on a three-year contract, and if he didn't like it he could get his mother to buy him out.

'Gettin fed up wi this dump,' he told Spasm. 'There's fuck all here.'

What clinched it was seeing his mother going into the lounge bar with Anderson. They were laughing. It was just a week after his father's funeral.

'That's it,' he said to Spasm. 'Next thing the cunt'll be moving in.'

Spasm thought that might not be too bad. 'Keep it in the family and that.' Eddie hated the thought of it. 'I'll see you later Spas.'

'Where you going?'

'Hame.'

Instead he took the subway into town and made his way to Central Station. He wouldn't be recognized there, and he might find a phone in working order. He had never made a phone-call in his life, and he felt really awkward about it. At first he thought he should dial 999, but the sign said that it was only for emergencies. Then he noticed there was a directory, and he looked up his local station under *Police.* He dialled the number, heard a single ring then pips and he shoved in the coin he had ready. A girl's voice asked what he wanted.

'Eh, I wanted to report something, somebody.'

The girl had a voice that sounded put on, clipped and nasal.

'And can I have your name, *sir*?'

'No, that doesnae matter.'

The girl gave a sigh, irritated. 'All right, what is it you want to report?'

'Eh . . .'

'Is it a crime?'

'It's no just the one, it's a few. And it's the same guy that's done them. Robberies and that.'

She put him through to somebody else, a man, and Eddie heard himself blurting out Andy's name and address and giving a few details. Then he hung up.

The next day he went into the recruiting office and got the papers for signing up. His mother thought it was a good idea. He could learn a trade. 'And anyway,' she said, 'you're as well gettin the hell out of here. If the polis have got that daft mate of yours, it's just a matter of time before they'll be round at the door.'

He had packed his things in his father's old suitcase, tied it with the same belt. Now that it was time, he just wanted to get away, quickly.

'This is it,' he said.

'Aye, well,' said his mother.

He felt there should be something more to say, but he didn't know what. 'I'll be hame on leave in six months.'

'Aye.'

'If I stick it that long.'

'You better. Where am I gonnae get twenty quid to bail you out?'

He was going to make some remark about Andy, but he decided to leave it alone. The police had gone round to Andy's house, found a whole batch of stuff he hadn't sold, and he was being charged. ('Bastards!' he'd said. 'Throwin the book at me. Thing is, they knew about the moneylending and that. Some cunt must've shopped me for the lot. First I thought it was Spasm but he said no, and I believe him. So I'm thinking it must've been that Bennett. There's prob-ably a couple of polis in his Lodge. Worse than the fuckin Mafia these people, so they are.'

'Terrible,' Eddie had said.)

'What are ye thinkin?' said his mother. 'You've went awful quiet.'

'Nothing,' he said. 'I better be going.'

On his way down to the subway he stopped at the place where his father had been killed. He stood for a minute or two staring at the space where the yellow line had been, but it had long since faded away.

Strawberry Fields Forever

Tam pushed open the door of the State Bar. Inside, through a fug of smoke, he found Bird holding court at his table in the corner. As always, he had gathered a crowd about him, and Tam was glad to see Ruby, the American girl, among them. She moved along the seat to make space for him. Bird, a pint mug in one hand, a roll-up cigarette in the other, was delivering a discourse on the *Tibetan Book of the Dead*.

'All these worlds,' he was saying. 'World after world that you go through after death. There's different states called *bardos . . .*'

'State Bardo,' said Tam, playing on the name of the pub. Bird grimaced, swigged more beer, went on.

'The book's like a manual to guide you through, to what they call the Clear Light.'

'It really is a far-out book,' said Ruby. 'Leary did a version of it called *Psychedelic Prayers.*'

Bird finished his pint, ordered up another round, a lager and lime for Tam.

'Might have something a bit more interesting for you later on,' he said. He tapped his forefinger to the side of his nose, and Tam did the same, in response. It was a gesture they'd picked up years ago from some character in a Dickens novel, serialized on TV. They grinned at each other, laughed.

'Cheers!' said Tam, raising his glass.

He looked around him, amazed again at this strange flowering. He remembered hearing the word *hippy* for the first time, a label like beatnik or teddyboy, rocker or mod. At first it had all seemed exotic, faraway. California dreaming. Now here they were, a sunburst in grey Glasgow, long hair and bright clothes. And the

113

heart of it, for Tam, was Ruby. She had brought the new gospel: brightness and freedom, life more abundant. She was New York Jewish, had more energy than anyone Tam had met, except perhaps Bird. She had been to San Francisco, spent time in Israel, working on a kibbutz. Bird called her Ruby Tuesday, after the song.

She touched Tam's arm now as she spoke to him, described a new Doors album she'd borrowed from Bird, told him it was *beautiful* and he *had* to hear it. He found her nearness intoxicating, the sweet scent of patchouli, her dark hair a haze of curls, an aura. On her forehead, third eye, she had stuck a silver star.

Across the table, Bird was raving again, picking up where he'd left off on the *Book of the Dead*, one arm round Claire, his latest girlfriend. No more than sixteen, she was thin, almost frail, long blonde hair and a pale face, beautiful and bland, that might easily have graced some Pre-Raphaelite canvas. Tam was quietly in love with her, almost as much as he was with Ruby.

'If you don't know the score,' Bird was saying, 'you get side-tracked, drawn in by these fainter lights, all different colours. The lights are from the different realms of being – *lokas* they're called – and it depends on your karma which one you end up in. Could be the loka of the gods, or the humans, or the hungry ghosts . . .'

'Here's Paki,' said Ruby.

'Talk of the devil!' said Bird.

Paki had sidled up to their table, looked furtive, as he always did. Tam was amazed he had never been arrested. He looked like every mother's nightmare vision of a drug pusher: glazed eyes and hollow cheeks. He was small and painfully skinny, lank hair hanging down each side of his dead, grey face.

'How's it going, Paki?' said Bird. 'How does it feel to be one of the beautiful people?'

Paki grinned, bared a row of rotten teeth.

His real name was Alex Black, but one of the lines he

pushed was a black cannabis resin from Pakistan: Paki Black. Bird had tagged him with the name and it had stuck.

'Got a minute?' he asked.

'Sure,' said Bird, getting up.

'Affairs of State?' said Tam.

'Right!' said Bird. That was the name they had given to his drug dealings, punning again on the name of the pub. The State was where he made most of his contacts. Tam watched him follow Paki across to a quieter corner, saw their heads together, haggling.

'I hear Paki's got some nice acid coming in.' Ruby spoke quietly, leaning close.

Patchouli.

He nodded. 'Bird said he would get me some.'

Bird took his place again among them, grinning, Affairs of State successfully resolved. With just a suggestion of formality, he passed to Tam and Ruby two tiny silver packages, shining; the precious sacrament, capsules wrapped in tinfoil. They put them away quickly, Tam in his pocket, Ruby in her purse.

'It's good stuff,' said Bird. 'Strawberry Fields.'

They paid him. He touched his finger to the side of his nose. They laughed.

From the other side of the bar came a burst of song, a crowd of students singing *Bandiera Rossa*. Tam knew most of them by sight, saw Malcolm among them, George's older brother. Malcolm saw them, waved over, raised his hand in a clenched-fist salute. Bird grinned back at him, held up his hand in the two-finger peace sign. Malcolm did the same, then turned his hand round so the gesture changed its meaning.

'Get it up ye!' shouted Bird, replying with his clenched fist, driving it up and slapping the forearm with his left hand. Malcolm called a truce, palms open, fingers spread.

'See how well we communicate!' said Bird, laughing, addressing all of them round the table. 'Who needs words?'

'Those guys are boring,' said Claire, pushing a strand of hair back from her face.

'They're just using a different language,' said Bird. 'That's all that separates us really.'

Two fingers. Clenched fist.

'Boring.'

Tam fingered the tinfoil in his pocket. As if tuning in to him, Ruby leaned close again, whispered in his ear.

'If you feel like dropping that acid tonight, we could take it together. It's good to be with somebody, especially your first trip.'

Tam nodded. 'Fine,' he said. 'Whenever you like.'

'Now?'

When they stood up to go, Bird gave them his benediction. 'Have a nice time,' he said. 'Strawberry Fields Forever!'

'Bastards!' said Eddie. 'Dirty fenian bastards! We should just go in and round them up. Shoot the fuckin lot of them.'

'Sure thing!' said Jack. 'We'll send you in a single-handed themorra. Give you a flamethrower and a map of the Falls Road.'

'I wouldnae need a map,' said Eddie. 'I could smell them. Sniff the bastards out. Telling ye, I can spot a fenian a mile away.'

'I bet you can!' Jack laughed. He was a few years older than Eddie, had been in the army that bit longer.

'Falls Road by Christ,' said Eddie. 'They want to just seal that place off and drop a bomb on it. Blow it to fuck.'

Heads down, they hurried across an open stretch of waste ground, battered by the rain, a sudden squall, past a giant mural painting of King Billy that filled a whole gable-end. REMEMBER 1690 was painted across the top, but lower down the wall was daubed with Republican graffiti, some of it scored out and painted in again. IRA. TROOPS OUT. FUCK THE QUEEN.

'Bastards!' said Eddie, again.

They had come this way as a shortcut to the pub nearest the barracks. But halfway across the rain had caught them out, unprepared, exposed. They were off duty and out of uniform, bareheaded in the needling rain. Eddie cursed at it all, his good suit soaked through, his suede shoes scuffed, spattered with mud. He cursed the Pope and the IRA, blamed them for the weather as well as everything else.

'Bastards!'

George checked himself in the mirror. He looked fine. Dark blue suit and tie. Crisp white shirt. Four neat peaks of royal blue silk at his breast pocket, the tips of an elaborately folded hanky. (No matter that it wasn't real silk and the peaks were stitched to a stiff piece of card in the pocket. The illusion worked. It looked good.) Hair brylcreemed slick into place.

Fine.

Except for the look on his face. Panic in the eyes. The tight mouth that went haywire when he tried to smile.

He told himself he was only going through with it to humour his father, keep the old man happy. He wasn't taking any of it seriously. Not for a minute. But still the fear was tugging at his guts. It was the stories he'd heard. And the not knowing.

'Nothing to it,' said his father. 'It's all over before you know it.'

'You make it sound like the dentist's,' said George. 'And I remember you telling me *that* was nothing.'

'What are you talking about?' said his father.

The sudden memory was vivid. The smell of the mask over his face. The bit of rubber in his mouth he'd had to bite into. The buzzing that vibrated through his teeth, his whole skull. The panic as he felt himself go under. Then the waking, to dull ache, rawness, the taste of blood.

'It was hell,' said George.

'What was?' His father was checking the contents of

117

his little black case, making sure it was neatly packed, everything in its place.

'The dentist's. First time I went.'

'You were just wee.'

'That's what I mean!'

'You were scared stiff.'

'Aye and no wonder!'

'We had to tell you something.'

'That's what I'm saying.'

'What's all this got to do with anything?'

'You said it was nothing.'

'Eh?'

'Same when I got my tonsils out.'

'Tonsils?' said his mother, coming into the room. She pulled the word out of the air, quizzical.

'You told me I'd get ice-cream after the operation. And so I did. But my throat was that raw I couldn't swallow a thing.' He heard the words spill out, his voice racing away from him.

'What *is* this?' His father slammed the case-lid hard shut. It was all going wrong. He hadn't meant to annoy his father. Tonight at least he'd thought he could stay on the right side of him.

'What's the matter?' asked his mother. 'What's all this about operations?'

'I don't know,' said his father. 'He's havering!'

'I didn't mean . . . I just . . .'

'What?'

'Nothing.'

'Suffering! Have we not been through enough nonsense with that brother of yours without *you* starting?'

Talk about Malcolm was a minefield. His mother was anxious to steer them clear of it. 'Och he'll just be a bit nervous about tonight. Aren't you George?'

'Aye,' he agreed, grateful. 'That's all it is.'

'Don't know what you've got to be nervous about,' said his father. 'It's perfectly straightforward. Just have to remember what I told you.'

'I know. I'm sorry.'

'Bloody dentist's by Christ.' Shaking his head. 'I don't know!'

'I said I'm sorry!'

'Aye OK. We'll say no more about it. But for God's sake act your age and stop behaving like a big wean.'

Not the way he had wanted it to be. Not at all.

'Now, are you ready?'

A last look in the mirror. Straighten the tie. Fine.

'Aye.'

'Right. So. It's time we were going.'

'Aye.'

'You'll be all right,' said his mother. 'You'll be fine.'

But now he had to turn away from her sympathy, harden himself against it.

'Aye.'

Brian was in the middle of exams, had forced himself to stay home and work. He had skimmed over his lecture-notes, was looking again at the books – *Lear,* the Metaphysicals, *Paradise Lost.* The temptation was just to lose himself in them, settle down for a good read, instead of paying attention to the list he'd drawn up of questions from past papers.

'All's cheerless, dark and deadly.' Discuss.

He had to distance himself from the works, keep them at arm's length, remember to treat them as *texts*. He balked at it, but had set himself to memorizing lines, to be dropped into his answers. Potent quotes. At least that way he could focus on the poetry, let the words resonate. He could walk around, declaiming in his head. 'All's cheerless, dark and deadly.'

Not that there was much space in his room to walk around. The bedsit was a cramped cell. A bed. A wardrobe. A table. A chair. He remembered a poem he had written at school. *Introvert* he had called it.

He is a prisoner / roaming his cell / wonders why / they've put the sky / behind bars.

That didn't sound too bad. But he hadn't been able

119

to sustain it, had ended up in a tangle of metaphor with a terrible line about a *padded self*.

Heard the one about the lonely prisoner? He was in his sel'. A Glasgow joke. Untranslatable. His cell.

The room was at the top of the house, under the roof, so the ceiling sloped down on one side, limiting the space even more. But cramped or not, he had to move about, had grown restless and fidgety, unable to sit still. He found himself scrumpling up a piece of paper into a ball and playing keepy-uppy with it. He could manage no more than a count of four without skiting it out of reach, on to the table, under the bed. It was too frustrating. He devised another game. He set up the chair as a goal at the end of the room, spun the paper ball as if it had been flighted towards him by some jinking winger. The perfect cross. The aim was to knock it down with his head or his chest and volley it low into the goal between chairlegs. He scored once in five attempts, cracked his shin on the edge of the bed and gave up, cursing.

'What a fucking way to spend a Friday night. Cheerless dark and deadly right enough.'

Ruby's room was another world. A Chinese paper lantern, hung low, threw a soft warm light. Heavy velvet curtains shut out the night. The bed and its recess and the two old armchairs were draped with Indian bedspreads, paisley-pattern shawls and scarves. The floor was spread with an Afghan rug. Books and records were stacked in old orange-boxes painted in bright primary colours.

Posters decorated the walls – psychedelia, art nouveau, Impressionist prints; Mucha's *Sarah Bernhardt*, Toulouse-Lautrec's *Moulin Rouge*, Bob Dylan Blowing in the Wind; and incongruously, amongst it all, Che Guevara, silhouetted black on a red background.

Ruby had collected bits and pieces on her travels – an Indian cushion embroidered with tiny mirrors, a

Mexican painting, done on bark, of birds and flowers intertwined.

The room was worlds away from Tam's taste for simplicity, clean lines, empty space. But something in him warmed to it, its ordered chaos, its fullness and clutter.

He picked up a tiny sandalwood figure of Krishna playing his flute. Ruby lit a stick of incense, patchouli, set it in a brass holder.

Tam scrutinized a snapshot propped on the mantelpiece – Ruby and Claire and between them Bird, an arm round each girl.

'That was in Skye,' she said. 'Few weeks ago. Whole bunch of us went up. Really really beautiful.'

'Never been,' he said.

'That's ridiculous!' she said. 'I've been here eight months and I've seen more of your country than you have!'

He peered at the picture, turned it over and read an inscription on the back.

> *Dying all the time. Lose your dreams and you may lose your mind in life unkind.*

'That's Bird being *meaningful*!' she said. 'Lines from the song.'

'*Ruby Tuesday*,' he said. 'I remember the Stones doing it at the London Palladium. Brian Jones was wearing this straw hat and playing the recorder. And they had a kind of strobe light flickering, like an old film.'

Ruby poured a little water into two Japanese cups and set them down on the floor. She sat cross-legged, unwrapped the capsule from its silver foil. Tam took the package from his pocket and did the same. Conducting her own ritual, she touched the capsule to her forehead then placed it on her tongue, and taking a sip of water from the cup, she swallowed it down.

'Space capsules,' he said, and he did the same, took his cup, sipped and swallowed.

'Blast off,' said Ruby.

*

Of man's first disobedience and the fruit
Of that forbidden tree . . .

Working for exams was always the same. He would set aside hours of time – whole afternoons, evenings – and fritter it away. It would suddenly seem a matter of some urgency that he dust the skirting board. Or wash his socks. Or rearrange his books alphabetically by author. Now he was in the middle of trying to untangle a knot in the lace of one of his training shoes. For weeks he had been untroubled by it, prising on the shoes in the morning, kicking them off at night. But now the knot had become an obsession. It had to be unfankled. Anything rather than concentrate on the work he had to do.

'One message of Paradise Lost is that we should see things in perspective.' Discuss.

The shoes had been wet, the laces soaked in the rain, and the knot had shrunk, tightened in on itself. The more he tugged at it the worse it got. It defied the grip of his fingernails. They were too long, might bend back, break to the quick. He grimaced at the thought. He would have to do an Alexander-the-Great on them. Cut the Gordian. Buy a new pair of laces. It occurred to him he might be able to make a poem out of it. Something about cutting his laces and cutting his losses. He grimaced again. He had been reading too much of the Liverpool poets. Cutting his losses! That was worse than his *padded self* effort.

Heard the one about the lonely prisoner?

Which way I fly is hell; myself am hell.

'Fuck it!'

He picked up both training shoes, threw them hard across the room to slam against the hollow wall.

'It's only two stops on the subway,' said his father. 'Then it's just a short walk. We'll be there in no time.'

George just wanted to get there, wanted the whole thing to be over. The journey was endless.

'No time at all,' said his father.

George stared straight ahead as the subway rattled and shook. He stared at their reflections in the glass opposite, side by side. The glass was a double thickness, so their images were distorted, unclear, double reflections overlapping, and blurred even more by the shaking of the train. To George, in this mood, it was an irritant, got on his nerves. Like watching an out-of-focus film.

His father sat upright, the black case resting on his lap.

He remembered a time. Years ago. He'd been very young. Watching Malcolm climb up and lift down the case from its hiding-place on top of the wardrobe, then click it open, empty it out. He had laughed as Malcolm clowned with his father's precious regalia, draped the Mason's apron over his head, pulled on the white gloves and went into an Al Jolson routine singing *Mammy*. Laughing, they hadn't heard their father come to the door. He had walloped the pair of them, told them it was sacrilege and they had no respect.

The guard came through the train, whistling to himself, clipping tickets. As he clipped theirs, two jagged flakes of confetti drifted on to his father's case. His father brushed them off. The guard caught George's eye, winked at him. That made him feel even worse.

Diagonally across from him were two young girls. He had noticed them get on the train and tried not to look too hard, just dart the odd glance, sideways. Short skirts. Nice legs. Dark shiny hair, just washed. He could smell their scent. Further along were a young couple, no older than himself. And the girls were probably younger. A year. Or two. And they were all going out to enjoy themselves, out on the town. Dancing maybe. Or a party. And here he was, stuck, in tow with his stupid father with his stupid case, letting himself be dragged along to this stupid meeting.

One of the girls saw him looking. She whispered

something to her friend and they laughed. He felt himself blush.

How much longer? One more stop. No time at all.

The guard made his way back along the carriage. He looked at the two girls, rolled his eyes in appreciation and winked again at George. George stared straight ahead, at himself, his father. The blurred reflections looked very much alike.

The guard passed them, whistling again. The green green grass of home. He slid open the doors, increasing the roar. The train slowed, came out of the tunnel into light, eased to a stop.

'Right,' said his father. 'This is us.'

The rain had stopped as quickly as it had started. Eddie and Jack stood drying off at the bar. They had knocked back quick halfs of whisky, to warm them, then ordered the same again and slugged their pints.

'Cheers!' said Jack.

'Aye, sure,' said Eddie. 'The beer tastes like pish. But never mind.'

'See you're in a great mood the night!'

'Ach it's this place man. I'll be glad to see the back of it, get hame on leave.'

'When do you go?'

'Couple of weeks. Just in time for going down to Wembley! I canny wait!'

'A glutton for punishment, eh?'

'Not at all. We'll get right in amongst them. Sort them out good style.'

'Oh aye?'

'They can keep their fuckin World Cup. They stole it anyway.'

'In extra time.'

'Whole thing was a carve-up. Anyway, we've beat them since they won it, haven't we?'

'So that makes us the best in the world!'

'Right! I'm telling you, there's nothing like beating

these people. Nothing. And this time we're gonnae destroy them.'

'That's what you said last year.'

'And so we did. We slaughtered them one each!'

Jack laughed. 'You're a headcase Eddie, you know that!'

Eddie smiled, took it as a compliment. He was mental. A headbanger. Pure mad.

'I'll tell you something funny,' he said. 'Last year I was at the Ireland game, at Hampden. That was before I knew we were getting sent over here. Didnae know I was living!'

'Anyway!' said Jack.

'Anyway,' Eddie continued. 'There I was on the terracing wi a bunch of the mates. And we're aw Rangers supporters like. But we're wearing the auld tartan scarves and that, cheering on Scotland. We'd let out a big roar every time John Greig got the baw. And we'd give wee Johnstone a right shirriking whenever he made an arse of it! So anyway, there we are giving it laldy, you know, *Scot-land! Scot-land!* And there's this bunch of Irish supporters along a wee bit, and they're giving it big licks as well. *Northern Ire-land!* And they start getting gallus, shouting louder. And we're trying to shout them doon. And a couple ae our boys are just about ready to get in and set about them. And then fuck me, do these Irish cunts no start singing The Sash!'

'Just to bamboozle you!' Jack laughed.

'It made your mind do a somersault kind of thing. Tumble its wulkies. Know what I mean?'

'Made your brain nip!' said Jack.

'So it did,' said Eddie. 'Then some brilliant bastard started shouting *If you hate the fucking English clap your hands!* And we all joined in thegether. Us and them.'

'Amazing!' said Jack.

'It was funny all the same,' said Eddie. 'Makes you think.'

'Oh you don't want to do that,' said Jack. 'Not in this place.'

'How d'you mean?'

'Have another pint!'

He was lost in the intricate patterns, the constant shift and change. The colours pulsed and flowed – an abstract expressionist canvas, neon-bright, contained in a circular silver frame. The shapes broke up, dissolved, re-formed in a dazzling mandala, worlds within worlds.

'God,' he said. 'This is incredible!'

Ruby came into the kitchen, behind him.

'Leftovers from last night's curry,' she said, and took away the frying pan he had sat staring into for the last half hour.

Brian had lost a page of his notes – one of the sheets of lines he was trying to memorize. He had been through all his folders, checked between the pages of his books. The sheet of paper was nowhere.

He was trying to stay calm, not get into a frenzy over it. But the page was an important one, had lots of lines from the Metaphysicals. He found himself looking through the same books, the same folders, for a second, a third time.

He was ready to believe there was a gremlin in the room, some malicious imp that moved things behind his back. It wouldn't be the first time.

On a table beside his bed was a stack of books he was planning to read after the exams were over. He didn't even dare to open them before that. They would be too much of a distraction. The books were mostly borrowed – Marxist texts from Malcolm, an odd, quirky assortment from Tam – existentialist novels, books on the 'new' psychology, guides to Hinduism and Zen.

There was no possibility that Brian's notes could be in amongst them. No possibility at all. But he set about looking just the same. And as he lifted the top books from the stack, he upset some precarious balance and knocked the whole pile on to the floor. He sat looking down at them, fanned out at his feet. He stared blankly at the titles of one or two that had landed face-up – *The Divided Self, One-Dimensional Man*. Then he set about picking them up, stacking them more carefully.

One book had landed under the bed, and as he reached out for it, down on his hands and knees, he saw, right back against the skirting-board, the ball of paper he had been kicking around earlier. And it occurred to him that it might be the missing page from his notes, that maybe he had been stupid enough to crumple it up and play football with it.

He couldn't move the bed without bumping the table and knocking over all the books again. So he got right down on his belly and crawled under the bed. It was thick with dust under there – he had never swept it – and it caught at his throat and made him cough and choke. But he managed to reach the paper – stretched out and grabbed it, brought it out and unravelled it, smoothed it out flat. And he scanned the page, the list of quotations in his own handwriting, the lines from Vaughan at the top.

I saw Eternity the other night

And his elation at finding the list faded into bleakness as he saw himself, crawling in the dust to fish out his little sheet of notes. Poetry reduced to the odd quotable line to be hammered into his head like the two-times table.

Education. Nothing to beat it.

'Hele, conceal and never reveal,' said his father. 'It's quite easy really.'

'Hele, conceal and never reveal,' repeated George, mechanically.

'Of course by that stage,' said his father, 'you're just repeating what's said to you. It's no problem. But it does no harm to memorize wee bits like that.'

'Aye.'

'It means you recognize them. You know where you are when you hear them.'

Words sounded funny. Know where you are. Hele. Conceal. Never reveal. All the way from the subway his father had been testing him on his responses, making sure everything was just right. And he knew it all, could rattle it off. But outside the hall his guts started churning again, the panic rising. The whole thing was ridiculous. He didn't have to go through with it. He could back out now. He pictured himself making a break for it, running down the street.

'So this is it,' said his father. He put his hand awkwardly on George's shoulder, took it away again hurriedly.

'You'll be all right son.' He cleared his throat. 'And believe me, you'll thank me for this. You'll see.'

'What I canny figure out,' said Eddie, 'is what we're here for.'

'Ours is not to reason why, my son,' said Jack. 'You know, when we got pulled out of Aden and the word went round it was Ireland next, I says *Ireland?* by fuck. What in the name are they sending us there for? And then I thought, ach well, it's practically hame. And anyway, whatever it is, it canny last. A six-month tour of duty and that'll be us. Some hopes!'

'You mean wi this carry-on in Derry?'

'Getting worse all the time.'

'Civil Rights by fuck. Think they were bastardn darkies the way they're going on. See that Bernadette fucking Devlin. I know what *she* needs awright.'

'Aye, and I know what *I* need?' said Jack. 'Telling you man, I'm ready for it the night.'

'You're *always* ready for it!' said Eddie.

'Listen,' said Jack. 'How about we go somewhere else? Somewhere wi a lounge and that. Find some talent.'

'Sure thing,' said Eddie. 'Lead me to it!'

She had re-heated the curry, served it up in earthenware bowls, laughing now and again at her own seriousness.

'Seems a shame to eat it,' said Tam. 'It's so beautiful.' And he felt a bleakness come in, felt himself grow sad at the passing of things. And he caught Ruby's eye and she was laughing, and he saw himself getting maudlin over nothing. And he heard what he had just said and tried to mimic himself. But he couldn't do it for laughing. And they ate the mandala curry, laughing, together. And in the laughter they were one, their separateness a tired old joke they had only just seen through.

It was the tone of that Vaughan poem he loved, the directness of it. He imagined himself using the opening line as a conversational gambit.

'Oh here, by the way, I saw Eternity the other night.'

'Oh did you now? What was it like?'

'Like a great ring of pure and endless light.'

'Is that a fact?'

His mind was wandering again. He couldn't seem to stay focused.

The poem didn't read like some overblown metaphor. It read like a transcription of direct experience, of something the poet had actually seen. A vision.

I saw Eternity.

He wondered what that meant. To see eternity. Pure and endless light. If he asked Tam he would grin and say something inscrutable about one hand clapping, or a finger pointing at the moon.

Malcolm would draw his attention to the lines further down the poem, about the *darksome statesman hung with weights and woe,* or the *fearfull miser on a heap of rust,* and give him a lecture on the dialectics of class struggle.

Brian put his notes to one side, went downstairs to the shared kitchen to make himself some tea.

He was on his own. His father had gone ahead, into the main hall, left him here in an ante-room. The room had the same kind of fusty smell as the church hall where the BB had met. Old wood panelling, stacks of musty books. A masonic scroll, framed, hung on one wall. At its centre, a single eye fixed him with its gaze. It made him feel uncomfortable. He turned his back on it, looked about the room, picked up a hymn-book, set it down again.

He remembered waiting for a flute lesson, in a Catholic school. Eddie had been there. And Brian and Tam.

A door opened behind him. He turned and his mind did a quick double-take as he saw Mr Bennett the bandmaster walk straight out of his memory into the room.

'Hello there George. How you doing?'

'That's really weird,' said George. 'I was just thinking about the time I came to your flute class.'

'Is that right?' He was smaller than George remembered him, older. 'That's going back a bit. Good few years.'

'Aye,' said George. 'So it is.'

'Still. Just shows you all the same. Quite a coincidence, eh?'

'Aye.'

'So anyway. Are you fit?'

George nodded, shrugged, awkward.

'Sure you are! Come on, we'll get you ready for the business. They're waiting for you.'

'I don't fancy yours much,' said Jack.

'Cheeky bastard!' said Eddie.

Jack laughed. 'Only kidding,' he said. 'See that big one but. I mean look at the tits on her!'

'The wee redheaded one's been giving me the eye,' said Eddie.

'The evil eye!' said Jack.

'What's that supposed to mean?'

'Nothing,' said Jack. 'She's lovely! You want to get right in there. Chat her up. I'll keep her big mate occupied.'

'She looks like she could keep *you* occupied for quite a while!'

'Occupied territory, eh?' said Jack. 'Telling you, I'd occupy her territory any day!'

'Are you game then?'

'Defi-nitely. I mean that's what we're here for. And anyway, what have we got to lose?'

'Nothing,' said Eddie. 'Absolutely fuck all!'

The drawing he had done was like a totem pole – head emerging from head emerging from head, and each one a cartoon version of himself – smiling, frowning, tightlipped, snarling, leering.

'It just keeps changing,' he said. 'On and on and on. Won't stay the same for a minute.' He remembered a childhood game. One potato two potato three potato four. Fist over fist. Five potato six potato seven potato more. 'Like, a minute ago I was this wee fellow here.' He pointed at one of the faces – smiling, benign. 'Now this guy's taken over.' He pointed at the topmost face – grim and unhappy. 'It's the same when I try to talk. Like, I'm saying something, right? But then it's as if it's not me that's speaking. It's somebody else, and I'm just listening. Then the me that's listening goes to say something, like *Aha! I know your game!* But there's another self behind that again, saying *Oh yeah?* And it keeps going on like that. Like this.' He indicated the drawing.

'For ever and ever,' said Ruby. She leaned over and took the piece of paper from him, and the pen. She looked at his drawing and made her own version of it, head emerging from head. But hers were caricatures of herself, each head haloed with dark curls, and instead of extending them vertically, up the page, she curved

131

them round to form a circle, the last head meeting the first.

'Yours goes on and on,' she said. 'Mine goes round and round.'

He looked at the two shapes, saw his totem pole tower, erect, saw her dark circle, open. He saw the ridiculously explicit sexuality of them, heard some-one's voice – his own – make a joke of it: 'We should put them together!'

Then there was that stepping back again, and he was mocking the posture he had just struck, some moustachioed Sir Jasper, stage villain from Victorian melodrama. He turned to share the joke with her but she was floating away again, off in her own universe.

George had taken off his jacket and tie, unbuttoned his shirt. He had rolled up his right sleeve past the elbow, his left trouser-leg past the knee. He had taken off his right shoe, replaced it with a slipper that was too big. He hoped it wouldn't slide off his foot.

'Just empty your pockets now,' said Mr Bennett, and George did as he was told, put his keys and money in the pocket of his jacket.

'Your stuff'll be safe enough here. See, you're not allowed to have any metal on you.'

'Aye, my father told me that.'

'Oh did he now?' said Mr Bennett. 'Giving away the secrets was he?'

'No really,' said George, miserable, confused. He should just keep his mouth shut.

'I suppose all this seems like a lot of old nonsense.'

'Aye!' said George, too quickly, too eager to agree.

'Aye, well,' said Mr Bennett. 'It is and it isn't.'

George just nodded. Safest to say nothing. The all-seeing eye still stared at him from the wall.

Mr Bennett held a blue silk rope, coiled into a noose. He placed it round George's neck, the end hanging down his back.

'That's everything,' said Mr Bennett, checking him

over. 'Just got to hoodwink you now, and we're away.'

His father had used the same word and with the same tone. He found it irritating. Hoodwink. Stupid nonsense. He looked down at the state he was in, the open shirt, the trouser-leg, the slipper, and he felt suddenly ridiculous.

Mr Bennett put the blindfold on him. Smell of nicotine from his fingers. Carbolic soap.

'Right son. Here we go.'

This was it. No going back.

'Over here, to the door.'

He followed the voice, in darkness took a hesitant step forward.

Downstairs in the kitchen, Brian met his neighbour, mad Rab. Rab was a third-year engineer, big and bearded. He enjoyed being called mad; in fact Brian thought he had probably coined the name for himself. ('Just call me Mad Rab!') His madness seemed to consist in drinking himself sick every weekend and bawling out rugby songs at the top of his voice. Brian had seen him the Saturday before, standing on a chair in the Beer Bar, and somehow keeping his balance as he led a mob of his mates singing *Dinah Dinah show us your leg, a yard above the knee.* He remembered Rab's face, beatific as he roared out the chorus of *In Mobile.*

Arseholes! Arseholes! Aaaarse-holes!

Tonight Rab was contained, seemed mellow. He had been drinking: that went without saying. But he was still coherent. And for a Friday night that was unusual.

'Quite compos mentis the night Rab.'

'Oh aye,' said Rab, grinning at him. 'Got to be. When you've got company!'

Brian noticed he was making instant coffee in two grubby mugs. So he had a girl back with him. That explained why he was home, and the pubs not yet closed.

'Right wee dolly she is,' Rab leered. 'First year

medic. Telling you man, if I don't score the night I'll chuck it.'

Brian felt an emptiness inside, part jealousy, part disgust. And in its black core something twisted into almost hate. But he managed to stretch his mouth into a kind of smile as he wished Rab the best of luck.

'What about yourself?' asked Rab. 'Nothing doing?' Now he was gloating, basking.

'Don't go out much these days. Exams and that.'

'Ach well,' said Rab. 'You know what they say. All work and no play!' He spooned powdered milk into the two cups of coffee. Little lumps and grains of the stuff, undissolved, floated on the surface. Spiral nebulae.

'Aye,' said Brian. 'Anyway.'

'Be seeing you.'

Brian turned away, took his cup of tea back upstairs to his room.

One more half and they were ready to try. Eddie led the way, Jack backing him up. They crossed to the girls' table. He spoke to the wee redhead.

'Can we buy yis a drink?'

The girls looked at each other, nodded, smiled as if at a private joke.

'OK,' she said. 'Sure.'

'Right,' said Eddie. 'What'll it be?'

'Whisky and green ginger,' said the redhead. Her friend asked for a vodka and orange.

Eddie ordered them up, two more pints for himself and Jack. He managed the four glasses at one go, back to the table. Jack had sat down beside Bigtits. Wee Redhead moved round to make space for him. He caught Jack's eye, grinned. Things were beginning to look good.

He heard Mr Bennett knock three times on the door to the other room, heard the door open, heard a voice from inside.

'Whom have you there?'

Mr Bennett, behind him, made his reply.

'Mr George Wilson, a poor candidate in a state of darkness, who has been well and worthily recommended, regularly proposed and approved in open Lodge and now comes of his own free will and accord, properly prepared, humbly soliciting to be admitted to the mysteries and privileges of Freemasonry.'

'How does he hope to obtain these privileges?'

He recognized the words. His first cue. Mr Bennett tapped him on the shoulder. He fought down the panic, heard his own voice, shaky and small. 'By the help of God.' He cleared his throat. 'Being free and of good report.'

'Halt while I report to the Worshipful Master.'

The door was closed. Words were exchanged in the room. The door was opened.

'Let him be admitted in due form.'

Mr Bennett pushed him gently from behind. He stepped forward, but stopped as he felt a sharp point jab at his bare chest. His father had warned him about this too. A poniard pointed at his heart. And another response coming up.

'Do you feel anything?'

He felt ridiculous, and irritated, and vulnerable, and scared. He felt like tearing off the blindfold, telling them they were all mad. He felt strange and unreal, as if in a dream. He felt terrible. He felt sick.

Do you feel anything?

'Yes.'

The point against his chest was removed. Someone took him by the right hand and led him into the room. Another voice spoke.

'Are you a free man and of full age?'

'I am.'

'Then I will thank you to kneel while the blessing of Heaven is invoked on our proceedings.'

He was guided forward to kneel on a low stool. He was conscious of movement round about him, people standing on either side, and he heard above his head a

135

quiet click, like two sticks hitting together. In a low drone, the voice began intoning a prayer. Lulled for a moment, his mind drifted and he found himself thinking about the two girls he'd seen on the subway. Maybe, just maybe, he thought, one of them had given him the eye. He started to fantasize a chance meeting. At a party maybe. Or if he went to the dancing. *Don't I know you?*

He forced his thoughts back from where they were leading, back to where he was, body clenched tight against its natural impulse. Please God no, not a hard-on, not here, not now. A telltale bulge in his tight trousers would be seen, by the unseen figures about him, by the all-seeing eye out there. And the thought of that was enough to put a stop to it. And he focused his attention once more on the droning voice.

'Endue him with a competency of Thy Divine Wisdom, that, assisted by the secrets of our Masonic art, he may the better be enabled to unfold the beauties of true Godliness, to the honour and glory of Thy Holy Name.'

And another voice again came out of the darkness.

'So mote it be.'

Nothing made any kind of sense. Here he was, stuck, poring over his books and his notes, so that he could rehash it all in a couple of days. Spew it out pat in the exam room.

And there was that big bastard Rab, only a few feet below him in space, in the room directly underneath, not caring about anything, luring some young girl into his bed. Brian had been in his room a couple of times. A pig-sty. The whole thing was too grotesque. How could anybody fancy that big animal? The girl must be desperate. She must be ugly. That was it. Hacket. But the word was too cruel, even just thinking it. Too harsh. *Hacket.* And anyway it probably wasn't true.

His mind was yapping round in circles, chasing its own tail. He wished he hadn't gone down to the kitchen, hadn't met Rab. But even if he hadn't, he'd be worrying away at something else.

To his annoyance, since he'd come back upstairs, the words of *In Mobile* kept running through his head.

In Mo- In Mo- In Mo- In Mobile

There must be something about Mobile. Dylan had written about it. Stuck inside of Mobile.

Oh mama, can this really be the end?

It must be one of those towns.

Rab had told him a joke. This guy comes up to him, a visitor to Glasgow, says, 'See this place man, it's the arsehole of the universe.'

'Oh well,' says Rab. 'You'll just be passing through then.'

Arseholes again. Something so Scottish about it. A whole nation anally fixated. Never got beyond it.

Still.

Can this really be the end?

At least Dylan had replaced Rab's Beer Bar doggerel.

Shakespeare's in the alley, with his pointed shoes and his bells.

Round in circles. Shakespeare was what he should be reading. He went back to his notes, switched from Vaughan with his ring of pure and endless light, back to past questions on *Lear*.

Who is it that can tell me who I am?

Discuss.

Who was he? Afloat in this dream. There was something he had forgotten. Something he had lost. He looked, could see the bones beneath his skin the tendons, muscles, veins, the pulse of the blood flowing through. He felt his breathing come and go. Whose breathing? His. But who was he? The breathing came and went, of itself. *It* was breathing *him*. He lay back, seemed to inhabit this hulk of a body. He felt his skull, great crag of bone. And somewhere inside it, *he* watched, listened. He touched his forehead, probing, opened a wound but felt no pain. And inside the wound a red jewel. And inside that was infinite space. Galaxies revolving. And somewhere, in one of the galaxies, a pinpoint of light, the sun, and the earth spinning round it, the life swarming on its surface. And part of that life was this country and this city and this room with him in it. And the whole universe, inside and out, was one vast mandala. And its centre was his forehead, third eye.

Wee Redhead was called Carol. Her big friend's name was Liz. Eddie launched into the old Neil Sedaka number, sending it up.

'Oh Carol, I am such a fool . . .'

'Oh no!' she said. 'I haven't heard that one for years!'

'Darling I love you, though you treat me cruel . . .'

'My brother used to sing that to annoy me,' she said. 'When I was about twelve.'

'You hurt me, and you make me cry . . .'

'Don't!'

'But if you leave me, I will surely die.'

On the next line Jack joined in and Eddie battered the rhythm on the table-top, jarred the empty glasses.

'I-will-al-ways-want-you-for-my sweetheart . . .'

'Easy there gents!' shouted the barman. 'A wee bit order!'

'Till the end of time . . .'

'It'll be the end of time for you son if you don't give that a chuck!'

'Aye OK,' said Eddie. 'Keep the heid.'

'Tornfaced auld cunt,' said Jack.

'Disnae recognize great drumming when he hears it,' said Eddie.

'So you're a drummer?' asked Carol.

'The best!' said Eddie. He did a quick flourish in the air with invisible sticks, a run round a drumkit, with sound effects, ended with a smash on the cymbals. 'When I get out of this I'm gonnae start my own group. Like the Stones and these guys.'

'Hey,' said Jack. 'The Stones did a song about Carol as well!'

'So they did!' said Eddie. 'She's famous!'

'Don't start that again!' said Carol.

> *'Oh Carol!*
> *Don't let him steal your heart away.'*

Stop!'

> *'I'm gonna learn to dance*
> *If it takes me all night and day.'*

'You'll get me a red face,' said Carol.

'And you'll get us all chucked out,' said Liz.

'How come there's no songs about Liz?' said Jack.

'It's not fair, is it?' she said.

'It's a dead liberty,' said Jack, and he slipped his arm round her.

Eddie looked at Carol. 'Another round?'

'Are you trying to get us girls drunk?'

'Now why would we want to do a thing like that?' he asked, all innocence.

Kneeling again, he had been given a pair of compasses to hold in his left hand, one sharp point resting against his heart. He had repeated a solemn obligation to keep the secrets and mysteries of Freemasonry. *Hele conceal and never reveal.* This he had promised before the Great Architect of the Universe and under pain of terrible punishment – his throat to be cut, his tongue torn out, or what they thought was worse – being branded as wilfully perjured and void of all moral worth. He couldn't help thinking he'd rather be an outcast than have his throat cut. Any day.

139

The compasses had been taken from his hand. A book had been held to his lips for him to kiss. The volume of the sacred law. Leather binding. That same old musty smell. His left knee was aching. He had pins and needles in his foot. The voice spoke again, with his cue for another response.

'Having been kept for a considerable time in a state of darkness, what in your present situation is the predominant wish of your heart?'

'Light,' he said.

'Let that blessing be restored to the candidate.'

The people round about clapped their hands, once. The blindfold was taken from his eyes, and he blinked in the sudden light.

Brian didn't want to switch on the light. Although it was beginning to darken in the room, there was still light outside, and there was something a bit depressing in the sudden switch from natural light to the pale glare of that weak bulb fixed to the ceiling. It couldn't be any more than 60 watts. He kept meaning to replace it with something brighter.

He stood on a chair and pushed open the skylight, looked out over the city rooftops. The long summer evenings were some compensation for being so far north, for the brutal shortness of those midwinter days when the dark came down hard at four in the afternoon.

He had a clear view across to the University tower, a fake-Gothic monstrosity against the sky, and further over, the cranes of the shipyards on the other side of the river, where he'd grown up. He'd been able to see the University, far in the distance, from their front window at home, and its spire had been like something from another world, magical, some higher realm he'd aspired towards and would one day reach.

And now he was here, getting on with it, grinding along. And it was all so much less than he had expected, the approach to everything so reductive, analytical. The poetry was hacked to bits, the magic lost.

A chaffinch, its breast feathers gold in the evening light, landed on the edge of the roof, a few feet away. It bounced along the gutter, weightless, jerked its head this way and that. Then it saw him, stopped, stared a moment, quizzical. And it shrugged and flurried off again, over his head and out of sight.

He closed the window and came back down into the room. It seemed gloomy now, his eyes not yet adjusted. But still he didn't want to switch on that dim light. There was a bit he'd tried to learn from *Paradise Lost*, about darkness and light. He had written it out. It would be in his notes. He flicked through them, standing under the skylight to see more clearly, found the page he was looking for, the quote.

A dungeon horrible on all sides round
As one great furnace flamed yet from those flames
No light, but rather darkness visible.

That was it. Darkness visible. He looked up at the square of sky, decided to go out and stretch his legs, clear his head.

The room was closing in on him, stifling him. Too many things. Not enough space. The place was a monstrous landscape inhabited by objects that mocked their names and stood there, threatening, separate. A grotesque assemblage in the corner, a 'chair', was somehow breathing, had a life of its own. An 'orange-box' bulked, self-existent, absurdly assertive in bright red. Everything in the room was watching him. The pattern at the heart of the Afghan rug resolved itself into a face, a wicked mischievous demon face, tongue out leering. Then the tongue was a snake that spat and hissed.

His own tongue moved, sluggish, round the great moist cavern of his mouth, probed the jagged edge of a tooth. And he watched the whole process, amazed, as his tongue flicked and darted in response to some panic signal flashed from his brain. And the sound came from somewhere deep, and the darting tongue gave it form, and his mouth filled with words. And he heard a voice, his own, speak.

'Got to get out.'

He watched Ruby with difficulty detach herself, come down from where she had been. She made her re-entry into their shared atmosphere. She brought him once more into focus.

'You said something?'

'Out,' he said. 'Got to get out.'

'Right!' she said. 'Way out!' She laughed. 'Far out!'

'No,' he said. 'I meant . . .' He searched for the word that would explain it. 'Out.'

'Oh, right,' she said, understanding at last.

'Outside,' he said. 'Out *there*.'

'Wow!' she said. 'You think you can handle it?'

'Got to,' he said. 'In here's getting too much.'

'Too much!' She laughed again, delighted.

Her laughter reached him, a reassurance, an ease.

'No wonder people *talk* like that,' he said. 'Words are ridiculous.'

And he too laughed, at the pompousness of his own pronouncement.

'Still want to go out?' she asked.

'I'd like to.'

'Right,' she said. 'But it could be complicated. Could take us a while to get organized.'

'That's OK,' he said. 'We can take our time.'

And he stopped, dazzled, genuinely astounded at the resonance of what he had just said. It was an entire philosophy, a message for all mankind. He heard himself repeat it, full of amazement and wonder.

'We can take our time.'

'Right,' said Ruby, miles away, across the room. 'All the time in the world.'

She *knew*.

'It's pure Zen.'

She knew what he was talking about. Exactly. Tears

came to his eyes, a rush of sheer mirth. But behind it was a sadness and a welter of emotion he couldn't even began to name.

'This stuff is amazing!' he said, settling again for the inadequacy of words.

'What stuff?'

What stuff did he mean? The stuff they had taken, how long ago? No time at all. All the time in the world. Now words were fireworks. A scatter of meanings.

'What stuff?'

'Stuff and nonsense!' He laughed. 'This stuff.' He meant the acid, but heard *this stuff* meaning everything. The stuff they were. The stuff of the universe. He was oh so close to understanding.

'Oh God,' he said.

'The acid,' said Ruby, answering her own question. 'I'd forgotten.'

'Forgotten,' he said. 'We've all forgotten.'

He could almost almost almost remember.

'Come and see *this* stuff,' said Ruby. He came back to where they were. She had negotiated the distance to the window, pulled open the heavy drapes.

'Toytown!' she said. 'Look!'

And he looked down through the open curtains, out through the window as if at images on a screen, the shimmering dance that passed for reality, the outside world, Byres Road on a Friday night.

'Scotch boys are nice,' said Liz.

'Have you known a few?' asked Jack.

'Oh, one or two!' she said, all coy. And she laughed.

'Did you know we were Scottish?' said Eddie. 'When we came in like.'

'I had a good idea,' said Carol.

'You *could* have been English,' said Liz.

'Not on yer life!' said Eddie.

'Once we heard your voices we knew,' said Carol.

'Right!' said Eddie.

'But we knew you were soldiers,' said Carol. 'Right away. The short hair and that.'

'Scottish soldiers!' said Jack, and he started singing.

'There was a soldier, a Scottish soldier . . .'

'Don't start giving us that shite,' said Eddie.

'What's wrong wi it?' said Jack, defensive.

'Nothing wrong wi the song,' said Eddie. 'Nothing wrong wi the *song*. It's aw that kiltie stuff. Pure crap so it is. Andy Stewart by fuck. The hoochter choochter bit. White fucking Heather Club. Heedrum fucking hodrum. Make you puke so it would.'

'The kilt is my delight!' said Jack.

'That's right,' said Eddie. 'Stuff like that. Pure shite the lot of it.'

'I like the kilt,' said Liz.

'You would!' said Jack, putting a hand on her knee.

'The Scots and the Irish are dead close in lots of ways,' she said.

'Oh aye,' said Jack. 'Definitely!'

'If you hate the fucking English clap your hands!' sang Eddie, but not too loud, as if just quoting something to himself.

'I mean,' said Liz, 'when I was wee I used to go to my auntie's, up on the coast. And you could *see* Scotland from there.'

'Away!' said Eddie.

'You *could*!' she said. 'You could see the sun shining off cars on the other side, on the coast road.'

'Amazing!' said Jack. And he started singing again, just for devilment.

'He's seen the glory, he's told the story
Of battles glorious and deeds victorious.'

'Ach!' said Eddie.

'Poison dwarves,' said Carol.

'Eh?' Eddie wondered if he'd heard right.

'Scottish soldiers,' she said. 'Poison dwarves.'

'That's no very nice,' said Eddie, wondering for the first time if she might be crazy.

'That's what the Germans called them a few years back,' she said.

'I remember that,' said Jack. 'Some of the boys stationed over there had been in a bit of bother. Fighting and that.'

'It was in the paper,' said Carol. 'That was what they called them. Because they were wee and vicious.'

'Some fucking cheek!' said Eddie. 'Nazi bastards.' He glowered at Carol.

'No, listen,' she said. 'I didn't mean anything! It just came into my head, when he sang that song.'

'See!' he said to Jack, accusing. 'You and your fucking song.'

'No offence,' said Carol, squeezing his arm, working hard to restore his good humour. 'It's funny the way the mind works,' she said. 'Isn't it? The way it makes connections. The way you just ... remember things. For no reason.'

'Well, it's funny the way *your* mind works,' said Eddie, beginning to come out of it. 'You're weird!'

She laughed and shoved him.

'Hey!' said Jack. 'The IRA are all wee smouts as well. Tell you how I know?'

'How?' said Liz.

'It's in that song they sing.' And he sang.

> *'Soldiers are wee*
> *Whose lives are pledged to Ireland.'*

Eddie laughed out loud and the barman yelled across at them.

'Right youse lot, that's it finished. No party songs or you're out!'

After the blindfold had been removed, someone had leaned over and shielded his eyes, directing his gaze to a bible held before him. The book he had kissed. The volume of the sacred law. Then as his eyes grew accustomed to the light, he looked up at the Worshipful Master, at last matching a face to the droning voice.

145

An old man, thinning grey hair, hornrimmed glasses and the face dour, the mouth a thin grim line.

The old man took him by the hand, helped him to his feet, and explained the significance of what he had just been through; he had escaped death twice, by stabbing and by strangling; he had taken a serious vow, to be broken on pain of death.

Then the old man initiated him into the secrets of the first degree. He told him to stand erect, his feet square.

'So that your body be an emblem of your mind.' The tight mouth hardly moved as he spoke. George's left foot had gone to sleep from kneeling so long.

The secrets consisted of a sign, a token and a word. The Master showed him first the sign, the hand drawn quickly across the throat. George almost smiled at that. He had known it as a child. Cut my throat and hope to die. Cross my heart.

The token was the masonic handshake. Pressure with the thumb. The grip.

The word was a password. BOAZ. During the ceremony he had to spell it out, cautiously, letter by letter.

Then he was given the pure white apron of the entered apprentice. It was handed to him by another older man, less grim-looking than the Master, who told him it was a badge more ancient than the Golden Fleece, the Roman Eagle. He called it the badge of innocence, the bond of friendship, and urged him never to disgrace it.

George caught sight of his father, across the room, not smiling, but giving him a nod of encouragement, approval.

Brian was going nowhere in particular, just wandering. He had walked the length of Byres Road and back, aimless, looking in shop windows at nothing. He was careful not to catch anyone's eye as they passed him in groups, in couples, in packs. They would think he was some kind of pervert, walking alone.

He was especially careful of a mob of young team boys, loud and raucous, on their way up from Partick. They all had cropped hair, wore sharp suits. They took up the whole pavement, inviting challenge. Brian crossed the road to avoid them, head down, looking away. One or two of them laughed at him, but no more. They weren't really interested in him. They were wound up tight and looking for *real* trouble, aggravation, bother.

He thought about going in somewhere for a drink, maybe catching the Rubaiyat before the last rush. But he knew if he did he would meet somebody he knew, talk till closing time, end up being dragged along to a party. So he moved on, gave the Bowl of Night a miss.

At the next corner he thought he saw Tam on the other side of the road, but a bus stopped at the lights and blocked his view. Then the traffic moved on and he saw him again. He waved but Tam didn't see him. He was with the American girl, Ruby, one of the hippy crowd. On the whole Brian didn't care for them. He had always felt uneasy with Bird, somehow didn't trust him. But he was glad to have linked up again with Tam.

They had drifted apart in their last years at school, had lost touch altogether since they'd left. They had met up again at the Maryland, at a benefit concert for something called an Arts Lab. Tam had hugged him, greeted him like a long-lost brother. Brian found out later he'd been stoned at the time. But they had arranged to meet, had seen each other a few times since. Tam had loaned him all those books, trying to initiate him into the mishmash that he called New Age Philosophy.

Tam looked stoned now. He was holding on to a lamppost, looking lost and confused. Ruby was trying to soothe him, stroking his face. She was very beautiful. Brian felt that pang again, that feeling of lack. He decided not to cross over. He probably couldn't help. He had no idea what Tam was going through. Better just to leave him to it. He didn't want to get involved.

Toytown she had called it, and the street had all the unreality of a cartoon film; buildings squat and dumpy, people moving like weird caricatures of themselves. Tam and Ruby stood marooned at a set of traffic lights, trying to cope with the complexity of crossing the road, as the traffic snarled and growled at them, baring its fangs.

The way he'd seen things as a child, cars with faces, headlamp eyes and radiator grins. His collection of toy cars, each with its own face, its own personality. What had happened to them? He found himself crying for his lost Dinky toys, his lost childhood.

'It's OK baby,' said Ruby. 'We'll get there.'

Baby. That was what he felt like. Vulnerable and small. Aloud, he said, 'Where?'

'Across,' she said. 'To the other side.'

'Wow!' he said, his mind groping beyond itself for meaning. The Other Side. But all she meant was across the road.

And across the road came a riot, of noise and colour and warmth. It had something to do with *them*. Their names were being called. Bird and his entourage from the pub swept round them, caught them, buoyed them up on a wave of energy and good humour.

Bird was cradling something under his jacket, something small and soft and warm.

'What's that?' asked Tam, wide-eyed, hoping it was a kitten, a puppy. He could *sense* the warmth.

'Fancy a chip?' asked Bird, producing a bag wrapped in greasy newspaper, stinking of vinegar.

'Barbaric bastard!' said Tam. But the harshness of the words shocked him, rang empty and fake. He felt regret and tried to explain.

'I thought it was some wee animal,' he said.

'Happiness is a warm puppy?' quoted Bird.

Bird understood!

'That's right!'

'Sentimental shite!' said Bird. 'Happiness is a fish supper!'

Somebody else started singing, 'Happiness is a warm gun.'

There were too many signals, too much to think about. He needed to simplify things again.

'So anyway,' said Bird, cutting through his confusion, 'how's the wee trippers? Been having a good time?'

And suddenly it was just as simple as that. No more to it. Having a good time. Tam laughed, felt a surge of love for Bird, for all of them. They were one, in complicity, sharing an age-old secret. Tam touched his finger to the side of his nose, and Bird laughed, a great roar of a laugh that shook every building in the street. Ruby and Claire were embracing each other in joyful reunion, tears streaming down Ruby's cheeks. They were both unutterably beautiful, two angels, one dark, one fair.

'Right,' said Bird. 'Now you've sorted out the universe, you can come and celebrate. We're going to a party.'

'Did you hear the one about the Irish Mafia?' said Eddie. 'They make you an offer you can't understand!'

'I hate Irish jokes,' said Carol, deadpan.

'Ach!' said Eddie. 'Where's your sense of humour?'

'They're just so stupid,' she said. 'It's like all these jokes about Scotsmen being mean.'

'They don't bother me,' he said.

'Well,' said Carol, 'you were bothered when I said that about poison dwarves.'

'That's different!'

'Is it?'

'In America they have Polish jokes,' said Liz. 'Same sort of thing.'

'Exactly!' said Carol. 'And nigger jokes and dago jokes. And the English have Paki jokes and Jewish jokes.'

'Christalmighty!' said Eddie. 'Somebody tell her a fucking elephant joke and keep her happy!'

Jack and Liz laughed, and even Carol untensed a bit, managed a tight smile.

'Heard the one about the Irish elephant?' said Jack.

It was all over. He had been initiated in the first degree. He was an entered apprentice. His father shook his hand, gave him the mason's grip, and he responded.

It was over, and there had only been one awkward moment. The master had explained to him the importance of charity, then asked him for a donation.

'Whatever you feel disposed to give.'

There had to be some mistake. He had left his money in the other room. Mr Bennett held out a dish to him and spoke, echoing the master's words.

'Have you anything to give in the cause of charity?'

Without thinking, he put his hands in his pockets, a reflex. In fact he almost turned the pockets out, to show he had nothing. But the whole thing was absurd. It was Mr Bennett who had *told* him to leave his money, his keys, everything.

Mr Bennett spoke again.

'Were you deprived of everything valuable before entering the Lodge?'

'Yes!' he said, almost querulous, as if to say *You know fine I was!* But now he realized it was another game, a test.

'If you had not been so deprived would you give freely?'

'Yes.'

They had, the master explained, been putting his principles to the test, making sure he had done as he was told and left his money outside; and they had acted so that he would always remember this 'peculiar moment' when he was received into masonry poor and penniless.

'You might have warned me about all that!' he said to his father as they shook hands.

'Och well,' said his father. 'You know how it is.'

'No I don't.' He heard that tone in his voice again, tried to fight it down. 'I was dead embarrassed. I didn't know *where* to look. Didn't know where to put my face.'

'They like to see how you respond.'

'You could have told me.'

'I couldn't. The candidate's not supposed to know. Anyway, you did fine. You got through it no bother.'

And his father was right. He shouldn't be making a fuss. It didn't matter. None of it mattered. It was all over.

'Aye,' he said. 'No bother at all.'

It was too dark in the room now to read, so reluctantly he switched on the light. He wanted to get through more of his notes, even if it meant staying up half the night. Rab's stereo was blaring down below, the bass turned up and thump thumping vibrations up through the floor. He had been through a strange assortment of records – folk, blues, a bit of hard rock. Now to Brian's surprise he was playing the Beach Boys. He must have the single of *Sloop John B* – he had played it twice. Now he had turned it over to the B-side. *You're so good to me.* It was playing for the fourth time. He had probably left the arm up so the needle automatically went back to the start, played it again. Brian was beginning to make out most of the words. *You're kinda small and you're such a doll.* He knew it would take him days to get the stupid song out of his head.

He had met Rab's girl on his way back upstairs. As he'd passed Rab's room, the door had opened and the girl had come out. There had been a momentary awkwardness as he'd stood aside to let her past on the narrow landing. Her eyes, a bit bleary and glazed with drink, had brought him into focus and she'd smiled at him, slightly flustered. She had moved with that too careful deliberation, an effort to keep things steady as they swayed and lurched away from her. With a crash she had shut the toilet door behind her, slammed it too hard.

He had glanced at her as she passed, a quick look up and down, appraising. She wasn't exactly beautiful, but then she wasn't exactly ugly either, and certainly not to be dismissed as *hacket*. If anything she was slightly old-fashioned. Something about the dress, the hair back-combed and lacquered, flicked out at the ends. But she was definitely too good for the likes of Rab.

> *You're my baby, oh yeah*
> *Don't mean maybe, oh yeah*

Thump Thump Thumpa Thumpa . . .

The song was playing for the fifth time. He found himself tapping his feet to the beat.

Bird had said they should come to the party to celebrate. And at first that was how it all seemed. A celebration. A coming together for no other reason than the sheer joy of it. There was music, the Stones singing *Dandelion*.

> *Dandelion will make you wise*

Bird was laughing, telling a story old as time.

'So anyway, there I was just standing there . . .'

Paki had showed up, sat grinning at everything. And Tam remembered, saw it clear, who Paki had always reminded him of. A boy he'd known when he was at primary school, small for his age, skinny and weak, the runt of a litter. One nostril always snottery, one lens of his National Health specs always cracked, the frames held together with elastoplast. A loser, a liability, always last to be picked when they ticktacked for sides at football.

The boy's name had been Feeny. Wee Mick Feeny. But somebody – the old man in the corner shop – had christened him Feeny Barbitone.

Feeny Barbitone and Paki Black, both named after drugs. Everything had a pattern to it, just waiting to be unravelled.

Paki looked out at him, oblivious, grinned his stoned grin, called to him across the room.

'Good stuff man, eh?'

He nodded. It *was* good stuff. He just had to relax into it, stay easy, have a good time. But something nagged, that there ought to be more to it. There was something else he should be doing, if only he could remember what it was.

And then the music changed. And the Beach Boys were picking up Good Vibrations, magically pulsing from the old recordplayer in the corner. And Claire was up and moving to the music, dancing in the circle of her own light and grace.

He looked around for Ruby and saw her by the recordplayer, her dark head pressed hard against the speaker, as if she couldn't get enough of the music. And he thought, for no reason, of his sister Moira. Then he realized it was the recordplayer – an old Dansette mono, two-tone, red with a grey lid. It was the same as Moira's, the one she'd had at home. Second-hand. A birthday present. They had bought him a flute. Moira had chipped in. He thought of his parents, of Moira, with a huge surge of compassion. A wee couple. A wee family. Doing their best. Getting by.

Ruby sat up, and there was something in the way she turned, in the tilt of her head. She too reminded him of Moira. More patterns to be unravelled, a dark tangle of interrelation.

But what did any of it matter? He loved Moira. He loved Ruby. He loved Claire. And he loved Bird, and even Paki, and *everybody*.

With a click the music stopped. Somebody groaned but Claire kept on dancing. Body swayed to music. Brightening glance. Ruby put the record on again. Good Good Good Good Vibrations. Right at that moment he loved the whole stupid world.

Eddie set down his glass, held it steady, the one still point in the room, as everything bucked and swayed

153

round about him. Jack's face came into focus, leering at him, mouthing words that sounded far away.

'You're pished ya bastard!'

'You're right!' said Eddie. 'It's a fact!'

Jack laughed out loud, his mouth all teeth. Everything was too loud, too harsh. Nothing would stay at peace. He was going to be sick. He had to concentrate again on the glass and his own hand clutching it. He had to hold on.

Slowly, carefully, he eased his eyes away from the glass, brought them up, looked around. Then he realized there was only Jack across from him.

'The lassies,' he slurred.

'What's that?' Jack's big face came close.

'They two birds,' said Eddie, as clearly as he could. 'Where'd they go?'

'Away to the bog,' said Jack. 'They'll be back in a minute.'

'Bog?' he asked.

'Aye,' said Jack. 'Hey, maybe it's the peat bog!' And he laughed again.

This time it was too much, too close. Even the glass wouldn't stay still, no matter how tight he held it. Jack's face swam away from him, started flicking up and up, like a TV screen with the vertical hold gone.

'What's the matter?' He heard Jack's voice. He managed to get the words out, to tell him.

'Spew my ring,' he heard himself say.

'Aw Christ!' said Jack. 'No here. At least make it to the lavvy.'

But it was too late. The spasm racked him. He doubled up from the waist, threw up between his legs, saw his own vomit hit the floor between his feet, spatter his shoes. He watched it all happening, as if it had nothing to do with him at all.

Apart from that 'peculiar moment' when the Worshipful Master had asked him for money for charity, he had had another peculiar moment of his own.

154

Just before the blindfold had been removed from his eyes, there had been a lull, a brief silence, when all he'd been conscious of was the beating of his own heart. And in that silence, in the space between heartbeats, it was as if he had forgotten who he was, and where. Then there was the light, and he remembered, came back to himself.

He was here. This was really happening.

And something of that strangeness had stayed with him, a sense of being outside himself, apart, as he looked at the master and the shadowy figures round the room. It was like something from a weird dream, faintly sinister. And that man over there, that stranger who was somehow familiar, was his father.

He felt the same unease as he had in front of that single eye on the scroll. And behind his father, on the wall, he had caught sight of another scroll – just a glimpse, but the images had registered: pillars, an archway, a pattern of stars, a skull. A sense of mystery had touched him for a second, emptiness in the pit of his stomach, that feeling again of looking at himself, detached. This was his life and this was him living it. And one day he would die.

Then the moment had passed, remained now as only a lingering discomfort, something he didn't want to look at too closely. The room was once more ordinary. The ceiling-lights had been switched on – dim bulbs in dusty plastic shades. A few men stood around in groups of two or three, no longer sinister, just ordinary. Middle-aged men in dark suits. And his father and the Worshipful Master were discussing the deeper mysteries of the bowling club, and the whist drive, and the bring-and-buy sale.

He picked up the top book from the stack beside his bed. It was one of the ones Malcolm had loaned him, a pocket edition of *The Thoughts of Chairman Mao*, with a red plastic cover. He flicked through the pages – thin paper, like a bible – read odd sentences at random.

Political power grows out of the barrel of a gun.

An image flashed in his head, of Malcolm waving a plastic machinegun. He had met Malcolm only recently, though he remembered him from years back. George's big brother. In those days he'd been intimidating, always surly, angry about something, always scathing towards his parents and George.

Although he had left University now, he hung around the campus a lot, selling books and newspapers, agitating. Brian had gone along to a meeting of the student socialist group, and Malcolm had been addressing them on how to organize themselves. He had spoken about Vietnam, said Ulster was shaping up as our own version of it. 'And so convenient too,' he'd said. 'Right on our own doorstep. No need to go halfway round the world to give the boys a bit of training in counter-guerrilla techniques. And don't you kid yourselves. One day these same techniques will be turned against *us*, or anybody else that steps out of line.'

There had been applause at that. He was good at working his audience up. Then he'd spoken about the student rising in France and what they could learn from it.

'It was the unions that chickened out,' he'd said. 'In the end they wouldn't go along with the students. Didn't trust them. So it's important to maintain credibility with the workers. Stick close to your roots.'

Brian had thought that was funny. Apart from himself and Malcolm, he didn't think anyone else in the room *had* workingclass roots. The ones he'd spoken to were from the middleclass suburbs, or were English. Brian found it hard to take them seriously, thought most of them were just posturing. If Bird and his crowd were too flippant, then this lot were too grim by far. The atmosphere at the meeting was earnest and dour.

Malcolm agreed there was a lot of play-acting going on.

'A bunch of wankers,' he'd said. 'But they've got brains. They can be educated. And then they can educate others.'

We can learn what we did not know. We are not only good at destroying the old world, we are also good at building the new.

Malcolm kept insisting they look to the French experience, learn from it. He had tried to make connections, forge links with the movement over there. Brian knew he had been instrumental in setting up Danny the Red as a candidate for the university rectorship. It had involved a midnight flight from London and a dash to the jail where Danny was being held. Malcolm had contrived to get Danny's signature on the necessary documents and the candidacy had gone ahead. It had all been highly dramatic, a real coup for Malcolm. The student socialists had been impressed.

At the rectorial elections they had been in high spirits, attacking the right-wingers with flour bombs and water-filled balloons. That was where he had seen Malcolm with the plastic machinegun. He'd produced it from under his jacket at the height of the fighting, brandished it in the air as he led a charge. A young policeman standing nearby had looked worried, till he'd realized it was only a toy. Malcolm had laughed in his face, rattled off a few rounds, sent harmless sparks flying.

A revolution is not a dinner-party, or writing an essay, or painting a picture, or doing embroidery. It cannot be so refined. A revolution is an insurrection, an act of violence.

Growing up where he had, it was inevitable his view of things would be a socialist one, thought there were exceptions – workingclass Tories, crazy Orangemen, Masons like Malcolm's father. Malcolm had spoken well about that in his summing up on Ulster – the madness of working people destroying each other, instead of uniting in the class war. *Atomization of the proletariat* he had called it.

And yet, whatever his gut feeling, Brian had difficulty taking himself seriously as a revolutionary. But then he had difficulty taking himself seriously as a writer, or as anything at all. Part of him always stood back, dismissive of any pretension, a wee crabbit Scottish gremlin that narked in his head. *Ach away ye go! Don't kid yourself. I know fine what you really are.*

He supposed it was a variant on the old put-down. *Him? A writer? He couldnae be. I kent his faither!* Only this was more insidious, was the end result of such programming, and the form it took was *Me? Ach, naw, no me. I couldnae.*

He was beginning to depress himself. He closed the red book, put it back on the pile. Rab was playing the Incredible String Band's first album.

You don't have to worry they sang. *Everything's fine right now.*

Everything had changed again. He had lost that sense of lightness. Things had a harder edge. A bare red lightbulb hanging from the ceiling had been switched on, and someone had set it swinging, to and fro. Caught up in its rhythm, Paki had picked up a guitar and he plucked and twanged his own accompaniment as he sang.

> *'See my baby all dressed in red*
> *She's a-drivin me outa my head*
> *Cocaine . . . all around my brain.'*

His voice was cracked and nasal, but surprisingly strong. His playing was halting, discordant, a jagged stammer that was its own statement: he would hang on to the beat, dogged; he would survive.

But Tam found it hard to take, too much raw melancholy. And someone else must have found it jarring, called out from across the room.

'Christsake Paki, give it a fucking rest!'

Tam turned and saw it was Raymond. Apparently it was his party, his flat. Tam didn't know him, knew only that he dabbled in dope, did some smalltime dealing on the side. He looked too straight for that – had short hair, wore an open-neck shirt, a cravat tucked in at the throat. Tam was ridiculously suspicious of him. Something to do with the cravat.

From another room came voices raised in song. *The Internationale.* The same crowd of students who'd been singing in the pub had showed up here.

'*Arise, ye starvelings from your slumbers*'

Tam had seen Malcolm, talking to Claire. She had laughed at him, at something he had said. Now he was haranguing Bird.

'Bourgeois individualism,' he said.

'Arseholes,' said Bird.

'You won't face up to reality,' said Malcolm.

'Whose reality?'

Out there. Right out. He looked for Ruby again, but she was gone. He felt stranded. The red light swung to and fro, lit briefly on a boy with the face of a satyr, leering, demonic; it lit on a young girl crying, a couple intertwined, two men arguing. One boy lay flat on his back, staring at the red light, mesmerized; another sat in the corner, reading a book of poems; another was being sick into a bowl of salted peanuts. A beautiful girl in a fur coat flashed it open to show she was wearing nothing else. Or had he just imagined it? So quick. A flash. 'Fur coat and nae knickers!' said a voice close to his ear. He turned and there was nobody there. Had the voice been his own? Inside his head?

Paki was still playing, a strangulated guitar-break between verses. But suddenly he stopped with a muffled yelp, a jangle of strings. Raymond had come up behind him with a plastic bag, rammed it over his head. One of his friends, satyr-face, had grabbed Paki in a bearhug, pinioned his arms to his side.

Tam started to panic. They were murdering Paki! He would suffocate! He stood up and shouted out, heard his voice fill the room.

'No!'

159

The two assassins stared at him, hard, their faces contorted, cruel masks.

'What's up wi you pal?' Ice in the voice.

He couldn't believe this was happening. Nobody else had said a word. Were they all in it? A conspiracy? Or had nobody noticed? A boy in his street had once drowned at the swimming baths, his friends playing round about. It could happen. Just like that.

'Did you think we were smothering him?' Raymond pulled the bag off Paki's head. Paki looked ruffled, but none the worse.

'The bag was ripped up the back pal. See? No problem. He could breathe, couldn't you Paki?'

Paki nodded, grinned.

'You should stick to the bevvy pal.'

Tam held his head in his hands, pressed it tight. He needed to calm himself, quiet his brain.

'What's up wi him anyway?'

'Daft cunt dropped some acid. He's out his fucking skull.'

Tam turned away towards the door, still holding his head. The door was frosted glass. He was aware for a moment of a shadow-figure, a silhouette on the other side. Then like something from a film the whole glass panel exploded into the room. Like something from a film and somehow in slow motion, smithereens of glass, glinting shards and particles, burst from the centre of disturbance where a fist came smashing through. And Tam stood dazzled by the sheer beauty of the spectacle. A glittering starburst, suspended, a moment. The noise of the room, a girl's scream, seemed far away, a background. Then the film picked up again, back into normal time, and the shimmering bits and splinters dispersed and fell. And Malcolm was looking through the shattered door into the room. His face was a bland mask, said nothing. He had punched through the door and that was that. He held up his fist, clenched in salute, as the blood began to well, flecked the fist with red jewels.

The tiles were cool against his forehead, but the stink of piss made him retch again.

'That's right' said Jack. 'Bring it up. You'll feel better.'

But there was nothing left to bring up. Just this dry heaving and the sour taste in his throat.

'You'll be OK. Get you out in the fresh air.'

'Fucking shoes,' said Eddie. 'Look at them. My good shoes.'

'Never mind,' said Jack. 'Come on. Splash your face and we'll get you out of here.'

He did as he was told, felt the shock of the cold water hit him between the eyes. He swilled his mouth out, spat. His own bleary reflection glowered back at him from a cracked mirror above the sink.

'Come on,' said Jack. 'They lassies are waiting for us.'

'Are they?'

'Said they'd see us outside. I heard them talking about a party. And they keep giving each other the wee looks and smiling and that. Telling you man, we're on a good thing the night. We are gonnae *score*!'

'It's important to think about these things,' said George's father. *These things* were contacts, connections. They would help him *get on*.

Now that the initiation was over, his father was already looking forward to the next stage, the second degree, when he would pass from apprentice to fellow craft mason.

'You've got to leave at least a month between the two,' he said. 'So we'll give it a few weeks. But you can start reading the books right away. Learning the responses.'

'Och give the boy a break!' said his mother.

'Do him no harm.'

'No, but at least let him get his breath back after tonight's business. I mean, it must have been a strain.'

'Not at all! He just sailed through it. Didn't you son?'

He nodded, gave a shrug towards his mother. She meant well. But. Her concern felt suddenly cloying, sentimental. Too much whine in the voice. He *had* sailed through it. No bother.

And although his father's smugness was just as likely to get on his nerves, although part of himself dismissed the whole evening as so much nonsense, still another part of him responded, felt a warm glow of belonging. He had been accepted into the company of men.

And for once his father was pleased with him. He had his head screwed on. Not like his brother. George just about knew the monologue by heart. Malcolm was a big waster. A no-user. He'd had every opportunity. They'd scrimped and scraped. Kept him on at school. Then the University. Could have got on. Made a career for himself. But no. Not him. Neither work nor want. Head full of nonsense. Up to God knows what with God knows who.

George heard it all for the hundredth time, let it wash over him, smiled to himself, grateful to be in his father's good books.

During the commotion he found Ruby again. She stood in the hall looking utterly confused, gaping at the jagged hole in the glass door. And through the hole Tam saw her. He went to her and they recognized, remembered each other. Long lost. They had embarked on this journey together, this crazy trip. They embraced, held each other close, and Tam wanted only to dissolve, to die into her soft warmth.

'I thought I'd lost you,' he said, the words absurd, as if spoken by the craggy hero in some women's magazine story.

'*You* thought you'd lost me?' she said. '*I* thought I'd lost me! Went through a rough time there. Thought I'd flipped out and wasn't going to get back.'

'It's this place,' he said.

162

'It is getting kinda heavy!'

Raymond, tight with rage, held Malcolm by the lapels, insisted that he pay for the door.

'Aye, sure,' said Malcolm. He could have brushed Raymond off, but he held back.

'Why did you do it?' Raymond's voice shook. 'What was the fucking point?' Malcolm stared at him, straight.

'No point at all. It was a fucking gratuitous act. All right?'

Nothing else to it. No more to be said.

Bird laughed, a harsh manic laugh. 'I like it!' he said. 'We'll make something out of you yet, ya big cunt!'

'He should get his hand fixed,' said Claire. 'It'll need stitches, at least.'

Malcolm's hand was a mess, dripped blood on to the carpet.

'And you'll pay to get that cleaned as well!' said Raymond.

The party was over. Time to call it a day.

The music had stopped.

He knew Rab's taste in music was varied and eclectic, but still it had been a surprise the first time he'd heard the strains of the String Band drifting up from downstairs. He had mentioned it to Rab the next time they'd met on the landing.

'Didn't know you were into the String Band, Rab.'

'Just their early stuff but. None of that poofy psychedelic shite they're coming out with now.'

Of course.

That last song he'd heard was a straightforward song of seduction. *Come a little closer to my breast.* A bit less subtle than *Had we but World enough and Time.* But probably just as effective.

O my my it looks kinda dark
Looks like the night's rolled on

After the song the recordplayer had been switched off. They hadn't even let the side play out. Then there

163

had been silence. Brian could picture the unfolding scenario, too clearly. He started to counteract it, weaving a fantasy of his own.

Rab is too insistent. She doesn't want. Not like this, so quick. But he won't take no. She pushes him off and runs out of the room, Rab after her. In a panic she turns the wrong way, turns back and Rab is blocking her. She runs up the stairs towards Brian's room. He hears the noise and comes out to see. She comes to him, pleading, for refuge. He takes her in, comes out again to face Rab, calm him down. But Rab has given up, yells at him. 'You're welcome to her. Nothing but a fucking prickteaser.' Now the girl is in his room, sitting on his bed. She looks shaken, dishevelled. He puts a comforting arm round her, makes reassuring noises. You don't have to worry. Everything's fine right now. Had we but world enough and time.

Enough. He had work to do. He had to stop this nonsense or he'd end up wanking himself into numbness and sleep.

Enough.

That way madness lies.

Jack had been right enough. The fresh air had cleared Eddie's head. He had a half bottle in his inside pocket, a few cans in a carry-out bag, an arm round Carol as he lurched along. He felt good.

Up ahead Jack was arm-in-arm with Liz, the two of them laughing away at something Jack had said. Eddie could feel Carol take his weight when he wasn't quite steady on his legs.

'Empty stomach,' he said. 'Should've ate something before we started bevvying.'

'You'll be OK,' she said. 'You'll be fine.'

'Is it far?' he asked.

'No,' she said. 'Be there in no time.'

Eddie had wanted to take a taxi, but the girls had said it was walking distance. Jack said the walk would do them good, sober Eddie up. Eddie said he didn't need sobered up, was completely *compos mentis.* But the words wouldn't come out right and Jack laughed. Sometimes Eddie hated him.

They were passing through a housing scheme. It felt like parts of Castlemilk, run down, the odd block derelict, boarded up. They rounded a corner, saw a chip-shop, open, across the road, bright light spilling out on to the pavement.

'Chips!' said Jack. 'I'm starving!'

Two soldiers came out of the shop with a boy about eighteen. They slammed him against the wall, made him stand facing it with his arms out. One of them kicked his legs apart, kept him covered while the other searched him.

'Couple of the boys,' said Eddie.

A handful of people came out of the shop, stood back, watching.

'Come on,' said Carol. 'Yous're off duty. You don't want to get involved.'

'What about my chips?' said Jack.

'You can have something when we get there,' said Liz.

'Promises!' said Jack. 'Promises!'

But they let the girls hustle them down a side-street, away from the shop.

'How much further is it?' said Eddie.

'We're nearly there,' said Carol.

'Going round in fucking circles,' he said.

'We are not. It's your imagination.'

'Everything looks the fucking same. I'd get lost if I had to find my way out.'

'So whose party is this we're going to?' asked Jack.

'Ours,' said Liz.

'It's a kind of a private party,' said Carol.

'Cosy,' said Liz.

'Intimate,' said Carol.

'Just the four of us,' said Liz.

'Aw hey!' said Jack. 'I like the sound of that! D'ye hear that Eddie? Intimate!'

'Brilliant!' said Eddie.

And so it was. And so was he. And so was everything. Brilliant.

Out in the street again they moved slowly, concentrated on taking their bearings, trying not to get lost. Tam held Ruby's arm, felt himself earthed in her, so he wouldn't fly away.

'Hope we can find our way home,' she said. 'Everything looks so weird.'

And words were playing tricks again, suggested other dimensions of meaning. *Find our way home.* That's what it was about, this journey they were on. But home to where?

'Once we get back to my place,' said Ruby, 'we'll be OK.'

Back to my place had other implications. Cheap line from a B-movie. Had she meant it that way, or not? He felt that leering Sir Jasper rise in him again. But he fought it down. He had been on the edge of something important. A glimpse. This journey home.

Then he saw himself again, as if at one remove, brow furrowed, trying to understand, to work it all out. And it seemed so ridiculous he threw back his head and laughed.

And as he did, he saw it, stretched out above them, the night sky. And he stood open-mouthed, stupefied in sheer amazement and wonder.

'Oh my God!' he heard himself say, heard those words too as if for the first time; for the first time spoke them with original awe.

The stars were Van Gogh flowers of light, pulses of cold fire in a swirling firmament. He looked out into vast space, felt afloat in it himself. He knew it was forever. And in that moment, in knowing it, so was he.

He wanted to write something. A poem. Not like his *padded self* nonsense, or that daft idea about *cutting his losses.* He wanted to break through to something more, something real.

He looked at his notes, his quotes from *Lear.*

> *Poor naked wretches whereso'er you are*
> *That bide the pelting of this pitiless storm*

The problem was he hadn't lived.

> *Why should a dog, a horse, a rat have life*
> *And thou no breath at all*

He would never be able to write like that. So what was the point? No point at all. And yet.

There was no sound now from downstairs. It was late. He flicked through his pages of quotes. The urge to write was a fever in his head and he had to ease it.

He would take his notes, and the books he'd been skimming, and the bits and scraps of songs that had drifted up, whatever came into his head, and he'd run it all together, make a cut-up, a collage of all the fragments, just follow the process through and see where it led, see if he could batter through to something, open himself up.

The flaring vision had faded. He was calm and still and almost sad. Ruby's flat was familiar. A haven. They had set out from it long ago, on a voyage. Now they were back, and all of that, out there, was unreal, a dream. All that mattered was this. Here. Now. Ruby had lit more incense. Patchouli. She was boiling a kettle of water, for tea. Simple things, tribal, the little ritual formalities of the everyday. A feeling of warmth towards her overwhelmed him. As if in tune with it she turned and smiled. And maybe, he thought, maybe there was no more to life than this. He looked about the room and it was friendly, no longer oppressive or threatening. In the pattern at the heart of the rug he could still see a face but it held no fear. He stuck out his tongue at it and laughed.

The little wooden figure of Krishna seemed alive. He looked at it with astonishment, felt *it* was looking at *him*. For the figure was more than just a piece of carved wood. It embodied a consciousness, was somehow the expression of a reality. And the nature of that reality was love. It was the silent melody played on this tiny flute.

He remembered his first flute lesson. Mr Bennett telling them how to blow. A wee half smile. 'It's not just a dod of wood,' he'd told Eddie.

The figure of Krishna, he knew, was a crude reproduction, a copy of a copy of a copy. But still it had caught some essence. Krishna himself smiled through it, the archetype behind this form. The grace and charm were there, in the angle of the head, the delineation of the limbs, the flute raised to the lips. 'I'm not just a dod of wood,' it said, with a wee half smile.

On the same shelf lay a bamboo flute. Tam picked it up and blew a single note.

'Nice,' said Ruby.

He tried a few more notes, a tune, heard each note shimmer, separate and clear, yet caught up with all the others in this greater whole, this melody. He was conscious of so much all at once. He felt his life-breath pass into the bamboo pipe, felt the air vibrate, modulated by the dance of his fingers. He felt the sheer physicality of the process, but what it became was birdsong, it soared. It sang in his head and it filled the room, a cascade. He closed his eyes, was a tiny bird flying in a Japanese landscape.

'Beautiful,' said Ruby.

He brought the melody back to that single note. The bird came to rest on a thin branch.

Ruby had made the tea and set it down between them on a tray. Again he felt that sense of the formal, the ceremonial. He watched as she poured from the squat brown teapot into two white mugs, added milk and sugar, stirred.

'Tea ceremony!' he said.

'Right!' she said, passing him his cup.

The tea had a fragrance to it he couldn't quite place –

some Indian herb or spice. A green seedpod floated on the surface. A tiny boat drifting. The African Queen.

The thought formulated itself in his head that Ruby might have spiked the tea with another drug, a booster to launch them further out. He pushed the thought away. But it surfaced again with the violence of sheer paranoia. He hardly knew her. She might be trying to poison him. The others had tried to suffocate Paki. They could all be in it together, a crazed freemasonry of acid psychotics, killing for kicks.

'Cardamom,' she said.

'Eh?'

'Cardamom seed. Gives the tea that amazing taste.'

'Bouquet!' he said. He heard himself savour the word and he laughed again, relieved at being back on an even keel, the moment of panic over. The mind was so delicate a mechanism, could flip itself out for no reason into manic elation, terror, despair. No reason.

'Do you just put some seeds in the pot?' he asked. He heard the note of polite enquiry in his voice, found it absurd.

'Yeah,' she said. 'When the tea's brewing. You just squish them and pop them in.'

'Squish!' he said, delighted, and they laughed.

'Actually,' she said, a look on her face he hadn't seen before, confessional, almost coy, 'I chewed em to a pulp. Best way to do it. Hope you don't mind.'

'Why should I mind?'

'No reason.'

They looked at each other direct, read recognition in each other's eyes.

'Sounds,' she said, and she was putting a record on the turntable. Music once more filled their shared space.

> *Let me take you down cause I'm going to*
> *Strawberry Fields. Nothing is real . . .*

The Beatles must have been *here*. They *knew*. The whole song was an expression of this other, this hidden reality. He felt tears of warmth and gratitude

169

fill his eyes. Through them he saw Ruby smiling at him. She shook a cardamom seed from a jar, popped it into her mouth.

'They use these in India,' she said. 'To sweeten the breath.'

And she came to him, and they understood what had been there between them, unspoken, all along. And her arms were round his neck, her body pressing into him. And her mouth was on his, and she passed the green seed to him on her probing tongue and its fragrance exploded in his mouth, as Lennon sang, reminding them, *Nothing is real.*

He was going through the ceremony again, back in the darkness, the hoodwink over his head, the noose around his neck. But something was different, felt wrong. Then he realized. He was naked. And the knowledge was a terror to him, panic in his heart. For he knew that out there the dark figures were watching him, judging. And behind them was the single eye that could see right through him. He stood exposed, unable to move. He wanted to cover himself, felt foolish. He wanted to tear off the hood, but the fear froze him, fear of what he would see.

Then he felt a gentle tug on the noose, heard someone behind him giggling. A girl. He took it as a sign. He had to move. He took off the hood, was dimly aware of the shadowy figures, the men in dark suits, as he turned and looked across the room, saw the two girls he'd seen on the subway. Somehow they had followed him here. He adjusted the noose, eased it round to the front. The blue silk cord was longer than he'd realized, stretched right across the room. And holding the other end of it was the girl who'd given him the eye. Her friend whispered something and they giggled again.

He turned and looked back over his shoulder at the men in dark suits. They were all seated, in a row, and the subway conductor came in and started clipping their tickets. He knew that his father was there, and Mr Bennett, and the Worshipful Master, but he couldn't make out any faces. The conductor winked at him. He was whistling *Please Release Me*.

There was another tug on the noose and he turned again. Now there was only the one girl, holding the cord. Her friend had gone. The girl was looking at him, and he saw that she too was naked, like him. And she pulled at the cord, reeling him in. And he went with it, moved towards her. There was no way he could stop now, no holding back. All in one movement he was on top of her and inside her, and he jerked once or twice and came into her in one long surge.

And as he subsided he half-woke and knew he had been grinding into the mattress. He felt the warm spread of wetness beneath him, felt the emptiness inside. And he turned over and drifted, went under again, sank back into sleep.

For the moment, sitting on the edge of the bed, he was able to view his own nakedness, and Ruby's, with a kind of amused detachment. These pale little bodies were what all the fuss was about.

What fuss?

In the simple act of undressing, he had relived it, in flashes of total recall.

The first shock to his little separate self newly emerged into life, pushed out cut off cast adrift. Too bright too harsh too rough too cold. Nothing but need, to merge back into that mothering warmth. The little body had struggled and kicked, a fish out of water, clenched tight around nothing but the first intake of breath and the first sharp cry of useless rage and pain.

Ruby had crossed the room to change the record, put on the Doors album she had told him about so long ago, a lifetime. *Strange Days*. He fought against the sense of unreality at seeing her move around, completely naked but absorbed in some mundane act, shaking the record from its sleeve, placing it on the

171

turntable. He fought down the sniggering schoolboy in him, and the grasping Sir Jasper, fought to see her simply, as she was. But his snake-eyes flicked over her, breasts and belly, the dark delta of hair.

The ache had been dulled, eased for a time by the closeness to his mother the comfort of her breast the sweetness of milk overflowing from herself into him, sweet intoxication as he'd sucked and gorged and was once more one with her, no separation, for a time, but too quickly over, too soon denied, pushed away.

Ruby had turned her back to him, had lit another joss-stick. She twirled it between finger and thumb, mesmerizing herself with the patterns, the lines of light she traced with its glowing tip, as the Doors sang *Light My Fire*, and he felt himself stiffen, his body rouse towards her.

A big boy now, on your own two feet. And keep yourself covered and keep buttoned up and don't look don't touch yourself there that's dirty. But Moira had touched him and showed him hers and they'd laughed, already guilty without knowing why, they'd laughed at the silly difference. But their mother had caught them and battered them both, and they had kept their distance, grown apart.

Ruby turned, and there again was that tilt of the head, reminding him of Moira. But she smiled at him, was completely and utterly herself, at once innocent and knowing, and he saw the immensity of her power, to fire him with this driving urge.

He had grown and contained himself, held himself back, denied responses, kept himself in check. Been a good boy. Tightened and tensed till he couldn't any more, had found brief release, at first in a lurid muddle of dreams, then with images conjured from pictures in magazines, in Reveille and News of the World. He had woven elaborate fantasies out of nothing, had come into utter emptiness.

He relived every pang of tortured adolescent self-consciousness. He could feel the effect in the set of his

172

body, the tightness in the shoulders, the stiffness in the hips. Hang-ups. Programmed into his very cells.

Ruby had lifted back the needle-arm on the record-player, was playing *Light My Fire* one more time. She seemed to inhabit the music, become the music itself, eyes closed, her face beatific, her dark head swaying to the pulse of the song, the sinuous insistence of Jim Morrison's voice.

> *Come on baby light my fire*
> *Come on baby light my fire*
> *Try to set the night on fire*

He watched her move and was conscious again that she was wholly other, a universe in herself, entire. And the nature of that otherness was wonderful, mysterious, the female principle embodied. He felt something close to reverence.

Girls he had known or half known or never known at all beyond the hesitant feel grope fumble in some back close or at a party. It was never enough, left him always feeling empty and alone and far inside himself. He saw their faces, was filled with a sadness that was real and deep. He had always been distanced, acting out some role, relating only to image image image in his head. Out of touch.

All these things surfacing that he didn't want to think about, didn't want to face.

That time at Bird's place with some young girl, too drunk to know or care about anything. She had come home with Bird after a gig, part of a crowd, had ended up instead with him. Bird had dismissed her as a scrubber and Tam's main concern next morning was whether he had caught anything from her. But still there had been a stupid sense of achievement, of conquest. He hadn't even known her name.

He caught himself, about to wallow in guilt. The uselessness of it all. Let it go.

He closed his eyes, lay back and drifted again. Boundaries were once more starting to dissolve. A sense of vastness. He was part of an endless flow.

173

The music was still playing but he felt far beyond it, removed from it. It was far away, sounded tinny and thin, had something to do with who he had once been, his little timebound self. The voice was petulant and cocksure, a dull American drawl. He focused on the words. An exhortation. *Light my fire.*

Then he remembered. The Doors. *Strange Days.* Ruby had played it long ago. An eternity.

The voice was becoming frenzied, but the frenzy was contained, a performance.

Try to set the night on fire

It worked itself up, built to a crescendo and stopped. Then the same song started all over again. Maybe they were caught inside the song forever. Eternal recurrence. Doomed to replay it again and again, until they understood. Revolving Doors! Words, meanings were playing with him again. Why *Doors*? Why not? Doors of perception. Had his doors of perception been cleansed? Wiped clean? Or had he punched a jagged hole, smashed his way through? He remembered Malcolm at the party, the shattered door and Ruby framed in it. Had any of that actually happened? Nothing was real. Nothing made sense. Shattered door. Je t'adore. *In the beginning was the pun.* Had Beckett written that, or Joyce? What would Joyce have written if he'd taken this stuff? *Finnegans Wake* probably!

riverrun past eve and Adam's

The words opened him out again, restored that sense of the vast. A return.

He was suddenly conscious of Ruby somewhere close to him, another galaxy approaching his own. He opened his eyes and the room was a glittering cave of brocades. She came towards him, reaching out, and he saw, this moment, now, the true nature of her being. The silver star in her forehead shone. Her eyes were as deep and dark as the night sky he had looked into, out there. In them he saw all the women she had been, would be, saw other lifetimes she had lived. She was

174

child and young girl, woman and withered crone. She was all women. She was womankind. He had known her before, other times. She was Indian squaw, Italian lady, a factory-girl in Russia, an Irish whore. In ancient Egypt she was high priestess, the keeper of secrets; she was handmaiden to Isis, had become Isis herself. He saw it all; she was priestess of her own temple, the entrance to the mystery and the mystery itself. He was being initiated. She pulled him into her, worked her magic, a spark, a charge. He was positive to her negative. He had to connect, complete the circuit, let the energy flow. *Try to set the night on fire.* He was hard and driving into her. Contact. Communion. The gates of the temple were open. He pushed through and entered.

Eddie laughed, shouted out 'Hello there! Ya beauty!' He shouted it at the stupid night, at the miserable street with its boarded-up windows.

'Shoosh!' said Carol. 'You'll get us hung!'

He booted a tin can, sent it clattering across the road, started chanting again. 'If you hate the fucking English clap your hands!'

Jack joined in, clapping.

'Come *on*!' said Carol.

Eddie laughed again, sang.

> *'Que sera sera*
> *Whatever will be will be*
> *We're going to Wem-b-ley*
> *Que sera sera'*

And Carol was guiding him into an entranceway and up a flight of stairs. And most of the block looked empty, the ground-floor windows bricked up. But she had a key, was opening a door, leading them into a flat. She switched on a light and they were in a drab living room, lit by a dim bare bulb. A table with a red formica top. Cold linoleum on the floor. A few old kitchen chairs. A beat-up three-piece suite.

'It's my brother's place,' said Carol. 'He's away right now and I've got his keys.'

'That's handy!' said Jack.

'Sorry it's a bit of a mess.'

'Not at all!'

'Is he the one that used to torment you?' said Eddie.

'Sorry?'

'Was it him that used to sing *Oh Carol* at you?'

'That's right!' she said. 'That's the one!'

Jack was looking round the place, checking it out. They had come in through a narrow hall. On one side it opened out to the room they were in, and then through to a bedroom. On the other side were a kitchen and bathroom.

'What was it you said about food?' he asked.

'I'll see what we've got,' said Carol.

'Got to keep our strength up, eh?' said Jack. The girls laughed, went through to the kitchen.

'What a dump!' said Eddie. 'Christ, I thought my ma's house was bad, but this place is a right hole.'

'Never mind,' said Jack. 'That's what you're here for, isn't it?'

'What?'

'Your *hole*!'

'I thought the Carol one was a bit nervous or something.'

'Must be love!'

'Aye, sure!'

Carol stuck her head round the door. 'We've just got to nip out for bread and milk. There's a wee place stays open.'

'Fucksake!' said Jack.

'We'll no be a minute,' she said. 'And anyway, you're the one that was anxious to feed your face!'

'OK,' said Jack. 'OK.' He fumbled in his pocket, handed her a crumpled pound note. 'Here, could you get us some fags. I'm running short.'

'Sure,' she said, taking the money. 'See yous in a minute.' And the girls were gone, out the door.

'You and your fucking stomach,' said Eddie, annoyed.

'What's up wi your face?' said Jack.

'Nothing.'

'They'll no be long.'

'Forget it.' He crossed to the window, pulled aside the shabby curtains, looked out.

'Hey!' said Jack. 'I've got a two bob bit. I'll toss you for the bedroom, OK?'

'OK.'

'The loser gets the couch in here, right?'

'Aye.'

'Heads or tails?'

'Tails.'

Jack spun the coin, caught it, slapped it down on the back of his hand. The Queen's head faced up.

'Heads!' he said. 'God bless the Queen!'

'What the fuck?' said Eddie. He was looking out the window again, saw the two girls run across the road and climb into a waiting van.

'What is it?' said Jack.

'They two lassies. They just got into a van and drove away.'

'Eh?'

'There's something weird going on here.'

'The bastards!' said Jack. 'They've fucking set us up. Next thing they'll be in mob-handed to do us in.'

'Jesus Christ!'

'Come on!' said Jack, heading for the door.

'I'm bringing a chib,' said Eddie. He started ransacking the room for something, anything.

'They've locked the fucking door,' said Jack. 'The cunts!' He put his boot to the lock but it didn't budge. He needed a hammer, a screwdriver. He turned to go back into the living room, where Eddie was. But he didn't make it, was thrown off his feet as the blast ripped the room apart.

Brian had dozed in his chair, felt chilled. The piece of

177

paper with his cut-up, collage, had slipped from his fingers and lay on the floor. He picked it up and read it through.

Tam lay awake, Ruby beside him, asleep. Just two people, clinging together for comfort and warmth. Out there was vast night, endless dark. But here, now, was haven. This moment, no more. And all he knew was they would die. But he had seen the way everything flowed together, was inextricably interwoven, interconnected, drops on a great spiderweb, shining.

Eddie was dead, killed outright. Police, firemen, an ambulance crew had arrived. Jack was carried out, smashed up but still alive.

George woke from a dream he couldn't remember. He sat up, staring, lay down again and slept.

had we but pure and endless light but rather darkness no not now the bowl of night on all sides round looks kinda dark looks like a dungeon horrible which way I fly a yard above eternity that forbidden tree the worst trip cheerless dark and deadly I wanna go home cannot be so good to me myself am hell and world enough time's winged chariot can't stop who I am political power a heap of rust but at my back the barrel of a gun don't mean revolution destroying the new poor naked wretches in the alley have life Shakespeare's writing an essay so refined such a doll with his worry about the rest hung with weights and woe first disobedience and a great ring of bells everything's fine act of violence visible like the old night feel so broke up in Mobile in pointed shoes no breath at all the arsehole of the universe its own place one-dimensional mind divided can't see maybe love a little closer can tell me right now who's that knocking who is it how come you are why should a dog a horse a rat can this really be nothing and thou the end

A Love Supreme

Tam had moved in with Ruby after that first trip together, what they called their *mystical wedding*. That same night some unlikely alchemy had happened between Malcolm and Claire as she'd bandaged his cut hand, and they too were now living together.

'Like a fucking game of *Stations*!' Bird had said. For all his talk of freedom and non-attachment, he'd been hurt in his pride at losing Claire, especially to Malcolm.

Not long after that, Bird had moved into a huge empty slum of a basement flat, near the University. With a flourish of irony, he had christened it *The Temple*, painted the name on a sign above the door in luminous dayglo orange and green. A few others had moved in with him – Paki among them – and the place had quickly become known as a hang-out, a crash-pad. Floor-space was always available to anyone passing through, and by means of some mysterious network the word had spread, so that there was a constant flow of visitors, some from as far away as London, or Amsterdam, even the occasional wandering American, backpacking round Europe.

One girl, Chris, had arrived from London, selling underground newspapers. She had planned to stay the night on her way to Edinburgh. Two years on, she was still staying, with Bird. She had a toughness about her that Bird liked, cropped hair, an Oxbridge accent blunted by an acquired Cockney drawl. She seemed to spark his energies, set him raving, dreaming up crazy schemes.

It was to talk about his latest idea that he'd invited a few of them round. His plan was to rent a space in

Edinburgh for the Festival, put on a performance at the Fringe.

'Everything is theatre,' he said. 'Everything.'

Conscious of what he was saying, and that his saying it was itself a performance, he paused. For dramatic effect.

The windows were covered over with black drapes, shutting out the daylight. The room was lit by a table-lamp, a candle stuck in a wine-bottle.

'I mean,' he continued, 'we should be able to create a space where it's possible to just go out there and do anything, say anything. And it'll be theatre because of the intention. Because of the consciousness.'

'What about structure?' asked Ruby. 'Don't we have to give it a shape?'

'That'll come as we work on it. As we work on ourselves.'

'How?' she asked.

'It's like jazz,' said Bird. 'Only we'll be the instruments.'

He took a deep drag on his joint, passed it on to Tam.

'You know what I'm saying man, don't you?'

Tam took in a quick sharp gasp, held, exhaled, passed the joint to Ruby.

'I think so,' he said. 'Yeah.'

The joint was passed round, to Claire, to Paki, to Chris and back to Bird, completing the circle.

'So anyway,' said Bird, to all of them. 'Are you with me?'

'A theatre group?' said Claire.

'Don't say it like *that*,' said Chris. 'You make it sound like amateur dramatics. And there is a *bit* more to it!'

'Guerrilla theatre,' said Bird.

'Agitprop sort of thing,' said Tam.

'Eejitprop!' said Paki.

'Listen pal,' said Bird. 'You weren't even invited to this meeting. You're only here on sufferance because you happened to be skulking about the place.'

Paki laughed, didn't let it touch him. He was in a

mellow haze from the dope and whatever else he'd ingested that day.

'Couldn't we open the curtains or something?' said Claire.

'Come on!' said Paki, laughing even more. 'Next thing you'll be wanting fresh air!'

'We don't want to spoil the atmosphere, do we?' said Bird.

Part of that atmosphere was the smell of the place: an uneasy amalgam of kitchen smells – spices and cooked food and something faintly rotten – mingled with tobacco and hashish, and wafting from the rooms an unnameable odour, stale and close, of bodies, and clothes, and bedding that had gone too long without being changed. And permeating it all was the sweet deodorizing fragrance of incense, sandalwood or patchouli, frangipani or musk.

'Oh no,' said Claire, deadpan. 'We don't want to spoil the atmosphere.'

One whole wall of the room was a huge montage – posters, photos, cuttings from newspapers and magazines. Chris had been to art School, could draw and paint, and she'd copied some of Bird's favourite comic-book characters directly on to the wall in bright acrylic colours. Doctor Strange stood, arms outstretched. The Silver Surfer crested a wave. Robert Crumb's rogue guru, Mr Natural, announced *The whole universe is completely insane.* And Bird had added some graffiti, with spray paint. KEEP ON TRUCKIN across the top in blue, and beneath it, in red, BIRD LIVES.

The whole thing was organic, changed from week to week, and Bird expected people to add to it, even provided felt-tip pens for the purpose.

Claire stood staring at it all, wrote *atmosphere* in small neat script. Then she found a space, drew a red clenched fist surrounded by the outline of a flower.

'So what happened to Malcolm?' said Bird. 'How come he's not here?'

'He's got other things to do,' said Claire.

'Not interested?'

'Depends what direction it takes.

'If it's ideologically sound you mean?'

'Something like that.'

Chris didn't quite choke back a harsh laugh, dry and derisive. Claire gave her a hard look, said nothing.

'He's such an old puritan!' said Bird. 'What is he these days? A crypto-anarcho-syndicalist or something?'

'Do you always have to be so *smart*?'

'Can't help it. It's my revisionist tendencies. Come the revolution I'll be strung up from the nearest lamp-post. And Malcolm'll be manning the barricades!'

'I think it's time I was going' said Claire.

'Aw come on baby! Don't get uptight. I mean I *love* Malcolm. And I think there's a place for him in what we're trying to do here.'

'That's big of you.'

'I mean we all want to change things, don't we?'

'Sure, sure.'

'Tell him it's a situation he can use.'

'Yeah.'

'And tell him my ideology is absolutely pure. I don't believe in *anything*!'

'He knows that already.'

Bird laughed, gave her a hug, turned to Tam.

'How about Brian?'

'He says he's into it,' said Tam. 'He just couldn't make it today.'

'Oh well,' said Bird. 'That's something.'

'Better than nothing,' said Paki, grinning.

'That you trying to be profound again?' said Bird. 'I've warned you about that already!'

'I really do have to be going,' said Claire.

'You know, you should all just move in here,' said Bird.

'No *thanks*!' said Ruby. 'Not after last time.'

'How do you mean?'

'We stayed the night after one of your parties,' said

Tam. 'Spent the next week wi disinfectant and a bone comb, getting the nits out of our hair.'

'Aw come on!' said Bird. 'The place has been gutted out since then. Chris gave it a good clean.'

'Smells like it!' said Claire.

'Ach, you're all fucking bourgies at heart,' said Bird. 'Except Paki! Listen, before you go, why don't you add something to the wall?'

'I've done my bit already,' said Claire.

'And very nice it is too!' said Bird.

Ruby took a green pen, drew an *aum* sign. Tam took the pen from her, drew five lines, a musical stave, and a little stylized bird on each line. Chris wrote YES in red. And Paki took the wrapper from his packet of cigarette-papers, tacked it up with a drawing-pin.

'Beautiful!' said Bird. 'I love you all!'

'So what do you make of it all?' asked Ruby. They were walking from Bird's place, back through the park.

Tam turned the question into something cosmic, stopped dead, stood, spaced-out, gaping at the sky. 'You mean what does *it* make of *me*!'

'Idiot!' she said, laughing, giving him a shove. 'I meant this thing Bird's dreamed up.'

'I don't know.' He shrugged. 'Sounds good to me. Anything for a laugh!'

Up ahead they heard the sound of a tin whistle, saw Martin coming towards them, playing it.

'Shit!' said Tam.

Martin was a crony of Paki's. He was dressed in a yellow kaftan, a floppy purple hat. He was trying to play *Greensleeves* but he kept hitting wrong notes, improvising little trills and halting runs, slurring up and down the scale.

'Maybe we could cut down here,' said Tam, grabbing Ruby's arm, indicating an escape route across the grass. But it was too late. Martin had seen them.

'Hi!' He was waving at them, flailing both arms, his

183

tin whistle in one hand, his purple hat in the other.

'Man!' he said, loping up to them. 'Isn't this a *beautiful* day!'

He was originally from Manchester, but had tried to bend his accent into something mid-Atlantic. The effect was grotesque.

'Aye,' said Tam, looking about him. 'Beautiful.'

'You just coming from Bird's place?'

'That's right.'

'Is Paki there?'

'He was when we left.'

'Great!' said Martin. 'I was hoping he might have some acid. Want to catch a horror movie tonight, and I'd like to drop a tab before I go.'

'Well, have a nice time,' said Tam. 'Or should I say a nasty time?'

'Right!'

'Well.'

'Anyway.'

'Be seeing you.'

'Yeah.'

When they were far enough away, Tam looked back, shook his head.

'God!' he said. 'How can he treat acid like that?'

The trips they had taken together had led them out, beyond themselves. But each time had left them more desolate afterwards, more fragile, less able to cope with the grey lingering sadness of comedown. The last time, three or four months back, they had both been genuinely terrified, thought they had done themselves permanent damage, trapped in a lasting paranoid psychosis, circuits blown, no way back. After that they had decided to leave it alone, at least for a while.

'Horror movies by fuck!' said Tam. 'I mean you've got to treat that stuff with respect. Like that last time, I thought it was the end of us.'

'Well it wasn't,' said Ruby.

'No, it wasn't.'

'And here we are.'

'Here we are!'

They walked on, up the hill, stopped and sat down on the grass.

'Listen,' she said.

'I'm listening.'

'If we do get involved in this theatre thing, that commits us to being here right through to the Fall.'

'I know.'

'And that means I'll be overstaying my welcome.'

'Yeah.'

'I mean my visa runs out August first.'

'I know, I know.'

'So what do you think we should do about it?'

'I don't know. What do *you* think?'

'Well,' she said. 'There's a few options.'

'Uh huh.'

'I could just stay on, as an illegal alien. That would be cool, until I try to go home. Then I could be in trouble.'

He nodded, said nothing.

'Or I could just stay legal, go back to the States, and you could come with me.'

'Then I'd have the same problem.'

'Eventually, yeah. Alternatively, *I* could just go back.'

'You mean we could split up?'

'I'm just listing the options.'

Again he said nothing, but this time the nothing sat there between them.

'There is another possibility,' she said.

'What?'

'We could get married.'

'Eh?'

'It would make me legitimate. No problem.'

'Are you serious?'

'Why not?'

'It's just . . .'

'I know. *It's so sudden!*'

He laughed. 'Right!'

185

'Well? *Whaddaya say*?'

'So this is a proposal?'

'If you like.'

'OK,' he said. 'I'm game. Anything for a laugh, eh?'

'That's what I love about you Scots,' she said. 'You're so fucking romantic!'

After graduation, Brian effectively dropped out. At first it meant confrontation with his parents. He was wasting his opportunities, his good education, throwing it away. But finally they realized there was no way through to him. His father shrugged it off. 'Sooner or later he'll grow out of it,' he said. 'Come to his senses. Settle down.' His mother was less philosophical, accepted it, but with a residue of bitterness. 'His heid's in the clouds,' she'd say, tightlipped and unforgiving, convinced he was spoiling his chances of a career.

The way he saw it, he just needed some time to himself. He had been on the treadmill called *education* for the best part of his life. He had to step off for a bit, take his bearings. No doubt someday he *would* get a job, *would* settle down. But not now. Not yet.

In some strange way it had been Eddie Logan's death that had made up his mind. He had read about it in the papers, felt a strange sense of displacement at seeing a face he knew staring out at him, a hard-eyed mugshot. Eddie, who no longer existed.

'Never know the minute,' Brian's father had said.

Brian had decided he would finish his degree, then embark on a crash-course in living, do the things he wanted to do. Life was too short. You never knew the minute.

First he took a summer job in a bakery, working nights. The work was hard – standing at a conveyor belt the whole shift, shunting great trays of cake-mix into a huge oven, wilting in the blast of its heat. But sometimes, at odd moments, the draining bodily exhaustion and the mind-numbing boredom would induce a kind of heightened awareness, a clarity of seeing. Things would be touched with a rare lightness, a humour. He would let his imagination go, follow an idea through beyond itself. And out of it all came a few short poems.

For the most part, though, it was dull repetitious grind. But because he worked nightshift it paid well. By the end of his two-month stint he had managed to save some money. After his last shift he walked clear, into the sunlight of a late summer morning. He was tired and he still smelled of the bakery, in his clothes, in his hair. But he felt buoyed up, elated. He had money in his pocket. He was free.

Next morning he woke with a sour mouth, a pounding head, the stink about him of stale cigarette smoke. Groaning, he sat up, stared without comprehension at a squat, bulky metal object, occupying the table. It sat, unfamiliar, like some kind of space-module that had just beamed down into his room. He stood up, let the sick throb subside, and crossed to the table for a closer look.

He read the lettering on the side – *Roneo*. He unfastened two clasps on top and the sides clattered open far too loudly for his nervous system.

'Jesus Christ!'

Now he knew what it was. He had seen one before. A duplicating machine. And some far faint memory of buying it was coming to the surface.

The day was a vague haze. He had started out with money – his last week's pay, two weeks' lying time. He hadn't come home, had gone into town and wandered around, gone into a café for breakfast, killed time till the pubs opened at eleven. He'd only intended having a pint or two, but he'd met Tam, then Bird had turned up. Bird had been raving. Something about a theatre group. It sounded wonderful.

He remembered the three of them lurching along the road, remembered them peering in a shop window at the duplicator. It was secondhand, reconditioned. A bargain. He remembered Bird encouraging him. 'Print

your own stuff. Start a magazine. Publish books even.'
In his liberated frame of mind it was all he needed to
hear. He had laid out the last of his money on a deposit,
walked out of the shop with the machine.

The thing had been heavy – they'd taken turns
lugging it, back to Bird's dump of a flat. The Temple.
Paki had been there and they'd all smoked dope,
blessed the duplicator, laughed at it. He remembered
swallowing a handful of mandrax, and the rest was a
blur. He had no idea how he had got home with his
machine, or dragged it upstairs to his attic room.

But here it sat, confronting him.

He had a momentary flash of being propped up in a
taxi, intoning 'Home James!' to the driver.

'Shit!'

He fingered the rollers, the drum that carried the ink,
the handle that cranked the whole thing into action. It
was his. He owned this piece of machinery. Or he
would when he'd finished paying for it. It was
ridiculous. He turned the handle, set the mechanism in
motion, the drum clanking round on its axis. And he
laughed at the total absurdity of it. But that started up
the dull throb in his head again, and he had to lie back
down in the hope that it would pass.

'It's great!' said Malcolm. 'It's putting the means of
production in the hands of the people.'

'In the hands of the artist,' said Bird.

'Wait a minute,' said Brian. 'I bought the fucking
thing. It's my machine!'

'Property is theft,' said Malcolm.

'But I paid for it! In fact I'm still paying it up. I've got
to get the money back one way or another.'

In the end it was agreed. Brian would do anti-
Apartheid leaflets for Malcolm, handbills for Bird for
his theatre project. They would provide the paper and
he would charge a basic rate for his time. That kept
everybody happy. For himself, he would run off a
poetry broadsheet. He had met a few others who were

writing, and he'd include some of his own stuff. He had already thought up a name for the paper. He would call it *Ion Engine.*

'Who?' said Malcolm.

'It's a line from an Eddie Morgan poem,' said Brian. *'What I love about poetry is its ion engine.'*

The duplicator had been moved into the Temple. It made more sense than keeping it in Brian's tiny room. In the big front room at the Temple it looked no more bizarre than anything else. It sat like some futurist sculpture, jostled for space alongside a paraffin heater and an old harp without any strings.

Bird had found a place in Edinburgh for their performance, a run-down church hall at a dirt-cheap rent. For the Festival they would call it the Magic Theatre, and Chris had already designed a handbill with the name across the top as if in neon letters. Underneath, in smaller print, it read *For madmen only! Price of admission your mind.* The central image was a door with a large eye where a peep-hole should be. The door was half open and beyond it could be glimpsed a surreal psychedelic landscape.

'It's beautiful,' said Brian. 'But I'll never be able to trace it on to one of these stencils. It's too intricate. It would just start coming to bits.'

'No problem,' said Bird. 'I know this chick that works in the University offices.'

'Oh aye?'

'She can make what they call a photo stencil. Take it direct from the original.'

'Incredible! Can she do it for you any time?'

'If I chat her up, yeah!'

Brian was quiet for a moment. Bird laughed.

'What is it?' said Brian.

'I can hear your brain grinding into action!'

'Oh can you now?'

'You were wondering if I could get these stencils done for you, for your poetry thing.'

'Christ!' said Brian. 'Am I that transparent?'

'When you've opened your third eye,' said Bird, tapping a finger to his forehead, 'you can read people like a book.'

'Third eye my arse!' said Malcolm.

'Well maybe *yours* is,' said Bird. 'That would explain quite a lot!'

'All that mystical crap is just physiological,' said Malcolm. 'It's all to do with the pineal gland.'

'Anyway!' said Brian. 'What about these stencils?'

'I'll tell you what,' said Bird.

'What?'

'You run off these handbills for free and I'll see what I can do.'

'It *would* make things a lot easier,' said Brian. 'I could use better drawings.'

'And you'd only have to type the stuff on to paper,' said Bird.

'Right.'

'You can even use letraset.'

'Wow!'

'You scratch his back, he'll scratch yours!' said Malcolm.

'Exactly,' said Bird.

'Meanwhile it's all based on the exploitation of some young girl at the Uni.'

'Exploitation!'

'Manipulation.'

'Ach come off it!' said Bird. 'The only ones getting ripped off are the University. We're just *using* the system.'

'And what if the "chick" gets into trouble, or loses her job, for doing you a favour?'

'Give me a break!' said Bird.

'Listen,' said Brian, cutting in. He didn't take their arguing seriously. Baiting each other was the only way they ever related. 'I'll do this duplicating for you if Chris'll do a cover design for my broadsheet.'

'Consider it done!' said Bird, shaking hands on it.

190

'More exploitation of women!' said Malcolm, moving towards the door. 'I'll leave you two businessmen to sort out the small print in your contract.'

'So you're not going to stick around for the rehearsal?' said Bird.

'No thanks.'

'Oh well,' said Bird. 'Pineal glands to you!'

Malcolm gave him the V-sign, banged the door shut behind him as he left.

2

At first it was formless, had no direction or shape and only the driving energy of Bird's vision to sustain it.

'It's all about making it sacred,' he said. 'We've got to find that spark inside ourselves, got to communicate it to an audience so *they* find it inside *them*.'

They agreed on a format for each evening. They would begin with music and a bit of poetry. Bird and Tam would provide the music, roping in any other musicians who happened to be free and willing to play.

'If we're feeling dada-esque we can unleash Paki on them,' said Bird. 'Give him a solo spot!'

Brian would be responsible for the poetry, reading himself or using the other writers he'd be publishing in *Ion Engine*. But the poetry and music would be no more than prelude, just to warm the audience up.

'Then we'll go out and wallop them!' said Bird. 'We'll break down the barriers till there's no separation between us and the audience. Just a shared consciousness. Communion. A realization that we're all one.'

'One what?' said Claire.

'It's all one tae me!' said Paki.

'We're going to change people's awareness,' said Bird, ignoring them. 'And we start by changing our own.'

They began by doing exercises. Ruby led them through a few basic yoga postures, *asanas*. She showed them the Cobra, the Lion, the Dog, and a cycle known as Sun-worship. They stretched and bent, tried to twist bodies that were stiff and unsupple. They stood on their heads, toppled over and tried again. They collapsed, laughing. And the hardest thing was self-consciousness, feeling foolish. And Bird fought it.

'Come on!' he said. 'This is serious. We've got to work at it.'

And they worked at it, till they ached.

Then Ruby, her voice a slow hypnotic drawl, talked them through the meditation techniques she'd picked up. She taught them breathing exercises and posture, visualization and mantra, an esoteric rag-bag, culled from books she'd read.

'Keep the back nice and straight. Breathe slow and even through the nose. Imagine you're breathing out all the garbage you've got inside you, and you're breathing in peace. Good.'

There was a bit of awkward shuffling, but they tried it, went through the motions.

'Now. Picture a flower, a rose, here in your heart. Feel it. Let it open out petal by petal.'

They sat in a circle, in a cleared floorspace, in the candlelit front room, a drift of incense fighting the smells from the stinking kitchen.

'Now chant with me the mantra, *aum*. The seed-sound of all creation.'

As she started to chant, it was too much for Paki and he burst out laughing.

Tam rounded on him. 'Give it a chuck or I'll rattle you one!'

'Aw that's really meditational!' said Paki, laughing even more.

'Listen!'

'Peace and love to you too man!'

'Paki's a Zen master,' said Bird. 'He thinks the Universe is a big joke.'

But the next day, when it was Bird's turn to lead the exercises, he kept Paki in check, wouldn't let him smoke dope before the rehearsal, told him to stay clear, to concentrate. And although Paki looked sullen, he did as he was told.

Bird too had gleaned some of his ideas from books.

'I picked these up in Smith's,' he said, chucking down two paperbacks – *An Actor Prepares* and *Towards a Poor Theatre.*

'You mean you nicked them?' said Brian, picking up the books.

'Liberated them,' said Bird. 'I'm a great believer in freedom of information!'

He had marked a few passages, underlined them in pencil, and his girl-who-worked-in-the-University-offices had made enough photocopies to go round.

Some of it felt like children's games. Be an animal, a cat say. Walk like a cat, stretch your back, *become* a cat. Now you're a dog. Roll around, bark, howl. Then they played with words. Take the first word that comes into your head. Repeat it over and over again till it loses all meaning, is just pure sound. Shout it. Scream it. Whisper it. Sing it.

They began to loosen up, feel more at ease with themselves and with each other. They worked in pairs and as a group, communicating at first in silence, by look and gesture and touch, moving through to improvised exchanges, encounters, confrontations. Then little tensions, hostilities, began to manifest, and nobody escaped.

Brian wrote some of it down, like dialogue in a play.

'I'm not working with Paki any more. He keeps trying to grope me.'

'Sometimes, Claire, you can be spectacularly vapid.'

'If Chris tries to put me down one more time . . .'

'For Christsake Tam . . .'

'For Christsake Ruby . . .'

'How come we all have to do what Bird says?'

'Come on Brian. How about participating instead of just writing everything down?'

After a few days of it, Bird suggested they have what

he called a 'truth session', say exactly what they thought of each other.

'Home truths,' he said. 'Slag each other. Clear the air. Let it all hang out.'

So they did, and it ended in tears, and tightlipped separation from each other. But the next day they admitted, tentatively, that there might, just, have been a little bit of truth in what had been said. And they looked at each other fresh, and started again.

They had been up all night. In the early morning stillness they straggled from the Temple through quiet, sleeping streets, and climbed the railings into Kelvingrove Park.

'Whose brilliant idea was this?' asked Paki, already out of breath with the effort.

Bird led them to a circle of rocks set in the grass.

'They're like wee standing stones,' he said. 'A scaled-down Stonehenge.'

'A Zen garden,' said Tam.

'Beautiful,' said Ruby, and she kicked off her sandals, ran barefoot across the grass.

There was still a chill in the air, the sun not yet up above the trees. The stone circle lay in shadow and the grass was still wet with cold dew. Ruby danced around, exhilarated at the shock of it to the soles of her feet and through her whole system.

'Come on in!' she yelled. 'The water's lovely!'

And they did. They peeled off shoes and socks, took a few steps and quickly realized they had to keep moving to keep warm. So they joined Ruby in her dance round the rocks. Tam had brought his bamboo flute and he squatted on the stone at the centre of the circle and he played, started with jigs and reels then moved on to freer forms, Indian modes. And they danced themselves to a standstill, laughing, exhausted.

'Now that you're warmed up we can try something else,' said Bird. 'I was reading about this thing Yoko Ono did years ago. *Dawn Chorus* she called it.'

194

'Sounds appropriate,' said Brian.

'What we do is, we each choose a word and we shout it out, repeat it over and over, so it becomes like a mantra.'

'Kind of thing we were doing last week,' said Claire.

'Yeah, but we do it all together,' said Bird. 'That's why it's a *chorus*. And doing it out here should be a gas.'

Ruby started it, chanted a long sustained *aum*. And over the top of it Paki spat out *shit shit shit,* again and again, rapid fire. Then Tam came in with *flute*, breathing the word out, holding it as long as he could, and Claire in a high clear voice almost sang *freedom*. Then Chris cut across her with *lies lies lies,* and Brian added *tree*, and Bird roared out *ach!* at the top of his voice.

And the cacophony of it became a strange atonal music. It contained its own harmonies and discords as words, voices, chimed together, or clashed and drowned each other out, in counterpoints of sense as well as sound. And one by one, as if they had agreed beforehand, the voices dropped out till only Ruby was left, chanting her *aum*.

'Wow!' said Bird, into the silence when she stopped.

'Wild!' said Paki.

'We're really opening up,' said Ruby. 'I think it would be good to do the *sun worship* now, then maybe have a meditation.'

'Sure thing,' said Bird, and Ruby led them again through the series of exercises, *asanas*, salutation to the sun. Then each of them sat on one of the rocks and tried to focus, to meditate, and even Paki sat silent, and Tam rounded it off with a slow, flowing melody on his flute, and the sun came up high enough to shine through the trees and touch their circle, warming them.

On their way out of the park, back to Bird's place for breakfast, they still carried that warmth. It was something tangible, something they had shared. It was there in their voices as they called out a Good morning to the bemused park-keeper who had just opened the gates.

'What we need now is a story,' said Bird. 'A myth. A theme. Something to build on.'

'Leitmotif,' said Tam.

'Exactly,' said Bird. 'And it just came to me, in a blinding flash of revelation!'

'What did?' asked Tam.

'It was down in the park there, when you were playing your flute. I saw it really clear.'

'Saw what?' said Ruby.

'The Magic Flute.'

'Eh?'

'That's our theme,' said Bird. 'Remember you were raving on to me about Mozart?'

Tam remembered. He had listened to *Die Zauber-flöte* on acid, come out of it raving that Mozart was an angel, that the opera had said it all.

'I was totally into it,' he said.

'Well that's it,' said Bird. 'You can tell us all about it!'

'I could research all the mythology and symbolism,' said Brian.

'I thought you might be into that!' said Bird.

'I'll go down to the Mitchell this afternoon, see what they've got.'

'Isn't there a lot about freemasonry in it?' asked Claire.

'That's right,' said Tam. 'They called it his masonic opera.'

'Malcolm knows a lot about all that stuff,' said Claire. 'His old man was heavily into it.'

'And George for Christsake!' said Brian. 'He's probably a Grand Master by this time!'

'He'd never tell us anything,' said Tam. 'Wouldn't want to risk getting his throat cut!'

'You can get it all from books anyway,' said Brian.

'What I'm really interested in is the ritual,' said Bird.

196

'Why?' said Chris.

'Eh?'

'Why ritual? Why get hung up on all these old empty forms?'

'Tying the cat to the bed!' said Tam.

'Sorry?' Chris had no idea what he was talking about.

'It's a Zen story,' said Tam. 'There was this master that used to have his disciples come to his place to meditate. But he had this crazy cat that would rush about the room and knock things over and generally disrupt everything. So the master tied it to the bed in his room, to keep it from getting in the way. Every time they came together, he would tie the cat to the bed, they would have their meeting, then he would set the cat free. This went on for years. And eventually the master died. But they kept on with their meetings – they would come together, tie the cat to the bed, and meditate. But gradually, in the course of time, some of the original energy went out of the thing, and they forgot what it was all about. And they ended up coming together once a week to tie the cat to the bed.'

'And that's religion!' said Bird, stealing the punch-line.

'OK,' said Chris. 'So why ritual?'

'Precisely *because* the old forms are dead,' said Bird. 'We've got to find new forms of our own.'

'Magic Theatre,' said Claire.

'Hey!' said Brian. 'We took that *Magic Theatre* bit from *Steppenwolf*, right?'

'For madmen only!' said Paki.

'And the character in that meets Mozart right at the end.' Brian was excited at seeing a sudden connection, a glimpse, things falling into place.

'You see!' said Bird. 'There's a pattern to it all!'

Brian came back from the Mitchell Library with pages of notes, on symbolic interpretations of the Mozart opera, on the rituals and forms of Freemasonry, on the cults of Isis and Osiris.

'Once you start looking into all this stuff it breenges off in so many different directions,' he said. 'This whole idea of music as a magic power is really ancient.'

'Orpheus,' said Bird, and Paki croaked out a line from an old String Band song.

'Orpheus made the sun rise
cos he knew how to play . . .'

'There's a story by Goethe about this boy with a magic flute,' continued Brian. 'He plays it and tames all these wild animals.'

'Music hath charms . . .' said Bird.

'Pied Piper sort of thing,' said Claire.

'Piper at the gates of dawn,' said Paki. 'The Floyd!'

'Then there's your cosmic flute players,' said Brian. 'Pan with his pipes.'

'Krishna,' said Tam.

'This is all very *interesting*,' said Chris. 'But what's it got to do with *us*, with what we're tryng to *do*?'

'It just gives the whole thing another dimension, baby,' said Bird. 'It's like we're dealing with all these archetypal images, and if we're aware of all that, it'll help us figure out what it is we're trying to express.'

'That was what blew me away in the Mozart opera,' said Tam. 'It was like . . . on the surface it was just this stupid pantomime story. But in behind that there was so much more going on.'

'Like what?' said Chris.

'Like all these polarities. Good and evil. Darkness and light.'

'Yin and Yang,' said Ruby, chipping it in.

Tam was trying very hard to articulate it, to hold on to his thread.

'And the really amazing thing was that at the same time, *at the same time*, it was expressing something beyond all that, something transcendent. Ach, I'm not explaining it very well. I just know it was there, in the music.'

'You're explaining it just fine man,' said Bird.

'I'll tell you one thing,' said Chris. 'From looking at this libretto thing, it's really sexist. I mean, the attitudes to women really stink.'

'Spirit of the times,' said Bird.

'Zeitgeist,' said Tam.

'No excuse,' said Chris. 'So anyway, what are you trying to say this opera's actually *about*?'

Tam thought for a moment. 'Initiation,' he said. 'Initiation into a higher realm. Through music. And love. And it ends with this sunburst. *Die Strahlen der Sonne vertreiben die Nacht.* The sun's rays drive away the night.'

'Too much!' said Paki.

Bird felt as if they were getting somewhere.

'This thing about initiation,' he said. 'Rites of passage. We've got to explore that.'

They explored it first by simply acting out some of the rituals that Brian had researched, with varying degrees of solemnity and mockery, swinging, as the mood took them, from high seriousness to knockabout clowning. The simplest of things could set them off – the ceremonial knocking, a masonic formula used in the opera, was translated into pop songs, *I hear ya knockin, Knock three times,* then led into a spate of *Knock-Knock* jokes.

Who's there?

Disney.

Disney who?

Disnae-matter-a-damn!

Chris was unhappy that they slipped so easily into a Glasgow mode, took refuge in patter.

'It's so reductive,' she said.

'That's what's good about it,' said Bird.

'Yeah, OK,' said Chris, 'but sometimes it's a cop-out, a refusal to see something through on its own terms.'

'I know what you mean,' said Bird. 'But it's something we've got to work through. We've got to find our

199

own voice, whatever that is.' He grinned at her. 'Trust me!'

His concern was to bring everything back, always, to their own experience. What rites of passage had *they* been through?

He wanted to try something. They stood around the perimeter of the room, as far apart as they could, and they faced outwards, away from each other, each one isolated in their own space. And Bird told them to take their time, and tell, in turn, something that had happened directly to them, something that felt like initiation.

After a silence, he kicked it off himself by talking about the loss of his virginity, at a party when he was sixteen.

'Brubeck's *Take Five* was playing in the next room.'

Then Paki spoke about the first time he'd smoked dope.

'In the school toilets it was, at dinnertime. First time I ever smiled through a double period of maths!'

Tam said a little about that first trip, with Ruby. 'The smell of patchouli always brings it back.'

There was a pause, then Ruby said, 'Seeing the Beatles at Shea Stadium. That was the nearest thing I'd had to a religious experience!'

There was a longer silence. Then Brian spoke.

'I don't know why this should come into my head. It was my first week at primary school and I got the belt for something I didn't do. The teacher wouldn't listen. I just had to take it. And the real killer was, my folks did nothing about it. Just sent me back next day and told me to forget it.'

Another pause, then Chris.

'When my father died. I was ten. Heart attack it was. Sudden like. Thing is, I didn't feel anything. It wasn't real. My mum wouldn't let me see him. Right up till the funeral, I was numb. Then at the last minute they started singing some stupid hymn and these curtains opened and the coffin moved through and I knew he was gone and I started crying and couldn't stop.'

Nobody was in a hurry to break the silence after that one, but finally Claire said 'There's nothing. Nothing I want to talk about. Nothing I want to say.'

'That's OK,' said Bird. 'No problem.'

That element of personal experience brought a new intensity to their improvisation. To a growing sense of structure, of pattern and form, they had added something stronger in the way of content, something of themselves. Bird's hope was that when they stepped in front of an audience those formal elements would be there only as framework, that they would find the freedom, from moment to moment, to express that *something* directly.

'We've been building everything round the *Magic Flute* idea,' he said. 'Now I want you to forget it.'

'Eh?' Paki was confused.

'How do you mean?' said Brian.

'I want to take away what we've been leaning on. Leave us out there with no preconceptions. Just wing it. See where it leads.'

Brian was unsure. 'Will that work?'

'Up to us to make it work, isn't it?'

Ruby had come up with an idea for a happening.

'Words in the trees,' she said.

'Eh?'

'There has to be a park near where we'll be doing the show, right?'

'There's the Meadows,' said Bird.

'So we bring along big bits of card, and string, and some brushes and paints, and everybody writes a word on a bit of card, and we hang them up in the trees.'

'Sounds good.'

'It'll be a ceremony, and you'll have to choose a word that means something special to you, and hang it with some kind of reverence.'

'I like it!' said Bird.

'I guess it's a kind of extension to that word thing we

201

were doing in the park,' said Ruby, 'the dawn chorus. But I like the idea of actually seeing the words up there, making a big poem.'

'It's great,' said Brian.

'And we can get people to join in,' said Ruby. 'Anybody that's passing by can add their words too.'

'That's nice,' said Claire. 'Opens the whole thing out.'

The idea of a *happening* shifted Bird into another gear. The next day he came back to them with an idea of his own.

'It's outrageous,' he said, 'but it could be really beautiful.'

'So tell us,' said Tam.

'OK. So. You're planning to get married, right?'

'Right.'

'And it has to be soon.'

'Uh huh.'

'And it's a marriage of convenience really, isn't it?'

'I wouldn't say that,' said Tam, defensive.

'But you know what I mean. You don't give a shit about the whole legal or religious side of it.'

'Right.'

'So what I'm saying is, why not have a ceremony that means something to you. Why not get married on stage, as part of the show?'

'Wow!' said Paki.

'You're kidding!' said Tam.

'No I'm not. It could be right at the end, the very last thing, like everything else was building towards it.'

'Big Finale,' said Chris.

'And *symbolically* it would be incredible,' said Bird. 'In terms of what Tam was saying about the opera, the way boy finds girl at the end.'

'*Mann und Weib*,' said Ruby.

'The only thing is,' said Tam, 'I'm not sure about our wedding being turned into a show for folk to come and gawp at. Know what I mean?'

'But it wouldn't be like that,' said Bird. 'Just for that

202

night we could invite family and friends and folk that are into what we're doing. It would be more like a congregation than an audience.'

'I'd be into it,' said Ruby.

Tam thought for a moment, looked at her. 'OK,' he said. 'You're on.'

'Married?' said his mother, immediately suspicious. 'Why now? Why the big rush all of a sudden?'

'I told you,' said Tam. 'Ruby's visa's about to run out.'

'Is that the only reason?'

'She's not pregnant if that's what you're asking.'

His mother looked relieved, then annoyed again. 'You might have given us some warning. Time to arrange things properly.'

'We've only just decided. Spur of the moment sort of thing.'

'Typical,' said his father.

Tam ignored him. 'And we don't want things arranged properly. We're doing it our own way.'

'On a stage?'

'It means something to us.'

'And to hell with everybody else,' said his father.

'A church wedding would just be hypocrisy.'

'Wouldn't have to be a church,' said his mother.

'Well then. Surely what we're doing's preferable to a Registry Office.'

'Nothing wrong with a Registry Office,' said his father. 'Was good enough for your sister.'

'That's fine,' he said. 'We just want to do it different.'

'No consideration.'

'I don't believe this! I mean what difference does it make to anybody?'

'Well if it makes no difference,' said his mother, 'why can't you have an ordinary wedding like anybody else?'

'That's far too simple,' said his father. 'Too straightforward for him.'

'I give up!' He picked up his jacket, ready to go.

'Spoiled rotten,' said his father. A parting shot.

At the door, his mother spoke quietly. 'It's just a bad time. All this talk of the yard shutting down, and the work-in, and hoping the order books'll stay full. I mean you see it on the news and it's all about fighting spirit and everything. But it's hard, you know. The uncertainty and that.'

'I know.'

'It gets that you just want everything normal. Uncomplicated. That's all.'

He nodded. 'But you'll come?'

'I'll talk to him,' she said. 'We'll see.'

The last week was chaos, madness. Rehearsals were going badly. They had lost sight of the process, felt adrift, no nearer to being ready than they had at the very beginning. The duplicator had packed up, so they hadn't printed the posters, or Brian's magazine. They hadn't found transport, or, alternatively, a place to stay. They couldn't get a minister to conduct the wedding. They were at each other's throats. Claire had walked out. They were ready to give up.

'I should have known', said Brian. 'It was never going to work.'

'Fuck off!' said Bird.

'I might just do that.'

Then somehow, miraculously, it all came together. Bird conjured up a van, borrowed from a band who were no longer on the road. Some friend of Paki knew an empty flat where they could squat. Someone recommended a Catholic priest for the wedding and, incredibly, he agreed. The duplicator started functioning again, as long as they kept the drum topped up with ink and didn't crank the handle too hard. They ran off the posters, handbills for Ruby's happening. In rehearsals they rediscovered what they had lost, a sense of exploration. Claire came back.

'OK,' said Bird. 'Let's get the show on the road!'

The flat had two rooms and a tiny kitchen, a toilet outside on the landing. There was running water but no electricity. Only one other flat in the building was still occupied, on the floor below. The rest lay empty.

'It'll do,' said Bird, and they set about cleaning it up, making it habitable. They had brought candles and a paraffin heater, a camping stove and a borrowed assortment of tin plates and mugs, bulk bags of lentils and brown rice. They all chipped in to a kitty and Chris took charge of the food, worked out a rota for helping to cook.

'As long as we keep things organized, we'll be fine,' she said.

The first morning Ruby was up early, getting everything ready for her happening. A week ago Brian had been talking about it to somebody he knew, who just happened to be working in a whisky bond, and just happened to know they threw out lots of good-quality stiff white card, off-cuts from great sheets of it used for packing. Brian's friend had rescued some. Now Ruby sat trimming it, cutting it to size. By the time the others started stirring in their sleeping-bags she had fitted each sheet with a bit of string, for hanging.

Chris had given her some powdered poster-paint in four bright colours – red, green, yellow and blue – and she had mixed them up in jam jars with water from the tap.

'Is that you making some tea?' asked Bird, propped up on one elbow.

'Not me!' she said. 'It's a magic potion!' She turned and held up to the light from the window a jar full of pure blue.

Tam sat up. 'You're like a wee kid going your holidays' he said. 'Up before everybody else in the house.'

'That's exactly how I feel!' she said, laughing.

Later they made their way in procession towards the Meadows, Ruby leading them, carrying her jar of blue and the jar of red. Chris carried the yellow and the green, Claire held a sheaf of paintbrushes, and the rest straggled out behind, awkwardly clutching the sheets of card which threatened to slip from their grasp or catch the wind and buffet them.

'Chalice-bearers,' said Ruby. 'That's what we are.'

'Bearing our little jam-jars full of poster colour?' said Chris.

'Yeah!' said Ruby. 'And these guys are our acolytes!'

'You're really into this, aren't you?' said Claire.

'Sure!'

Paki's sheets of card were sliding from under his arm. He cursed.

'Acolytes!' said Chris.

'What you've got to realize,' said Ruby, 'is that this stuff is lethally potent.'

'Poster-paint?'

'Colour. This place is so grey, there's no telling what might happen if we unleash vast quantities of the stuff, splash it around. I mean, people could go insane!'

Nobody had turned up.

They had sent out press releases the week before, left piles of leaflets in cafés, bookshops, galleries. Ruby had called the event *Ceremony*, had described its form and its purpose with the help of quotations from John Cage, D.T. Suzuki.

To symbolize an awakening of the consciousness to the significance of every personal act/utterance . . .

'Shite!' said Paki, finally dropping all his card.

A way of waking up to the very life we are living

'Shite! Shite! Shite!'

'OK,' said Ruby. 'I guess we should start.'

'Maybe we could give it a few more minutes,' said Tam. 'In case anybody comes.'

'I guess so.'

'I mean, you never know.'

Ruby laid out all the card in a circle, put the paints

and brushes in the middle, stood back pleased with it.

'There!'

People passed by, along the path, but nobody stopped. A few small boys played football, ignoring them. Then a young couple came over.

'Is this the words thing?'

'Yeah!' said Ruby. 'Yeah! It is!'

A girl appeared with two small children, introduced herself as Sally, the children as Peter and Sue.

'Hi!'

Then came a group of five or six who looked like art students.

'Hey!' Ruby clapped her hands. 'It's happening!'

She began it herself, kneeled down and took the jar of blue. The paint was watery so she stirred it to mix the sediment that had settled to the bottom, then with quick strokes she wrote DANCE on a piece of card and hung it from a low branch.

The others laughed, cheered, set about joining in. Up went their words, higher into the tree. HAPPY LOVE STAR SONG. Brian climbed up among the branches, took the words up higher still. PEACE HIGH ZEN BLUE.

Two old women passed, looked over, disapproving.

'Damt disgrace,' said one.

'Weird,' said the other.

'Foreigners likely.'

And up into the tree went FOREIGN WEIRD DISGRACE.

A BBC van pulled up and a man stepped out. He was clutching one of the leaflets for the Ceremony.

'I take it I'm in the right place,' he said.

'Right place, right time!' said Ruby, and a camera crew piled out of the van, set up their equipment ready for filming. First they took Ruby to one side and the interviewer asked her a few questions, and she raved at him that the Ceremony was to celebrate the dawn of a new age. Then they moved around, filming from different angles – Paki grinning at camera, holding up the word DOPE, the two children covering a card with tiny handprints after spilling the jar of green paint, others painting with their fingers, with leaves and bits of twig, Brian up in the tree, hanging their words. Tam had his bamboo flute with him and he started to play. The mob of small boys had abandoned their game of football. Drawn by the camera, they crowded round.

Then into the middle of it all came a park-keeper striding across towards them.

'What's this?' he demanded. 'Who's in charge here?'

'Just a spot of painting,' said Ruby.

'Oh aye? Have yis got permission?'

'It's for the Festival,' said Ruby. 'Part of the Fringe.'

'Look, man,' said Bird. 'The BBC are here. You can't get much more official than that!'

'I don't care who's here. You've got to have written permission.'

'OK,' said Bird. 'Hold on.' And he took a brush and wrote PERMISSION in red on one of the cards and handed it to the man.

'There you are!'

'Now don't try and get smart wi me, son! And you!' he yelled at Brian. 'Get down out of there!'

'Come on, man,' said Bird. 'Take it easy.'

'I'm not having folk damaging these trees.'

'But we're not damaging them,' said Ruby. 'We're honouring them.'

The cameras continued to roll. The little girl, Sue, stood in front of the park-keeper, grinned up at him.

'Man?' she said, pointing at him, naming him. He was caught in mid-attitude. The beginning of a smile twitched at the corner of his mouth.

Ruby sensed the moment, felt him weaken.

'That's right,' she said. 'He's a *nice* man. He looks after all these lovely trees.'

'Man!' said the child again, waving a hand at him. And without thinking he took the hand, found his own smeared with green paint. And the mood broke and he smiled, giving up

'That's it,' said Bird. 'That's you implicated along with the rest of us.'

'Yeah!' said Ruby. 'We're all in it together!'

'You might as well join in,' said Tam. 'Hang a word in the tree.'

'It's *me* that'll get hung,' said the man. 'No thanks!'

Tam wrote PARKIE on a card, placed it in the tree. 'There!' he said. 'That's you hung!'

The two boldest of the footballers had worked out what was happening, wanted to take part. They fought over a brush, wrote CELTIC and HEARTS on separate cards.

'OK,' said the park-keeper. 'I'll leave yis to it. As long as you clean up after you.'

'Sure,' said Ruby. 'Thanks!'

He called up to Brian, 'And no damage to that tree or you're dead!'

'Right!'

'I hope yis haven't been filming everything,' he said, as he turned to go.

'It's OK,' said the interviewer. 'We'll edit it.'

Later they all sat crowded round a table in the corner of a pub, directly under the TV, waiting for the six o'clock News.

'Hope they show it,' said Bird. 'Sometimes they film things and don't use them.'

'Are we on the right channel?' asked Chris.

'Yeah,' said Bird. 'The guy switched it over specially.'

'Wish they had colour,' said Ruby.

Black and white images flickered above them, the voice of the announcer carefully modulated against the reality of what was being presented – the latest horror from Belfast, Uganda, Bangladesh. Then came the local news, a report on the Upper Clyde work-in – familiar shipyard skyline, a banner above the yard gate, overalled men streaming out at the end of a working day, waving at camera, giving thumbs-up or clenched-fist salute.

'Right on,' said Claire.

'Think there's hope for Scotland yet?' asked Bird.

'Could be.'

'Hey Tam,' said Brian. 'Maybe we'll see your old man.'

'Aye, maybe,' said Tam. He stared into his pint then back at the screen.

The news item gave way to another, a look back at the Ibrox disaster and forward at the new season just beginning.

'Come *on*!' said Tam.

'And finally,' said the announcer, 'it's that time of year again, our very own silly season . . . Yes, I'm talking about the Edinburgh Festival and its lunatic Fringe . . .'

'Hey!' said Paki. 'He's talking about us!'

Everybody shooshed him, craned closer to the screen. And there they were, dabbing paint on their bits of card, hanging them in the trees. Cut to Ruby raving about the New Age and the awakening of consciousness, her voice continuing over images of the children making handprints, Paki with the word DOPE, Brian up in the tree, Tam playing his flute. Cut to the park-keeper looking angry. 'You've got to have written permission.' Cut. 'And you! Get down out of there!' Cut. 'No damage to that tree or you're dead!' Cut. A final montage of words among the branches PARKIE PERMISSION HAPPY FOREIGN DANCE ZEN DISGRACE CELTIC HEARTS HIGH. Close on WEIRD filling the screen. Cut.

They cheered and hugged each other, drowning out the announcer's parting remark.

'Probably a put-down anyway!' said Ruby.

'Who cares?' said Bird. 'We're in business!'

The mood of optimism carried them through the next day, through what passed for a last rehearsal. They were as ready as they would ever be, nervous, with that necessary edge, the rush of adrenalin.

'All we need now's an audience,' said Chris.

They opened the doors at seven. By half past – the time they were due to start – there were three people in the hall, one of them the girl Sally who'd been at their happening in the park. Another fifteen minutes brought the numbers up to five, all sitting in the back row.

'We've still got them outnumbered,' said Paki.

'Should we give it a wee bit longer?' asked Tam.

'Fuck it,' said Bird. 'We might as well start.'

Tam began it, doodled improvisations on his flute. Then Brian read a few poems while Tam continued to play. Then one by one the others came on stage, started clapping or beating or stamping out a rhythm. Bird picked up his guitar, struck harsh discords that cut across Tam's melody. At a signal from Bird they stopped playing, put their instruments down, stared at the audience. Paki moved to pick up the guitar and they rounded on him, pushed him back. He crouched down in the corner; they stood towering over him, threatening. Brian tore up the poems he'd just read, threw the scraps of paper in the air. Meanwhile Ruby sat cross-legged, Chris and Claire stretched, did yoga asanas. Bird nodded to Tam and they sidled over towards the girls, went into a Saturday-night-at-the-dancehall routine, gum-chewing, gallus. They mimed slicking back their hair, straightening their ties.

'Don't fancy yours much,' said Bird, looking down at Ruby who still sat, eyes closed, doing alternate-nostril breathing.

Tam ignored him, checked himself again in an imaginary mirror, then stood in front of Ruby.

'Ye dancin?' he asked.

She opened her eyes, chanted *aum*.

Bird laughed, turned to Chris.

'Ye dancin?'

'No,' she said. 'It's just the way I'm standing.'

Brian decided to join in, try Claire.

'Ye dancin?' he said.

'Ye askin?'

'I'm askin.'

'I'm dancin.'

With Paki still lying in the corner where he'd been

211

dumped, the others, paired off, moved into the kind of exchanges they'd worked through in the early rehearsals. Tam and Ruby, with a gently erotic familiarity, stroked each other's faces, touched fingertips to eyes, lips, hair. Brian and Claire, more tentative, pressed hands together, palm to palm, traced graceful shapes in the air. Bird and Chris circled each other like animals, sniffing, prodding. Then he made a grab at her, practically grappled her to the floor, made as if to mount her from behind, but she pushed him back and he laughed.

'There was that time when I was sixteen,' he said, to the audience. 'At a party. Brubeck playing in the next room.'

Tam picked up his flute, started playing *Take Five*. Ruby took her cue from Bird.

'There was that time at my first high school dance. Bobby Vee singing *The night has a thousand eyes.*'

'One eye,' said Tam. 'His eye is single.'

'A single eye,' said Ruby, 'on the Godalmighty dollar. Oh say can you see. In God we trust!'

'There was the time I got my first flute,' said Tam. 'My father brought it home. I played my first note on it, and it was good.' He raised the flute to his lips, played one note.

'That time I fought Eddie Logan,' said Brian. 'He was the hardest guy in our class. And for some reason he just had it in for me. Called me brainbox, stuff like that. He must have niggled at me for a month. Threatened me. Said he was going to get me. I was shit-scared. Then one day it just broke. He tripped me up in the playground. Right, I said, that's it. A square go. A crowd was round us in no time and we were swinging away at each other. He gave me a right hammering too. And then we both got the belt for fighting. But he left me alone after that.'

Brian had been miming the fight, jabbing with his fists, reeling from blows to the head. He stopped, let his arms drop to his sides.

'Eddie's dead now. Got blown to fuck in Belfast.'

'The guy I was with at that dance,' said Ruby. 'His name was Vinny. Came back from Vietnam in a box.'

'The time I keep coming back to,' said Chris. 'The curtains opening and the coffin sliding through. A hum of machinery and that was it. My father was gone.'

'Christ we're getting morbid!' said Bird.

'Got to face it,' said Chris. 'We're going to die.'

'So we've got to live,' said Bird.

'Gonna die.'

'Got to live.'

'Blown to fuck.'

'Back in a box.'

'Here comes the night.'

'A thousand eyes.'

'Take five.'

Claire had said nothing, now she spoke. 'There was that time.' The others looked at her and she stopped, then continued. 'Dusty bluebells.'

Tam chanted, quietly. 'In and out those dusty bluebells.'

'I was maybe about nine,' said Claire. 'I went to the Bluebell Woods to play. My father had told me not to go there on my own. Said it was dangerous. But I went anyway. And I played there all day, and I guess I lost all track of time. It was so . . . magical. Anyway, I must have realized it was late, and I picked a bunch of bluebells and started running home. When I got to the end of the street I still had the bluebells in my hand. I threw them away, into the gutter, but my father was standing at the close looking out for me. He had seen the bluebells. He knew where I had been. I tried to smile but he gave me a look that shrivelled me up. He never said a word. Just took me up to the house and battered the living daylights out of me.'

A silence, then Tam singing again, softly.

> *'In and out those dusty bluebells*
> *I am the master.'*

213

Claire joined in, and Brian, and they moved into the childhood game that went along with the chant.

> *'Rippa Rippa Rapper on my shoulder*
> *I am the master.'*

Claire skipped round them, ducked under the archway they made with their arms. When Brian tapped the rhythm on her shoulders she fell to her knees, hid her face in her hands.

'Dancing on the roof of hell,' said Tam, 'and picking the flowers.'

'We're going to die,' said Chris.

'There with fantastic garlands did she come,' said Brian.

'We're going to die.'

'This cunt's dead already!' said Bird, breaking the mood, aiming a kick at Paki who still lay in the corner. 'Come on ya lazy bastard!'

Paki turned over on his side, curled up. Bird grabbed him by the feet and dragged him to the front of the stage. 'We're all slogging our guts out,' he yelled, 'and you're just lying there, copping out. Well it's not fucking on!'

'We'll have to raise him up from the dead,' said Claire. 'Make him levitate.'

She straightened Paki out, laid him prone like a corpse, made them all kneel on either side of him.

'A whole bunch of us used to do this at school,' she said. 'Then the Mother Superior found out and threatened to expel us. Said it was black magic!'

Paki twitched, uneasy. She told him to lie still, relax.

'Now,' she said. 'We've all got to concentrate really hard.'

There was silence except for their breathing, someone in the audience shifting, the creak of a chair.

'He looks sick,' she said, leaning over him. 'Chant it.'

And they joined her, chanting. 'He looks sick . . . He looks sick . . .'

214

'He *is* sick,' she said, and again they joined in.

'He is sick . . . He is sick . . .'

'He looks dead.'

'He looks dead . . . He looks dead . . .'

'He *is* dead.'

'He is dead . . . He is dead . . .'

'Now,' she said. 'We can raise him up. It just takes the first finger of each hand, underneath him. Now, lift!'

With what felt like no effort at all, they lifted him a foot from the ground. They paused for a moment then lifted him higher. They stood up and he seemed almost to float upward. He was four feet from the ground when he opened his eyes and panicked and started to struggle. They couldn't hold him then and he crashed to the floor with a yell.

'Ladeez an genulmen!' said Bird, clutching an imaginary microphone. 'Back from the dead! Back to the land of the living! I give you . . . the amazing . . . Paki Black!'

The others applauded and the audience joined in, the girl Sally enthusiastically, the rest with a desultory politeness. Brian and Tam helped Paki up, dusted him off. He took a bow and at a nod from Bird, they all did the same.

'I thank yow!' said Bird, the master of ceremonies, bowing with a flourish. Then in his own voice he said 'OK, I think that's it for just now.' Tam picked up his flute and played them out, closing the session.

The talk afterwards was of how it could be better.

'We were just a bit nervous,' said Ruby.

'Stiff,' said Chris.

'It'll come,' said Tam.

Bird was still angry at Paki for opting out; Paki sulked at the way Bird had treated him.

'It worked out fine,' said Brian. 'Gave you something to react against.'

'That's right,' said Claire. 'I don't know what you're

moaning about. The whole thing was brilliant.'

'It had it's moments,' said Bird.

And it had its moments for the rest of the run.

The time the whole performance was made up of lines from Shakespeare, and Beckett, and pop songs, and nursery rhymes. And somehow, without planning it, the whole thing ran together, and so did all their separate, self-absorbed moments, as if it had all been carefully structured.

The times when they blundered around, leaden and awkward, achieving nothing, and all they shared with their audience was embarrassment.

The time they struggled and ground their way through an hour of trying to make it happen, and getting nowhere, and losing patience with one another, till Ruby yelled at them all, 'Why are we making this so difficult? It should be *easy*! And Tam chanted, 'Ea-sy! Ea-sy!' and Chris said 'It *is* easy!' And the others took it up, told each other it was easy, sharing the realization, the shift of awareness. And they linked hands, moved among the audience, told everyone how easy it suddenly was.

The time they had an audience of twenty or more and the place felt packed, and right from the first note on Tam's flute they knew instinctively they could do anything at all – they had moved through into that freedom they had been striving for. And into the middle of it came a tiny bird, a sparrow, in through the open window, and it flustered round the room, panicking this way and that, then settled on the edge of the stage. And they stood, or sat, or crouched, and watched it. And Bird crept forward, made a lunge, but it flapped clear of his grasp. He stalked it round the room, crawled forward on his belly into the audience. He shooshed everyone to silence, became the focus of all their concentration as he tracked the bird with ferocious intensity and it hopped and bounced away from him, just beyond his reach. The others tried to head the bird off, direct it back towards him, but always it was too quick, darted past.

Tam played a scatter of notes on his flute, repeated it, birdsong. Bird closed again on the sparrow, grabbed, missed. Sweat drenched him, stuck his shirt to his back. Still he persisted. Tam played the opening line of Papageno's song. *Der Vögelfänger bin ich ja.* The birdcatcher am I. He repeated it, and again. Bird looked at him, astonished. 'I'm the birdcatcher,' he said. 'And I'm Bird. I'm trying to catch myself!' And he burst out laughing, and the sparrow flew away from him again, straight towards Claire who caught it, a moment. But she couldn't hold it, yelped and let it go as it struggled in her hands, and this time Bird pounced, and caught, and held it firm, and the audience cheered.

He stroked its head and made soothing noises, carried it to the window. He motioned to Brian to open the window wide. It led out into an overgrown garden. He turned to the audience, held the bird towards them at arm's length, like an offering.

'When I was about twelve,' he said, quietly, 'I killed one of these. No reason. Just . . . badness. Snuffed it out. Just like that.'

He turned and let the bird go, out through the open window, watched it fly free. The audience applauded. Tam played *Der Vögelfänger* again. Bird grinned.

It had its moments.

Brian woke, not quite sure at first where he was. Then the room defined itself, and he knew from the light that streaked through the grimy window, and from the traffic noise outside, that he'd slept late. The place was deserted, sleeping bags jettisoned as if they'd been left in a hurry, cups left lying here and there. Then he remembered it was signing-on day and Bird had taken the van, driven back to Glasgow with the others, first thing. The noise of their going had half-wakened him but he'd been sunk too deep to surface.

Brian wasn't signing on yet himself. Time enough

when all this was over, when they went home, when the last of his money ran out. He sat up, stiff in the neck and shoulders from lying on the hard floor. His pillow was his jacket, rolled up in a bundle, but somehow it had unfolded, spread out, gave no support for his head. He pulled on his jeans, sat up. The copies of *Ion Engine* were stacked in the corner beside the duplicator. He picked one up, flicked through it. A sudden noise made him jump. The door to the other room opened and Claire came out, stopped dead, looked even more startled than he was.

'God, what a fright!' she said. 'I thought everybody was away out!'

'Me too! Thought you'd gone with the rest of them.'

She shook her head. 'Don't sign on till Friday.'

She was wearing a man's shirt, a couple of sizes too big. She still had a soft sleepy vagueness about her, a warmth. There was a slightly awkward silence and she became uncomfortable, aware of his eyes on her. She put a hand to her throat, clutching the shirtfront closed. With the other hand she smoothed the shirt down, front and back, as if to lengthen it.

'The bog,' she said, and hurried out of the room. He listened, heard the toilet on the landing clank and clank and flush, and she scurried back in, through to her own room, closing the door behind her.

He looked out of the window at the blank grey face of the building opposite. He turned the pages of his magazine again but he couldn't settle, chucked it back on the pile. He knocked the door to the other room.

'Yeah?' He thought her voice sounded wary, unsure. He pushed open the door.

'Thought I'd make some tea. Bit of breakfast maybe.'

'Sounds great.' She'd gone back inside her sleeping bag, but she sat up smoking, propped against the wall. She had managed to get hold of a few cushions to spread underneath her. So had Ruby, and Chris had found herself a length of foam.

'Got all the comforts in here,' he said. 'Luxury!'

He sat on the cushion at her feet. She pulled up her knees to make space. Again that silence.

'I like your shirt,' he said at last, the words sounding ridiculous, even to him.

'It's an old one of Malcolm's,' she said.

'You must be missing him.'

She flicked off ash, took a deep drag, blew out smoke.

'He said he'd be through sometime. To see the show.'

'Listen,' he said. 'I . . .'

'What?'

He had no words. He reached out, tentative, put a selfconscious hand on her shoulder.

'Ye dancin?' he said, trying to sound light, but a choke in his voice.

'Ye askin?'

'I'm askin.'

She looked at him, hard. She stubbed out her cigarette.

'Fuck it,' she said. 'Why not?'

When the others came back in the van that afternoon they had brought Malcolm.

'Found him wandering down Byres Road like a fart in a trance,' said Bird. 'Obviously pining for Claire.'

'Fuck off,' said Malcolm. 'Where is she?'

'She went to the baths,' said Brian, trying to sound natural.

'For a swim?'

'Just a hot bath I think.'

'That's what I had this morning,' said Ruby. 'Went back to the flat, filled the tub up to here and just *wallowed*!'

'How do you manage here?' said Malcolm. 'Washing and that.'

'Kettle on the camping stove,' said Bird. 'Wash down at the sink. Everybody just averts their gaze. Except this disgusting creature here!' He slapped Paki on the back. 'In fact, come to think of it, I don't believe I've even seen him wash since we got here.'

'Well you wouldn't,' said Paki. 'Not if you averted your gaze.'

'Nice one Paki!' said Tam.

Malcolm turned to Brian. 'You'll never guess who we saw down in Princes Street.'

'Who?'

'That turdy little brother of mine.'

'George?'

'The very same.'

'What's he doing through here?'

'Said he had some holidays due and he thought he'd do Edinburgh. Take in the Festival.'

'Never thought he was into culture.'

'He's not.'

'I gave him a leaflet for the show,' said Tam. 'He said he'd come along.'

'I'll believe that when I see it,' said Malcolm. He picked up a copy of *Ion Engine*, skimmed through it then stopped, and listened. And they heard Claire coming up the stairs, singing to herself, *Love the one you're with*.

George had come through to Edinburgh for the day. He had been working a lot of overtime. He was due time off. He had seen something on TV about the Festival. It had looked good. A cheap day-return on the train and here he was.

The freedom of it felt strange, unreal, as he walked down unfamiliar streets. He tried to buy a ticket for the Tattoo but it was booked up solid. He went into a pub off Princes Street for a pie and a pint, had two pies and three pints. He wasn't used to drinking during the day and that added even more to his sense of unreality. He couldn't get rid of the feeling that he shouldn't be here, that he really ought to be somewhere else. Like the one and only time he had taken a day off school, gone into town to see a film, come out of the darkened cinema to blink at the unexpected daylight. He remembered the sense of being displaced inside an utterly ordinary day. And that same sense of displacement was what he felt now. This was him in Edinburgh, walking around.

He had passed through the city once as a child. He had gone on a mystery tour with his mother and Malcolm, had ended up in Portobello. Somewhere in a drawer at home there was still an old black-and-white snapshot of himself and Malcolm squinting at the camera, faces screwed up, the sun in their eyes. Just after the photo had been taken, he remembered, they had fallen out and fought. Malcolm had beaten him, held him down and forced sand into his mouth till he gagged.

Apart from the mystery tour, he had only been in the city once before, for the Masons' annual gathering a year ago – hundreds of them assembled in a huge chandeliered hall, the guests of honour at the top table raised high on a special platform built above the stage. Below them was another, longer table for the next rank of dignitaries, then down at ground level the rest. George had been at the back of the hall, miles away, but still happy to be part of the occasion, the ceremonial. That sense of tradition, of richness, was what had stayed with him. It was what he associated with Edinburgh.

But this other Edinburgh he was seeing now was a different place altogether, had a colour and an atmosphere that was almost continental. Very un-Scottish. And not like anything he had ever felt in Glasgow. The city was letting its hair down. He could see it, was aware of it all about him, but still he felt distanced, not quite part of it. Being alone didn't help, not knowing anyone. What he really needed was female company. He knew that. He hadn't been out with anyone in two months. And here in this place he was overwhelmed by the sheer number of girls who caught his eye. At one point, in Princes Street, he started counting the ones he fancied, quickly reached 250, realized he was being ridiculous, and stopped.

At a set of traffic lights, as he waited to cross, he thought he heard his name being called. He looked, saw someone waving at him from a van that had pulled up, eventually recognized him as Tam Rae. Beside him sat a girl with a mass of dark hair, and beyond her a redhaired man in the driving seat.

'Hey!' shouted Tam. 'Incredible!'

And there was Malcolm in the back of the van, leaning forward between Tam and the girl to say hello. Tam was right. It was incredible.

They asked him what he was doing, shoved a leaflet at him, drove off, waving back at him as they went. He read the leaflet. *Magic Theatre. For Madmen Only* . . .

'Weird!' he said, out loud.

Further down it read *A Magical Mystery Tour. An Amazing Journey.* He remembered again the photo of himself and Malcolm on Portobello beach. A mystery tour. The gritty taste of sand in his mouth.

For madmen only.

Still, he might go along and see the show, out of curiosity. He had nothing better to do.

That night the show had been going well enough, though Claire seemed inhibited and Brian was locked in a mode that was merely functional, going-through-the-motions. Bird didn't try to break them down. Instead he worked hard at leading the others through now-familiar routines, till the audience responded, began to open up.

They were conscious, however, of Malcolm, shifting uncomfortably in his front-row seat, and of an older man, further along the row, who seemed to be taking notes. George too had showed up, arrived late and slipped in at the back where he sat looking bewildered, completely ill-at-ease. Some devilment sent Bird straight towards him. He clutched his imaginary microphone, went into a routine as a chat-show host.

'Well ladiesangenulmen, it's so wonderful to be back with you again this evening.' He thrust the invisible microphone at George. 'Can I ask you sir, how you're enjoying the show?'

George writhed, squirmed. 'It's, eh, very interesting.'

'Very *interesting*!' said Bird. 'Thank you sir for that penetrating, in-depth analysis of the performance!' Then he switched roles, became Doctor Benway, character from a Burroughs novel.

'Innaresting, huh? Do you think I'm innarested in your horrible old condition? Do you think I give a shit about your slimy opinion?' Then in a flat, deadpan monotone, 'Who programs you? Who plays back your old humiliations and defeats holding you in pre-recorded present time?' He leered, cracked the bland mask, was suddenly the chat-show host again leaning over a girl in the second row. 'And tell me, where are you from?'

'Paisley,' she said.

'Paisley!' He grinned. 'Oh well, there's always somebody worse off than yourself!'

By now he had worked his way to the front, towards Malcolm, ready for a confrontation. 'And now,' he said, 'to put things in perspective with a hardline Marxist critique . . .'

'Biggest load of self-indulgent crap I've seen in my life,' said Malcolm, and he stood up and shoved past Bird with a suddenness and ferocity that caught him off balance.

'Hey!' said Bird as he staggered back, brushed aside. He made a grab at Malcolm's arm. 'Come on man!' Malcolm turned, swung a punch, caught him full on the jaw. Bird, raging, hit back and they stood there slugging till the others managed to grapple them apart. Claire hustled Malcolm out the door, turned and threw back an apologetic look as she went. Bird felt his jaw, wiped a smear of blood from the corner of his mouth.

'What the fuck's got into him?' he said, then as if remembering they were still in front of an audience, he shrugged towards them. 'Critics!'

Tam picked up on his tone. 'Real blood!' he said. 'I

mean, is this the theatre of the here and now or isn't it?'

But nobody had the energy to take it on. The show was over and they let it wind down, a slow fade. There was a spatter of applause. George left quickly, avoiding eye-contact.

Claire had gone back to Glasgow with Malcolm, left a message to say she would see them when she'd sorted things out.

'What a fucking night!' said Bird.

'What was with the old guy in the suit?' asked Paki. 'Looked as if he was writing it all down.'

'Probably from the drug squad, Paki!' said Tam. 'Or else he'll be a psychiatrist!'

'Actually he was from the *Scotsman*,' said Chris.

'You're kidding!'

'I was on the door,' she said. 'I let him in.'

'You might have told us,' said Bird.

'Didn't get a chance, did I? Had to go straight on. Anyway what difference would it have made?'

'Not much I suppose. Wonder what he made of it?'

George stood waiting on the platform for the last train back to Glasgow. A voice over the tannoy had announced it was running late. Due to the late departure of the twenty-two hundred hours from Glasgow. But the train he was waiting for *was* the twenty-two hundred hours from Glasgow. The train was running late because the train was running late. He was tired. He wanted to be home. Forty miles and an hour's journey away.

A few other people stood here and there on the platform. Separate. He looked along, saw Malcolm and his girlfriend Claire coming through the ticket barrier. They hadn't seen him. He turned and walked further out, moved behind a pillar. The last thing he felt like was travelling back through with them, having to talk. After a while he risked looking out, saw them about halfway back, standing together but not talking. He was safe enough behind his pillar.

224

Near his feet, a plastic cup, discarded, was caught by the wind, scuttered in a circle round its own base. Water dripped steadily from the roof, smacked into a puddle. He couldn't work out where it came from. It wasn't raining and the rest of the platform was dry. The kind of thing that could irritate him if he let it. Up ahead he saw lights coming out of the tunnel and the train was hissing and roaring past him. At last. Thank fuck. A quick look back over his shoulder, Malcolm and Claire climbing on in the middle of the train. He sat in the end compartment, the corner seat, as far away as he could get. Claire had been part of the show and he didn't want to be caught between the two of them arguing.

It wasn't often he understood Malcolm, but when he'd punched that redhaired man, George had felt like cheering. Up out of his seat. *Yes!* George had been uncomfortable all through the show. Hadn't understood it. There had been no shape to it. No story. A load of nonsense. The redhaired man had made fun of him. *Interesting? Do you think I give a shit about your slimy old opinion?* Somebody else with an education.

The carriage door slid open, made him jump. The guard came through, checked his ticket, clipped it. For some reason a memory came to him. Travelling on the subway with his father, on his way to be initiated in the First Degree. And moments in the show had brought that back as well. It was as if they had known he would be in the audience, were homing in on him. Brian and Tam had gone through a pantomime ritual, with all the right Masonic questions and responses, but played like a Monty Python sketch. Trousers rolled up. Nudge Nudge. Knock Knock. Nod's as good as a wink. Say no more.

But then in the middle of their knockabout clowning, they had mimed being blindfolded, kneeling down with their hands over their eyes. And George had remembered kneeling in the dark at his own initiation, that silence, the strange sense of unease, a kind of emptiness.

On stage, for a moment, it had been quiet, Tam and Brian kneeling there, the others standing behind them. Claire had started singing, her voice sweet. *A love like yours don't come knock knock knock knocking.* Then somebody had broken the mood with another knock knock routine.

Madam who?

Madam foot's stuck in the door.

Magic Theatre. For Madmen Only. That wasn't far wrong. In his pocket he still had the leaflet for the show. He took it out and read it, annoyed. A Magical Mystery Tour. He tore it up, stuffed the pieces down the side of the table. He leaned close to the window, cupped his hands to his eyes to look out. But there was nothing to see. The odd light flashing past in the dark. Leaning his elbows on the table, he looked sideways at his own reflection in the glass. Himself. George. And the strangeness was there again, and he turned away from it, didn't want to know.

When the train finally pulled in to Queen Street, he was the first one off. Before it had even come to a stop he had let himself down on to the platform, dropping slightly backwards, the momentum making him run on a few steps. He didn't look back, hurried on through the barrier and out into George Square. He was sure Malcolm and Claire would take a taxi from the station, and he cut across the Square to wait for a latenight bus. A good way to avoid them. And anyway the bus was cheaper. The day had cost him enough already. A total waste.

The review appeared next day, described the show as mindless, shapeless and pointless, said that the member of the audience who attacked one of the cast had the right idea.

'The worst show on the Fringe,' said Bird, reading it out.

'I guess that's something,' said Chris.

'Yeah,' said Ruby. 'Quite a distinction!'

'Bastard!' Bird chucked the paper across the room. 'What does he know about anything?'

Brian picked up the paper, smoothed it out, read over the review, twice.

'Says it's all been done before. Mentions the Living Theatre. The People Show.'

'Of course,' said Bird. 'They're from New York and London, so they're OK.'

'I'll buy that!' said Ruby.

'Me too!' said Chris.

Bird glared at them. 'Yeah. Sure.'

'Come on,' said Ruby. 'Lighten up! I mean at least this guy's putting us in some kind of context. What's gone before.'

'But we don't *want* put in context,' said Bird. 'That's the fucking point! OK, certain things have been done before, but not *this*. Not us here now.' He took the paper from Brian, read it again, threw it down. 'Bastard!'

The black mood that was on him threatened to fill their space, so they all found reasons for going and left him alone with Chris.

Brian just walked, with no clear idea of where he was going. He didn't know the city well, found himself heading down the High Street towards Holyrood. Even this early the place was busy with tourists and with hustlers from other Fringe groups. He passed a busker in a kilt and T-shirt playing jigs on a penny whistle; a boy in a clown-suit juggled, miraculously, with a grapefruit, a saucepan and a paperback book.

And the mood of it, the atmosphere, began to work on him, open him out from the clenched tight state he had been in. He knew the whole place would shut down dead after the Festival, knew it was a cold and tightlipped bitch of a city in winter. But right now it was happening, was alive.

A tall girl in a tophat and tails, fishnet tights and high heels, shoved a leaflet at him, advertising the Oxford Revue. He took it, gave her a slightly crumpled one of theirs in return. She smiled at him, all teeth.

'Great! Super!'

Up ahead a group of American tourists drew back to let an old tramp pass through their midst. The old man wore layers of clothes topped by a stinking greasy trenchcoat. On his back he carried a huge pack tied together with string. On his head he wore a soldier's tin helmet and round his neck was a tartan scarf. He muttered and cursed as he passed by the Americans, snarled and laughed, away in his own world. Brian picked up bits of it.

'Ach Ach Ach Ach! . . . Away and fuck the lot of yis . . . Yanks is it? . . . Yankee fuckin doodle . . . Oh aye mind my fuckin grammar . . . Aye Aye Aye Aye! . . . Who you talkin tae pal? Who d'ye think yer shovin? Who d'ye think you are?'

He was squaring up to nobody, jabbing the air.

'A man's a man's a man's a man, eh? For a that an a that. D'ye know who I am?'

He looked straight at Brian, and through him, not seeing him at all.

'Nice to be nice, eh? Know what I mean?' He turned away. 'Ach, fuck it. Who cares?' He spat, moved on up the hill. The Americans regrouped. One woman clicked a camera at the old man's back.

'Guess he's what you'd call an old worthy,' she said.

Brian couldn't help it, he laughed out loud, felt suddenly, ridiculously exhilarated. The woman glared at him. He looked over her head, away down the clear vista to the Firth. He knew that down behind the palace was the park, and Arthur's Seat, and he made up his mind to climb to the top.

From an open window came the blast of a radio, a record he'd heard before.

> *Knock down the old grey wall*
> *Be a part of it all*

It caught his new mood, exactly.

The climb was easy enough, the slope gentle. Only the last section was steep and he had to scramble over rocks, loose stones. At the very top, the sheer force of the wind surprised him. A sudden gust slapped him, almost knocked him off balance and he clutched at the stone marker to steady himself then sat down resting his back against it. The vertigo passed and he eased round, took in the full sweep of the view on all sides, looked out across the city, out to the Firth and the open sea.

A few others were clambering about the summit, a German family, a middleaged American couple, a group of half a dozen Japanese.

'Quite a view!' said the American, turning from his wife to address Brian.

'It is that,' he said. 'Beautiful.'

'You local?' asked the man. 'Or just here for the Festival?'

'I'm from Glasgow,' he said. He supposed the American would think that was local, but as he said it he felt like a foreigner, as much a tourist as the rest of them. Glasgow was another reality, another world entirely.

'You can probably *see* Glasgow from here!' said the American.

'Just about!' he said.

'So you just taking in a few shows?'

'Actually I'm part of a show at the Fringe.'

'No kidding! You an actor or what?'

'Well, sort of. It's a kind of improvised theatre thing. And I do some poetry and stuff.'

'How about that! A poet! Hey, what's your show called?'

Brian fumbled in his pocket for a leaflet, his last. It was even more crumpled than the one he'd given the girl with the legs and the teeth. He tried to smooth it out, handed it to the man.

'Looks real . . . interesting,' said the man, obviously

229

thrown by Chris's artwork. 'See this honey . . .?' He handed it to his wife who nodded, managed a smile.

'Maybe we'll get to see it,' she said.

'Maybe,' said Brian. The wind was whipping his hair across his face, beginning to be an irritant, getting in his eyes, in his mouth.

'Well anyway,' he said. 'Be seeing you.'

'Nice talking to you,' said the man.

'Yeah,' said his wife.

Brian picked his way down over the rocks, found a sheltered spot, out of the wind. He sat down and realized how tired he actually was. He lay back, his hands behind his head, and it was as if the wind had been switched off. He let himself sink into the earth, let the sun warm him, let his mind drift.

Talking to the American had been an aggravation, had completely punctured his mood. He could hear himself, apologetic, trying to explain what they were doing. Sort of. Kind of. Poetry and stuff. It must have sounded pathetic. Worst show on the Fringe. The review must have cut him more than he had admitted. They would have to pick it up again, raise the energy level, push it through to the big finale, the wedding.

He recognized, admitted to himself, that he had no enthusiasm for it any more, that somewhere inside him was a tight knot of pain at the thought of Claire. He knew it was ridiculous, that a couple of days ago there had been nothing much between them beyond an ordinary flirtation, an innocent intimacy from their contact on stage. He tried to tell himself too that what had happened was nothing. He should be grateful to have taken what he could get. Slice from a cut loaf. Love the one you're with. But that didn't change the way he felt, an emptiness inside, ache at the thought she wouldn't come back.

And in behind all that, he knew, was a deeper malaise. Something to do with the fight, and what it meant. He remembered Bird and Malcolm haggling over his duplicating machine, Bird making a joke of it.

Brian had been happy enough to work with them both. He had even seen himself as a link between them, a bridge. Now he saw that was only stupid vanity. They were on different roads and he didn't want to walk down either of them. Bird's creative energy would dissipate itself in vapid self-indulgence. Malcolm's politics had a dark side, destructiveness, a dour intolerance. He reran the fight, Claire's look back as she left.

He rubbed his eyes with his knuckles, hard, as if he could bore right in to his thoughts, rub them out. The rubbing made colours, patterns of light, pulse behind his eyes. He blinked and stared at the sky, the high clouds drifting, and was overwhelmed by a sense of his own insignificance. This tiny figure that was himself lay on a lump of rock that was the core of a dead volcano, gouged and shaped by glaciers, aeons back. From that kind of perspective nothing much mattered. Or, paradoxically, everything did. In the face of the great implacable glacier that was time and change and death, the only meaning was the moment, this now. He imagined the sky opening and a great Hollywood God-voice booming out a message, for all mankind, *The Show Must Go On!*

He laughed and sat up. He would have to write a poem out of this. He would make it a wedding-song for Ruby and Tam. An epithalamium. He would write it in a style they would like. Something to go with Tam's music.

When he stood up the wind whipped him again. The American couple had gone. The Germans had found a spot in the lee of the hill and were sitting down to a systematic picnic. The Japanese were photographing each other, each one in turn snapping the other five.

He turned back down the hill, felt the return of that gratuitous exhilaration he'd felt earlier. He picked up his pace, let his momentum carry him faster, into a loping run. He remembered a bit from a Kerouac novel – *Dharma Bums* or *Desolation Angels*, he wasn't sure which. The one where Kerouac and the character who was Gary Snyder went careering down a sheer slope, yelling, crazy, *You can't fall off the mountain!* He bounded, surefooted, felt he was flying. Near the bottom he rushed on past the American and his wife, startled them with a wave and a shouted *Hello there!* When he hit the flat he stumbled, pitched forward, rolled over and just lay there, out of breath but laughing, staring up at the spinning sky.

4

The hall was completely transformed. Ruby had kept all the sheets of card with the words they'd hung in the trees, and she'd stuck them round three of the walls. On the fourth wall, behind the stage, Chris had worked a miracle. On the nights when the rubbish was left out in the street for collection she loved to go scavenging. And one night she had turned up half a dozen rolls of wallpaper. Now she had tacked them to this back wall, covered the whole space and painted over it an immense mural as backdrop for the last show, the wedding.

The central motif was a huge stylized figure of Krishna playing the flute, straddling images of Glasgow and New York – on one side shipyard cranes, tenement buildings, TAM spraypainted across it like graffiti, on the other a skyscraper, Brooklyn Bridge, RUBY as if in Broadway neon lights. A winding road, a river spanned by a Chinese bridge, led away from Glasgow and New York, away into the far distance through fabulous magical landscapes. Bright-plumed birds led the eye on and up, through patterns of cloud to a night sky studded with stars. And placed here and there in the firmament were religious symbols – a cross, an *aum* sign, an Egyptian *ankh*, a Star of David, a lotus flower, and above Krishna's head, a single eye.

Father Thomas, the priest who was to conduct the ceremony, stood staring up at it.

'It's certainly impressive!' He sounded as if he meant it.

He was a small man, but strong-looking, muscular, his white hair cropped close to his head. They'd heard he ran a boys' club in one of the schemes, was known to take part in wrestling bouts with some of the older boys, give them a chance to let off steam. Brian had read an article he'd written for some magazine about his conversion to Catholicism. It seemed he'd had some kind of mystical experience – the article had been called *Encountering the Ineffable*.

'This has to be a first,' he said, to Ruby and Tam. 'A Protestant and a Jewess being married by a Catholic in front of a Hindu image!'

He was giving them a last briefing, making sure they all knew what was happening, how the ceremony fitted into the evening as a whole.

'I'm sure it'll be all right on the night!' he said. 'Just a matter of timing.' He stepped back, taking in the whole mural.

'Definitely,' he said. 'Most impressive. There's certainly something there. I mean, I'm not completely sold on this whole hippy thing. I think there's a dark side to it. Demonic. Like that Manson fellow in the States, ritual murders and all that. Horrible. Horrible.' He shook his head. 'But still. There's something trying to emerge. There's a genuine searching here, a seeking.' He smiled. 'But some of us have to work within the system. That's how we can change things.'

Brian had read another article by him. *Social acceptability – the knife-edge between revolution and reform?* After his encounter with the ineffable he had decided he had a vocation, had to work things through in the context of Catholicism.

He looked at Tam and Ruby, fatherly. 'Find your own way,' he said. 'And for God's sake don't make a mess of things.'

The place was jampacked, buzzing, with friends from

Glasgow, and friends of friends, and new friends they'd made in Edinburgh. Crazy Martin had swept in wearing an embroidered poncho.

'Man!' he said, 'I am so mellowed out it's not true!'

'So you think this'll get you higher than a horror movie?' said Tam.

'Oh, no contest! This one is going to be *beautiful*!'

Brian was hanging a piece of sculpture on the wall. He too had found something left out with the rubbish – an old gilt picture-frame of heavy carved wood. He had cleaned it up, backed it with a sheet of card covered in tinfoil. In the middle he had mounted a slice from a pan loaf, the ender, outsider. Underneath he had stuck a piece of card with the title done in Letraset – *l'étranger*.

'I'm afraid I don't get it,' said Father Thomas, looking at it over Brian's shoulder.

'The Outsider,' said Brian, and he laughed, pleased at his own joke.

'Oh yes,' said the priest. 'Of course.'

'It's a kind of visual poem,' said Brian.

'And in the course of time it'll go stale. And mouldy. And hard.'

'That's it.'

Claire had arrived, with Malcolm. Malcolm, looking solemn, was shaking hands with Bird who laughed and slapped him on the back. Claire flitted about the room, hugging people she knew. She came over to Brian, kissed him on the mouth. 'Love you,' she said, and turned away, waving to Ruby and Tam.

Tam waved back, was about to go and talk to her when he stopped, stared at his parents and his sister coming into the hall. They stood in the doorway, hesitant, unsure. They had dressed in their best clothes, and that in itself was almost too much for Tam as a great wave of emotion threatened to break him. As if to compensate, a sense of unreality took over. They were all taking part in some strange movie, and his family, incongruous, had wandered on to the wrong set. He went to them, kissed Moira on the cheek, hugged his mother, shook his father's hand.

'You came!' he said.

'You always were good at stating the obvious!' said Moira, and he loved her for it, for trying to break the ice. He laughed, nervously loud, and Ruby came over, said 'Hi!' and grinned at them all.

'Let me introduce you to Father Thomas,' said Tam, thinking the priest might be some kind of reassurance, an island of normality in this ocean of the weird. And his father at least seemed to brighten, shaking hands with the priest. But his mother looked even more appalled. It was all of it equally alien to her – the Catholic priest, the image of Krishna, the smell of incense. She gaped at Paki and Martin sitting cross-legged against the wall and laughing as if demented.

'No doubt you'd have preferred a more . . . traditional wedding' said Father Thomas, seeing she was upset. 'But the youngsters now, they're determined to go to hell in their own way!'

She hardly heard him. She was staring past his head at Brian's sculpture on the wall.

'It's a slice of bread,' she said. 'In a frame.'

The lights were flicked off and on, off and on, and Tam guided his family to seats in the front row, and Bird was on stage, calling for order as people applauded, cheered.

'I can't tell you how good it is to see you all,' he said. 'It's just blowing me away!'

More cheers.

'You all know why we're here.'

('Yeah!')

'It's not for a performance. It's to take part in a ceremony. And it's a celebration, a sharing, of love. And remember, that's all you need!'

A roar.

'It's going to be a beautiful evening. And here's the man himself. Tam Rae, to start it all off.'

Tam came to the stage, said nothing, but stilled the

cheering by raising his flute to his lips, playing one long note. Then he moved into a piece from *Die Zauberflöte*, the melody for flute that leads the young couple through their trials and into the temple of wisdom. He played it simply, without embellishment, and when it was finished he acknowledged the applause with a quick bow, and introduced Brian to read his poem.

'This is an epithalamium,' said Brian, exaggerating his Glasgow accent to cope with the word, saying it in inverted commas. 'That means a marriage-poem, and it's for Ruby and Tam.'

He cleared his throat, read.

> 'In the beginning was the sound—
> a single note on the flute
> piercing clear across the void,
> made time, made space,
> sparked atoms into being,
> made them dance.
>
> Into silence came sound.
> Into darkness came light.
>
> One became many, the elemental dance
> of earth fire water air
> spun down aeons.
>
> Fires cooled, waters rose,
> ice flowed, ground mountains down.
> Continents drifted, oceans apart.
>
> The flute played, was heard
> in cave and mudhut.
> Temples were raised to it, fell.
> Down ages more its sound was lost,
> found again, lost,
> in cycles of peace and war,
> heard faintly in the roar of cities
> till Tam played it in Glasgow,
> Ruby heard in New York,
> they danced to its tune
> and it led them here.'

Tam still sat at the side of the stage, and he played again the opening line of the Mozart melody, and he continued playing it, the one line over and over, and Brian went on reading, above the music.

> 'Within this sacred hall
> within these hallowed walls
> let them enter the temple
> hand in hand.
> Let them know the mysteries,
> no fear of night or death.
> Let the magic flute lead them
> through darkness to light.
> Let them always hear its melody,
> a love supreme.'

The other musicians had come on stage now. At Brian's last line, Bird nodded to Rob who laid down the bass-line from Coltrane's *A Love Supreme*, a single phrase, repeated, hypnotic riff, undercutting Tam's melody. Tam carried on playing, against it, then let the phrase dissolve into separate, random notes. Then Mike came in, a touch on the cymbals, shock of hi-hats, a leisurely trundle round his whole kit, beat here, hit there, thud of the bass drum punctuating, and everything right, fit, in its place.

Bird struck chords across it, tangents to the bass riff, then soared into a high-flying solo. Tam blew, flew up beside him, wove counterpoint, response. They discovered their instruments, threw themes back and forward, a laughing question-and-answer, and Mike built intricate structures underneath, and the whole thing was earthed, grounded, in that constant unchanging bass, sustaining, *A Love Supreme*.

Brian picked up on it, chanted refrain, *A Love Supreme*, changed it to *A Magic Flute*, then to *A Marriage Feast*, again to *Ruby and Tam*, and back to *A Love Supreme*. And by now the audience, congregation, were joining in, clapping time. Tam and Bird stopped playing, clapped and chanted with the rest. Then Mike too dropped out, left only the bass. *A Love Supreme.* They beat and clapped, and stamped their feet, Bird nodded to Mike to come back in, and he mouthed at the others, 'Burn-out!' and they wound it up to a big frenzied finish, climactic, overstated, a last crash on the drums to bring it all down and end.

The cheering at that took time to subside, the musicians grinning at each other, shaking hands. Eventually Bird raised his arms, called for hush.

'OK,' he said. 'Now this is it. This is the serious bit.'

A few people clapped, whistled. But as the priest stood up, and Tam and Ruby came forward, the atmosphere changed to a quiet that was almost solemn. Tam felt it, a stillness, a sudden distance from what was happening. He watched what was going on, and himself in it. To his right was Brian, the best man. To Ruby's left was Bird, to give away the bride. Father Thomas asked everyone to stand, and he said a short prayer. Behind him, the painted image of Krishna smiled as the priest read from Saint Paul on the nature of love.

> *'Love suffereth long and is kind: love envieth not: love vaunteth not itself, is not puffed up, doth not behave itself unseemly, seeketh not its own, is not provoked, taketh not account of evil: rejoiceth not in unrighteousness, but rejoiceth with truth: beareth all things, hopeth all things, endureth all things. Love never faileth.'*

The words seemed to Tam to come from another dimension, another realm. They carried an authority, a certainty, that was absolute.

Here they were, on a tacky stage set, acting out parts. And yet, in behind it all was something real, something these words had the power to invoke. He found himself staring at the floor, at the priest's feet, as he heard the words resonate. The priest's shoes were scuffed at the toes; the trouser-cuffs that showed beneath the robes were old and worn, beginning to fray. Noticing, Tam was absurdly moved. This reality. This. Here. Now.

And yet.

The priest droned, intoned the transfiguring words. It was time for them to make their responses, pledge themselves. Brian was handing over the ring. Take Ruby's hand, repeat the formula, counting from the thumb, *In the name of the Father*, to the first finger, *and of the Son*, to the second, *and of the Holy Ghost*, to the third, *Amen*. And on with the ring. And it was done. Man and wife. They embraced, chastely. Tam looked around, at his parents and his sister, at his friends, at people he had never met. And in every face, from his mother's furrowed forehead to Paki's stoned grin, he saw that they too were moved, even the most crazed and freaked-out of them, moved by the simple ceremony, moved in spite of themselves. And the priest made the sign of the cross, blessing them, and Krishna smiled, a wee half-smile, playing his silent flute.

A Lotus on Irish Streams

1

Ruby made Europe small. She just seemed to operate from a different perspective, an American sense of scale. The first summer after they were married they hitch-hiked to Italy, the next year they made it down through Spain and Morocco. Ruby's father still sent her money from time to time, an allowance, and through winter into spring they would work, take whatever jobs they could find. Ruby didn't care what she did, would work as a waitress, a barmaid, anything. Tam found it harder at first, having to work as a hotel porter, a nursing auxiliary, serve behind the counter in a boutique. But he knew it was buying those precious months of freedom in the summer, and that kept him going, through another bitter winter.

This last one had been worse than most. Sustained strikes had meant power cuts and blackouts, a three-day working week. In the four o'clock dark one particularly bleak afternoon, Tam had waded through slush, beaten by freezing sleet, to queue in the corner shop for candles.

'You're lucky son,' said the man behind the counter. 'No too many of these left. Have to start rationing them!'

The shop itself was lit by oil lamps, hung from the shelves.

'It's a disgrace,' said an old woman in the queue. 'It's getting like the Blitz all over again.'

'Never you mind, hen,' said the man. 'This'll all be worth it if it sinks Heath and his bloody crew.'

'Won't make a blind bit of difference,' she said. 'One lot's as bad as the next.'

'Not at all,' said the man. 'You'll see.'

She shook her head and he laughed. 'Och well. We're all in it together, eh? Never died a winter yet!'

Back at the flat, Ruby sat close to the paraffin heater, warming her hands. The heavy curtains were drawn shut. A stub of candle guttered on the mantelpiece.

'I'm thinking about summer,' she said.

'Wonder why!'

'How about France this time? We've only ever passed through and I'd like to really check it out.'

'Sounds fine.'

'We could be there in no time,' she said. 'I mean it's right on our doorstep.'

At one of the snackbars where she'd worked, Ruby had met a young girl, a student, who had been to Avignon the summer before, had worked on a farm picking pears.

'She gave me the address,' said Ruby. 'Says it's just a matter of turning up. I figure we can go there first, work for a couple of weeks, make a few extra bucks.'

'Francs.'

'Whatever. Then we take off, do France.'

'Check it out.'

'Right!'

Ruby travelled better than Tam. She'd had more practice, was more at ease. Tam was always slightly out of phase with himself for the first few days. They arrived in Avignon in the halflight of early morning and he felt grubby, had the tight beginnings of a headache. They had travelled the last stretch of the journey, from Lyon, in the cabin of a grain lorry, and Ruby had nudged him awake a few times, saying 'Talk to me!' Finally she had asked him to switch seats with her. She said she didn't like the way the driver kept leering at her.

'You want him to stop and let us out?'

'In the middle of nowhere? In the middle of the night?'

'I wish I'd done French at school instead of German. Could have given him a mouthful.'

'I think it's just as well you didn't.'

They were glad to be out of the lorry, to watch it disappear into the distance. Although it was early, there was a warmth in the air, a mildness. Ruby was excited just at being there.

'Can't you just feel the atmosphere?' she said. 'You can smell it!'

Tam was tired and hungry and couldn't tell which was which. He was prickly and irritable, the pain in his head a dull dead ache that throbbed if he moved too quickly. He wanted a meal and a bath and a sleep. Nothing was open anywhere.

'Let's go,' said Ruby.

'Where?'

'Who knows? Who cares?' She picked up her rucksack. 'Stop being such a goddam baby.'

They crossed a square, wandered through narrow winding streets, eventually found themselves down by the river.

'Wow!' said Ruby. 'This is neat!'

They found a spot, sat down on the bank. Tam lay back, resting on his pack.

'That must be the bridge,' she said. 'The one in the song.'

To their left, a great span of concrete arched over the river.

'Too modern,' he said, half asleep.

'Not that one,' she said. 'There.' And she pointed upstream at the ruin of an older bridge, red stone. She sang to herself.

> Sur le pont d'Avignon
> On y danse . . . On y danse . . .

It made him smile. He was fighting sleep, then he let go. When he woke he sat up suddenly. The sun was up further. People were beginning to appear, a trickle of traffic across the main bridge – cars, bikes, mopeds.

'Hi!' said Ruby. 'Guess we conked.'

He rubbed his eyes, felt gritty, but at least his head had eased a bit.

'Let's eat.'

To Tam it was still unreal, a dream. The pavement café was a stage set, a cliché of Frenchness, the proprietor was an actor, playing a part. But they drank bowls of real café-au-lait, ate actual croissants, and Tam felt better for it, more alive. He listened to Ruby ask directions, in her highschool French with its American rhythms, intonations, painstakingly making herself understood.

Once, in a bad mood, he had told her Americans were as bad as the English when it came to speaking languages. They had no ear for the subtleties, no real willingness to listen. It was a kind of linguistic imperialism, he'd said. Everyone spoke in funny accents except them. She had thrown that back at him more than once – times on their travels when he'd been floundering, unable to make himself understood, and she would laugh and refuse to help him out. 'What an ear!' she would say. 'So fucking subtle! So refined!'

'OK,' she said. 'I think I know where we're going.'

'That's handy!'

They took a bus from the main square, sat at the back on hard seats, their rucksacks tucked in at their feet. The bus rattled and shook, jolted them with every bump. A few miles out it stopped in a small village. Ruby checked with the driver.

'We're here,' she said.

The heat was intense, poured over them. Ruby asked the way from an old woman dressed in thick black from head to foot, and they found themselves walking down a lane, a rutted track. They came in at a gate and an Asian girl slipped past them on her way out.

The house was incongruously modern, anonymous. A middleaged man peered down at them from a wrought-iron balcony. He called something, interrogating, his voice rough and guttural. Ruby fumbled for the bit of paper with the address. Tam could follow what they were saying, more from the tone than anything else. Ruby was persistent, the man was getting annoyed. At last he gestured at them, told them, unmistakably, to go.

'I guess that's it,' said Ruby.

'No work?'

'Got it in one! Says he doesn't need anybody. Especially not foreigners.'

'Bastard!'

Back at the village square they bought a litre bottle of Perrier, dumped their packs in the shade and sat down on them.

'What now?' said Tam.

'Back to Avignon I guess. Looks like a nice place. We could stick around for a few days, then see what's what. See how the money goes. Sound OK to you?'

'We're here,' said Tam. 'Might as well enjoy it.' They passed the bottle between them, finished it off.

'There's that girl again,' he said.

The Asian girl they had seen at the farm was coming towards them, wheeling a bike. She wore a loose smock and baggy trousers, a big straw hat on her head. A shiny black pigtail hung down her back. She smiled at them, tentative.

'Hi!' said Ruby.

'You were looking for work back there?' asked the girl.

'That's right.'

'No luck?'

They shook their heads.

'Me too,' she said. 'But I know where to try. Good chance. If you still want.'

That afternoon in the same square, they stood self-consciously beside the girl, tagging on to the end of a line of men. There were groups of men all over the square, a lot of arguing, haggling going on. The girl had told them this was where the farmers came to deal, to bargain, to look for casual labour.

'We just have to wait,' she said. 'Be patient.'

Her name was Lee and she came from Vietnam. She studied at the Sorbonne, came down here in summer to stay with friends, to pick up work when she could. More than that she hadn't told them.

'Talk about a cattle market!' said Ruby as another potential employer came along the line, picked out the two men he wanted.

'I don't fancy our chances,' said Tam. 'These guys look like the real thing.'

Ruby shrugged. 'We could luck out. Who knows?'

A younger man came along the line then, stopped in front of Lee, nodded. She started talking to him, quietly, and he turned to Tam and Ruby, looked them up and down.

'She's putting in a word for us,' said Ruby.

'*Anglais*?' asked the man, addressing them.

'*Américaine*,' said Ruby.

'*Ecossais*,' said Tam.

The man grinned. 'Good!' he said. 'You come, work.'

They followed him across to a small truck and he motioned to them to get in the back. Lee lifted her bike on board, climbed in beside them.

'Thanks,' said Tam.

'That's OK,' she said. 'He like to think he's educated. Probably want to practise his English on you.'

'Great,' said Tam. 'I'll teach him Scottish, Ruby can teach him American. Bamboozle him completely.'

'Bamboo?' said Lee, and they laughed, explained what they meant. They had turned into the grounds of the man's farm, swung round past rows and rows of pear trees, pulled up outside a stone-built cottage. He unlocked the door, beckoned them to come inside.

'You are married?' he asked.

'Sure are!' said Ruby, showing him her wedding ring.

He nodded. 'You stay here then. Start work tomorrow. Eight o'clock. OK?'

'OK!' said Tam.

When he'd gone, Ruby let out a whoop. 'This is incredible!' she said, running from room to room. There was the big room they were standing in, two smaller rooms to the back, all with beds or mattresses. Then there was a kitchen with running water, a toilet with a shower.

'I guess the shower be cold,' said Lee. 'But it so hot outside you don't mind.'

'Will you be staying here too?' asked Ruby.

She shook her head.

'Why not?' said Tam.

'He only ask you two. Not me.'

'But there's plenty space.'

'Is all right. I stay in town with friends. Take no time on bike.'

'Whatever you say,' said Ruby.

'Maybe sometimes I stay here. Is OK with you?'

'Sure it is.'

'Only don't tell boss.'

'If you say so.'

'Now. You tired from travelling. Want to rest?'

'You're not kidding!' said Tam.

'No cooker in the kitchen,' said Lee. 'Or I bring back food to cook.'

'No problem,' said Tam, and he unpacked their tiny camping-gaz stove, a set of pots that nested inside each other like Chinese boxes, like Russian dolls.

'Great!' she said, laughing. 'I find food. See you later.'

'What a character!' said Tam when she'd gone.

'Tough cookie,' said Ruby. 'A survivor.'

They lay down. Tam felt a wave of tiredness sweep over him. He let go, slept deep.

When he woke he didn't recognize the room, had no idea where they were. Then he pieced it together, remembered. The sunlight through the window was softer. A smell of cooking wafted from the kitchen, tang of onions, mingling of herbs. Ruby too was awake. 'Smells fantastic,' she said. 'I guess Lee's been busy.'

They got up and went through. Lee was hunkered down, stirring what looked like a stew or a thick soup, the pot bubbling away on the stove set down on the stone floor.

'Amazing,' said Tam. 'What is it?'

'Ratatouille Niçoise,' said Lee. 'It's a speciality from this part of the world.'

'What's in it?'

'Aubergine, courgette, onion, pepper, tomato. And a little garlic, some herbs.'

'How much do we owe you for the stuff?' asked Ruby.

'I don't buy much,' said Lee. 'The garlic. Bay leaf. Oh, and the rice to go with it.' She tapped one of the other pots, set aside, lifted the lid to show them the fluffy rice, already cooked. 'This,' she said, holding a sprig towards them, 'you call thyme. It grow on the hillside back there. You pick it for free.'

'And the rest?' asked Ruby. 'The vegetables?'

'Some grow here on the farm. He don't miss a little bit. Some grow on back of truck!'

'You know what she's saying?' said Tam.

'Sure do!' said Ruby.

'Fell off the back of a lorry!'

'I don't steal,' said Lee. 'I just good at finding.'

'I told you,' said Ruby. 'This one's a survivor!'

Lee had found plates in a cupboard, and she dished out the food.

'You must show us how to make this,' said Ruby, between mouthfuls. 'It's delicious.'

'Sure,' said Lee. 'It's easy.'

'Isn't this great!' said Ruby, turning to Tam. 'What did I say about lucking out!'

The work was backbreaking slog – climbing up shaky ladders, getting snagged and tangled among branches, jabbed and scratched, choking on weedkiller dusted

247

on the leaves. They each had a gauge, a small metal ring, for measuring the size of the pears. If they were small enough to slip through the ring, they weren't yet big enough to pick. Sometimes they would check a whole tree and find nothing the right size. Then they would have to climb down emptyhanded, move on. The hours were long, 8 till 6 with a break in the middle of the day when it was too hot even to move. At night they dreamed of pears.

'Waves of them,' said Ruby.

'Me too,' said Tam. 'Swarms.'

'Hordes.'

'Droves.'

Their first day off, at the weekend, was relief. They slept late, took their time. They wandered down through the village, up into the hills beyond, came on the bleached white ruins of a chateau.

'Isn't this just beautiful?' said Ruby. 'It's like real Van Gogh country.'

'You can see what these guys were into,' said Tam. 'The Impressionists. I mean, they just painted what they saw.'

It was something in the quality of the light, a clarity, a burning intensity of colour. The sky was the deepest blue, seemed vast, the few clouds drifting high and far. A breeze wafted the scent of thyme – Tam recognized it from the sprigs Lee had brought. And there was another, sweeter smell that seemed familiar.

'Lavender,' said Ruby.

Tam breathed it in. A lizard darted up the wall behind them. Two white butterflies flickered past. The sun in his eyes made him sneeze, and he laughed. Ruby picked a few wild flowers, all yellows and bright blues, and Tam moved out from the shelter of the wall, climbed up to the edge of the ruin, a single arch left standing in what might once have been a colonnade. He stood looking out across the countryside as a cool dry wind whipped about him. And he realized he knew this, knew what it was called. A memory had surfaced of a dank grey day in Glasgow long ago, a Geography lesson at school, end of the day and the lights on in the classroom, the early dark coming down outside. The teacher, a humourless, dour old man called Bryce, was giving them a blank map test on France, asking questions round the class. Tam's attention must have drifted – he was startled to realize Bryce was talking to him, pointing with his ruler at the board, at a red arrow marked on his outline map.

'Well?'

'Sorry sir, I can't remember.'

'Can't remember what it *is* or what it's *called*?'

'Neither sir.'

'All right, I'll help you. It's a cool dry wind.'

Nothing.

'Blowing south.'

Total blank.

'In the Rhône-Saône Corridor.'

No.

'Maybe if you were to write it out 500 times it might help imprint it in your mind.'

He had written it. He remembered. *Mistral*. Now here it was, the reality, blowing into his face, tugging at his hair.

'What are you laughing at?' Ruby called to him, shielding her eyes from the sun with the bunch of flowers she had picked.

'My education!' he shouted down to her. 'Hey! I bet you don't know what this wind's called!'

Lee had more or less moved in to the cottage, though she still kept it secret from the farmer. She kept to herself, moved around silently in her rope-soled shoes. When they came back from the hill, she asked them to come with her to the main road.

'What for?' asked Ruby.

'Potatoes,' she said, handing them each a plastic bag, tucking another, folded neat, in her pocket. On the way she explained. 'It's the farmers. They get mad at the government. Price of potatoes not high enough. So they make protest.'

The protest was to dump truckloads of potatoes on to the road, block it for a hundred yards. A few local people were already out, filling up baskets and sacks, an unexpected harvest. Tam and Ruby waded in, following Lee, picked out the best ones they could lay hands on.

'I told you,' said Lee. 'I just good at finding things!'

Later she cooked another dish for them, potatoes provençale, filling the house once more with the smell of onions and garlic.

'Later I make tisane,' she said. She held out two bags stuffed with dried leaves, petals. 'Which you prefer? This one *verveine*. I don't know what you call it.'

They shook their heads, shrugged.

'The other one *tilleul*. I think you call it lime?'

They sniffed, both chose the *verveine* with its sharp bitter tang.

'Is good for digestion,' said Lee. 'Other one calm you down, make for good sleep.'

Ruby was arranging her wild flowers in an old wine-bottle.

'You pick these up the hill today?' asked Lee.

'How d'you know that?'

'I saw you. From distance. You easy to see. Both stand out, like bad thumb.'

'Sore!' said Tam, laughing. 'Bad penny. Sore thumb.'

'OK,' said Lee. 'But you stand out. Is better sometimes to be invisible. You say merge?'

'Yeah,' said Tam. 'Blend in.'

'OK.' She suddenly stopped, alert and listening, then hurried through to her room at the back of the house. They heard footsteps outside, a knock at the front door, and their boss, the young farmer, came in. He was slightly awkward, standing there. 'Smells good,' he said, then to Ruby, 'Good cook!'

She nodded, picked up a knife and prodded at the

potatoes sizzling in the pan. In a halting mixture of English and French he said he could give them work for two more weeks. The apricot crop would be ready a few weeks after that, if they wanted to come back. They said they would see. Still awkward, he wished them *bon appétit* and left.

'Suits me,' said Tam. 'Two more weeks is probably as much as I could take.'

'Yeah. Be good to move on.' She shook the pan to stop the potatoes from sticking. 'Where did Lee get to?'

'Merging,' said Tam. 'Making herself invisible!'

The door to her room was open and the one window had been pushed up about a foot. Apart from her sleeping bag, rolled up and left in the corner, there was no sign that she had ever been there.

'Amazing,' he said, coming back through. 'She must have gone out the window.'

'She's weird,' said Ruby.

'How d'you mean?'

'All this skulking about, hiding, lying low. She's totally paranoid.'

'But who knows what she's been through? I mean it can't exactly have been easy, growing up in Vietnam.'

'OK, so maybe there's reasons for her weirdness. She's still weird!'

'Come on!'

'Plus she doesn't like me.'

'How can you say that?'

'It's true. I can feel it. The way she says things, looks at me. It's like a kick in the stomach.'

'Well I think she's all right.'

'Yeah, I've noticed.'

'Give me a break!'

Lee came back in as quietly as she had gone, asked what the boss had wanted. Ruby shook the pan again, banged it down on the stove.

When they'd eaten – Ruby in a sullen silence – Lee cleared up the dishes.

'Maybe the other tea be better,' she said. 'For calm.'

Lee had heard Tam play his flute, in the evening after work, and one day she said he should meet her friend in Avignon. She said there might be a little bit of money in it, not much.

'He need a musician for his play.'

Her friend was called René, and Tam took a liking to him straight away. He had long hair, a bushy beard. There was a bigness about him, an easy laugh, a deep contagious chuckle.

He was putting on a play at the local Festival.

'We use music to create atmosphere,' he said. 'Percussion and flute. Now my fluteplayer is injured. Nothing serious. He skidded on his Solex, you know, the moped. He broke his finger, cut his lip. Means he can't play. But now Lee finds you! It's a great coincidence, no?'

The work at the farm was finished and they were grateful to move in with René. He lived in one huge long room, a kind of studio. He screened off one end for them, and the other end, where a Vietcong flag covered most of the back wall, he shared with Lee. Sometimes Philippe, the injured fluteplayer, would stay as well, bedding down somewhere in the middle. René had let Tam hear a tape of Philippe playing. The theatre piece they were doing had borrowed elements from Japanese *No*, and the flute Philippe played was a traditional *shakuhachi*.

'It's great!' said Tam. The music was atonal, the quality rough and breathy. 'I could probably get the same sort of effect, overblowing, bending the notes. Or maybe I could borrow this Japanese flute from Philippe.'

'No chance!' said René. 'He hardly lets anyone touch it, never mind play it. Sounds crazy, but he says for him it's sacred.'

Philippe seemed in many ways the opposite of René. He was thin and morose, nervy.

'He's into Zen,' said René. 'But he doesn't talk too much about it.'

'That's fair enough,' said Tam. 'In fact it's very Zen!'

René translated for Philippe, who spoke no English at all. He nodded in reply.

'Could you ask him to show me his flute?' said Tam.

René asked. Philippe looked hesitant a moment, then opened up his duffle-bag, brought out the flute wrapped in a purple cloth, decorated with Japanese calligraphy in white. He carefully unwrapped it, held out the flute towards Tam.

'It's beautiful,' he said, reaching out to take it from him, asking permission with his eyes, a quizzical look. Again Philippe seemed to hesitate, then he handed it over.

Tam turned it this way and that, admired it, noticed the inside was lacquered. He covered the finger-holes, worked out that the mouthpiece was at the end. Before he could even think about blowing it, Philippe reached across and grabbed it back.

'Thanks,' said Tam. '*Merci!*'

'Poor Philippe,' said René. 'These stupid injuries. Now he'll have to play the iron flute.'

'What's that?' asked Tam.

'You don't know the iron flute?'

Tam shook his head. 'Don't think so.'

'It's a Zen koan,' said René. 'It says, You can play sweet melodies on the flute of bamboo, or the flute of wood. They are hollow and have a hole to blow into and holes for your fingers. But how do you play the flute of solid iron, with no mouthpiece and no holes?'

Tam found the image strangely disturbing. A solid lump of iron.

Later the five of them sat drinking at a café in the main square. It was the square they had wandered across that first morning they'd arrived in the town. Already that seemed long ago. The square was a different place now, crowded with people who swirled and eddied round little groups of performers – musicians, dancers, a juggler, a clown. Near where they sat, a group of Algerians, all men, were dancing in a circle, taking turns to move to the centre and dance solo, snapping their fingers and swaying their hips.

'Isn't this great!' said Ruby.

He was glad to see her happy. She had said no more about Lee, seemed reconciled. After all, Lee had really looked after them, had brought them here.

'You like it?' called René, grinning across at him. 'You like Festival?'

'Beats Edinburgh for atmosphere any day!'

Back at René's place they drank more wine, passed round a pipe of sweet Moroccan grass and sat back on huge cushions.

'God I'm smashed!' said Tam, and he heard himself laughing. But then something started to niggle, unease, grit at the edge of his consciousness that wouldn't let him relax. He looked round the room, trying hard to locate it. René was laughing, his arm round Lee, whose smile was completely inward, entirely to herself. Ruby too was in her own space, her smile vague, her eyes puffy, half-shut. Philippe lay curled up on the floor. Tam remembered the koan, the Iron Flute, and he wanted to understand it.

'I want to know what it means!' he demanded.

'What?' asked Ruby, turning to him.

'Fucking koan,' he said.

'Some guy in the States published a book of answers to all the koans,' she said. 'Can you believe that?'

'It's absolutely typical,' he said. 'Disgusting.'

'That's California for you!' She laughed, but somehow the grit, the irritation, was growing.

'How many Californians does it take to change a lightbulb?' said Ruby.

'Another koan?' asked René. 'Tell us the answer!'

'Five,' said Ruby. 'One to change it, and four to share the experience!'

'What about the *real* koan?' said Tam, surly. 'I want to know what it's about.'

'The answer is music!' said René, and he detached

himself from Lee, dragged out a cardboard box full of record albums and flicked through them, found the one he was looking for.

'Here it is!'

Twice he made them jump with false starts, put the stylus down in the wrong place letting loud guitar-noise shriek out at them. Then at last he judged it right, placed the needle just so in the space between the tracks with its soft expectant click and hiss.

'Now,' he said, and the music began. And after a few bars Tam felt the tension in his gut begin to ease. He let the music carry him, flow round him like water. It was nothing he had heard before, had a quality about it that might have been Indian, or Celtic, though the playing, the phrasing, suggested jazz.

'What is it?' he asked. 'It's beautiful.'

René handed him the cover. Mahavishnu Orchestra. *The Inner Mounting Flame.*

'Which track?'

'A Lotus on Irish Streams.'

René put the needle back to the start of the record, a harder-edged piece of jazz-rock, soaring.

Philippe turned over, groaned, mumbled something.

'He wants the other track again,' said René. 'The gentle one.'

'Play it again,' said Tam. 'One more time!'

The play turned out to be a mixture of mime and dance, the only words a chanted chorus. Ruby translated for Tam, explained it was all about tearing the veil of illusion, seeing things clear.

'So that's all the cavorting about with lengths of gauze?' he said. 'Veils of illusion?'

'I guess so. They get all tangled up in it then work their way free.'

'Then there's all these trials they go through.'

'René says it's like evolution. Moving through different levels. From darkness to light.'

'Sounds like our Magic Theatre!'

'Madmen only!'

'Price of admission your mind!'

'That was a good time,' said Ruby.

'Weird.'

'Yeah,' she said. 'Weird. But good. Well, sort of!'

'Sometimes I think every wee bit of your life is weird when you look back at it.'

'I know what you mean.'

'Something reminds you, and you think, God that was a strange time!'

'Strange Days!'

He smiled. 'I guess that's what it's like on your deathbed. You look back at your whole life and think, Oh well, that was pretty weird!'

'Then it's over,' she said. 'Zap!'

'Just like that.'

'I don't like to think about it,' she said.

'Comes to us all,' said Tam, remembering a musty classroom, a blackboard covered with mathematics. Dust. 'It must be great to be like these old Zen masters. Knowing the score. I mean, they would announce the date of their deaths a few days in advance, quite matter-of-fact, you know – *Oh, by the way, I'm leaving the body on Monday!* Then they'd have the grave dug, climb into the coffin, recite a death-verse they'd composed for the occasion, and just lie down and die.'

'Way to go!' said Ruby.

'It's just such a different perspective on things.'

'It's a nice way to think of it,' she said. 'Leaving the body.'

'Imagine it,' he said. 'Sitting up in your coffin.' He tried to look inscrutable, intoned *'Life . . .'* He paused. *'. . . is weird.'*

'Some death-verse!'

'But good!' he concluded.

'Right,' she said. 'Don't forget good!'

'Sort of! Hey, how many Zen masters does it take to change a lightbulb?'

'Tell me.'

'Two.'

'Well?'

'One to change it, one *not* to change it! Good, eh?'

'Yeah.' She grinned. 'Good!'

The show had three more nights to run. After that they would probably move on, hitch back up to Paris, then home. Before they left, Ruby wanted to stage an event, a happening. She would call it *Earth and Water*, and the idea had come to her with simple clarity as she'd stood one day on the bridge, looking down at the river flowing underneath.

'It's a beautiful idea,' she'd said. 'And it'll cost nothing.'

She had already bought what she would need – a few reels of coloured thread – and she was beginning to get excited. She'd had other ideas for happenings, usually on their travels, but she'd never seen them through. This would be the first one she'd done since her ceremony *Words in the Trees*.

'It must be something to do with being around a theatre group again,' said Tam.

'I think you're right,' she said. 'It reminds you that it's just a matter of going out and doing it.'

'Getting away with it!'

They roped in René and Philippe, and a slightly reluctant Lee.

Ruby divided the event into two sections, *Earth* to be done at noon, *Water* at midnight. In the full bright heat of the day, they crossed the bridge to the place she had chosen, a bare dusty stretch of the riverbank. She lined up the three men, gave each of them a reel of red thread; and she asked them to walk, parallel to the river, unwinding the thread as they went, let it trail out behind them on the ground.

'Good!' she said. 'Good!'

Here and there the threads had blown, tangled. But it didn't matter. She gave a reel to Lee, kept one herself, and they took up positions, further apart, with their backs to the river. She gave a nod and they too walked forward, letting out their threads, crossing the lines of the other threads at right angles, to make a grid.

'There!' she said. 'That's it.'

That night they all went for a drink after the show, and towards midnight they headed once more for the bridge. She placed them all at intervals across it, facing downstream, and this time she gave them each a spool of blue thread.

'Right!' she said, and at her signal they dropped their spools over the parapet, holding on to the loose ends so the threads unravelled, spun out. And as the bobbins hit the water, the current carried them, tugging the threads away and out, and they let them go, to drift and fall to the river, disappear.

'Wow!' said Ruby. 'Beautiful!'

Her face was shining, and Tam saw that her excitement, her nervous energy, had been replaced by something else, a stillness and a calm. She had touched some centre in herself, a source of poise, delight. He saw it clear, felt it from her, knew that for her the whole thing had been an active meditation, an opening out.

A group of people raving across the bridge had noticed them. Now they were throwing out remarks. René shouted something back and they laughed.

Tam asked Ruby what they had said.

'One of them asked how the fishing was. Another one said, Don't do it, don't jump!'

'And René?'

He was talking some kind of *argot*, some dialect. I couldn't make it out.'

'Probably just as well!'

'Yeah!'

René came up then, hugged Ruby. 'Thank you for a very nice happening!'

Lee appeared behind him, said, 'Only thing is, for this river the threads should be brown, like shit.'

'It is kind of murky,' said Tam.

'Well, we're not exactly talking social realism here!' said Ruby. 'Let's say we're celebrating the *spirit* of the river, its essence. The principle of water.'

'It's a kind of sculpture you've made,' said René. 'Earth and Water. And the wind had a big part too, blowing the threads around. That's Air. So all that's missing is Fire!'

'Yes,' said Lee. 'That's what's missing. It had no fire.'

René muttered something to her, low and gruff, and she argued back. Tam heard the word *bourgeois*, looked at Ruby, his eyes questioning. She shrugged and shook her head.

'More *argot*?' he asked.

'Right,' she said. 'But I'm sure you get the drift.'

René turned to them. 'This one is the critic! She always gives me the hard time also, about my plays. Next time you have to make a happening just for her, with fire!'

Philippe had sauntered up from his station, wondered what was going on. René produced a bottle of wine from his shoulder-bag, said, 'Let's drink!' He opened the bottle and handed it to Ruby. 'To Earth and Water!'

'And Air!' she said, and took a swig.

'And the fire next time!' said René.

'Hey, that's a novel!' said Tam.

'I know,' said René. 'James Baldwin. He lives in Saint-Paul-de-Vence. Is a friend of mine.'

'The fire next time!' said Tam, taking the bottle and drinking, then passing it on to Lee, who smiled, drank.

When the bottle had been round all of them, twice, and finally drained, Tam blew across the neck of it, a deep mellow note, then pitched it higher so it pierced, sharp.

'Always music!' said René. 'Everything is your flute!'

'Maybe even the lump of iron you were talking about,' said Tam. 'Someday I'll figure that one out.'

He tossed up the bottle, spun it like a juggler. But

before it could return to his hand, René caught it, said, 'All right, let's make another happening!'

'Great!' said Ruby.

And René drew his arm back, hurled the bottle arching into the air. And they watched as it rose, turning in space, seemed to hang a moment then fall, flashing and glinting as it turned, to finish its arc and splash down into the river.

Next morning Tam woke late. He had lain for a while, his mind alert and restless, his body still slumped in its warm torpor, unwilling to shift though he needed to empty his bladder. It was hot in the room, stuffy, the sunlight glaring in through gaps in the closed curtains, the drawn blinds. Ruby lay beside him, still asleep. Even the single sheet that had covered them had been too much and had been kicked off, lay in a tangle.

They had all come back here, stayed up half the night, raving, setting the universe to rights. A heap on the floor, in the middle part of the room, must be Philippe. At the far end the Vietcong flag had been taken down from the wall, strung across as a makeshift screen to curtain off the corner where Lee and René slept.

Tam sat up, the pressure in his bladder insistent. He stood up, groggy. Ruby moaned something, turned over. He thought about throwing on some clothes, but nobody would see him anyway, and what did it matter? The bathroom was in the far corner, and as he made his way towards it, stepping carefully, the door clicked open and he realized he had heard someone in the shower, but it hadn't registered, had just been background noise, like the voices in the courtyard, like the drone of faraway traffic.

The door swung open and Lee stepped out. She was naked, like him, and was towelling the ends of her hair. When she saw him she stopped, not startled, not selfconscious. He was aware of himself standing awkward and staring as she looked at him, smiled in that way of hers that was turned in, to herself. Her hair was still wet and sleek. Loosed from its tight pigtail it hung long, down past her waist. She carried on patting the ends of it dry, her head to one side. He saw her look past him, stop and wrap the towel round herself. He turned and saw that Ruby had sat up, was looking the length of the room at them.

'Toilet,' he said, explaining.

When he turned back, Lee had silently disappeared, in behind the screen, the flag.

Later in the afternoon Tam and Ruby wandered across the bridge. Ruby had wanted a last look at the grid of threads they had laid on the other side, wanted to see if they were still there.

'I don't think Lee meant anything by what she said last night,' said Tam.

'Oh no?'

'She was just surprised at how subtle the whole thing was.'

'Subtle meaning insipid. Pointless. Self-indulgent.'

'That's not what she said.'

'No fire.'

'It wasn't what she expected.'

'No. From an American she doesn't expect subtle. She expects gross, brash, overstated. Do you know what she said to me? She said in the jungle the Cong could smell the Americans miles away, cigarettes, aftershave, chewing-gum. Then she pointed at that flag of hers, said *Soon this fly over Saigon*. I mean who the fuck does she think she's talking to? Some fucking redneck?'

Tam was hot and tired, still felt fuzzy from the night before. He had been stung by mosquitoes, on his knuckles, his ankles, and the more he rubbed and scratched the more it itched and burned. Ruby's voice, whining, was grating on his nerves.

'I'm sure she wasn't getting at you,' he said. 'It's just her way.'

'Oh yeah? Got to know her pretty well have you?'

'What's that supposed to mean?'

'Quite an eyeful she was giving you this morning.'

'For God's sake. She just came out the shower. I was going to the fucking bog. That's all.'

'Yeah?'

'Listen, I'm not going on about you and René, am I?'

'So what's to go on about?'

'Just the way he was all over you.'

'He was enthusiastic, about the happening!'

'Arm round you.'

'This is ridiculous!'

'That's what I'm saying.'

'It's nothing.'

'Exactly.'

She stopped and took a deep breath, leaned on the parapet looking down at the river. He touched her shoulder, said, 'This is crazy.'

'I know,' she said.

'Just as well we're moving on.'

'Living on top of people. It's no good.'

'Propinquity,' he said. 'Good word, eh?'

She smiled. 'Yeah!' And they walked down over the bridge. 'Kind of an odd couple, don't you think?'

'Us?'

She shoved him. 'Them! René and Lee.'

'I guess they're not really a couple. She just turns up when it suits her.'

'He's quite an interesting character.'

'Got to know him pretty well did you?'

'Smartass!' She shoved him again, harder. 'No, but it seems he used to be quite a radical. He was talking about *Les Événements* in '68. Like he was really involved, you know. The barricades, the petrol bombs, the whole bit.'

'I thought there was a bit of flair about the way he lobbed that bottle off the bridge!'

'They really thought it was going to happen.'

'Didn't we all?'

'Now he stays down here, works on his plays.'

'And Lee gives him a hard time, tells him he's sold out.'

'Is that what she says?'

'No fire.'

They scuffed along in the dust of the riverbank, looking for the pattern of red thread.

'Wind must have blown it away,' said Ruby.

'Probably drove folk crazy,' said Tam. 'Imagine getting your feet tangled up in all that thread!'

'I like the idea of it being trampled,' she said.

A few yards from where they had laid the thread, they found a strand of it, then another, almost hidden by the dust.

'Hey!' said Ruby. 'Some of it's still here. That's neat!' She crouched down for a closer look. 'Not that it matters of course. I mean it's the doing of it.'

'But still,' said Tam.

'Yeah,' she said. 'Still!' She stood up, seemed lost for a moment in her own thoughts, silent. Absently she drew a line in the dust with the toe of her red canvas shoe. 'It's amazing, isn't it?'

'What is?'

'The way there's no straight lines in nature. No squares. No triangles. No perfect circles.' She tapped her head. 'It's all in here.'

She had just seen something, realized it for the first time. She looked at him, astonished. 'I mean, it's like nature *approximates* to all these geometric forms, but they're never absolutely perfect. God, I'm not explaining it.'

'You are so. I know what you mean.'

'It's like that idea of perfection is what we bring to things. That order. It's actually a function of the way we perceive.'

'Dead Platonic!' he said.

'It's incredible!'

He was touched again by her capacity for sheer wonder at some revelation, and he remembered the way she had looked last night at the happening, her

263

pure delight at the simple formal beauty of it. He laughed to cover up the sudden rush of emotion he felt, hugged her, held her tight.

In the morning they set out early. René and Lee said goodbye, saw them off. René gave Tam a hug, kissed both his cheeks, slapped him on the back. He embraced Ruby, gave her an extra kiss on the mouth. Lee came to Tam then, put her arms round his neck and held her cheek lightly against his, placed one small kiss on his neck, just below the ear. Then she turned to Ruby, took both her hands, kissed her cheek.

'Don't be wrong about me,' she said, smiling. 'I like you. Both.'

Ruby nodded. 'Yeah.'

'It's just, you're innocent,' said Lee. 'Naïve maybe. But could be no bad thing.'

'Thanks for everything,' said Ruby. 'You too René. It's been nice.'

'Maybe we see you again,' said René.

'Who knows,' said Tam.

'So *au revoir*.'

'See you.'

They lugged their packs down to the square, took a bus to the main road out of town.

By the time they reached Paris, these last few weeks were already beginning to seem unreal. They would never see these people again. They were moving on and leaving this behind, a time, like any other, a time to look back at and half-remember. Blue threads carried by the river. Red threads trampled in the dust. Another weird time, but good. Sort of.

2

The main thing was finding a place to stay. Brian hadn't realized it would be so difficult, and his timing had been all wrong. He had waited until after the Festival, the last theatre group packed up and gone. He had left time for the tourists to clear out. But he hadn't allowed for the flood of students coming back into town, all, like himself, looking for rooms, flats, bedsits, anything at all.

He didn't even know anyone in the city, hadn't been back in Edinburgh since they'd done their show at the Fringe. Three years ago. It seemed like no time, or forever. Magic Theatre.

He had given up his rented room in Glasgow. Might as well jump in feet first. He had packed all his belongings, mostly books, into cardboard boxes, left them with his parents. Just for a week, he'd said, till he got settled. They were glad to hear him talk like that – *settled* was a comforting word. But his mother didn't understand why he couldn't do his Teacher Training in Glasgow, stay where he was, go to Jordanhill. And he couldn't really explain, said he just felt like a change. That was all. A change.

Obscurely he knew he was trying to get back in touch with something in himself, some spark. He hadn't written much, a few poems, an unfinished story. He had pushed out another two issues of *Ion Engine*, then let it die. He didn't have the money, or the inclination, to sustain it.

An exchange from that Fringe show – Tam and Bird as stand-up comics.

You got the time?
If you've got the money!

Then they would turn away, do a Groucho Marx duckwalk round the stage, meet up again in the middle.

You got the time?
If you've got the inclination!

He remembered Claire. *You dancing?* And there it was, surfacing again, that time in Edinburgh, doing the show. And he knew it was the last time he'd been really fully alive.

You dancing? He wondered where Claire was now. She had gone off to Ireland with Malcolm, but he couldn't imagine them still being together. The same with Bird and Chris, who had gone to London. Paki was in jail, for dealing. Tam and Ruby were travelling again, had sent a postcard from the south of France – an avenue of cypress trees, the sky impossibly blue.

The wind that whipped along Princes Street had a cold cutting edge to it. It tried to rip the newspaper out of his hands, crackled and billowed the pages against him as he looked for the list of accommodation to let.

Fuck this for a caper. He crossed the road to Woolworth's, went upstairs to the café and bought a cup of tea, cleared himself some space at a table by the window where he could look out. That was better. Right. He opened up the paper, scanned the list.

Some of the rents were a disgrace. Superior. Spacious. Luxury. Executive. All meant expensive. Executive Bedsits! No Children No Students No Animals No Couples. Next it would be No Catholics No Women No Blacks.

He ticked off four that were possible, made sure he had enough change and went down to the station to phone. After half an hour of it he had finally succeeded in getting through to all four numbers, only to be told there was nothing doing, the rooms had been taken, hours ago. He chucked his newspaper in a rubbish bin, sat down on a hard plastic bench in the waiting room.

What to do next was the problem. He didn't want to go back to Glasgow, back home. That would be defeat. So he checked in at the Youth Hostel, spent a restless night, not sleeping. When the place closed next morning, he set out walking, down across the Meadows where they'd once hung words in the trees, past the University, past the building where they'd squatted, now boarded up, a big FOR SALE sign outside, pasted over with SOLD in red. Then he bought himself a map-book. A to Z. Today he would be ready. And he phoned the newspaper office, found out that the first edition of the *News* came out at 1.30. He could buy it at the back door, in Market Street, across the road from the station. Today he would find something, anything.

The steps down into Market Street were a dark spiral littered with chip-papers and stinking of urine, a mess of vomit on every landing. The Scotsman Steps! He ran down them, holding his breath, emerged into the street to find a queue of people already waiting for the paper. He took his place, counted twelve in front of him. Delivery vans backed up to the open doorways, started to load up with great bales of the paper, tied with thick string. One bundle was slung over and cut open for sale. The first few people in the queue grabbed their copies and ran, sprinted, across the road and down into the station.

'What's the rush?' he asked the boy ahead of him in the line. 'What are they running for?'

'The phones,' said the boy. 'Got to be quick off the mark.'

'God! Is it that desperate?'

By the time he got there the phones were all in use. The accommodation list was much the same as it had been the day before, except for two he didn't recognize that might be worth trying. The first number was engaged. At the second, a woman's voice, irritated, told him the phone hadn't stopped ringing and half a dozen people were on their way to see the room and he would probably be too late but it was up to him if he wanted to bother. He took the address. He tried the first number again, and again, and one last time, and banged down the receiver.

'Fuck it!'

The address he had taken down was in a back street off Leith Walk. He checked it in his map-book and it didn't look too far, so he walked, and it was further than he'd thought, took him half an hour. The woman seemed even more annoyed than she'd been on the phone.

'Are you the one I told not to bother?'

267

'Not me. Must have been somebody else.'

'Well you're too late. The room's gone.'

'Could I have a look anyway?'

'What for?' She eased the door a fraction shut on him, suspicious. 'I told you, it's taken.'

'I'd just like to see it, that's all. See what's on offer for that kind of money.'

'I've had folk traipsing through here all day.' She pushed the door to as she spoke, slammed it on a curt 'Thank you.'

'And thank you too,' he said, loud enough for her to hear. 'Auld bag!'

He walked half a mile back up towards town before he found an unvandalized phonebox, tried the other number again. Still engaged. They must have taken it off the hook. There was nothing else for it. He would have to book in for another night at the hostel.

The next afternoon he was first in the queue, arrived a good half hour before the papers were due out. The boy who'd been ahead of him the day before turned up at five past.

'On the ball today!' said the boy.

'Both got the same idea!'

'It's murder all the same. What you've got to do to get a roof over your head.'

'How come it's so bad?'

The boy shrugged. 'It's a seller's market. I mean it's not that big a town really. And the thing is, the rents get bumped up sky-high at Festival time. Folk can just charge what they like and they know they'll get away with it. Then they get greedy on it, you know. And even though the rents come down again after the Festival, they always settle that wee bit higher than they were before.'

'Sicken you,' said Brian.

'Then there's the foreign students coming in. Including the English! No, but take your Americans and that. They think nothing of it, paying these rents. Even compared to London it probably doesn't seem too bad.'

'This is it,' said Brian.

'So one way or another it just keeps spiralling.'

A few others had joined the queue behind them.

'You wouldn't believe the place I'm staying in,' said the boy. 'A right pig-sty. That's why I'm looking for something else. Pronto.'

There was a shout from inside the building and the first batch of papers came down the rollers from upstairs.

'Good luck!' said Brian.

'Same to yourself!'

Brian had the right money, exact. He timed his run to avoid two vans pulling out, made it into the station ahead of the pack.

That afternoon he saw three places. The first was in the New Town and the landlord was Indian. He showed Brian into a wide hall that looked as if it had recently been papered and painted. That much at least was encouraging.

'The room is up top,' said the man, leading him upstairs. After the third floor was a last short flight of bare wooden steps to a tiny room, maybe eight feet by six, that looked as if it hadn't been decorated in twenty years. A bed took up most of the space, covered with a shabby candlewick spread. The floor was bare linoleum, worn through in patches to strands of hessian. The one chair and a chest of drawers looked as if they had been dragged from a rubbish tip. In the corner stood a big old wardrobe with a door that swung open, refusing to shut. A pane of glass was missing from the window, had been replaced with a piece of stiff card that had buckled and warped. A single-bar electric fire lay unplugged.

'I don't think so,' said Brian.

'Is good for the money,' said the man. 'You won't get any better for that price.'

'We'll see.'

'Plenty people interested.'

'I'm sure.'

On his way out, along the hall, he caught a glimpse into the man's sitting room. It was garish and over-plush, but comfortable and warm. The man's family were watching TV. As Brian passed, they stared out at him, blankly.

The second place he saw was a dull basement in Leith – bars on the windows, a patch of mouldy damp on the ceiling, wallpaper curling away from the walls. A middleaged Englishman had met him with the keys, let him in. He was offhanded about it, checked his watch as if anxious to be elsewhere.

'Forget it,' said Brian.

'Suit yourself.'

The last place he looked at was in Marchmont, near the Meadows, not too far from the hostel. He knew he had no chance. It was a whole flat, not just a bed-sit. It would be far too expensive. But he came to look anyway. By the time he arrived there was a queue halfway down the stairs – young couples, groups of students. He took his turn to file round, poke his head into the three rooms, the kitchen, the bathroom. He registered the tackiness of the way it had been done up, the cheap ugly lightweight furniture, all chipboard and veneer. But the flat itself was solid and spacious and clean, the rooms high-ceilinged and light. If only there was some way. Maybe that boy would be back again tomorrow queuing for the paper. He might know others who were looking. But then tomorrow would be too late. The woman showing the flat was announcing that they would accept offers, in writing.

'Offers?' he asked.

'In writing,' said the woman.

'You're asking people to bid? For a rented flat?'

'Exactly.'

'But that's disgusting!'

The woman ignored him completely, carried on with her announcement – offers would close on Friday, first post, and the successful applicants would be notified next week.

Successful applicants! Brian looked about him, unbelieving. But if he had expected any show of solidarity he was disappointed. All the others were busy writing down the details, ready to make their bids. He felt the anger rise up in him and he had to get out. Leaving the close into the street, he tugged at the heavy wooden door, swung it wide so it hit the wall and fell shut behind him with a crash.

In the pub he sat on his own, feeling bleak, fighting back the anger that kept welling up. He started at Moray House next week. He couldn't stay on at the hostel. Commuting from Glasgow was out of the question. He had to find a place.

He thought of the flat in Marchmont. Bids. Offers over. Sometimes he could understand the position someone like Malcolm had taken. Smash the lot. Blow it all to fuck and start again. It had a certain simplistic appeal, a ruthless clarity and logic. Not that clarity and logic were everything. Still, there were times.

He knocked back his half of whisky, banged down the glass, took a sip from his pint. Even the pub was beginning to annoy him, the voices raised in conversation, hard laughter. And every voice that obtruded into his consciousness seemed to be English.

He was about to leave when somebody tapped him on the shoulder.

'Hey!'

He turned, saw the boy he had met in the queue for the paper.

'Found a place yet?'

'No,' he said. 'Nothing. Yourself?'

The boy shook his head. 'Fuck all.'

'Terrible, eh?'

'You just on your tod?'

'Yeah.'

'Come on then,' said the boy. 'We've got a table over in the corner there. What are you drinking?'

'Lager,' he said. 'Thanks. That's good of you.'

271

'Ach!' said the boy. 'Rubbish!'

'My name's Brian by the way.'

'Kenny.'

Brian picked up his hold-all, slung it over his shoulder, helped Kenny back to his table with the drinks. Kenny introduced the two girls he was with – Linda his girlfriend, and Sally. Sally would be in her late twenties, was big and a bit on the heavy side. An evaluation. She wore a poncho made from a blanket. Her hair was in pigtails tied with odd scraps of coloured wool. It was as if she'd been stuck a few years back. Out of time. Brian was aware of her looking at him as he sat down.

'Don't I know you?' she asked, her accent maybe London.

'I don't know anybody in Edinburgh,' he said. 'Not a soul.'

He suddenly realized they made a foursome.

'I'm sure I know you from somewhere,' she said.

He shrugged. 'Can't think where.'

'God!' she said, laughing. 'Sounds like a really corny come-on, doesn't it? *Hey, haven't we met someplace!*'

And her laughter was so goodhumoured that Brian laughed too, and he started to relax, glad to be in company. By asking, and by listening, and by filling in gaps, he found out that Sally had moved up from London five years ago, had two kids and no man, Linda was from Motherwell and studied at Art School, Kenny was from Dundee and worked in a jeans shop.

'Doesn't anybody in Edinburgh actually come from the fucking place?' he asked, and he knew himself to be just the slightest bit drunk. He ordered up a round, laughed as the room spun about him, and he heard himself agreeing that it was Scotland's Oil, and the game was a bogey, and if Bremner had knocked it in from six inches against Brazil we'd have won the World Cup, and Wilson was as bad as Heath, he could stuff his Social Contract, and the Bay City Rollers were a load of absolute shite.

When they all left at closing time, out into the shock of the suddenly cold night air and a damp clinging mist, he found himself walking beside Sally, the other two up ahead.

'I've got it!' she said, putting a hand on his arm.

'Hope it's not catching!' he said.

'No, listen. I've remembered where I know you from.'

'Where?'

'Fringe show, couple of years back. You did a happening, at the Meadows.'

'That's right.'

'Then I came to your show. And the last night that couple got married.'

'Amazing!' He remembered her vaguely, her two kids making handprints on the sheets of card.

'It was really beautiful,' she said. 'The whole thing.'

'Well, I'm glad somebody liked it!'

They had walked down a steep hill to a part of town he didn't know. Sally lived in a basement flat in a narrow cobbled street lined with shops that seemed to sell nothing but antiques and secondhand clothes. The flat was warm, stuffy after the chill of the mist. The place had a friendly messiness about it, too many things in not enough space. Children's books, clothes, toys lay everywhere. But in one corner, in its own clearing, stood a small harp, a Scottish clarsach.

A young girl sat curled in an armchair, gave a lazy wave as they came in.

'Kids OK?' asked Sally.

'Fine,' said the girl, stretching and yawning. 'Took a while to settle down, but they've been asleep for a while.'

'Great,' said Sally. 'Thanks again.'

'No problem.'

'Like some coffee?'

'No thanks,' said the girl. 'If I drink any more it'll be coming out my ears! Anyway, I better be going.'

Sally saw her out, went through to the kitchen and put on the kettle.

'Christ!' said Brian, looking at his watch. 'I should be going as well.'

'What's the rush?' asked Kenny.

'Hostel,' he said. 'They shut the doors at eleven or something.'

The couch he was slumped in was draped with an old velour bedspread. The soft comfort of it, the warmth of the room, had sapped his strength, the will to move. To get up again, to go out in the cold, seemed beyond him.

'Doubt if you'll make it,' said Kenny.

'You're welcome to stay where you are,' shouted Sally, from the kitchen. 'Kip on the couch there.'

'There you are,' said Kenny. 'Very comfortable it is too. Many's the night I've crashed there.'

'Me too,' said Linda.

'Must have been a tight squeeze.'

'Cosy,' said Kenny.

Brian shouted through to Sally. 'Thanks, that's brilliant!' He shifted a child's toy, a dismembered Action Man, from the seat beside him, spread himself out and subsided further, back into the depths of the couch.

Somewhere in the middle of the night he woke, feeling cold. He was inside a thin sleeping bag, and the blanket he'd been given, a patchwork of knitted squares, had slipped off onto the floor. He sat up, groping for the blanket, and he found himself staring at the harp, the clarsach. It had been left, on its base, in the middle of the room where Sally had sat playing it. She was just learning, she'd said, couldn't play anything complicated and it might not be perfectly in tune. But she'd plucked out a simple Irish melody, haltingly embellished it with runs, glissandos, stroking the strings. Just the sound of it had been magic in itself. And Brian had found himself moved. In the midst of

274

this clutter she had cleared a space for herself, to make music.

Now the harp sat, in what at first he thought was moonlight, but was only the light from a streetlamp across the road, shining in through the window. Picked out in the strange stark light, it looked even more amazing, out of place, its curves, the form of it, like something from another dimension altogether.

He was wide awake now and realized he had a thirst on him. He stood up and picked his way carefully through to the kitchen. He couldn't find the light-switch, fumbled in the dark towards the sink. There was a smell of sour milk. He took his bearings, moved slowly, afraid of making a noise that would wake Sally and her kids, asleep in the only other room, through to the back. Feeling his way, he found a cup on the draining-board, poured out the dregs of coffee from it. The tap made more noise than he'd anticipated, clanked and juddered, let the water out in a rush. He gave the cup a quick rinse, then filled it up and drained it three times. He stood and listened. No sound from the back room. Good. He eased his way out of the kitchen again. The soles of his bare feet picked up crumbs, grit. He stood on something moist, didn't want to know what it was. As he tried to wipe it off he lost his balance, bumped the harp as he stumbled, made a lunge and a grab to right it miraculously and stop himself falling. In jarring the harp he'd set its strings vibrating, a discord that faded into a low drone.

He was shaking as the sound subsided. He knew how easily he might have knocked it over, smashed it. He wondered how it survived with children rampaging about, then remembered its usual place in the corner of the room, suspected it was sacrosanct, not to be touched. His hands were sweating. He wiped them on his shirt, reached out and touched the harp, gently. Clarsach. The Gaelic meant tree of strings. Another dimension. He plucked a single string of it, let the pure clear cold note resonate, fade. He shivered. He wiped his feet on the rug he stood on, climbed inside his sleeping bag and pulled the patchwork cover tight about him. He clenched and lay still, trying to generate a little warmth.

When he woke again he felt he had hardly slept, but the morning grey was getting lighter and occasional footsteps passed by on the pavement outside, sounding loud and close. He heard a noise across the room, looked and saw a small girl in the kitchen doorway. She was watching him, wary.

'Hello,' he said. 'You must be Sue.'

She said nothing, stared.

'My name's Brian. I'm a friend of your mum's.'

She slid into the room, keeping her back to the wall.

'I came here with Kenny and Linda. Do you know them?'

She nodded.

'Actually, I've met you before. But you won't remember. It was ages and ages ago. Years.'

'I'm six,' she said, assertive. 'And a bit.'

'That's big. When I met you before, you must only have been three.'

'Three!' It was almost a shriek, was followed by a high tinkle of a laugh. 'That's tiny!' From the heights of six and a bit, the thought of her three-year-old self was wonderfully funny.

'I met your brother too,' he said. 'Peter.'

'He's seven and a half.'

'So back then he must have been four.'

'Four!' This was even better. Her big brother four. Younger than she was now. 'That's just a tiddler!' She laughed again, delighted, and Brian laughed too, caught up for a moment in her way of seeing.

'Tiddler!' he said. 'That's a brilliant word. Magic!'

He was suddenly aware of the boy, Peter, standing in the doorway, glaring.

'Hi! I'm Brian,' he said. The boy crossed to the couch and picked up the bits of his Action Man, started piecing them together. Brian thought about going, leaving a note for Sally to say Thanks. He looked at the harp, still sitting in the middle of the room, decided he should put it back in its safe place in the corner. As he picked it up with great care, Peter said, 'That's Sally's! Nobody's to touch it!'

'That's why I'm moving it,' said Brian. 'So nothing happens to it.'

The boy had dressed his Action Man in combat uniform, a red beret, a camouflage flak jacket. He twisted the arms, placed a machinegun in the hands. Then he held the figure up, pointing, made firing noises in his throat. And he used the soldier to rattle off a salvo that wiped out Brian and Sue and shattered the harp.

'That's charming!' said Sally, coming into the room. 'That's very nice! Hardly know the man and you're gunning him down!' She turned to Brian, apologetic. 'I really shouldn't buy him these things I suppose. But, *Everybody else has got them*, so what can you do? Anything for a quiet life, eh?'

'Do him no harm,' said Brian. 'Let off steam and that. You can take things too far.'

'Guess so. Anyway. You'll stay for a bit of breakfast?'

He caught again the sourmilk smell from the kitchen. 'I should really be getting a move on. Got a lot to do.'

'Cup of tea then? You must have something.'

'Cup of tea would be fine, thanks.'

'Right. I've just got to get this pair ready for school.'

'God!' he said. 'School. Just the sound of the word makes me shudder!'

'And you training to be a teacher too!'

'I know,' he said. 'Don't remind me.'

He didn't like the idea, but finally he came round to it. He would try an agency. There was one that had advertised in the paper, with a fancy West End address. He phoned and they told him to come along.

The office was one of twenty sharing the same accommodation address. There was a list of them in the entrance hall. The one he was looking for was on the top floor, at the end of a long corridor. The office was tiny. Behind the only desk sat a thin balding man in a grey suit.

'Yes, can I help you?'

A cigarette end smouldered in an ashtray, acrid.

'Yeah, my name's Ritchie. I phoned you about a room.'

'Oh, yes. You're a student.'

'Teacher Training.'

'Well, there's lots of places won't take students.'

'I know.'

'But I might have something that would suit you.' He looked in his filing cabinet, found the details. 'Bedsit,' he said. 'Southside.' He passed the card across.

'Sounds OK,' said Brian, reading it.

'So when do you want to view it?'

'Right away.'

He had to put down a deposit, refundable on return of the keys. The weight of the keys in his hand felt good as he half-ran down to the bus stop. The excitement of it lifted him on the journey out.

The address was a main-door terraced house, divided up into bedsits. The room was on the second floor, and something in him sank as he pushed open the door and stepped inside. The room was small, but jammed with big old heavy ugly furniture – a three-piece suite, its pale covers grubby and stained, a sagging bed in the corner, a huge dark wardrobe, a chest of drawers. By the one window, which refused to open, sat a yellow formica-top table, a brown plastic stacking-chair. But worst of all was the wallpaper, bright red and patterned with a repeated Chinese motif in white and gold, willowpattern kitsch with a temple, a pagoda, a bridge over a running stream. The thought of having to live with it was depressing. But so was the thought of finding somewhere else.

278

He looked out of the window, and at least there was a view. Over the rooftops opposite he could see Arthur's Seat, and somehow it was a reminder to him. He turned back to the room, took it in, managed a halfhearted laugh at the hellish red walls, the endless pagodas. He slapped the arm of the couch, raised dust. He fumbled in his pocket for two pence, to ring the agency on the payphone downstairs and tell them he was taking the room.

There was something wrong with the gas fire. He couldn't get it to light. There was no other heating and it was too late to call the agency. He would have to see to it in the morning. He went out and bought a fish supper, came back and ate it, sitting on the couch in his coat and scarf. He didn't think he could take a miserable evening of it, so he took a bus into town, went to the pub where he'd met the others the night before. But none of them showed up, and he sat till closing time on his own.

Out in the street, in the dank seep of the cold, he thought about going back down to Sally's place. She had said he was welcome. Any time. The couch was there. He knew he might even get something going with her, was tempted by the soft numbing comfort and warmth, the company. He pictured the kitchen, the kids, the sticky domesticity. He turned and walked the other way, back up to Princes Street.

The mist had come down again, a clinging east coast haar. He stood waiting for a bus to take him back to his drab cold room with its pagoda wallpaper. Above him, outside one of the big stores, a saltire flag hung limp. It looked old, its edges tattered from flicking in the wind. It drifted, sagged. The mist swirled about the crags and battlements, the castle on its plug of rock. The wind rose for a moment, billowed the flag, swirled the mist. And a strange image came, vivid and clear, like something remembered, something he knew. He saw this castle, this street, these buildings, destroyed, reduced to rubble, as if in some desolate future. And he seemed to know that this same mist, that had been before the city ever was, would still hang over its ruin. Somehow the thought put things in perspective, reconciled him to this time, this place, himself here.

3

George drooped, nodded forward, jerked awake again, whiplashed upright in his hard chair. He had gone beyond all comfort, but he shifted anyway, tried to find ease. The scrape of the chairlegs echoed along the corridor. Somewhere a door opened, closed. The young night-nurse passed by, shoes squeaking on the polished floor.

'Any more word yet?'

She smiled, reassuring. 'Shouldn't be too much longer now.'

He had been here waiting for over three hours. Shouldn't be too much longer.

'You can still go in,' she said. 'It's not too late. And it might be a help to your wife.'

'No,' he said. 'It's OK. I don't. I couldn't. I . . .'

'Fair enough.'

He felt gritty and raw, irritated at her for trying to pressure him, to make him go in and watch.

'We'll let you know,' she said. 'As soon as there's any word.' And she was away again, brisk, disappearing round a corner. He listened to the squeak of her shoes, fading, heard another door click open, shut. Not too late, she had said. A help to your wife.

Six months married and it still sounded strange to him. His wife. Mary. His eyes closed again and he saw her, coming into the drawing office on her first day. The new typist, all bright and pert. She had smiled at him.

Something clattered, metal on metal, startled him alert with an image of surgical instruments dropped on a steel tray. There was something metallic too in the smell of the place, sterilized and clinical, ether and disinfectant, methylated spirit. It had made him feel frightened, a tightness in the stomach, brought back the only time he had ever been in hospital, to have his tonsils cut out. He remembered the gauze mask, chloroform, and waking afterwards, whimpering and sore.

He rubbed his eyes hard, stretched and shifted again in his chair. The tiredness had reached the stage where his legs were twitching, his nerves frayed. He stood up, walked across to the reception area, put another coin in the hot drinks machine. The other times he had used it he had bought tea, and the last twice it had tasted faintly of coffee. Maybe if he tried coffee, the stronger taste of it would make the mixture less disgusting. He hit the button, watched with a kind of blank concentration as the paper cup filled up with dark khaki liquid. He raised it to his lips, blowing to cool it, took a sip. It was even worse, the same bitter mixture as before, but now with an aftertaste of oxtail soup.

'Graugh!'

The nurse at the reception desk, an older woman, looked across at him over the top of her glasses. 'I know what you mean!' she said. 'Still. It's hot and wet, eh?'

'Aye. That's something I suppose.'

He went back to his seat, carried on sipping the drink in spite of himself, but he baulked at the last half inch of powdery sludge, set the cup down beside him on the floor.

He had asked Mary out in her second week at the job, and she had said yes. They had gone to the pictures a couple of times, then it was New Year and the office party. And they'd both had a drink at dinnertime, and another in the afternoon, and by the time the party started they'd already had too much, and later they would use that as an excuse. It had been the drink. They hadn't been responsible. And they'd slipped away from the crowd and the noise in the staff canteen, let themselves in to the empty drawing office. He'd fumbled across in the dark, holding her hand, to his desk, his drawing-board, switched on his worklight. The drawing he'd been working on still lay where he'd left it. He unclipped it from the board, held it up to show her. 'All my own work.'

'Etchings is it?' she asked, and he hadn't understood, but she'd laughed so it must have been a joke. And she'd kissed him and he'd let the drawing slip from his hands, not caring, and they'd lain down on top of it. And then they were doing it, right there on the floor, and it all felt wrong, tense and uncomfortable and awkward and tight and over so quick and done.

He had to tear up the drawing. It was crumpled and torn, smeared. He would have to start it all over again. He walked Mary home, said nothing much.

'The waters have broken.'

He looked up at the night-nurse. 'Sorry?'

'Could be any time now. Half an hour. An hour at the most.'

He shook himself awake. 'Thanks. That's great.'

'You haven't changed your mind yet?'

'Eh?'

'About going in.'

'No. I don't think so.'

'Fine.'

Half an hour. An hour. He was that close to being a father. He could picture Mary, a few yards away, legs splayed, pushing down and down and out. He didn't want to look, didn't want to know about the pain and the mess.

'I'm pregnant,' she had said, just like that, right out. She had sat down facing him, across the table in the canteen. He had looked about, this way and that, but the table was half empty and nobody seemed to have heard.

'What do you mean?' he'd said, and the words had sounded stupid, even to him.

'What in God's name do you think I mean?'

'Are you sure?'

'Of course I'm bloody well sure. Otherwise I wouldn't be telling you, would I?'

She had never spoken to him like this, impatient, cutting. A different person. He stared at her, looked away.

'Just from that one time?'

'That's all it takes.'

It had been nothing. Not them, the drink.

'So what are we going to do?' he asked.

'That's what we need to talk about.'

He hadn't finished eating, was halfway through a sickly pink pudding. Angel Delight. He pushed it away, stood up.

'Where you going?'

'Outside,' he said. 'Come on.'

Out behind the factory it was rutted, muddy, sloped down to a stagnant burn. They walked along the path by the side of it, not talking. A few seagulls circled in the grey sky. All kinds of junk had been dumped in the shallow water, broke its scummy surface – an old tyre, an oil drum, the frame of a pram.

'Well?' said Mary.

'Well what?'

'We came out here to talk, didn't we?'

'Right,' he said. 'We've got to sort things out.'

'Just like that!'

'You know what I mean.'

They walked a bit further. Something darted across the path in front of them, a mouse, heading for the water's edge. They stopped again, stood. George looked down at a used contraceptive, just at his feet, and the sight of it annoyed him, disgusted him. He kicked it away into the mud, then wished he hadn't. He drew back his foot, recoiling as if contaminated by the contact, without thinking wiped his shoe in the dirt.

'I'm not getting rid of it,' she said.

'No.'

'It's not right. It's murder.'

He should have realized. As a Catholic she wouldn't believe in it. He hadn't thought anything through, didn't know where to begin.

He looked at her. 'So it's a matter of whether we want to get married, or what.'

'Suppose so,' she said, turning away.

There was a sudden flurry just above them. A seagull dived to the edge of the burn, flapped up again, something small and dark wriggling, caught in its beak.

'Jesus Christ!' he said. 'It's that wee mouse!' He gaped at it, amazed, saw the bird rise, the mouse struggle and writhe. Then the bird let go, dropped its prey, and the tiny black shape plummeted, hit the water with a dull plop and disappeared. The ripples settled, the green scum closing over. The stink wafted a moment, from the water being stirred. The gull circled round and flew off.

'Godalmighty!' said George, and he turned to say something to Mary, but she had her back to him, and he heard her sniff and knew she was crying.

'Hey,' he said. 'Don't greet. Don't.' And he went to her and she sank against him, letting it all out. 'It's OK,' he said. 'It's all right. Everything'll be fine.'

The hooter went for the end of the dinner break.

'Shite!' he said. 'Got to get back to work.'

She dabbed at her eyes, managed a kind of smile. 'Back to the drawing-board!'

A phone ringing jangled him. It was still the middle of the night, still the hospital corridor. He checked his watch. A few more minutes had passed. The nurse had said half an hour, an hour. No more than that. A father.

He saw his own father's face, vivid. His father had given him a hard time over the whole thing, had reduced it to a choice between two evils. Abort the baby or marry a Catholic. And he'd said to George there were ways and means. There were doctors who did it. He would find out where. If it was just a matter of the money. George had said no, it wasn't on, she wouldn't.

'Oh, of course,' his father had said. 'It'll be against her religion! Just like it's against her religion to take sensible precautions. But then shouldn't it have been against her religion to have got into this situation in the first place? I mean, if she can forget her principles once, why can't she forget them again and save everybody a whole lot of bother? Or is it a different kind of sin we're talking about here? What is it they call them? Mortal and venial is it? Doesn't seem to make a blind bit of difference. All they have to do is confess it and say a couple of Hail Marys and there you are, Bob's your uncle, away you go and don't do it again!'

There was no arguing with his father's anger, blank and stupid. When George finally told him they were going to be married, and the ceremony was to be in a Catholic church because that was what Mary wanted, he said he would have nothing to do with it, refused to come to the wedding.

His mother at least had the gumption to defy him, came to the church and then to the reception after-wards. Malcolm had long since lost touch, and nobody knew where he was. But he must have heard through some kind of grapevine, sent a telegram, from London. It read *All the best to my wee brother. Never thought you had it in you.*

Somewhere a baby screamed, and he wondered if that might just be it, but nobody came rushing to fetch him. A trolley was trundled past by an orderly in a grubby white coat. He looked tired and bored. George stared, mindless. The trolley was on hard rubber wheels, almost soundless, but something rattled, clanked.

He should stay awake, especially now, at the last. But the sleep came at him in waves, dragging him down. Mary lay back on the floor of the drawing-office, her legs apart, knees up. She ground her hips and her breath came in short gasping sobs. He knew he was somewhere in the picture, knew all this had something to do with him, but he couldn't figure it out and all he could do was watch. Now she was crying and he heard his own voice say, 'Don't greet. Don't.' And he was down there with her, down on the floor, lying on top of her and it all felt wrong. An old witch of a woman said, 'Still, it's hot and wet, eh!' and laughed, a harsh cackle. And then he was standing, looking down at Mary, and a man's voice he thought he should know said, 'All your own work. Never thought you had it in you.' And he felt another presence, threatening, somewhere close, looked up and saw his father. He was wearing his masonic apron but it was spattered with red ink. He was glaring and George couldn't meet his eye. 'Look,' he said. 'See.'

Something dark, a tiny creature, darted from between Mary's legs, disappeared. And something beaked and vicious hovered near, ready to swoop down, to stab and tear. Then it wasn't just that he was watching it all. At the same time he was there, he was in it. He had darted across the floor, he was hiding. He was circling above, claws and beak ready. He was his own father, felt the grim anger as his own. He was himself with his compasses and setsquares, working on a drawing that wouldn't come right. Its lines refused to come together, take shape. He was lying back, now in a hospital bed, legs spread open. This was Mary but he was living it, a gauze mask over his face, the smell of chloroform, going under. He was circling round looking down at it all from somewhere high above. He was down there in the hot close dark pushing pushing to be born. He opened his mouth to scream but nothing came.

'Mr Wilson.'

The night-nurse. The hospital. Yes, this now.

'Congratulations.'

The word was strange.

'Your wife's just had a wee boy.'
Yes, this was happening.
'You're a father.'
Now he would go in.

A Walk on the Wild Side

1

At the first stop in Manhattan, 53rd and Lexington, the subway emptied a little and Tam managed to grab a seat by the door. The old man vacating the space had chucked down his copy of the *Daily News* on the seat as he went. The way he threw it down said he was finished with it, had read enough. Tam picked it up and slid into the seat, propped his kit-bag between his feet. He had bought the bag specially. It was old and anonymous, looked as if he might be carrying his laundry in it, instead of his flute and his soprano sax, packed away inside it in their hard black cases. Would-be muggers wouldn't look twice at him carrying it.

He seldom bought a paper these days, couldn't be bothered with it all. He flicked through the pages, looking for cartoons. One showed a weary New Yorker crawling across a desert marked SUMMER OF '77 towards the oasis of Labor Day. Over his head were clouds reading BLACKOUT, BOMBINGS, SON OF SAM, and the caption underneath read 'We made it!' Tam didn't know yet if he and Ruby had made it through.

Blackout.

A year now they had been here. An American wife qualified him for a green card. He was legal. The first month they had stayed with Ruby's father in White Plains. Her mother was long-since dead, and the old man had grown cantankerous. He took an instant unreasoning dislike towards Tam, nothing spoken, but always there behind what was said. He would act exasperated at Tam's accent, making out he couldn't understand him.

'Thought you Brits invented the goddam language.'

'I'm not a Brit. I'm Scottish.'

'So that's why you don't talk right.'

'No such thing as talking right.'

'Sure there is.'

'I talk one kind of Scottish English. And that's just as valid as Lithuanian American English.'

'You saying *I* don't talk right?'

'It's not a matter of talking right. You got to listen right. I can understand you just fine.'

They held their smiles, pretended it was all just banter, but Tam could feel the cutting edge, the resentment. Somehow the old man had always expected Ruby to settle down after all her travelling around, marry some nice Jewish boy, a doctor maybe, or a lawyer. Buy a house. Raise a family. When they'd found out Ruby was pregnant, they knew it was time for them to move out, find a place of their own. They spent a desolate month looking for somewhere cheap but habitable in a neighbourhood where they might feel safe. They found nothing, and even Ruby was shocked at some of the places they'd seen – total unremitting squalor, the city's darkside, its underbelly.

'It's like lifting up a stone,' said Tam. 'Having a look at what's crawling underneath.'

'I had no idea,' she said. 'I'd just never seen it.'

Finally her father had come up with something. He had an old friend who owned an apartment in Flushing. For years he had spent his summers in the Catskills, and now he had more or less retired there. The apartment lay empty. What with the crime rate and the threat to his property, didn't it make sense to have somebody move in? A nice young couple? They could be caretakers, look after the place for him, plus they would pay him rent, and hey, didn't every little bit help? So what did he think?

He thought *Sure*, he thought *Great*, and they moved in.

The figure in the cartoon was crawling, half dead. *Blackout*. The word brought too much back, stabbed and twisted in his guts. He folded up the newspaper, shoved it under the seat. The train stopped at 5th Avenue, emptied out a few more passengers.

A skinny Hispanic, maybe in his forties, was walking the length of the car, handing out cards to anybody who would take one. He shoved one into Tam's hand. It was grubby from handling, creased at one corner. *Hello*! it read, under smudged stars and stripes. *I am a deaf person. Please buy this Deaf Education System Card to help me make my living.* On the other side was the alphabet in sign language, crudely drawn. A few more drawings showed the signs for particular words. *Good. Bad. Perfect. Chance. Girl. Boy. Sweetheart. Marry. Right. OK. No Good.*

The man was going round the car again. He wore a flak jacket over a thick checked lumberjack shirt. Outside in the heat he would be drenched with sweat. But maybe he spent all day down here, riding the air-conditioned trains. Most people handed the cards back to him. One or two gave him a quarter, shoved the card away in a pocket. Tam had no change, and wasn't about to hand over a dollar. He held out the card, shrugged. The man grabbed it from him, gave what was meant to be a look of contempt, but without the self-belief to bring it off. The eyes were dead and dull, not even cunning left. The lips twitched into a snarl that was half animal. Tam remembered Paki Black, wondered if the man was an addict with a habit to feed, and not deaf and dumb at all.

He leaned back his head and shut his eyes, tried to block out the man's image. The city was teeming with them, the casualties, the losers, swept aside like so much detritus, garbage. Bring me your poor, your huddled masses. Home of the free. There were times when everything looked to him like the photos of Diane Arbus. He had seen an exhibition in the Village, had flicked through the glossy expensive book of reproductions. It was a way of seeing things, stark and grey, reality distorted to make it more real. Days at a stretch he would see things that way, a passing freak show, a bad trip. *People look ugly, when you're strange.* His fear was that he would end up stuck there, locked in to that mode of perceiving.

Then there was the other side, freedom, the light. More and more it was music that took him there, lifted him up into it.

The night he had found himself, by a series of coincidences worthy of a Hesse novel, wandering lost down streets he didn't know, paranoid and looking for a way to get out, to get home.

He had gone along to play with a band – he had sat in with them a few times and they'd asked him to join them for this session at some New Age centre in Harlem. Barnie the piano-player had said, 'It's a wild place, man. Bird of Paradise it's called. Real voodoo vibe!' Tam had come in by subway and bus, found what he thought was the address, but the premises were burnt out, gutted, the whole face of the building blackened and charred, the smell of burning, of smoke, still hanging in the air. As Tam had stood there staring at it, a young Rastafarian had stopped beside him, grinned.

'Woh! Guess they really barbecued that bird!'

'Is that the Bird of Paradise then?'

'It was, man. Till yesterday.'

'What happened?'

'I hear somebody firebomb the place.'

'Anybody hurt?'

'Don't ax me man. I don't know nothin!'

As Tam had turned to go, the boy had called after him. 'Hey, you need anything? Smack? Coke? Good grass?'

'No thanks. I'm fine.'

If the fire had only been yesterday, Barnie had probably just found out, been unable to contact him and tell him not to come. Now he had to trek all the way back.

He had walked a few blocks when he'd realized he

was going the wrong way. He turned down a side street, saw two men walking down the middle of the road. One was carrying a baseball bat, the other an iron bar. Nobody paid them any attention, but he changed direction again, seemed to come round in a circle and out on to a main avenue. Up ahead he saw some big buildings, some kind of institution, and he thought he could take his bearings from there. It turned out to be Columbia University, and he cut across the campus, thinking he would just sit somewhere and gather himself.

That was when he had seen the poster. White lettering on a blue background *Let the music-bird fly in your heart-sky*. A brush-drawing of a bird in flight. It was advertising a concert of Indian music. He just happened to be outside the church where it was just about to start. A few people were drifting inside. He found himself following them in, found himself sitting there.

It seemed the solo performer was some kind of spiritual teacher. Tam didn't notice him come out, but a change in the atmosphere, a reverent expectancy from the people round about, made him look up and the man was there. Dressed all in white, he stood, his hands folded in prayer, facing the audience in absolute silence. Then he bowed, picked up a flute and began to play. And the melody was simple and pure, with somehow an immense dignity as the notes hung and resonated in the natural acoustic of the high vaulted space.

By the end of the concert the man had played an assortment of flutes – a small Indian one, made of wood, a double-flute of bamboo with a gourd that made a built-in drone, a set of pan-pipes, a tiny ceramic ocarina. At some points he seemed to be just doodling, repeating some phrase that appealed to him, over and over again, just for the joy of it. Then it would open out into something more, an intense piercing sweetness. And Tam realized it had nothing to do with technique. Beyond that, the man was in tune with some vast consciousness, was still enough and poised enough to let it breathe through him. He himself was the instrument being played. And Tam felt the music unlock the door to a space inside himself, a familiar room he had long forgotten.

Once he opened his eyes, saw the man sharp and clear in a glow of blue light, and he thought it must be his eyes playing tricks, but he blinked and the aura persisted, was definitely coming off the man. He finished playing, and put down his flute. He stood in silence. He bowed, and smiled. It was over, and not one word had been spoken. On the way out, someone handed Tam a little printed card. It read *Keep your heart's door wide open*.

That had been months ago, and the memory of it had stayed, a stillness he would try to return to, an oasis.

The subway rumbled on. He heard a cracked voice raised in song.

Poetry in motion
Walking next to me

The accent, the inflections, were unmistakable. The drunk was from Glasgow. Arms out, swaying, somehow staying upright as the train bucked and shook.

A vision of devotion
Is what you mean to me.

Were those really the words? A vision of devotion.

The man had broken off from his singing. 'Come on now!' he said. 'A wee bit order there. One singer one song.' Nobody was taking any notice. He threw back his head, shouted out, 'OK Scotty! For fucksake beam me up!'

Tam laughed as he stepped from the train at Bleecker Street, and the man yelled after him. 'Have a nice day ya bastard!'

The heat in the station was sticky after the cool of the train. The drunk had reminded him in some obscure way of his father, and he wondered how in God's name the man had ended up here. He imagined himself, if

293

things went wrong, ten years down the road, or twenty, an alien, trying to survive on welfare. He shut the thought out, dismissed it, before it led him back into Arbus country. But he seemed to be in for a day of it. A bag-lady shoved past him, talking to herself, muttered something about anchovies. A young black tried to panhandle him. 'Come on man. Reach out and touch somebody.' Then the crowds parted as another crazy came through. He was fat and redfaced, wore cut-off denims, a torn shirt flapping open at the front. 'Get outa my way,' he growled, raging. 'Don't make me mad or I'll turn into the Hulk!'

As Tam reached the top of the subway steps, the full blast of the heat hit him, like an oven door opening, like walking into another element. It stifled, mugged him as he stepped out into it. Have a nice day.

The air-conditioning made Barnie's apartment a haven from the heat, but the place was a mess. Every available surface was heaped with papers, books, records separated from their sleeves. Shoes, clothes, lay discarded. Here and there, where a patch of carpet showed through, it was littered with crumbs, clots of dust, the contents of a spilled ashtray. But standing among it all, rising out of it, were a grand piano, a colour TV, a sophisticated stereo system with giant speakers.

Barnie sat tinkering at the piano. The TV, as always, was switched on with the volume turned down, an inconsequential stream of images flickering on the screen. Tam slumped into the couch, closed his eyes to it all, tried to shut it out. He had once stayed the night on the same couch, the night of the blackout.

Shut it out. Enjoy the artificial cool.

When Mack arrived, dragging in his drumkit, he cleared a space for himself, set up. 'How can you live in this pit?' he said. Barnie's reply was to incorporate *No place like home* into what he was playing, build an improvisation on the tune.

'Sure,' said Mack, looking about him. 'No place like it. Thank fuck!' He had been in New York for ten years, but still had a Glasgow edge to his accent, even though the vowels had been dragged out, flattened. He turned to Tam. 'How you doing, man?'

'Och, you know. Fine.'

'Here,' said Mack. 'I brought you this.' And he chucked a book on to the couch. Tam picked it up, read the cover. *The Real Book.*

'Used to be a kind of bootleg version of it called *The Fake Book*,' said Mack. 'Just all these different songs, ripped off, photocopied and that. Then some bright bastard thought of doing it properly, publishing it.'

'Looks great,' said Tam.

'Good for session work. It's got all the standard stuff you're likely to need.'

Tam flicked through the book, saw *My Way* and *Yesterday* and *Fool on the Hill.*

'Thanks a lot.'

Mack had put some recording work his way, the odd session, filling in.

'It's nothing,' he said. 'I know it's not what you really want to be doing. But hey, it pays the rent. Better than fucking barmitzvahs any day!'

Barnie played *Hava Nagila*, vamping with the left hand.

'Oy fucking vay!' said Mack. He cleared space at the other end of the couch, dumped some papers on to the floor, sat himself down.

'I doubt if Ben's going to make it,' he said. 'He's smacked out of his brains. Totally incoherent.'

'So what else is new?' said Tam.

'Shit!' said Barnie. 'Have to rehearse without him.'

'Again,' said Tam.

Ben was the bass player, made electric bass sound mellower than Tam would have believed possible. Or he could slap it with a funky strutting authority if the music needed it. But the problem was his habit, and the fact that he didn't recognize it as a problem. He had

295

swallowed the myth, believed his music couldn't flow without the hit the rush the surge through his veins.

'Sad,' said Mack. 'Stupid bastard's wasting himself.'

Barnie played the riff from *Man with the golden arm*.

'How about a couple of cold beers?' said Mack, stretching out. 'I'm totally wrung out. Dehydrated.'

'Refrigerator's packed in,' said Barnie. 'You can have a warm coke.'

Mack groaned. 'Fucking heat. It's killing me. Don't think I'll ever get used to it.' He picked up the remote control handset for the TV, started flicking from channel to channel. A cowboy rode through Marlboro country. A girl wriggled into Sergio Valente jeans. Joe DiMaggio smiled, avuncular, selling bonds.

'Where have you gone Joe DiMaggio?' said Mack. Like Tam, he had a head full of old songs, was forever quoting from them. They could have whole conversations, throwing lines back and forth. It had been the same with Brian.

'A nation turns its lonely eyes to you,' said Tam. But Mack was changing channels again, picking up the pace.

A weather map of America. Shrieking contestants in a game show. A soap-opera starlet, glycerin tears catching the light. A car crashing through a roadblock. *Star Trek. Top Cat. Bonanza.* A home run. A Big Apple, labelled NY.

'If you can make it here,' said Mack.

'You can make it anywhere.'

Barnie stopped playing. 'How about we rehearse?'

'I think we shouldn't bother,' said Mack. 'The way things are going with all this punk stuff, I mean we'll lose all our credibility if we're too together!'

'We've got no credibility with these guys anyway,' said Tam. 'Old hippies are definitely bombed out.'

'Crazy,' said Mack. 'A lot of it sounds to me like it's from Dylan out of Lennon by Lou Reed.'

'I actually saw Lennon the other day,' said Barnie. 'Coming out of a Soho gallery. He looked pretty strung out.'

'The last I heard he was up in Maine or somewhere, communing with angels,' said Mack.

'Imagine there's no heaven,' said Tam.

'It's easy if you try!'

'I heard he was putting money into Noraid, to fund the IRA,' said Barnie.

'Is that what the angels told him to do?' asked Tam.

Mack laughed. 'A working-class hero is something to be!'

'Have you heard Sid Vicious singing *My Way*?' said Tam. His *Real Book* happened to be open at the song. 'It's brilliant.'

'I like the energy of all that,' said Mack. 'But it's just being turned into another commodity, hyped up and sold.'

'What's mad is all these Scottish kids getting into it,' said Tam. 'Only instead of faking American accents, they're faking Cockney accents!'

'Nothing really changes,' said Mack. 'I mean, even when I started out playing way back, like late Fifties, early Sixties, there was this whole feeling that you had to play it *right*, you know? Like there was a set way it had to be, like rigid. Sort of Calvinistic bebop!'

'No freedom.'

'That's right. And that's why I like the way you play, man. You're breaking through that.'

'Yeah. I'm learning to fly!'

'It's good you came here, man. It's just so open.'

'Yeah,' said Tam. 'You get session work, barmitz-vahs, the lot!'

'That's just buying time,' said Mack. 'Time for the real work. And the thing about here is they let you get on with it. Whatever *it* happens to be. I'll tell you something. See whenever I think about going back to Scotland, I hear this voice saying, *Ach naw son.* Doesn't matter what it is, that's the response you get. *Ach naw!* But here's different. You just do it. And OK, maybe you go under.'

'Like Ben.'

'But at least you go for it.'

'Sink or swim.'

'If you can make it here!'

'Big Apple.'

Mack had continued idly channel-popping as he talked, only half watching. Now he started speeding it up again.

'I remember reading this thing by Lorca,' said Tam, 'where he described America as an apple smelling faintly of gasoline.'

'Wild!' said Barnie, who had just been sitting listening to them, saying nothing. Now the three of them watched the images jump/flick/jerk on the screen. A girl's throat gulping Coke / fist smashed into a face / a young Judy Garland / cute kids / Lassie / Van Gogh sunflowers / Bilko / Mr Spock / Fred Flintstone / a burger with fries / guns blazing / a smile / teeth / eyes / lips / hair / an aircraft carrier / Elvis / ice cream

'Hold it,' said Barnie. 'What's that about Elvis?'

Mack took it back to the right station, turned up the sound.

The young Elvis, ripping through *Jailhouse Rock*, was replaced by his older self, squeezed into his white rhinestone-studded jumpsuit, and crooning *Always on my mind.* A voice-over announced, *Three weeks after his death, the mourning goes on . . .*

'It's an anniversary show,' said Tam. 'Three whole weeks.'

A man being interviewed, Southern redneck, maybe fifty, was saying, 'Elvis is the King. Always was. Always will be. Won't never be another one like him.'

A young woman, wild-eyed, raved at the camera. 'He's not dead! I know it. I saw it with my inner vision. He went in a UFO to Alpha Centauri, and at the Second Coming he'll return with Christ and Buddy Holly, and they'll be a new holy trinity ruling in majesty from Graceland.'

'Woh!' said Mack. 'Too much!'

Now Jimmy Carter was talking. 'Elvis Presley changed the face of American culture. He was unique and irreplaceable.'

Cut to pilgrims filing past the gates of Graceland, laying wreaths, tributes. The funeral cortege. Pall-bearers almost staggering under the weight of the coffin.

The King is dead, said the voice-over. *Long live the King. More coming up, after this.*

'I heard somebody was selling a bootleg film of the autopsy,' said Barnie.

'Jesus!' said Tam. 'That's sick!'

'Hey, this is America!'

On the screen, a fat actor was going berserk over a special offer on hi-fi equipment. He jumped up and down, scattered dollar bills in the air, yelled, 'Crazy Eddy! His prices are INSANE!'

'Let's play,' said Barnie.

'Sure,' said Mack, turning off the sound. 'Enough is enough.'

On the way back on the subway, Tam was hustled by the same man he'd encountered on the way in, selling his Deaf Education cards. This time Tam gave him a quarter, kept the card. The man grunted what Tam took to be thanks, moved on.

The rehearsal had gone well, once they had finally got down to it. Barnie was good at leading them, talked them through it in terms of visualization. 'OK, we're moving up now, a progression, like climbing a big wide flight of stairs . . .'

'Giant steps to heaven!' Mack had said.

'Up and out.'

And Tam had hit a melody that he couldn't believe, that seemed to have come from nowhere, sang itself through his soprano, full and rich and achingly sweet. And he'd played it again, and 'Hey!' Barnie had shouted. 'Nice!'

When they'd finished Mack had said, 'Great wee

tune you came up with there. You should call it Gasoline Apple.'

'That's good!' Tam had said. 'I like it. Good!'

Now he fumbled in his pocket for a pen, wrote the sequence of notes along the edge of the Deaf Alphabet card. He didn't think he would forget it, but better to be safe.

He hated the way the dark came down, so quick and sudden. One minute it was day, the next it was night, with nothing in between. That was one thing he missed about home, the slow fade of twilight. Just a song. Love's old sweet.

On the last block before their apartment he stopped to buy pizza. Ruby never seemed to feel much like cooking these days, and usually he didn't mind, actually enjoyed taking it on. But tonight he couldn't be bothered with the time it would take.

He ordered a whole pie – mushrooms / peppers / black olives. He watched Carlo, the owner, sprinkle on the toppings, shovel the pie into the oven. He ordered a small Coke while he waited, sat behind the fan at the end of the counter.

'Hot!' said Carlo, raising his voice against the noise. Above the clank of the oven, the whirr of the fan backed up by streetnoise through the open door, the radio, turned up loud, was blasting out Lou Reed, *Walk on the Wild Side*.

'Bad enough out there,' said Tam. 'In here must be hellish.'

'Right,' said Carlo. 'Is like a furnace.'

Tam shut his eyes for a moment, breathed in the warm fresh-bread smell of the dough. The mix of herbs – oregano, garlic, thyme – always brought back the summer they'd spent in France. Ratatouille Niçoise. Scent of the hillside. A weird time but good.

Carlo sang along with the radio, word-perfect.

'A hustle here and a hustle there
New York City is the place where

300

> *They say, Hey babe*
> *Take a walk on the wild side'*

Tam was singing the *doo-doo-doo* chorus out in the
street, walking that last block home, when a soccer ball
bounced across towards him. A few young Greek boys
had been kicking it around, and one of them had sent a
wild miskick in Tam's direction. Even with his kit-bag
slung over his shoulder, and the pizza in its box
carried high on his fingertips like a tray, he still had the
poise and balance to bring the ball down and trap it,
chip it back across the road.

'Pele!' shouted one of the boys. 'Cosmos!'

Tam laughed, waved. He had been to watch the
Cosmos once, against some international all-star eleven.
But the game had just been an exhibition, all skill and
no passion. He had sat on his plastic seat, watching
Pele and Beckenbauer and the rest go through the
motions, as electronic organ accompanied attacking
moves, and cheerleaders flounced on the track, and
messages flashed on a huge video screen – COSMOS!
and GOAL! and ALL RIGHT! And round about him
families on a night out ate hot dogs, drank Coke. And
Tam remembered halftime pies and Bovril, and standing on the terracing at Ibrox in the pouring rain,
soaked to the skin and shouting himself hoarse on a
New Year's Day, long ago and half a world away.

He realized he was tired, had a headache beginning,
tight in his shoulders and neck. Just being in the city
could do that to him. The radio report, giving the
pollution count, had said that today the air was only
marginally unsafe. He rotated his head, felt something
click where the neck met the skull. If Ruby was in a
good mood he might ask her to work on it. She had
learned *shiatsu* massage, knew all the acupressure
points.

As he turned the key in the door, he knew she wasn't
home yet. The place was dark, empty. He had a
momentary sense of it, stark. This was how it would be
if he lived alone. He sat in the kitchen where the

striplight was too bright, ate half the pizza while it was still warm. Then he took a shower, let the rush of water batter the top of his head, bent forward to let it hit his neck, then across the shoulders and down the length of the spine, and back up to that point, the join with the skull, convergence of nerve-ends, and up again to the crown. He turned the jet up full, let the pressure smash down on him. It needled, drummed, on the roof of his brain, where the gap had once been, fontanelle, before it had closed, gates of the prison-house, closed tight, location of the crown chakra, sahasrara, thousand-petal lotus, doorway through to silence, light, if only he could batter it open.

To finish he turned off the hot, yelped and couldn't catch his breath at the sudden shock of the cold. He towelled himself dry, changed into a clean T-shirt, shorts made out of old denims, cut down ragged at the knee. Through in the living room he lay back on the couch, feet up. They hadn't been able to do much to the room, make it their own. It still belonged to their landlord, the friend of Ruby's father, and his heavy old furniture bulked, took up too much space. But the first thing Ruby had done was buy half a dozen plants in clay pots, place them about the room. They staked out the territory, defined it as theirs. And a few things had survived all their travelling, were scattered here and there – posters, a Moroccan rug, a sandalwood figure of Krishna. Tam was resting his head on one of Ruby's Indian cushion-covers, decorated with little mirrors. It had lasted well, though a few of the mirrors were cracked, broken in half. From upstairs came the sound of a violin, the old man on the next floor playing *Moonlight and Roses*. Tam's head still ached. He turned over on his side. The cushion-cover still smelled faintly, faintly, of patchouli.

He jumped up, wakened out of a dream he was already forgetting. Something terrible had happened to Ruby. But here she was, coming in the door.

'You OK?' she asked.

She was here. She seemed fine. Unharmed.

'Guess I was conked,' he said. 'Must be the heat.'

'Have a good day?' she asked.

'Sure,' he said, stretching, rubbing his neck. His head still hurt. 'Hey, I got pizza. Left half for you.'

'I already ate,' she said. 'Tony took me to this great Japanese place.'

Of course. He remembered. Tony.

'Had sushi, noodles, tempura.'

'The works.'

'Right.'

Tony ran a gallery, in SoHo. Tam had met him through Barnie, at a party. He had been talking about happenings, not as something dead, played out, but as the coming thing. He talked of installations, performance art. Tam had told him about Ruby's work and he'd been interested, wanted to meet her, to talk. Tam had set it up.

'So how'd it go?'

'Good,' she said. 'I told him about my stuff and he liked it. Said if I can come up with something he'll be open.'

'That's great!'

She nodded. She still looked pale, tired. But he saw something there, in her eyes, just a glimmer. And he saw that she didn't trust it, was guarded, unsure. But still it was there, a spark, light, hope.

Ruby had a healing touch, even now, when she wasn't fully strong in herself. She had worked on the pressure-points on the soles of his feet, sent waves of ease through his whole system, numbed the deep root of the pain.

Now she lay beside him, asleep and turned away, as he lay awake, too hot, and wishing she'd been able to reach deeper still, numb his brain, stop its fevered racing. And always it was the same dark malaise, the same nagging discomfort at the edge of his awareness,

303

that came at this bleak ebb of the night, till he couldn't shut it out, had to face it as the same cycle of images played itself out again, reran the night of the blackout.

The blackout came in the middle of a gig and they all found it funny, especially Ben who was flying anyway. Tam heard him shriek and laugh in the sudden total dark. 'Yoh man! What the fuck!' Then he started singing the old Ray Charles number, *Take these chains from my heart.* 'This is what it's like for that cat all the time. Can't see a fucking thing!'

The club owner came out, shining a flashlight. He had no idea what the problem was, or how long it would take to set it right. If they wanted to leave their equipment, he would make sure it was locked up safe. Tam kept his instruments with him, packed in his kitbag, and they headed out with three girls that Ben had in tow. One of them, Liza, stumbled at the door, grabbed hold of Tam's arm, laughed.

The street was like a war-zone, cars smashed, shops being looted. Fires had been started in alleyways, on vacant lots, made the whole scene infernal, grotesque. A fire hydrant, ripped out, gushed water across the street.

'Word is the whole city's down,' said Barnie. 'Some power point got hit by lightning.'

'Wild!' yelled Ben. And it was. Total chaos, out of control. A man ran past carrying two ghettoblasters, one under each arm. Another followed with a TV set, staggered and dropped it, and the screen shattered to bits on the sidewalk. He left it, ran back the way he had come. Round the corner, they saw him trying to fight his way into Crazy Eddy's, but by now the place had been gutted, picked clean. A display banner, its giant red letters screaming INSANE, lay trampled. Further along the block, a car showroom was pillaged, new cars broken into, started up somehow and driven away.

Ben was in a shop doorway, his hand up to his face. Tam went over, saw he was snorting coke.

'Hey man! Want a hit?'

And although Tam usually left the stuff alone, these days didn't even smoke dope with the rest, the manic charged-up energy of the night was getting to him, and he stepped into the doorway. 'What the hell!'

The hit was a rush of white light straight to the cerebral cortex, a sudden searing clarity. 'Man!' he said to Ben, expressing it. 'Woh!'

In the street the madness continued. Outside a supermarket a fight had broken out, loaded trollies were overturned.

'Things fall apart,' he announced, and he turned towards Mack, expecting a response. 'Come on, man. Give me the bit about mere anarchy being loosed upon the world.'

'Don't know that one,' said Mack. 'Is it another Sex Pistols number?'

When he came down from his brief high, Tam realized there was no way he could get home. 'No problem' said Liza. We're all going back to Barnie's place.'

Ruby turned over, moaned something in her sleep. Tam lay still, stared at nothing. He kept his eyes wide open, unblinking as long as he could, till he couldn't hold it any longer and they twitched and his eyelids flickered shut. And each time he blinked he forced his eyes open again. He'd read it somewhere. A trick, a technique, for getting to sleep. And he held it for less and less time, the blinks came closer together till his eyes stayed shut.

He was going under again, and this was the hard part he didn't want to face. It came at him in vivid images as memory edged into dream and he didn't know which was which.

Fire on the wasteground, water running in the

streets. Shattered windows. White light to his brain. Back to Barnie's place, Liza on his arm. Barnie finding candles. Miraculous. A circle of light. And sounds, a ghettoblaster that ran on batteries. Liza emptying a cassette-rack on the carpet, picking out Dylan's *Desire*, playing it loud. Liza sitting beside him on the couch. Ben passing round a joint, then disappearing for a long time to the bathroom where they knew he was fixing up, would be zonked into oblivion. And that meant simple arithmetic. *Ah ha!* Three of them and three girls. And Liza turning the tape and coming back to him. Liza with her long hair hennaed red, her face a white mask and eyelids painted black. And Dylan singing *Isis, O Isis, you're a mystical child.* Liza with her earrings, cheap amulet round her neck. Arms round him, pulling him down. *She said, You gonna stay? I said, If you want me to, yeah!* The others gone, faded out, and Liza moving on top of him.

Waking, the candles burned down, the music stopped. Liza beside him, turned away.

But no, that had been Liza, this was Ruby. This was now.

He sat up, still halfway between the two realities. Ruby slept deep. He got out of bed, padded through to the living room, and sat there naked, in the dark.

The morning after the blackout he had come home and found the place empty, no sign of Ruby. A knock had come at the door and he'd thought it must be her. She had gone to the shops maybe, forgotten to take her key. But when he answered it he did a quick double-take. Not Ruby, but the old lady next door, Mrs Heller.

'Hi,' she said. 'I thought I heard you come in. Guess you just got home.'

'Yeah. With the blackout. Got kind of stranded.'

'Yeah. The blackout. So, you didn't hear about what happened?'

'Happened?'

'Listen, your wife is gonna be OK. I called the hospital a half hour ago.'

'Hospital?'

'Maybe I should come in. You wanna sit down?'

And she told him the whole story. Just after the power-cut she had heard the noise and what sounded like a scream but she hadn't paid any heed, what with the racket from the street, the car horns and people yelling. But after a while had come a tapping at the door, and she hadn't answered, had sat there, too scared.

'The things you read, you know.'

'I know,' he said, numbed, staring at her.

'Anyway,' she said. 'Next thing it's like somebody's crying out there. A woman's voice, and she's saying *Please, God!* Like that. And I get my flashlight and I open the door this much, with the chain on the bolt. And I look out and it's your wife.'

'Ruby.'

'And she looks terrible.'

'God!'

Then the old woman came out with the rest of it, all in a rush. Ruby was in the shower when the lights went out. She slipped and fell. She managed to get up, pull her wrap around her, drag herself to the door.

'She gets in here, she collapses. What do I do? I call the hospital but what with all that craziness going on out there the ambulance takes forever. But finally it gets here and they take her away.'

Tam shut his eyes, tried to breathe deep. He knew what was coming, what the old woman was trying to say to him. Her hands had a life of their own, nervous.

'Listen, you oughtta call the hospital. I got the number. You can use my phone.'

'You said you called earlier. What did they say?'

'You should call.'

'Did she . . . lose the baby?'

The old woman nodded.

'Call.'

He thought he was beginning to get over it, but then

307

came nights like this, when the guilt and the loss still ate at his innards like some two-headed beast, tore his sleep to shreds.

Rehearsing at Barnie's hadn't helped, then coming home to the empty flat. It was all still too close to the surface. He could rationalize the whole thing away. What had happened with the girl Liza had been nothing. He hadn't even seen her again, probably never would. It was meaningless, unrelated to anything else. But then there was that other, deeper knowledge, the primitive certainty that the baby's death had been retribution visited on him. He knew this was nonsense, knew it was absolutely true.

The irony was he had argued Ruby out of blaming herself for the miscarriage, argued the utter uselessness of guilt.

'It was my fault,' she'd said. 'I should have been more careful.'

'For Christ's sake!' he'd said. 'It was an accident. Pure and simple.'

'If I'd kept my cool.'

'If If If! Where does it end? If you hadn't been in the shower. If there hadn't been a blackout. If lightning hadn't struck a transformer. Who you going to blame for that?'

'It's what they call an Act of God.'

'So blame God!'

'Yeah,' she'd said quietly. 'I do.'

This would pass. Like everything else. Tonight there had been that faint glimmer of light he'd seen in Ruby, the first since it had all happened. He'd been right to arrange the meeting with Tony. Maybe something would come of it.

He switched on a table lamp. His pale skinny body was somehow strange to him, alien, something he inhabited. He was tired.

Beside the lamp were a few things he'd emptied from his pockets – a little money, his keys, scraps of paper. Among them, folded and creased, was the card he'd picked up back at that concert in the church at Columbia. *Keep your heart's door wide open.* Stillness. Oasis.

Beside the card was the one he'd been given today on the subway, with the deaf alphabet, the words spelled out on the back. *Good. Bad. Perfect. Chance. Girl. Boy. Sweetheart. Marry. Right. OK. No. Good.* Along the edge was his reminder to himself of the tune that had come to him from nowhere. Gasoline Apple. He put down the card and switched off the light, went back through and lay down again beside Ruby, moving very carefully so he wouldn't wake her.

2

George had been half asleep in front of the TV when the knock came at the door. He wondered for a moment where Mary was, then remembered she was through in the kids' room, trying to get John to sleep without waking the baby. The knock came again, louder, more insistent. It annoyed him. Nobody ever came, unexpected, to visit. It could only be Jehovah's Witnesses, or men selling locks or insurance.

There were two of them, hard-looking, in dark suits, overcoats.

'Mr George Wilson?' The one who spoke was stocky, thickset, grey hair cropped short. The one behind him was taller and younger, dark.

'That's right,' said George, confused.

'Police.' He held up a card, the way they did on TV. 'Special Branch. Wonder if we could have a word?'

'What about?' said George. 'What's wrong?'

'Nothing wrong,' said the man. 'Just want a wee chat, that's all.'

'But what about? I don't understand.'

'It's about your brother.'

'Malcolm?'

'Got any other brothers have you?'

309

'No.'

'Well then.'

'But I haven't seen Malcolm for years. Don't even know where he is.'

'Listen,' said the younger man. 'Maybe if we could come in.'

'But my wife's just got the kids off to sleep.'

'We weren't planning to take the place apart,' said greyhair. 'Not just yet.' The mouth smiled, but not the eyes. 'Like I said. Just a word. A wee chat.'

'What is it George?' said Mary, behind him.

'Mrs Wilson? Sorry to bother you. We're police officers.'

'Name of God!' she said. 'What's happened?'

He tried smiling again. 'Nothing. There's no problem. Can we come in a minute?'

In the living room, the two men sat forward on the couch, arms resting on their knees. They were completely out of place. An intrusion.

'That's the thing,' the older one was saying. 'Police at the door, folk think the worst. We get it all the time. And mostly it's just routine enquiries we're making. Nothing to worry about.'

'Nothing at all,' said the other one.

'So, we're just trying to contact your brother.'

'Want to talk to him.'

'Think he might be able to help with our enquiries.'

It was true. They really did talk like that.

'What enquiries?' said George.

'I'm afraid we can't go into that. Reasons of security.'

'No real need for you to know.'

'Now. When was the last time you saw Malcolm?'

'I told you. Years ago.'

'You haven't seen him recently?'

'No.'

'Hasn't been in touch?'

'Written?'

'Phoned?'

'No.'

'Not a very close family then?'

'Not really. Me and Malcolm never got on.' He shrugged. 'Just lost touch. He moved away and that was that.'

'Where did he move to?'

'Well, first he went to Ireland. That would be five, maybe six years ago.'

'Why Ireland?'

'Don't know. He had a girlfriend. Claire. They went there together.'

'So at that time you were still in contact with him?'

'No. Like I said, we lost touch.'

'So how do you know all this about Ireland?'

'Well, I met him not long after that. Just bumped into him in the street.'

'In Glasgow?'

'That's right.'

'When would that be?'

'Can't remember.'

'Try.'

It was an order, a threat.

'Time's funny, you know.'

They waited.

'I suppose it was four years ago. In the summer.'

'Summer of '73?'

'Right.'

'And he'd already been to Ireland?'

'Aye.'

'So why was he back in Glasgow?'

'Don't know. Said he was just visiting. Business or something.'

'What kind of business?'

'He never said.'

The intake of breath was long-suffering, patient.

'And you haven't seen him since this chance meeting in the street?'

'No.'

'Haven't heard from him?'

'No. I think he went to London.'

311

'What makes you think that?'

'Don't know. Maybe somebody said.'

'Somebody?'

'I don't know. I can't remember.'

'And he definitely hasn't been in touch?'

The same questions, again.

'No.'

'Not a word?'

'Nothing.'

They let a silence hang there. And this time it was Mary who broke it.

'Except.'

'Except what?' said George.

'The telegram.'

'What telegram's this?' said the older man. The look he threw at George was an accusation, a charge of withholding information.

'Just the one he sent when we got married,' she said. 'Wedding telegram, you know.'

'That's right,' said George. 'I'd forgotten all about that.' He hated the way they made him feel guilty, for no reason. 'Came as quite a surprise.'

'Is that something you'd hold on to?' asked the man. 'Keepsake sort of thing?'

'We did keep it,' said Mary. 'Kept them all. Stuck them in the album with the photos.'

'Would you mind if we had a look at it?'

She went through to the bedroom, came back with the album, open at the page. George looked at the telegram over the man's shoulder. 'That's it there.'

All the best to my wee brother. Never thought you had it in you.

'Quite a surprise,' he said again. 'Out the blue.'

Greyhair was showing the telegram to the younger man. They seemed to be interested in the date, and the name of the London office it had been sent from.

'Can we borrow this?' he asked.

'Our wedding album?'

'Just the telegram. The book's looseleaf, so we can just take the page out.'

As he spoke, he was prising open the hinges, easing out the page. 'We'll take care of it. Get it back to you.' He turned over the page, looked at the two snapshots on the other side. A group shot, outside the church. A close-up of George and Mary, their tense smiles held fixed.

'Nice,' he said, trying his own smile again. 'So that's that.' He handed the album back to Mary, gave the page to the younger man who held it carefully. 'Sorry to have bothered you. And thanks for your time.'

At the door he stopped. 'If you *should* happen to hear from your brother, don't mention this, eh? And let us know.' He took a small card from his pocket, scribbled his name and phone number, gave it to George. 'I'm sure we understand each other. No love lost between you and Malcolm anyway, am I right? And you could be in trouble if you help him out. So.' He shook George's hand, the familiar grip, pressing with the thumb. George supposed it was meant to reassure him, but the feeling in his stomach was mistrust, unease.

As he closed the door behind them, the baby started to cry.

'Christ! Give us peace!' said Mary. 'You and your bloody family!'

His father talked and George listened.

'Ach aye, they came round here as well. Just about battered the door down. Looking for that clown. That headcase. Don't know why they thought they'd find him here. I told them. No uncertain terms. Bloody no-user. If I never see him again it'll be too soon. I think they got the picture. No love lost. The older one seemed to understand. Sharper than a serpent's tooth he said. Probably got a son of his own that's turned out a bad lot. That's the way it goes he said. *Que sera sera*.

313

Seemed a decent enough bloke. Gave me the old handshake. The grip. Hele and conceal, eh? Never reveal. Decent enough. But something a wee bit sleekit about the eyes. And a bit heavyhanded the way they came barging in with all their questions. When did I see him last? When did I hear from him? Trying to trip me up. As if I knew anything. As if I cared. Never seen hide nor hair of him. Not for years. And never a word. Scrape of a pen even. Nothing. I don't know. Makes you wonder. Families.'

'And how's the weans? Wee John got over the cold? And Caroline still all right? Six months already. Hard to believe. And John nearly three. That's where you really see it, in the kids. See how quick it goes. No time at all. You should bring them round again. Keep your mother happy. She's been bad with her nerves, but I'm sure she'd cope all right if you just brought them for a wee while. Mary too, if she'd come. But I don't suppose she would. Still no talking to me, eh? The thing is, it was nothing personal. Just the situation. Didn't want you to go making a mess of things. Nice enough lassie. Even if she won't turn. No harm I suppose, as long as you bring the kids up right. That's the main thing. Bring them up in the faith. God knows we tried. Then you look at that nutter. Police round at the door. And you wonder where you went wrong. I don't know. You do your best. Scrimp and scrape. And for what? Thankless. Don't know what the world's coming to. Now the factory shutting down. Folk laid off. I'm just taking the redundancy money and packing it in. Chucking it. Early retirement. Golden handshake. Too old to start again. You'll be all right though. Get another job no bother. I'll pass the word that you're looking. Land on your feet. No bother at all. See you right. Ach aye, if we can't look out for one another it's a bad day.'

George supposed his father was right. He would be able to find a job. No shortage of work. And with connections, a word here. No bother. Easy. Say no more. But still, the worry was there, nagged at him.

'You should start looking now,' said Mary.

'Won't be happening for another year,' he said. 'Maybe more.'

'No point in waiting till you're out on your ear.'

'I'll find something soon. You'll see.'

'Unless *you* want to look after the kids, let me go back to work.'

'No chance!'

'You're sounding more like your old man every day.'

'What's that supposed to mean?'

'Set in your ways.'

He was too tired for this, didn't want to know.

'Don't start,' he said.

'Start what?'

'Being so pass-remarkable. Again.'

'Few home truths,' she said. 'Never hurt anybody.'

But they did, and she knew it. She had been like this since Caroline had been born. Fine one minute, stabbing at him the next. He was never on solid ground with her, never knew where he stood.

'OK,' he said. 'Just leave it.'

'That's your answer to everything, isn't it? Just leave it. It'll go away. Anything for a quiet life.'

'What *is* this?'

'Nothing!' she said. 'Nothing at all!'

From the pitch of her voice he knew she was cranking herself up, would end up screaming at him.

'I don't understand,' he said.

'No, you don't,' she said. 'Not one damn thing!' And she was out of the room, and he was picking up a cup and throwing it, with a sudden rage he couldn't believe, hurling it at where she'd been standing, watching it smash against the wall.

Shaken, he kneeled down to pick up the bits, without thinking used his hand to sweep up the smallest of them, nicked the tip of his finger on a sharp edge.

'Shite!' He dumped the broken pieces in the bin. He

looked at his finger, squeezed a glob of blood from the tiny cut, licked it.

Somebody rattled at the letterbox.

'Christ!'

Mary shouted through, 'You get it. And tell them to go away. We don't know anything about your stupid brother!'

But when he opened the door, it was a young man and woman standing there.

'Hello!' said the man, smiling at him. 'We're from your local church. 'I wonder if—'

'This is a bad time,' said George.

'It certainly is!' said the man. 'And that's why—'

'No, I mean it's a bad time for me. You've come at a bad time. Awkward like.'

'Oh I see!' said the man. 'Sorry!'

'So.'

'Well. Maybe we could call again. Some other time.'

'No it's OK. Thanks all the same.'

The man's smile faltered.

'Would you like one of these?' said the woman, handing him a leaflet, a tract.

'Fine,' he said. 'Thanks.'

He closed the door, stood listening as they made their way up the stairs to the next landing.

He looked at the tract. *The City of God.* And under the title, the words of an old hymn he remembered from Sunday School.

In that city
Built four square

The text was about building God's City on earth, using bricks of Faith and Love, Hope and Trust. A drawing showed smiling children working on it, all different nationalities, with trowels and mortar, hods full of the bricks.

He turned it over and saw a smear of blood on the back, remembered his cut finger, licked it again.

Mary was through in the kids' room, looking out the window at the street.

'Who was it?' she said, without turning round.

'Local God Squad. Trying to save us.'

It was almost dark in the room. They both spoke quietly, not to wake the kids.

'Are you coming through?' he said.

'Sure. In a minute.' But she didn't move, stayed with her back to the room, looking out. Her voice sounded strange, as if she had been crying. The children breathed heavy. A dog barked in the street. Somebody kicked a tin can. She was right. He didn't understand one damn thing. Another drop of blood had formed on his finger, and again he licked it, tasted it salt and warm.

As he came out of the factory gates, George saw a man in a hooded anorak, coming towards him. Instead of passing, the man stopped right in front of him, pulled back the hood. George looked again and saw it was Malcolm.

'Should see your face!'

'Well,' said George. 'It's been a while.'

'Suppose so.'

'So what is it?'

'What's what?'

'You didn't just happen-to-be-passing.'

'No.'

'So what do you want?'

'Straight to the point, eh?'

'Listen Malcolm, I haven't got time for this. I've already had enough aggravation over you.'

'What do you mean?'

'Only the Special Branch round at the house, that's all.'

Malcolm tensed, stared at him. '*Your* house? When?'

'Last week.'

'What did they want?'

'Asked if I'd seen you.'

'What did you tell them?'

'What *could* I tell them? I haven't seen you for years.'

'Good.'

'They went to the old man's house as well.'

'Bet that got up his nostrils, eh?'

'It's not funny. I've got kids you know.'

Malcolm nodded. 'Listen, George, I need a favour.'

'You're not roping me into anything.'

'I just need to borrow a few quid, that's all. I wouldn't ask if it wasn't desperate.'

'I might have known.'

'Just whatever you can manage. Fifty would be great.'

'Fifty quid! You're kidding!'

'There's other folk I can ask. I just thought. Family and that. How about twenty?'

'I haven't got it!'

'And even if you did.'

'It's out the question.'

'Fine,' said Malcolm, his voice quiet. 'I know where I stand.'

'Always did know how to make me feel bad,' said George.

'Not me,' said Malcolm. 'Your conscience.'

'What sort of trouble is it you're in?'

'Nothing you'd understand.' The way he had always talked to him, talked down. 'There's a war on, you know. Whether you realize it or not.' He pulled up his hood. 'See you.'

George stood watching him go, felt sick in his stomach, as if he had been punched.

'Fifty quid?' said Mary. 'Where did he think you'd get fifty quid to throw away?'

'I think he's just lost touch with reality,' said George. 'Got no idea.'

'How does it happen?' she said. 'Intelligent boy. Educated.'

George shook his head. 'He was always a bit mental to tell you the truth.'

'Mental's the word,' said Mary. 'Still, with a bit of

luck he'll have got the message. Won't bother you again.'

At dinnertime George came out for a breath of air. The stodge he had eaten, spam fritter and chips, lay heavy on his stomach, and he wanted to walk it off. The air was cold, first real chill of autumn. He should have worn his coat. But if he kept his walk quick, brisk.

Standing at the gate, where Malcolm had been the day before, was the crewcut policeman, waiting.

'Hoped I might catch you,' said the man. 'A word?'

They walked round behind the factory, down to the path beside what had once been a burn. Now it had almost completely dried up, a slimy mudbed used as a dump, a rubbish tip. The smell was worse than ever. George had come here once with Mary, when she'd told him she was pregnant. They'd seen a seagull catch a mouse. It didn't seem real now. Something he had dreamed.

'Smoke?' said the man, offering.

'No thanks.'

The man lit up, sucked in smoke. 'So, have you seen him?'

'Sorry?'

'Have you seen your brother?'

He probably knew. Somebody must have seen them. A word.

'I saw him yesterday. Out in the street there.'

'He came here to meet you?'

'Suppose so.'

'What did he want?'

'Said he was skint. Wanted to borrow money.'

'How much?'

'Few quid.'

'And did you give it to him?'

'No. Told him I didn't have it. And it's true. I don't.'

'How did he react?'

George shrugged. 'Didn't say much. Wasn't too pleased.'

'Did he say he'd be in touch again? Give you an address?'

'No.'

'Not even a phone number?'

'Nothing.'

'Didn't mention any names?'

'No.'

'You sure?'

'Of course I'm sure! What is this?'

'OK,' said the man. 'I'll be straight with you. On the level.'

The words were a formula, a sign.

'Right.'

'I'll keep it simple. You know your brother's politics. He's been dabbling for a long time. Only now he's in with some real nutters. Kind of folk that stop at nothing. Just want to destroy. Take a situation and use it. Right now they're working with the IRA.'

'Dear God!'

'I don't have to spell it out. You read the papers. These people don't mess about.'

'No.'

'Malcolm's out his depth. Let's face it, he's just a wanker. But these people he's working with, they're the real thing. They're the ones we want.'

'And Malcolm?'

'We want to talk to him. See if we can do business. Seriously, you'd be doing us a favour if you put us in touch with him.'

'And how could I do that?'

'If he contacts you again.'

'But he won't.'

'If he does.'

'If.'

'Get an address, a number, anything.'

'I'll see.'

'Here's my hand on it,' said the man. 'A sure pledge, eh?'

320

'Aye, sure,' said George, not sure at all, but shaking hands anyway.

The food had made him feel squeamish, greasy. He needed to wash his face and hands in hot water.

He knew he could never talk it out with his father. There was too much there. Instead, one night when his father hadn't come to the Lodge, George spoke to Mr Bennett, asked if he could have a word.

'Sure thing, son. Nothing wrong is there?'

George shook his head.

After the meeting, they went to the pub and George told him the story. The old man knocked back his half, sipped at his pint, dragged at his cigarette, picked a shred of tobacco from his lip.

'Hell of a thing all the same.'

George nodded. 'The thing is, I really didn't like this policeman. Didn't take to him.'

'Didn't trust him?'

'Oh, he gave me the handshake and that. But still. Doesn't mean much nowadays.'

'I wouldn't say that son. Still counts for something.'

'I was reading about these trials in London. Porn Squad detectives taking their cut. Making all their contacts through the Lodge.'

'Terrible that. Mind you, some of the folk that put them away were on the square as well. It's just, you get folk that'll misuse anything. Rotten apple in every barrel.'

George laughed. 'Sounds like my old man talking about Malcolm!'

'So. Do you know what it is he's mixed up in?'

'Not exactly.'

'Must be political, if it's the Special Branch.'

'Something to do with Ireland.'

'Uh huh.' Mr Bennett ordered up another round, their third.

'You won't mention this to anybody?' said George. The drink was beginning to affect him.

'Not me,' said Mr Bennett. 'My lips are sealed!' He shooshed, his finger to his lips.

'You're all right,' said George. 'It's good to talk to somebody about it. It's just not knowing what's for the best.'

'Stick to your masonic principles, son. You can't go wrong.'

'Aye but.'

'Brotherly Love. Relief. Truth.'

This was difficult, holding his thought. 'But where do you draw the line?'

'Am I my brother's keeper sort of thing?'

'Exactly.'

'Tough one.'

'And Malcolm is my actual brother.'

'Man to man the world owre
Shall brothers be for a that!'

'Then there's this polis.'

'That you don't trust.'

'And he's talking principles as well. Law of the land. Defence of the realm. Preserving a way of life.'

'Hobson's choice, eh?'

'Sorry?'

'Whatever you do is wrong.'

'Hiding to nothing.'

'It's like that old lawyer's question. Have you stopped beating your wife yet?'

'Eh?' All he'd done was throw a cup, and it hadn't hit her.

'Answer aye or no to it, you're still in trouble.'

'Oh aye. I see what you mean.'

'No easy answers.'

'No.'

When he got home, Mary was listening to the radio. 'Lodge meeting must have went on late,' she said.

'Aye, well. Went for a wee snifter.'

'I'd never have guessed.'

'Had a wee talk to Mr Bennett.'

'What about?'

'Och, you know. This and that. Nothing much.'

'All secret stuff was it?'

'Not at all. Just a blether.'

'Oh well.'

He became aware of the radio. 'What you listening to?'

'The wireless.'

'No! But what's the programme?'

'Just music. Golden Oldies. This is the Beatles. *In my life.*'

'Thought it was familiar.'

'You're not really that into music, are you?' she said. 'It's funny. I've only just realized it.'

'Well, I sometimes hear things I quite like. But I don't remember them. I mean I wouldn't go out and buy a record.'

Mary laughed. 'I quite like it but I wouldn't buy it and I'll give it five!'

'Eh?'

'*Juke Box Jury*. Remember?'

'Vaguely.'

'Janice Nicholls. It's gorra good beat. You could dance to it.'

'Any chance of a cup of tea?' he said.

'There's some in the pot. Shouldn't be stewed. No like you!'

'What?'

'A joke!'

'Oh aye.' He poured himself a cup, carefully. 'Kids OK?'

'Fine. Got them down ages ago.'

'You wonder sometimes, don't you?'

'What?'

'How they'll turn out. What they'll grow up into.'

'What *were* you talking about in the pub?'

'Brotherhood and Truth.'

'God!'

'Yes?' He pronounced it deep and resonant, as if from far away. 'No, we left Him out of it! But funnily enough I was just thinking there about that leaflet thing they Christians left. About building the City. Foursquare. The kids and that.'

'What's brought this on? It's no like you talking like this. Even if it is the drink.'

'Mr Bennett's quite sort of wise you know. Quotes Burns and stuff.'

'Wise? How much *did* you have to drink?'

'Listen,' said George. 'I never told you. The polis came to see me at work. The older one that was round here.'

'Asking about your brother again?'

'That's right.'

'So what did you say?'

'Said I'd seen him in the street, that was all.'

'Christ! It's got nothing to do with you. You should just have kept your mouth shut.'

'The thing is,' he said.

'What?'

The radio was still playing, another old song he half knew. *Listen. Doo Da Doo. Do you want to know a secret?* Mary looked tired. He didn't know what he was trying to say.

'Nothing.'

He didn't really expect to see Malcolm again. But a week later, end of the day, there he was at the gate.

'Coast clear?' asked Malcolm, with almost a laugh.

'It's no funny,' said George. 'These guys could be hanging about.'

'What guys?' Now he was serious.

'Polis.'

'They've been round here?'

'One of them. A week ago.'

'Jesus Christ.' He took George by the arm. 'Come on. You can buy me a pint.'

In the pub, Malcolm sat at a corner table. 'Wild Bill

324

Hickok sort of style!' said George, setting down their drinks.

'What?'

'Back to the wall. Sit where you can see the door.'

'Makes sense,' said Malcolm, picking up his pint. 'Cheers.'

For a while they said nothing, sipped their drinks. At the far end of the bar, a voice was raised above a burst of laughter. *A menace so he is. Any more of that and he's barred.*

'Remember years ago,' said George at last, 'you roped me into that thing you were doing with the food. I got you leftovers out the supermarket.'

'Seemed like a good idea at the time!' said Malcolm. 'I guess I was more naive then.'

'Maybe that was no bad thing.' George looked at him straight. 'Have you come to ask for the money again?'

'I need all I can get. I'm going away.'

'Where?'

'Better if you don't know.'

'You know I don't believe in what you're doing.'

'What else is new?'

There was no point in this. No point at all.

'I should be going,' said George.

'Sure.'

'Listen. I don't know if this means anything, but when these guys came to the house, they took something, a page out our wedding album.'

'They what?'

'The telegram you sent us.'

Malcolm looked puzzled, then it fell into place. 'Oh, that's good!' he said, and let out a laugh again, bitter. 'That's a nice one!'

As he stood up to go, George took a five pound note from his pocket, shoved it into Malcolm's hand. 'I don't know why I'm doing this,' he said.

'Thanks,' said Malcolm. 'Cheers.'

'Right,' said George.

He shook his brother's hand, got out of the pub

quickly before he could think twice about it.

Brian stood at the staffroom window, stared out across the teeming playground at the bridges and flyovers, the tower blocks of the scheme. As usual he was the first one here. The times of the buses meant he had the choice of being twenty minutes early or fifteen minutes late. So he came early, switched on the kettle, stared out of the window.

This was his third year of it and he still felt a sinking, an emptiness inside, every time he stepped into the building. He felt it most here in the staffroom, with its smell of stale tobacco smoke and banda fluid, its tired atmosphere.

The window was stiff but he managed to budge it, shove it open a fraction to let in some air. The playground noise that had been muffled invaded the room. Voices carried clear. A yell. A shriek. Laughter. He thought he recognized a couple of his third-year girls.

'You're dead meat!'

'Fuck off or I'll waste ye.'

A boy's voice rose louder, singing to the tune of *Clementine*.

> *I'm a failure, I'm a failure*
> *I'm a fai-ai-ai-ailure.*

And cutting across that came the jangle of a radio, tinny at this distance, snarling out something punk.

The door behind him swung open and Knox, his principal teacher, breezed in.

'Still staring at far horizons? Thinking big thoughts?'

'You know, from the Maths department you can see Arthur's Seat.'

'Wasted on that lot,' said Knox.

'Isn't *scheme* a funny word to use for an estate? When you think about it?'

'Can't say I've ever thought about it.'

'The planners should really be called schemers!'

'You're not trying to tell me this place was planned!'

'Too much too quick,' said Brian. 'Never learned from the mistakes they made in Glasgow. Just throw up the houses and dump folk out here with bugger-all amenities.'

'O brave new world!' Knox looked past Brian, down at the playground, and screwed up his face with exaggerated disgust. 'Such creatures in it!'

'From up here it looks like one of those Lowry paintings,' said Brian. 'All the wee figures. Or maybe a Breughel.'

'Close up it's more like a Bosch. Positively infernal! Did I tell you I had to chuck an alsation out of my class the other day?'

'I've seen it wandering about the corridors,' said Brian. 'Seems quite a docile big thing.'

'That's hardly the point! Then one of my first year had his jacket set on fire in the playground. And yes, he *was* wearing it at the time!'

He pulled the window shut, turned the handle to lock it. 'Keep out the noise.'

'I *was* trying to let in some fresh air,' said Brian.

'Losing battle,' said Knox. 'Couple of fags, a whiff of body odour and the place is reeking again.'

The door opened and Sheila came in, followed by Janet. A swish of coats. Bags, papers dumped.

'Good morning *ladies*!' said Knox, pronouncing it in italics. They had pulled him up for calling them girls, said they were women.

'Is it?' said Sheila.

Knox enjoyed baiting them, as he did everyone else, but with them it always had a harder edge, was more barbed.

'Hi!' said Brian, and they nodded, smiled. 'Hi.'

With a rush of steam and a rattling of its lid, the kettle came to the boil. 'Good timing,' said Brian, switching it off.

'Where's my cup?' asked Knox, accusing.

'You don't think we'd use it, do you?' said Janet.

'Wouldn't even touch it,' said Sheila.

Brian joined in. 'Is that the one with the thick scum round the inside?'

'Talking about my CSE class again?' said Knox.

'Sorry?'

'Thick scum.'

'Not bad for a Monday morning.'

'But *have* you seen my cup?'

'I think I saw it crawling along the corridor of its own volition,' said Brian.

Sheila lifted a dish-towel, recoiled in horror. 'It's here! It was hiding under the towel!'

'Just about the level of wit I get from my first year,' said Knox.

'Thank you sir,' said Sheila, curtsying. 'So we've gone up in your estimation.'

Janet lit a cigarette. Knox gave Brian a knowing look. 'See?'

'What?' said Janet.

'Oh, nothing. It's just that Brian was trying to let in some fresh air. I told him not to waste his time.'

'Christ!' said Janet. 'It's getting that you can't light up without being made to feel guilty.'

'I had this idea for a novel,' said Brian, quickly. 'Kind of science fiction thing, about the last surviving smoker, being hounded to death!'

'Well I'll buy it,' said Janet. 'If you ever write it.'

'You could call it *Last Gasp*,' said Knox.

'That's good!' said Brian. 'I like it!'

Mary looked at her watch. 'Ian's cutting it fine. He better not be off again. I'm damned if I'm doing another please-take for him.'

'I'm afraid you'll have to, my dear,' said Knox. 'If you have a free period.'

'No I don't have to. And I'm not your dear. And how come Ian always gets sick at the start of the week?'

'He's allergic to Mondays,' said Sheila.

Ian arrived as the bell was ringing for registration.

'Another major crisis averted,' said Brian.

Ian looked puzzled. 'Eh?'

'Never mind.'

'Any of you girls got an aspirin?'

'Sorry,' said Sheila. 'Try these *boys*.' She and Janet laughed as they left the room.

'You look terrible,' said Knox. 'Been on the batter again?'

Ian groaned. 'Rough.'

'Itchy teeth?' said Knox. 'Sore hair?'

'You've been there!' said Ian.

Brian still couldn't believe the way they talked about drinking, compared hangovers with a kind of rueful delight. Somehow it was part of the way they defined themselves as men. It reminded Brian of how he had been at eighteen, and the thought depressed him.

He remembered the grey men who had taught him. This vicious bastard. That boring turd. A good education. Getting on. He picked up his briefcase, the pile of jotters he had marked at the weekend.

'Once more into the breach,' said Knox.

Ian had poured himself a coffee, gulped it down. 'Another day another dollar.'

'A dirty job,' said Brian. 'But somebody's got to do it.'

A frame from a comic. The Bash Street Kids. He took in the whole scene, registered a few of its individual components.

A cluster of girls, huddled round a magazine, giggling. Tracy, Mandy, Kathleen, Ann. Two boys playing headers with a ball of paper. Paul and Scott. Two more, grappling, Stephen grabbing Mark in a head-hold. Louise combing her hair. Garry climbing on to the windowsill. Jim waving a Hibs scarf. Davie shouting that the Stranglers were crap. Danny playing a screeching solo on invisible guitar as he jumped up and down, pogoing and headbanging. Brian had 3G for the double period before lunch. He was planning to read poetry with them.

'Right!' he shouted, slamming the door. 'Settle down!'

A few of them made moves towards their seats with a kind of ostentatious reluctance.

'OK girls, break it up. You can read that later. Right Stephen, you win by two submissions to a pinfall. Louise, your hair's lovely.'

Yells, wolfwhistles.

'Davie, I happen to think the Stranglers are not bad. And Jim, that's more than I can say for Hibs.'

A cheer, some booing.

'Danny, slamdancing causes brain damage. Do you want me to confiscate that guitar?'

'Eh? What guitar?'

'Garry, if you're going to jump out the window, do you mind opening it first? Right, come on the lot of you. Sit down and shut up!'

In their own time they subsided, broke it up, slid into their chairs, scraping them on the floor.

'So. We're going to look at some poetry.'

A few moans, an exaggerated yawn.

'Aw naw!'

'Poetry?'

'No again?'

'Boring!'

'We're talking about good stuff here. Edwin Morgan.'

'Who?'

'Never heard of him.'

'Listen, we've done three of his poems already! Can anybody tell me the name of one of them?'

Louise waved a languid hand in the air.

'Yes?'

' "*In the Snack Bar.*" '

'Very good.'

'That's the one about the old guy going for a pee, isn't it sir.'

'Yes Danny, that's exactly what it's about. And I don't know why the rest of you find that funny.'

Dear Christ, to be born for this!

'He wrote that dirty one as well sir, didn't he?'

'What dirty one's that Danny?'

'The one about Glasgow Green or something.'

'That is *not* dirty.'

'You said it was about homosexual rape.'

'God help me, so I did.'

'Well then.'

'That's one element in a very complex, beautiful and compassionate poem.'

'You could get your books for reading us dirty poems.'

'Complain to the Education Department. They set questions on it in the Higher.'

'I think that's terrible so it is.'

'Such a sensitive wee soul, aren't you Danny!'

'So I am.'

He raised his voice again. 'Listen! Right, that's better. Now, if you cast your minds back, all the way back to Friday, you'll remember we read another one called *A View of Things*.'

'Was it another dirty one?'

'No Danny, it was not! Anybody remember it?'

'What I love and what I hate.'

'That's the one, Tracy.'

'What I love about Hank is his string vest.'

'What I hate about the twins is their three gloves.'

'Good! Good! Well thank God some of you were listening.' Looking at the poem, he had a sudden, dazzling inspiration. 'What I'd like you to do is make up your own version of it.'

'Eh?'

'Write a poem?'

'It's too hard.'

'Nonsense. We can make it a joint effort. A class poem.'

'Is it for the school magazine?'

'Could be. If it's good enough.'

'Does that mean we'd all get our names in?'

'If you contribute a line, yes. Now stop trying to

331

stall me and let's get on with it.'

He turned to the blackboard, where STERILE PROMON-TORY was chalked. He took the duster and wiped it off.

'So, it's a simple formula.' He wrote across the top of the board.

WHAT I LOVE ABOUT (   ) IS ITS (   )

WHAT I HATE ABOUT (   ) IS ITS (   )

'It's just a matter of filling in these blanks with what *you* love and what *you* hate. Just think for a minute. Use your imagination.'

Their faces registered nothing.

'It can be anything. Anything at all.'

'I hate eggs,' said Louise.

'Well, that's a start. What do you hate about eggs?'

'I hate the yolk when it's all runny.'

'So how can we fit that into this formula?'

She thought about it. 'What I hate about egg is its runny yolk?'

'Right! Good!' He wrote it up, first line of the poem. 'And that's got a good sound to it too. If you remember the original, a lot of the lines depend on their sound. In fact, have a look at the copies I gave you. Might find some inspiration.'

'Havenae got it.'

'Lost it.'

'You never told us to bring it.'

'It should be in your folders. Has *anybody* got it?'

A shuffling through papers. A few hands raised.

'All right, you can share. Look at the one nearest you.'

'What's an ion engine?' asked Tracy.

'You tell me!'

'But you're the teacher.'

'Doesn't mean I know everything.'

'But.'

'What's an ion?' he asked her.

'It's from science. It's an atom or something.'

332

'With an electrical charge. And what's an engine?'

She looked guarded, as if it might be a trick question. 'Everybody knows what an engine is.'

'Right. It powers a machine. Drives it along. So what's an ion engine?'

'Don't know.'

Brian laughed. He was seeing an old hand-cranked duplicator, churning out pages of poetry. A pile of magazines with a psychedelic design on the cover. 'An ion engine is an ion engine is an ion engine!'

'Eh?'

'Words don't always mean just the one thing. They can spark things off in your imagination.'

Now her suspicions were confirmed. He was daft.

'So let's see what this can spark off. Get on with *our* poem. We've got a good first line here. How can we follow it up?'

Mandy raised her hand. 'What I hate about stew is its gristle.'

'Good!'

'What I hate about mince is its grease.'

'Yes, Ann, that's great.'

'What I hate about custard is its skin.'

'Yes, Davie, good.'

He scribbled up each line, pushed up the board.

Danny called out. 'What I hate about black pudding is its boke.'

'Boke?' he asked, over the laughter

'Aye. Black pudding gies me the dry boke.'

'All right!'

Danny looked pleased as Brian wrote it.

'What I hate about beer is its belch.'

'At your age, Stephen! Terrible!'

'What I hate about Coke is its fizz.'

'Fine, Louise. That's nice. These are all good lines. But can we not get away from eating and drinking? There must be more to your life than that! And how about something you love? It's been all hate hate hate so far.'

333

Danny grinned. 'What I love about Louise is her tits!'

This time there was uproar, and he had to shout. 'Come on now, keep it clean!'

'But you said *anything*!'

'I also said it might end up in the school magazine, Danny. Do you want to get me hung?'

Danny glared at him. 'Crapper!'

'That's enough!'

'What I hate about Danny is his rotten patter.'

'Louise! I don't want the whole thing brought down to that level! You can slag each other all you want outside, but right now can we just get on with this poem?'

'What I hate about school is its lessons.'

'All right, Mark.'

'What I love about Hibs is they're great!'

'OK Jim. Just have to change *their* to they're and that's fine. It's also the first LOVE.'

'Except mine,' said Danny, still in the huff.

Brian ignored him. 'So we're into football now. What about other things you like? How about music?'

'What I love about Reggae is its beat.'

'Good, Kathleen, good!'

Encouraged, she came up with another one. 'What I love about swimming is its splash.'

'Excellent!'

'What I love about Punk is its puke,' said Davie.

'God, we're fairly getting it, aren't we? Belch Boke Puke! Still, it's a good line. It *sounds* good. Punk and puke.'

'Do you *really* like the Stranglers sir?'

'Sook!' said Danny.

'They're all right,' said Brian. 'Got a good bass-player.'

'I've got a line,' said Danny. 'What I love about glue is its buzz!'

'You're determined to get this school magazine banned, aren't you?'

'I've got another one,' said Jim. 'What I love about Scotland is its football.'

'Nice!' said Brian, writing it up.

'What I hate about England is its voice.'

'That's a sharp one, Kathleen. Cutting!'

'What I hate about this place is it stinks!' said Danny.

'All right,' said Brian. 'I'll buy that.'

'Yes!' Danny jabbed both his fists in the air, then held them out, still clenched, to show Louise what he had written across the knuckles, tattooed in black felt-tip. Brian took a closer look, read LOVE on the left hand, HATE on the right.

'As if it's not hard enough getting them to write anything,' said Knox, 'without other departments handing out punishment essays. It just reinforces the idea that writing's an imposition, something inflicted on them.'

'We should retaliate,' said Ian. 'Give out punishment Maths exercises, or Physics experiments'

'Brilliant!' said Knox. 'Of course, it would make life easier if we just brought back the belt.'

'Should never have scrapped it in the first place. Now it's all this farting about with detentions and suspensions. And the extra paperwork. Reports. Referral slips. Letters home. Sicken you so it would.'

'The belt's simpler,' said Knox. 'Instant retribution. Kids know where they stand.'

Brian remembered knowing where he stood. In Latin, for making a mistake in conjugating *amare*. In Physics, for messing up an experiment. In Music, for not being able to sightread. Every Good Boy Deserves Favour. Skelp!

'Brutal,' he said.

'Wondered when you'd throw in your tuppence-worth,' said Ian.

'The threat was usually enough,' said Knox. 'Didn't actually have to use it all that often. If you got them in first year and put the fear of death into them, that was it.'

Brian remembered Danny Connor in first year,

pushing him, testing him, seeing how much he could get away with. There had been a moment when Brian had broken, grabbed him by the front of his jacket, breathed a threat right into his face. And he'd seen the look of triumph in Danny's eyes. He had won, reduced Brian to this anger, to the straight threat that was something he understood, could cope with. Parameters defined. This far and no further. He realized Danny reminded him of Eddie Logan.

'Only language they understand,' said Ian.

'Think I'll get out for a breath of fresh air,' said Brian.

He couldn't face the canteen, the stink of fried food, the constant noise of the kids. So he headed for the shopping centre where he could pick up a filled roll from the Lite Bite. The way to the centre led down through an underpass, a tunnel blitzed with graffiti like the side of a New York subway. At the end of the tunnel, silhouetted, he saw the skinny figure of a man, standing. He was dragging on a cigarette, seemed to be waiting. He wore an old leather jacket turned up at the collar, a woollen hat pulled down over his ears. Brian thought there was something familiar about him, the slight stoop, the jerky way he moved. But before he could get close, the man turned and hurried away. By the time Brian came out at the other side, he had disappeared.

The shopping centre was drab and inhuman. Rumour had it the original planner had died. Work had fallen behind schedule and they'd rushed at it, cut costs. Everything had been done in a hurry, on the cheap. The place had been thrown up. 'As in *vomited*!' Knox had said. From the outside it was a featureless concrete box. Inside, its square was divided into bland indistinguishable shop-units on ground floor and gallery – newsagents and sweetshop, TV rentals, licensed grocers, a betting-shop, the Jobcentre. Although the place was only a few years old, it had a scuffed and grubby look, already run down. From somewhere canned music piped out *Welcome to my world.*

The bakery shop Brian wanted was on the first floor, the gallery, and the escalators leading to it had long since broken down, never been repaired. They stood there, stuck, locked rigid, two narrow flights of steep and awkward stairs. Brian hurried up them, had to flatten back halfway up to let a young woman bump a push-chair past him. He bought his roll and came back down the main staircase – a longer way round but easier to negotiate. He peeled off the clingfilm, started eating as he went. He didn't have much of his dinnerbreak left. The roll was cheese and tomato, tasted fresh enough but soggy where the tomato had soaked through.

As he came back down through the underpass, he saw Danny Connor, talking to the skinny man he'd seen before. The man was handing something to Danny, who shoved it in his pocket, headed off towards the school. The man turned the opposite way, towards Brian, and as they passed, he caught his eye.

'Paki!'

Paki stared at him, not sure. Then he realized.

'Brian?'

'Right! Christ, I thought you looked familiar!'

'Didn't recognize you at all, man. You look so fucking straight!'

Brian shrugged. 'Got to earn a living.'

'Aye.'

'So, what are you doing here? Don't tell me you've moved through?'

'Just doing a bit of business in the scheme here.'

'What sort of business?'

'Come on man, you know me!'

Yes, he knew, with a sudden sick emptiness in his stomach, he knew what he had just seen in the underpass.

'You're not dealing to these kids are you?'

Paki registered the change in Brian's tone. The smile stayed fixed on the thin lips, but the eyes were wary, hard.

'What kids?'

'I saw you talking to Danny.'

'Good boy that.'

'*Boy* is right. He's fourteen.'

'Start them young, eh?'

'Listen, Paki, are you pushing the hard stuff at them? Smack and that?'

'What's it to you?'

'I don't believe this!'

'You said it yourself. Got to earn a living.'

'But they're *kids*!'

'So was I when I started.'

'Exactly. And look at the state of you!'

The mask had dropped now. The eyes were vicious, sly. An animal, cornered.

'You've changed your fucking tune.'

'All that hippy-shit is finished,' said Brian. 'Disappeared up its own arsehole. And that's what you'll do if I see you about here again.'

'Sounds like a threat.'

'No, it's a promise.'

'We're not on a fucking stage now, man. You canny just pick me up and dump me in a fucking corner.'

'I've warned you Paki. Now beat it.'

Paki shook his head, spat. 'Fucksake!'

'I mean it.'

'I know you do, man. That's what's unbelievable about it.'

'I teach these kids.'

'Fucking brainwash them you mean. To turn out as straight as yourself.'

Brian looked at the twisted face, the hate. There was no talking to him, no way to reach. They lived in different worlds, with Danny Connor the only point of contact.

'Just bugger off Paki. Don't come back.'

338

Paki snorted what was meant to be a laugh, arid and harsh and utterly humourless.

'Nice seeing you again, man. *Really* nice!'

Back at the school he felt drained. The encounter with Paki had shaken him. As he headed upstairs, he scanned the faces in the tide that seethed past him. He caught sight of Garry, the windowsill-climber from Danny's class.

'Where are you lot next period?'

'Maths,' said Garry, surprised at being stopped and asked.

'Tell Danny Connor to come and see me in the staff base. Now!'

He stuck his head round the classroom door, to tell his Sixth-Year Studies group he would be a few minutes late. Only one of them, Siobhan, had arrived.

As he sat in the staffroom waiting, Ian came in, started shuffling through papers.

'Still here?'

'No,' said Brian. 'I left about ten minutes ago.'

'Sorry I spoke!'

'Just got something to sort out.' Brian looked at his watch. 'Bloody kids. Treat everything as a skive.'

'Must be important, to keep you from your CSYS group,' said Ian. 'Those luscious young ladies.'

Brian managed a laugh. 'Dirtyminded sod!'

'If Siobhan wants any help with her dissertation, you know, like private tuition after school, tell her I'm available.'

'Forgetting the old *in loco parentis* bit?' said Brian.

'Meaning what?'

'Meaning responsibility.'

'For all the little bastards in our care?'

'Exactly. And that means keeping your manky hands to yourself!'

There was a quiet rap at the door. 'That'll be Danny Connor.' But it was Garry standing there. 'Well?'

'Danny never showed up yet.'

'Are you sure?'

'He never came back after dinnertime.'

'OK Garry. Thanks.'

The wandering alsatian passed along the corridor. Brian shut the door. 'Bastard!'

'Connor in trouble again?' said Ian.

'Just want to talk to him.'

'He's a headbanger. A nutter. A budding psychopath. I wouldn't give him the time of day.' He had found the papers he was looking for, was moving towards the door. 'Don't keep your young ladies waiting now!'

'No.'

'I mean look what I've got next. Second year. Fucking module on the *Marie Céleste*! You don't know you're living.'

Siobhan was still alone in the classroom. The other three girls hadn't turned up.

'Are they *all* off sick?' he asked.

She shrugged, smiled.

'Or maybe they're lying low because I asked you to come up with your dissertation titles.'

'Could be,' she said, sliding into a chair.

'Have you come up with yours?'

'I think so.'

'So what is it?'

'I want to do the portrayal of women in Scottish novels.'

'Sounds good.'

'I thought I'd called it *Mothers and Virgins, Hags and Sluts*.'

'I like it!' He laughed and so did she. Her hair was a mass of tight blonde curls. It hung, heavy, to her shoulders. She had a way of letting it fall across her face, a way of shaking it back with a jerk of her head, a way of pushing it behind her ears. She had a way too of meeting his gaze and looking away with a half smile, an innocent knowingness that could turn him inside out. She could amaze him with the sharp edge of her intelligence that could still be overridden by a surge of unreason, brighteyed enthusiasm. Her own poetry and prose were lush and overstated, lurching into purple. And here she was, talking about anima figures and earth mothers, complaining about stereotyped male perceptions, romanticized images, as he watched the sweet shapes her mouth made forming the words.

Danny had almost killed himself. He had been rushed to hospital. They were talking about it in the staffroom at morning break.

'I told you he was a mental case,' said Ian. 'Wasn't I just saying to you yesterday?'

'So you were,' said Brian.

'There you are then.'

'Psychopath you said. Wouldn't give him the time of day.'

'Well, was I right or was I right?'

'Poor kid,' said Sheila.

'Poor kid nothing. He's a dangerous loonie.'

'So how did it happen?' asked Mary.

'Seems he broke into an empty house,' said Ian. 'At the far end of the scheme. Apparently he went there to take drugs or sniff glue or something. And the story is he got inspired to rip out some piping. Probably thought he could sell it. Anyway, he caused a gas leak. And at some point he must have struck a match.'

'Boom!' said Knox.

'Blew all the windows out.'

'Dear God!' said Sheila.

'They're saying he was lucky. I mean, he's badly burned, but they reckon he'll live.'

The bell rang for the end of break.

Brian was seeing Paki, handing over the package to Danny in the underpass. If he'd realized sooner what was happening. If he'd gone after Danny, caught up with him. He should have known he wouldn't head back to school with it.

'Funny thing that,' Ian was saying.

'What?'

'The fact that you were trying to track him down, yesterday afternoon.'

'Isn't it.'

'Probably just about the time it was happening.'

'Probably.'

Ian could see that Brian had nothing more to say. 'Well anyway,' he went on. 'You won't have any problems finding him for the next couple of weeks. He's not going anywhere, that's for sure!'

'No,' said Brian.

Later in the day he phoned the hospital, was told Danny was *satisfactory*.

'More than his work's ever been,' said Knox.

Brian checked the visiting hours, and in the evening he headed out, selfconsciously carrying a bottle of Lucozade.

Danny's hands and arms were bandaged. A dressing covered part of his face. When he saw Brian he looked surprised, then confused, then suspicious.

'Just thought I'd come and see how you were getting on.'

Danny watched him, didn't speak.

'I brought you this.' He set down the Lucozade on the bedside locker. 'Thought it might perk you up a bit.'

Danny looked at the bottle, nodded, still didn't speak. Brian too stared at it sitting there, sparkling gold, wrapped in yellow cellophane. He suddenly saw the strangeness of it, as if through Danny's eyes. He had probably never had a whole bottle of the stuff in his life.

Brian shrugged. 'It's sort of traditional, for folk in hospital. Like grapes. Or flowers.'

Danny still said nothing.

'Didn't think you'd fancy a bunch of flowers somehow!'

'No.'

It was the first word he'd said since Brian had come in, and he spoke it with a total absence of irony, flat and matter-of-fact. But at least it was a response, a breakthrough.

'Do you want a glass just now?'

Danny shook his head. 'I'll get some after.'

He probably thought if he opened it now he would have to share it.

'It's all yours,' said Brian, staring again at the bottle, and beginning to feel uncomfortable. 'I was only ever in hospital once,' he said. 'For scarlet fever. And my auntie brought me a bottle of this. Rationed it out like medicine, a wee half glass at a time!' He remembered the exact taste. 'The bottle used to come with a foil wrapper round the top. If you took it off carefully and flattened it out, it made a circle, like a sort of rosette. Gold on one side, silver on the other. I remember thinking it was like the sun, then if you turned it over it was the moon.' He had no idea why he was telling any of this to Danny Connor. It couldn't possibly be of the slightest interest. The sun and the moon. 'I kept the one off the bottle my auntie gave me. Smoothed it out. Kept it beside my bed. Then she snaffled it. Crushed it into a ball. Said she would add it to her collection of silver paper and milkbottle tops. Something to do with buying guide-dogs for the blind.'

Strangely, for a moment, he thought Danny looked interested. He was talking to a young boy who might, just, be curious, about dogs, or the market value of silver paper, or whatever. Then it was gone, and the eyes were hard again, the look guarded.

Brian changed the subject. 'Had any other visitors yet?'

'My ma came in yesterday.'

'When's she coming again?'

'No till the weekend. And my da's away the now.'

Away meant down the road in Saughton, doing time for breaking and entering. The more he looked at Danny, the more he saw Eddie Logan. He could see

343

him heading down the same road, his options reduced to the army or the jail. Already the boy had come close to destroying himself, blowing himself to bits. Another sacrificial victim to the way things were.

'I don't suppose Paki Black'll be in to see you, will he?'

'Who?' The way he asked it was too quick, too innocent.

'Paki.'

'Who's that?'

'Don't come it, Danny. I saw you talking to him down the underpass.'

'Oh, *that* guy? He was just asking me something.'

'Don't act it. I was talking to him.'

'Aye, talking shite!'

'Listen, I know him. And I know what he was selling you.'

'You know him?'

'From way back. Seven, eight years ago. Used to think he was a bit of a joke. But he doesn't seem so funny now.'

He could see Danny was trying to come to terms with this sudden shift, two separate segments of his life overlapping.

'And if I see him hanging about the school again I'll kick his arse right out the scheme.'

Danny almost smiled at that, probably picturing it.

'Chasing the dragon were you?'

'Eh?'

'Isn't that what they call it now? Heating it up on the old silver paper. Sniffing up the fumes.'

Danny looked away. 'I'm saying nothing.'

'Then Paki'll say, try it this way, it's a better buzz. And he'll give you a needle. And that'll be you, on your way. And if you're lucky you'll end up a leech like him. But the way you're going you won't even manage that. What d'you think it'll be? A straightforward overdose? Infection from a dirty needle? Choke on your own vomit? Or maybe you'll get so

344

zonked you'll set yourself on fire again, only this time you'll finish it off.'

'Better than getting old,' said Danny. 'Wasting away.'

Brian saw then the uselessness of what he'd been saying. The very things he'd been stressing were what made it all exciting, were part of the buzz. Blood, vomit, danger, fear, death, the ritual of the fix. Lurid as images in a horror film, they fed the same dumb craving as the junk. He looked at Danny, saw the bleak reality of the boy's life. *What I hate about this place is it stinks.*

'Listen,' he said.

'What?'

'Nothing.'

A handbell rang in the corridor, announcing the end of visiting.

'Just take it easy,' he said. 'And get better.'

The next day, school over, he was heading towards the shopping centre to wait for his bus home. As he cut down through the underpass, he saw Paki coming towards him. There was a moment when they both hesitated, then Paki stopped, turned back the way he had come. Brian hurried after him, shouted out. 'Hey! You!'

Again Paki hesitated, looked as if he'd thought of making a run for it. Instead he stopped and turned, facing him down.

'What's up this time? Still got your fucking knickers in a twist?'

'I told you to fuck off Paki. Stop hanging about the school.'

'It's a free country.'

'First I've heard of it. And even if it was, you'd be out of order.'

'You're starting to get on my nerves, pal.'

Brian grabbed him by the jacket, the way he had once grabbed Danny back in first year. He slammed Paki against the wall of the tunnel.

345

'Fucksake man, take it easy!'

'That boy you sold the stuff to. He's in hospital. He's lucky to be still alive.'

'How?' said Paki. 'What happened? Did the daft cunt o-d?'

'He was out his head and he caused an explosion. Nearly blew himself to fuck.'

'And you're blaming me for that?'

'You sold him the stuff.'

'You might as well say it's the barman's fault if some cunt gets drunk in the pub and then drives away and runs somebody over.'

This was becoming surreal. He still had a grip on Paki's jacket, still held him pinned to the spraypainted wall, and here was Paki trying to raise things to the level of moral debate.

'Damned disgrace that!' said an old woman passing behind them. 'Grown men too!'

Brian relaxed his grip, let Paki go. It was all ridiculous, his anger, everything. But he didn't want to back down.

'Go,' he said. 'And this time stay away or I'll get you busted.'

'You'd shop me?'

'Fucking right I would.'

Paki held his stare, then turned away. As he moved off he called back. 'Hey!'

'What?'

'Tell the boy I'm sorry he got hurt.'

'Fuck off.'

As Brian walked on, he heard quick, light footsteps behind him. He thought it might be Paki coming after him, and he braced himself, ready. But he looked back and saw it was Siobhan, and he waited, let her catch up.

'What was all that about?' she asked.

'It's a long story,' he said. 'Maybe sometime when you've got a couple of hours to spare.'

'I've got a couple of hours to spare,' she said. 'You heading into town?'

'Yeah.'

'Me too.' She smiled, that way. 'I'll get you in on the bus.'

She had just been coming in to windowshop, maybe buy a book. He went with her to the bookshop. The reading-list for her dissertation was as good an excuse as any. Then he took her for a coffee and he wound up telling her the whole story about Paki, right back to when he had known him before.

'And there I am arguing the morality of it all in this stinking underpass. I mean the whole thing's ludicrous! And that wee wifie passing by just set the seal on it.'

Siobhan laughed, shook her head, those curls. She saw him watching her, for a moment was almost shy. She finished her coffee, set down the cup. 'So.'

It was his move again. He didn't want her to go. 'Listen.' He looked at his watch. 'I can't be bothered going home and cooking anything. D'you fancy a chinkie or a curry or something?'

'OK,' she said. 'That would be nice.'

This early, the restaurant had only just opened, was empty. They had the place to themselves.

'Nice,' she said. She included it all, the red flock wallpaper, hanging plastic lanterns, framed pictures of Chinese landscapes. The one above their table was a tinted photo of a temple, a golden pagoda seen through a massive wooden gateway.

'So tell me about your writing,' she said. In talking about Paki he had told her about the Magic Theatre, and *Ion Engine*, and his own poetry.

'Nothing much to tell. You start off seeing yourself as this writer who just happens to be teaching for a living. Then you think you're a teacher that does a bit of writing from time to time. Then finally.' He shrugged. 'You realize.'

'You mean you've given up writing altogether?'

'*It's* given *me* up.'

'That's a shame.'

'No great loss. Too many books as it is.'

'That's a terrible thing to say. And you a teacher too.'

'I know,' he said. 'I know.' The chopsticks he was trying to manoeuvre squirmed in his fingers, skited across each other like knitting needles, and he spilled the mouthful of rice he'd been trying to shovel up. Siobhan had been smart enough to use the boat-shaped spoon that had come with the rice. She tried to stifle her laugh but couldn't. He asked the waiter for a fork, and that set her off again.

'Right,' he said. 'That's you scrubbed. D-minus for your Creative Writing prelim.'

'No fair!' she said, and laughed again.

When they'd finished eating and he'd paid the bill, he said he would walk her to the bus-stop. As they stood in Princes Street waiting, that same old damp mist was beginning to come down, and he told her the way he'd once imagined it, hanging over the ruins of the city.

'Make a good poem,' she said.

'I suppose it would.'

On the other side of the road, a bus painted silver passed by.

'Jubilee,' he said. 'Here's a health unto her Majesty!' He mimed raising a glass. 'Make you sick so it would. Street parties and everything. What a con!'

'I went up Arthur's Seat for that bonfire thing,' she said.

'Did you now? You're not a secret royalist are you?'

She shook her head. 'Just thought it would be nice.'

'Actually. To tell you the truth. So did I.' A linked chain of beacons on hilltops, each one visible from the next, running the whole length of the country. Like a happening, he'd thought. Ruby would have approved. 'Only thing was, with it being such a miserable wet night, I thought they'd have problems getting the fire lit.'

'Maybe they used a lot of paraffin or something.'

'Sent out for a wee packet of firelighters!'

'There was a lot of smoke and sparks and that, but it was still really great. And you could see the glow from the next fire down, on Berwick Law. That was the signal.'

He found the image strangely haunting. A blaze on the hilltop, in the pouring rain.

'Here's my bus,' she said, and he was suddenly, absurdly awkward.

'Maybe we could do this again sometime.'

'I'd like that.'

She leaned forward, surprised him with a small quick kiss to the mouth. Then she was on the bus, fumbling her exact change into the ticket machine. And the doors were closed, and he stood waving as the bus moved off. Turning away, he shook his head, wondered what in God's name he was doing. Anima figures by fuck! He laughed. What he loved about many waters was their inability to quench love.

Starting Over

1

A bunch of kids were playing softball in the street. Three years on, the brief craze for football had passed. The Cosmos were history. By the entranceway to the apartment block, old Mr Zabrowski sat, upright in a kitchen chair he had brought out on to the sidewalk. He wore slippers and a soft hat, a baggy cardigan and a shirt buttoned up to the neck. He was savouring the mild autumn evening, watching everyone come and go.

'The Fall,' he said, as Tam came up. 'The best time. Even in the city.'

Tam set down his bag and nodded.

'A comfortable time,' said the old man. 'Doesn't melt you down. Doesn't freeze your ass off. You can just sit out here and watch things happen.'

Tam moved his bag over and sat down on the step.

'You been away,' said the old man. 'A whole month I didn't see you.'

'Yeah,' said Tam. 'I was staying with friends. Up in Connecticut.'

'How's Ruby?'

Tam hesitated. 'She's OK. Fine.'

'She left you, huh?'

Tam turned and stared at him. 'Yeah,' he said, at last.

'I thought so.' The old man nodded. 'I don't miss much.'

The softball was hit high, curved in an arc, a slow parabola, bounced on the roof of a parked car and landed almost at their feet.

'Goddam kids,' said the old man. 'Wreck somebody's car and who cares?'

A little Puerto Rican boy in a Yankees T-shirt rushed over, stopped, looked around, frantic. The others were yelling at him to hurry.

'Where'd it go man?'

Tam pointed to the ball, nestling against the step.

'Forchrissakes Jose, move yer ass!'

Jose gathered it up, lobbed it towards the manhole cover that was third base. The black kid who had shouted caught the ball, then fumbled and dropped it, and the batter went charging past, on to home base.

Tam was back home, in Glasgow, long ago. Eleven years old, an autumn evening just like this, an endless game of football in the street. Brian cleared the ball out of defence towards Tam on the left wing. The ball was bright red vinyl. It took an awkward bounce from the edge of the pavement, squirmed past a defender, and Tam was clear, the ball at his feet. Head down he ran for the byeline, and without looking up hit a cross with his weaker foot, the left. The ball floated over as if in slow motion, a dream of perfection, and rising to meet it was Eddie, to head past the keeper, out of his reach, between the lamppost and the factory wall. Eddie turned towards Tam, his arms raised in exultation. The exact feeling. How it was.

'Get themselves killed!'

Tam thought for a moment Mr Zabrowski was reading his mind, could see Eddie. But the old man was talking about the kids, scattering out of the path of a car that shuddered its way along the street bumping and jolting at every pot-hole. The kids yelled after it and re-started their game.

'Don't let it worry you,' said the old man. 'Ruby I mean. It'll pass. Same as everything else.'

'Were you ever married Mr Zabrowski?'

'Oy! Was I ever married! Only three times I was married, that's all. Don't talk to me about it!'

'How did they . . . What happened?'

'The first. She went in the Holocaust. They sent us to different camps. I never saw her again. For two years

351

after the War I tried to find out. Nobody knew. Then I figured it was hopeless. I came here.'

Tam was silent. It all seemed worlds away from this quiet old man, sitting here in his slippers and cardigan.

'I still see her sometimes.' He tapped his head. 'In here.'

Tam imagined her like Ruby, dark Jewess.

'She's still young,' said the old man. 'Always.'

'Had you any children?'

'Not then. But here, my second had a son.' He laughed. 'Oish! What a life they led me. Her and the boy both. The life of a dog!'

'Did she . . . die?'

'I should be so lucky! She went to live with her sister in Miami. Took the boy – he must have been twelve or thirteen. Few years later she got married again.'

'What about your third? You said you were married three times.'

'A jewel,' said the old man. 'A gem. We really had good times. But different. We were both getting older. Wasn't so frantic. Was quieter. Good times.'

'And she?'

'Died four years ago. Cancer.'

Somewhere a police car wailed, a mad banshee. Tam became aware of the city around them, its pulse and throb and never a silence.

'So now I just sit here, wait out my time. Soon be too cold and I have to stay inside. Turn on the heating. Look out the window.'

A faint wind shook the one scraggy tree in the street. Tam felt the first touch of coolness. Autumn. The Fall. A jet plane trailed across the sky.

'I'd better get moving Mr Zabrowski. Get myself sorted out.' He stood up to go.

'You still play the flute?' said the old man.

'Yeah. Sure.'

'I still got the fiddle. Don't play so great now, but not bad. You should come down see me. Bring the flute. I teach you some of the old Broadway hits. The old movie songs. Now that's *real* music!'

The apartment seemed smaller, felt empty. He went from room to room, mechanically setting things straight. He crumpled up a paper bag, stacked a few dishes in the sink, checked the fridge but there was nothing – old milk and a shrivelled apple, nothing.

The potted plants, half a dozen about the place, were wilting, leaves hanging limp, the soil in the clay pots dried up. He ran tapwater into a plastic basin, carefully placed the plants in it, and let them stand. Ruby had told him it was a good thing to do.

The place was unbearably familiar. It all seemed long ago, another life. This is how it was. The things he knew stared back at him, remorseless. They occupied space. They impinged. He recognized and remembered them. The low table. The couch. The wicker chair. The cushions embroidered with tiny mirrors.

He sat down amongst it, felt suddenly exhausted.

They were caught in a burning building. Now it was their New York apartment, now it was the tenement where he grew up in Glasgow. Ruby was leading him from room to room. Somewhere below them was screaming, the sound of breaking glass.

His parents and sister were trapped. There was no way back to them. Ruby led him out through a door and up a flight of steps. Away above he could hear a flute, a pure clear melody. An old man's voice grouched in his ear. 'Doesn't that guy know there's a war on? What's with the music at a time like this?' Tam laughed out loud then stopped, suddenly guilty. The old man was right. The situation was serious. A war on. No time for music. No time for mirth.

The fire had been started by a bomb-blast on the ground floor. Two young soldiers had been killed. Tam kept climbing from floor to floor, and each floor, as he left it, fell away beneath him, till at last he stood with Ruby on the roof, and they faced a wall of flame.

'Right,' she said. She took his hand and they walked through unscathed. The flute music was all around them. The music was the fire caressing them.

They came up to the edge of the roof. The building stood alone, a high tower in the middle of a lake.

'We have to jump,' said Tam.

'No,' said Ruby. She let go of his hand. She was suddenly changed, afraid. Her face was set hard against him. He didn't understand. He reached out again but she shook her head and turned away.

'Hell and High Water,' she said. 'But not with you baby. Enough is enough.'

Her words cut him deep – utter pain of rejection. He called her name once more but she turned her back. He jumped over the edge, out into space. He floated a moment like a skydiver, then plummeted towards the lake. He fell a long time, his arms out to his sides, a rushing in his ears. The surface of the water was smooth and still. He saw his own reflection come rushing up towards him and he met it head on.

He plunged deep then surfaced again. He drew a deep breath. He was still alive! All around was endless expanse of water, no building, no shore, nothing. He floated on the surface, all alone. The flute he had heard played one sustained note.

The sound still lingered as he woke. It changed to a soft hum he couldn't quite place, like a drone in Indian music, a shruti box, a tamboura. Still tired, he opened his eyes. His head rested on the embroidered cushion, and in one of the tiny mirrors close to his eye he peered as if through a spyhole at the darkening room reflected, the street light framed in the window.

He sat up, awake now, feeling cold. The dream was still vivid and he looked around for Ruby. Then he remembered she was gone for good.

He crossed to the window and looked out. The kids were gone from the street. The neon sign above the allnight DINER flashed on and off, on and off. Beneath it ran the message *Pizza . . . Heros . . . Soda . . .* the words chasing each other, endlessly repeated. Further away, on a rooftop, shone another sign advertising cigarettes. They were called *Golden Lights.* But the final *s* was broken, blacked out, so the sign flashed out GOLDEN LIGHT again and again. A mantra. Golden Light. Golden Light. And under it the time, 9.47. And the temperature, 54°.

The lights of a jet plane moved slowly up the sky, and another, fainter, higher up. At Kennedy they queued up to take off, one every two minutes.

He turned back to the room. He could still hear the soft drone and he wondered what it was. It wasn't the fridge or the central heating. He knew their clanking and jarring and this was none of them, was too gentle, harmonic. It seemed to be coming from the kitchen. He switched on the light and half a dozen cockroaches scattered to the dark corners. The sound was slightly louder. Getting warm. Over by the window it was softer. Cold again. Then he located it, exactly – the plastic basin where he'd placed the potted plants. The clay pots were porous, absorbed the water, and each one gave off its own quiet note.

He stood there staring at the pots, listening, amazed. There was something so mysterious in it, the accidental harmony, the remorseless life of things. And yet behind that there was something comic. Half a dozen plant pots, in a plastic basin, in the sink, sitting there humming to themselves.

And behind that again was the mystery, and behind that again was the absurdity, and the two were inseparable, meaningless meaning, purposeless purpose.

He felt himself smile. He pressed down the moist earth in one of the pots. He dipped his hands in the basin, cupped water and splashed his face. Refreshed, he went through to the other room. For the first time in weeks he actually felt like playing music.

The last time he'd played was the night before Ruby left. His sax had wailed and screeched and growled as he'd sent a barrage of noise against the walls of the apartment, raging and howling into the night, till Ruby had begged him to stop and give her peace.

The sax was too raucous for the way he felt now. He picked up the concert flute in its black case, then put it down again, unopened, and rummaged in the cupboard for the old bamboo flute. The bamboo was split at one end, but he'd carefully taped it. He blew a note. The flute had kept its tone, its piercing sweetness, for all its lightness still mellow and full. He settled to play, let his fingers get the feel of the open holes. He remembered the instrument, rediscovered its range, played scales and arpeggios, threw off grace-notes and trills. Then he found himself playing tunes, bits and snatches of old songs, on into *A Love Supreme*, the simple refrain, the riff repeated, again and again. A Love Supreme. A Love Supreme. He improvised, wove intricate patterns round the thread of the melody. But always he came back to it, found his way home, complexities resolved in simplicity. A Love Supreme. He played it softer, fading. And softer. Again. A Love Supreme.

His ear caught the drone from the plant pots and he moved into something else, another mode again. With the drone it sounded Indian, an evening raga, slow and calm. And he felt a rightness in whatever he played, wherever he placed the notes, just so. And suddenly he himself was an instrument, and the music was playing itself through him.

Behind the drone he became aware of other sounds, the refrigerator shuddering, the clank of the central heating coming to life, and from other apartments the sound of the TV, and Mr Zabrowski's violin, scraping away at *Secondhand Rose*, and beyond his window the street sounds, the traffic noise, raised voices, laughter, and behind it the endless drone of the city itself, electric, vibrating, like some great machine, and the music included it all, included himself as part of it.

He ended his raga with one note, held. He went to the window, looked out. The city still flashed back its signals. Diner. Pizza. Heros. Soda. And the mantra shone, bright neon against the dark. *Golden Light.* 10.52. 48°.

I'll give you a definition of New Age music,' said Barnie. 'Hold down the sustain pedal and just play on the white notes!'

'What about that Philip Glass stuff we were listening to?' said Tam. 'I thought you'd like that.'

'Too clinical,' said Barnie. 'Music by numbers.'

'No balls,' said Mack.

'Well I like it,' said Tam. 'All that repetition. It's kind of meditative.'

'Boring,' said Mack.

'Can do it all with synthesizers,' said Barnie. 'Sequencers, Program it all in.'

'Drum machines by fuck!' said Mack.

Tam laughed. 'Come back Punk, all is forgiven!'

'One gig Glass did,' said Barnie, 'some guy from the audience attacked him. Just couldn't take any more. So there he was, playing away with one hand and fighting the guy off with the other!'

'Well at least it was a response,' said Tam. 'The music got through to him!'

'Aye, sure,' said Mack.

'I remember years ago some guy slashed that Dali in the Glasgow Art Gallery. *Christ of St John of the Cross.*'

'Right enough,' said Mack. 'I remember that as well.'

'Anyway, it seems Dali was quite pleased when he heard. Said he was glad the painting had got a reaction.'

'Some reaction!'

'The funny thing was, it turned out the guy that did it was some Protestant headbanger. Just objected to crucifixes in general.'

'Absolutely fucking typical.'

Tam started singing. *'Scotland! Scotland! Scotland aye sae braw.'*

'Don't!' said Mack. 'I can't take it!'

'My hert is aye in Scotland, though I am far awa.'

'Enough!'

Barnie laughed. 'You guys!'

'We'll have to watch Tam at this gig,' said Mack. 'He'll be giving us a New Age version of an auld Scotch song.'

'You got it,' said Tam, and he wondered how much longer they could play as a group. In a strange way Ben's death had made them work at it, try to keep it going. Ben had finally overdosed, been found face down in his bath, a year back. That might have been a good time to split up. But a sense of loyalty, of loss, had pulled the three of them closer, for a while. Now the differences were asserting themselves, were always there, just under the surface. Tam thought this next time they played together might be the last. Things were running down. Another time, ending.

'So,' said Barnie. 'Do we rehearse, or what?'

He met Ruby in the street one day, near Tony's gallery in SoHo. She was friendly enough, more relaxed now they'd made the break.

'How you doing?' she said.

'OK. You?'

'Oh, you know.'

'And Tony?'

'He's fine. I'm doing a new performance at the gallery.'

'It figures.'

'You should come and see it.'

'Maybe I will.'

'It's called *Naked City.*'

'As in *There are eight million stories in*?'

'Right. And that's what it is. Stories. I've taped all these different people just telling something. A joke

358

maybe. Or a dream. Or just something that's happened to them.'

'And you play the tapes?'

She nodded. 'All these voices. It's so *real*. And I also tell some of the stories myself, along with a few of my own! And I'll have big projected images on the gallery walls. Right round. And synthesizer music.'

'Sounds good.'

'I think it will be. Have you seen any of Laurie Anderson's stuff?'

'Read about it.'

'Well, it's moving in the same direction. But different!'

Her hair was cut shorter, streaked. He couldn't think of much to say. 'Still jogging?' he asked.

'Running,' she said.

'Sorry. Running.'

'I'm getting back into it.'

He had tried running with her a few times in Flushing Meadow Park, but he'd found it too painful. Each time he'd hurt for days afterwards, his calf muscles knotted, clenched. He remembered her gliding away from him, picking up the pace.

'Come on!' she'd yelled. 'Just one more time round the world!' And she'd raced ahead, done a last lap of the giant globe, a leftover from the World's Fair back in the Sixties, and he'd dragged himself round after her, through fine spray blown from the fountain.

Ten years they'd been together. Now it was over. They stood here in the street making smalltalk.

'I guess I'll be moving out of the apartment,' he said.

'You got someplace else?'

'Not yet. I might go home for a while.'

'Home as in Scotland?'

'Only home I've got.'

She was quiet for a moment, then said, 'Oh well. Might be a good time to be away from here. Things are getting kind of strange.'

'You're not kidding.'

'Don't suppose you saw that Reagan-Carter debate on TV?'

'Funnily enough I did. Well, part of it. Watched it at Barnie's after our last rehearsal.' He had watched, been shocked at the utter vacuousness of what he was seeing and hearing.

'Did you check out that lie-detector stuff?' she asked.

'Oh God! I could not believe that was happening! Slap a fucking lie-detector on the pair of them, then analyse what it says.'

'At random of course. All fair and balanced.'

'Right! They ask Carter some really delicate question about the hostages, and the guy knows he can't put a foot wrong or he'll prejudice negotiations. And the machine says, This man's response is hesitant. He's prevaricating.'

'And they ask Reagan something like, What'll you do for America if you're elected?'

'And he says, Everything in my power, so help me God.'

'And it's all over the paper the next day.'

'Carter's a liar. Reagan is honest-as-the-day-is-long.'

'You better believe it.'

'It's insane!'

'It's America!'

The way she laughed brought it home to him. His loss. Too late.

'Another weird time,' he said.

She nodded. 'Weird but maybe not so good.'

The club was dimly lit by fake, electric candles on the tables. The ceiling was low, the atmosphere thick with smoke.

'Can hardly fucking breathe in here,' said Tam, 'never mind fucking blow.'

'Never bothered you before, man,' said Mack.

'Aye, well. Maybe I'm just seeing it different. I mean look at it! It's such a fucking cliché. Like a crummy scene from some two-bit movie. *The jazz club.*'

Mack shrugged. 'The punters like it. Place is packed. It's what they want.'

'Ach, what do they know?'

'They pay your wages. One way or another.'

'Keep the customer satisfied, eh? Is that all it's about?'

'Look, man, I know you've been through a hard time, but you just got to get out there and keep doing the business.'

'I know what you're saying Mack. But there has to be something else.'

'Like what?'

'Fucked if I know. But not this. Not this.'

'You guys ready?' said Barnie, coming out behind them on stage.

'Ready as we'll ever be,' said Mack.

They began with old standards, *Favourite Things* running into *On a Clear Day*. Mack kept it driving along, and Barnie did his best to make up for the lack of a bass-line. But Tam's heart wasn't in it. He was going through the motions and he knew it, couldn't seem to spark it into life. He shrugged an apology and they nodded, looked at each other, knowing. But the audience howled and cheered anyway.

After the break he came out first. He picked up his soprano and blew a single note, held it as long as he could then played it again, and again, and he kept on playing it as the other two came out and sat down. He closed his eyes, swayed and grew lightheaded as he kept on playing the note. It came out of him like a chant, a mantra, as he gave it all the breath he had. He kept his eyes shut, kept on blowing, heard Barnie and Mack come in, not sure, behind him, make a shimmer of texture, isolated notes. Then he launched into it. He grunted, screamed, thrashed, ran frantic up the instrument's whole range, battered at its boundaries, hammered at its gates, tried to break the barriers that held him in, held him down, then he was through to clear free space, vast emptiness and light, simplicity, a pure melodic line. And he let the melody sing itself out, brought it all back down to that one note, held it and let it fade right down to nothing, and the audience howled and cheered just the same.

Overnight the weather had turned. The cold was a greyness, made his head feel like concrete. The wind that slashed him was vicious. It punched a cold hole in his chest, seared his lungs. He had chosen a bad day. But now that he was out he had to keep going, slog his way round the park. He jogged and walked, once or twice had to stop altogether. But he made it to the globe, sat down on the rim of the fountain, now drained and turned off for the winter. He stared up at the greymetal framework of the globe, said 'What the fuck am I doing here?'

A jetplane roared low overhead, coming into La Guardia. The noise of it deafened him, filled the whole sky, and he yelled out loud, his voice swallowed up in it. 'Jesuschristalfuckingmighty!' As the roaring died out, he heard a radio blaring near and a young black boy glided past him on rollerskates, a red ghettoblaster perched easy on his shoulder. Tam recognized the song as one he had heard a lot, Blondie singing *Heart of Glass*. The boy must have heard Tam yelling, shouted 'Yoh, man! Let it out!' Tam watched him coasting away, effortlessly circle the globe, the words of the song fading. *Once had a love, thought it was divine* . . .

He looked up at the globe above him. Britain was mis-shapen, Scotland ill-defined. The radio got louder again as the boy came back round, completing his orbit. *Lost inside adorable illusion and I cannot hide* . . . Tam waved, called out to him. 'I come from up there!' As if that somehow explained something. He was pointing up.

'From outer space?' the boy called back.

'Sure!' he shouted. 'Beam me up!' He remembered a drunk on the subway. Poetry in motion. When the boy came round for the third time, his red box was still playing *Heart of Glass*. It had to be the 12-inch version, or he was listening to a tape loop playing it again. *Riding high on love's true blueish light* ... He gave Tam a last wave, called out 'Take it easy!' and he was away, striding out.

Take it easy. He knew that was right. But how to take it easy by trying? He started to shiver. The sweat had dried, on his scalp and neck, in the small of his back. He had to move, to get himself home, all the way back across the park. Sitting he had started to stiffen. He should never have come out. Some madness had grabbed him. He wanted to cry. The sky was the colour of bone, of ash. Pale sunlight diffused through grey pollution-haze hurt his eyes, made them ache. The colour was drained from everything. Even the grass, the trees, looked grey. The taste in his mouth was like iron. To get home. All the way back. One foot after another, hurting. Another plane roared over.

'Ach!' he shouted. 'Ach!'

The little cinema was half empty. He had read in the *Village Voice* that Bergman's *Magic Flute* was showing. He had travelled almost an hour to get here. He would have the same journey back. A man's languid voice from two rows behind was saying, 'I've seen it before and it's not bad. But of course it's not the real thing. I mean opera on film just doesn't work.' Tam knew he shouldn't have come.

But as the lights came down, and the curtain opened on a country house seen through trees, a summer evening, soft northern twilight, faint birdsong in the background, he began to relax into it, let the familiar overture flow round him. And the scene changed to the inside of the building, a theatre, and the camera focused on a child in the audience, a girl with the face of a Botticelli cherub. It framed her in close-up, wide shining eyes, mouth turned up in a faint half smile, an astonishing combination of serenity and mischief. And it cut to a picture of Mozart with the selfsame expression, then moved into a montage of other faces in the audience, all different ages, nationalities, all caught off-guard, absorbed in the music, in all their humanity, their beauty and vulnerability, seen with the eye of compassion. Then the opera itself began, like a stage production filmed, and Tam found himself drawn further in, enchanted. So much the music brought back. It hurt, like a thorn being pulled out. But beyond the hurt was release. It took him out beyond the mundane, beyond his everyday self, but at the same time it reconciled him to it, was total forgiveness, absolution.

When it was over, the lights back on in the half empty cinema, the voice from two rows behind said, 'It never was my favourite Mozart. I mean is it sublime or ridiculous or what?'

Tam couldn't resist turning round. 'Of course it is.'

'Sorry?' said the man.

'It's sublime *and* ridiculous *and* what,' said Tam. 'Especially *what*!'

'Asshole,' said the man.

Outside, the cold wind had him almost whimpering as it rushed at him unchecked down avenues that went on forever. It stung his face and hands, even his legs through his jeans. It chafed, dry and abrasive, stretched the skin taut across his cheekbones. Head down and butting into it, eyes watering, he ran the last half-block to the subway.

As he sat on the train clattering through the night, the melodies from the opera still sang in his head, and he tried to hold on to what it had given him, hold it inside. He glanced at the faces opposite, saw them like the montage at the start of the film, all the different races, backgrounds. But here he read the fears and doubts and stresses, the weariness and desolation. Eight million stories in the naked city. And every one a spark of the divine, all somehow moving towards light, if he believed the music. Sublime and ridiculous and what.

At the top of the subway steps, he braced himself to step out into the freezing wind. As he passed the pizza place, Carlo was putting his garbage out in the street. He waved at Tam, called 'Hey! You hear about John Lennon?'

'What about him?'

'Some guy just shot him. I heard it on the news. Just walked right up to him outside his apartment. Shot him dead. Bam! Just like that. Crazy, huh?'

'Yeah,' said Tam. 'Crazy.'

2

Knox was doing his crossword in the staffroom. 'Young worker in a muddle with his rent. Things running down. Seven letters.'

'Sounds like a headline from the *Socialist Worker*,' said Brian.

'Afraid I wouldn't know about that.'

'Anybody seen *The Goalkeeper's Revenge*?' said Ian, coming into the room.

'Don't tell me they've made a film of it,' said Brian.

'I meant the book, smartarse.'

'It walked,' said Knox.

'The whole set?'

'The lot. Somebody must have nicked them.'

'What in God's name would anybody want with thirty copies of *The Goalkeeper's Revenge*?' said Brian.

'Takes all sorts,' said Knox.

'Probably sold them to some other school,' said Ian. 'One that's worse off than us.'

'There's no such thing,' said Brian. 'Not possible.'

'Things running down.' Knox was trying to retreat back into his crossword.

'You said it,' said Brian.

'Don't start.'

'Why not? You helped vote in this bloody government.'

'Muddle with his rent. Could be an anagram. Rent plus something else.'

'And the gall of that woman! Misquoting St Francis as she took over! What was it? Where there is discord, may we bring harmony.'

'Where there is despair, may we bring hope.'

'Make you sick. The hypocrisy of it.'

'What am I going to use instead of *The Goalkeeper's Revenge*?'

'Get Knox to give them a crossword.'

'Three letters meaning young worker.'

'How about YOP?' said Brian.

'YOP?'

'A young person participating in the government's Youth Opportunities Programme.'

'I know what it means,' said Knox.

'Right. We've sent enough poor little bastards from this place straight on to the scheme.'

'Just didn't think they'd use something like that in a crossword.'

'Twelve months down the road they're booted out. No real skills. A year older. And another whole mob leaving school after them, chasing up the few lousy jobs that are going.'

'Rent plus YOP. Things running down.'

'Youth Opportunities. Talk about fucking new-speak!'

'It has to be an anagram. *In a muddle* gives it away.'

'Entropy,' said Brian.

'Who?' said Ian.

'It's a science word.'

'Thought it had that kind of ring to it.'

'It means a general tendency towards formlessness, chaos.'

'Oh aye?'

'A running down of the energy level in the universe.'

'That'll be it then,' said Knox, filling in the squares.

'Factory closures,' said Brian. 'Redundancy. It's all part of it. Decay. Death. Paint flaking off the walls. The sun burning itself out. It's only a matter of time you know.'

'Five across,' said Knox. 'In a net I am peculiarly lifeless.'

'Just need to take a walk through this scheme. Go into the shopping centre. Talk to anybody that lives here. Hey missis! See this place? See entropy? This place is hotching wi it!'

'Nine letters. The second one's the *n* from *entropy*.'

On one corner of the staffroom wall, Brian had pinned a few newspaper cuttings, headlines, made a kind of collage of bits and pieces. A picture of Willie Johnston, head down, sent off against Peru in the World Cup, was stuck next to the headline from the day after the Devolution Referendum, NO in huge letters.

Ian was scanning the bookshelves. 'What *can* I use?'

'Get them to write an essay,' said Brian. 'Man's anti-entropic function in the universe.'

'Eh?'

'Buckminster Fuller. *Man's function in the universe is anti-entropic*. Means we're supposed to counteract all that running down.'

'Very Sixties,' said Ian.

'I think this is another anagram,' said Knox. 'That's where *peculiarly* comes in. *In a net I am*.'

'I *could* get them to write something,' said Ian.

'Show them how to fill in their UB40s,' said Brian. 'That's all the writing most of them are ever going to need.'

'Lifeless,' said Knox, tapping at the newspaper with his pen. 'Got it!' He scribbled. 'Inanimate!'

'Says it all,' said Brian. He turned to Ian. 'What you should do is go out there and tell them you've got absolutely nothing to teach them. You haven't a clue!'

'What *is* it with you today?' said Ian.

'Nothing,' he said. 'Nowt. Zero. Zilch. Sweet Fuck All.'

'Bad as that?' said Knox.

Going to see his parents had started it. Brian noticed the difference in them, even since he'd last been to visit, a couple of months back. His father had been laid off when the factory shut down. Sixty was too old to start again, and five years short of drawing his pension. But he had the redundancy money as a cushion, could get by on Social Security, eke things out, make do.

For his father, *making do* had become an obsession. He would walk half a mile to a bakery that sold yesterday's bread cheap. He would keep every FREE OFFER coupon that came through the door, every voucher promising 5p off next purchase, and he would use them regularly, claim every discount that was going. He had changed all the light bulbs from 100 watt to 60, to save electricity, and he would get upset if a light was left on, in the toilet, in the hall. Brian realized that somehow all of this was his father's way of still being the provider, of being useful. The need was deep. That foraging trip to the bakery, to the supermarket, was the hunt. What he brought back was his kill, on special offer.

The scrimping, economizing, was remorseless. The only thing exempt was the TV. It was on as constant background, from afternoon till late at night, and any conversation had to be cranked up over its noise. His parents seldom spoke to anyone, apart from each other, and when Brian came they bombarded him, in stereo, hit him with a stream-of-consciousness barrage, relentless in its manic triviality. They talked at the same time, butted in and cut across each other, drowned each other out, as they bludgeoned him with all the unedited detail of their day-to-day existence. What they'd had for breakfast and who they'd seen on the bus and the convoluted story-line of a sitcom on TV and the riffraff that had moved in next door and the price of frozen peas.

Then somewhere in the middle of it all his mother

was saying, 'Just dropped dead in the street. Heart attack. Just like that.'

'Sorry,' he said. 'Who?'

'Mr Wilson,' she said. 'George's father.'

'Laid off the same time as me,' said his father. 'Chucked on the scrapheap when the factory shut down. Redundant. The old early retirement. Golden handshake sort of thing.'

'Everything to live for,' said his mother.

His father nodded. 'No an old man either. A year younger than me.'

'Just like that,' she said again.

'Sudden.'

'Never know the minute.'

'No.'

'Don't suppose you ever see George these days?'

'Haven't seen him in donkeys.'

'That's the way of it,' said his father. 'Folk just lose touch.'

'Think he's doing all right,' said his mother. 'Married. Couple of kids.' It sounded like a simple statement, but Brian knew in behind it, implied, was expectation.

'I guess he must have been laid off as well,' he said, quickly. 'Did he get himself another job all right?'

'Is the Pope a Catholic?' said his father. 'Different ball game for him. He's young enough for starters. Plus he's got the old contacts and that.'

'Nudge Nudge,' said Brian. 'Say no more.'

'Mind when you were wee it was always the four of you. You and Tam, and George, and that Eddie character.'

'Poor boy,' said his mother.

'Remember you all went to learn the flute in that band?'

'That's right. I got to bring the flute home.'

'And the boss here put her foot down and that was you scrubbed!'

'Quite right too,' said his mother. 'All these nutters.'

'Still,' said his father. 'Shame in a way. Was a chance to learn music. I played the trumpet in the Sally Army band you know.'

'We know,' said his mother.

'Bare feet,' said Brian. 'Bye Bye Blackbird.'

'Aye. Well. It was the greatest.'

'Tam's in America these days.'

'Is that a fact?' said his mother.

'Playing jazz.'

'Ach aye,' said his father. 'Funny the different roads you ended up taking.'

When his father went through to the kitchen to fill the kettle, Brian breathed in a brief moment of silence. But his mother couldn't leave it.

'Still seeing that girl?' she asked, offhanded.

'Siobhan,' he said. 'Yeah. We're still together.'

Siobhan was 21 now, in her third year at university. It had taken his mother this time to stop thinking of her as some child he'd led astray, see her instead as a potential daughter-in-law.

'Next thing you'll be getting married,' she said, still trying to make it sound casual.

He shrugged. 'Maybe someday. Who knows?'

'Och well,' she said. 'It's your life.'

When his father came back through he said, 'Great wee kettle that. Electric. Turns out cheaper than using the cooker. I worked it out. Made a note of the units on the meter. And the likes of the morning, I heat up enough for a pot of tea, use the rest for my boiled egg, and when the egg's ready, the same water does me for shaving. Two birds with the one stone sort of thing.'

'Great,' said Brian.

'It can't be a midlife crisis,' said Knox. 'You're too young.'

'Thirty,' said Brian.

Knox was dismissive. 'A mere boy. Callow, beardless.'

'According to the Romans, it was the end of your

370

youth,' said Brian. 'At thirty you were no longer *adolescens*. You became *vir*, and that was it. Official.'

'That you flashing your classical education at us again?' said Ian. 'If it's not that, you're dazzling us with science.'

'*Scientia*,' said Brian. 'Was our school motto.'

'There you are then.'

'Comes in handy for doing crosswords and that.'

'There speaks a disenchanted man,' said Knox.

'That's the word,' said Brian.

'Siobhan must be making you feel your age,' said Ian, a leer in his voice.

'Just leave her out of your manky imaginings.'

'Siobhan,' said Knox. 'A *rara avis*.'

'Don't you start,' said Ian. 'What does it mean anyway?'

'Means she's a rare wee bird!' said Brian.

'Better not let the weird sisters hear you talking like that,' said Ian. He was talking about Sheila and Ann. 'Have your balls off quick as look at you.'

'Is it any wonder they've stopped coming in here?' said Brian. 'Except when they have to.'

'Prefer the company in the main staffroom.'

'I wonder why!'

'Talking of loony feminist nonsense,' said Knox, 'there was a beauty in the paper the other day. Woman whose surname was Cooperman, changing it by deed poll to Cooperperson.'

In spite of himself Brian laughed at the idiocy of it.

'Careful there,' said Knox. 'Your ideology's slipping!'

When he'd left his parents, with that old familiar mixture of sadness and release, a rush of magnanimity now he was finally getting out the door, he had taken the blue train into town, gone into a pub across from the station, to wind down.

As he sat staring at his pint, he had a curious feeling the man at the next table was watching him. He flicked a quick glance across, careful not to catch his eye. Nobody he recognized. Thin and gaunt, bearded. Hair receding but long at the back. The man stood up and came across towards him. Fuck it. He would finish his pint quickly and go.

'Brian?'

Surprised, he looked up. He thought he knew the voice. The eyes had a hardness in them, gave nothing away. The man looked down at him across a great distance. The mouth was tight, unsmiling, tense.

'Malcolm,' said the voice he almost knew. And yes, it was, in behind that drawn mask, thinner and much older.

'Jesus Christ!' he said. 'So it is! I didn't know you.'

'A long time,' said Malcolm. 'Folk change.' He looked about him, seemed edgy. 'Another pint?'

'Thanks,' said Brian. He watched Malcolm cross to the bar, amazed at the change in him, and at meeting him at all.

'Cheers!' he said, as Malcolm brought the drinks over.

'Yeah.' The voice was as cold, noncommittal, as that hard stare.

'One of those coincidences, eh? What do they call it, synchronicity?'

'You mean us bumping into each other?'

'The thing is, I was just out seeing my folks and they mentioned George. Told me what happened to your dad. I was sorry to hear about it.'

'Were you?' The look made Brian uncomfortable. It was strangely detached, analytic. 'Just the fact of it I suppose. Somebody you knew. He was, now he's not. Dead as everybody else that's ever died. History. But the truth of it is he was a pompous old get and he's no great loss. If there's anything sad about it, it's what he did with his life.' He looked at Brian again. 'So, how you been wasting yours?'

'Teaching,' he said, then as some kind of justification added, 'Housing scheme. In Edinburgh.'

'An area of multiple deprivation no doubt!'

'It is actually.'

'So you turn out dole queue material. Or cannon fodder like Eddie Logan.'

'I do what I can within the system. Helped organize the strike over wages.'

'But essentially it's just one big control mechanism. And you've been programmed to keep it going.'

'So tell me something I don't know!'

'I always thought you had possibilities.'

'Hell of a sorry if I've disappointed you.'

'The old repressive tolerance trap. Gets just about everybody. You just said it. You settle for doing what you can within the system.'

'Well that's me summed up and dismissed. What have *you* been doing with your life?'

'This and that. Carrying on the struggle.' Again he looked around. 'Bastards are trying to nail me.'

'What for?'

'It's a long story. Right now I'm out on bail. That's why Mutt and Jeff over there are keeping an eye on me.'

Brian looked across at two men in the far corner, sitting, not talking. One middleaged, grey hair cut short in a fierce crewcut, the other younger, dark.

'I wouldn't stare,' said Malcolm. 'Probably arrest you for it.'

'Are they really watching you?'

'You think I'd make it up?'

Brian didn't answer. He had no way of knowing. This stranger spouting jargon at him might well be completely paranoid, psychotic.

'How come they let you out?'

'Good lawyer. Found a loophole. A technicality.'

He talked like someone in a play. And the place itself added to the sense of unreality. Brian became aware of it, the tacky veneer of the decor, the muffled thud of disco beat, pulse of coloured lights above a fruit machine.

'I'll tell you the funny thing,' said Malcolm. 'The ironic bit.'

'Tell me.'

'It was George that gave them a lead.'

'George?'

'Was my own stupid fault. I got a daft notion to send him a telegram when he got married.'

'So?'

'So these guys paid him a visit. Got hold of the telegram.'

'I'm not following this.'

'It was sent from London you see. But I'd told them I was somewhere else at the time. And they were trying to tie me in to something that happened down there. Not that the telegram proved anything. But as far as they were concerned it was another link.'

'How come you're telling me all this?' said Brian.

'Passing the time of day. No, you're right. It is kind of stupid. Like sending that telegram.'

There was a lull then, a silence, and again that distance between them.

'Don't suppose you ever see anybody from the old days?' said Brian, breaking it.

'Like Claire?'

He shrugged. 'Anybody.'

'Claire and I went our own ways long ago. And I never really knew the rest of them.'

'I saw Bird on TV a while back. Looking fat and middleaged! He's running a theatre in London. And there he was, being interviewed by Chris!'

'Cosy.'

'Right.'

'What did he have to say for himself?'

'He was talking about the way forward. Business sponsorship in the arts!'

'Always knew he was a chancer.'

'Remember you punched him on stage?'

'Had more to do with my state of mind than anything else.'

'Magic Theatre!'

'Wasn't your show based on *The Magic Flute*?'

'Very loosely!'

'It's just that I read something recently by one of the few Scottish journalists that's actually got a mind. And he was talking about going to a performance of it – the Mozart I mean – in Berlin in '67. What they call a gala occasion, laid on for the visit of the Shah of Iran. And the journalist came out of the Opera House really uplifted by it all, and ran smack into a student demonstration against the visit. And the police were wading in to break it up, and the whole thing escalated into a full-blown riot. Like Paris a year later. Fires in the street. And at one point a young student was shot dead. In some ways that was the start of it all. Red Brigade. Baader-Meinhof. Anyway, the journalist could never quite see *The Magic Flute* in the same way after that night. In fact he's never been to see it again.'

'I know what you're saying,' said Brian. 'But you can't just deny the other thing, kill off a part of you.'

'You've got to.'

'I don't believe that.'

'No. I don't suppose you do.' The look Malcolm gave him was almost pitying.

'Anyway.' Brian looked at his watch. 'I've got a train to catch.'

'You were talking about coincidences,' said Malcolm. 'I'll tell you one you won't believe.'

'Try me.'

'That business in London, the thing they want to get me for. It was all to do with a consignment on its way to Ireland. And I ended up going over there, making sure it arrived.'

'You're doing it again. Telling me too much.'

'Maybe I still think there's hope for you. Who knows? Anyway, the person in charge of the operation was this woman. Called herself Carol. Been involved since she was really young. I mean totally committed. And we got talking about this and that. And with me

375

being from here, she told me the first job she ever did was to set up these two Scottish soldiers. And she remembered it all really vividly, I suppose because it was her first time. Every little detail. And the way she described one of them started bells ringing in my head. And I worked it all out, the date and everything. And sure enough, she was talking about Eddie Logan.'

'God Almighty!'

'Now that's what I'd *call* a coincidence. Amazing really. The way things link up.'

The disco beat thudded. The coloured lights pulsed. Blue. Green. Red. Green. Blue.

'I've got to go,' said Brian, standing.

'Right,' said Malcolm. 'Maybe see you in another ten years.'

'Maybe.'

As he left, he glanced across at the two men in the corner. The older one looked over, watched him go.

The past was everywhere he turned.

At parents' night at the school, a big hefty woman came up to him. She seemed a few years older than himself, frizzy greying hair tied back in a ponytail. He remembered a basement flat, an Irish harp.

'Sally!'

'I thought it was you!' she said, and she hugged him. 'So you wound up teaching after all.'

'Don't make it sound so final! What are you doing here?'

'We live in the scheme now. I'm with a really nice guy, and he's got a couple of kids too. So out here we could get a place with enough rooms.'

'And your kids are here at the school?'

'Sue starts in the summer. Peter's in second year.'

'Peter Edwards?'

She nodded. 'Yup!'

'He's in my class, for English.'

'So *you're* Mr Ritchie!'

'What's he been telling you about me?'

'Tell you the truth, he never talks much about school.'

The boy was difficult, uncommunicative, withdrawn. 'He's quiet,' said Brian.

Sally laughed. 'You mean he's a sullen little sod!'

'So you won't be needing a report on him!'

'Reports I don't need.' She took both his hands. 'Come round and see us. You married?'

'Sort of.'

'So bring her.'

'I will.' He knew he wouldn't.

Later, Ian asked. 'Who was the big momma?'

'Earth mother,' said Knox.

'Just an old friend,' he said. Another old friend.

Next morning in the staff base, a headline in the paper caught his eye. *Drug Link in Bizarre Killing.* And as he read mindlessly, he realized the article was about Paki. *Glasgow-born Alex Black, aged 33.* Paki Black.

'Christ!' he said.

'Something stunning on Page 3?' said Ian.

'This guy that got murdered. I used to know him.'

'Murdered?'

'They found him dead in his kitchen. Somebody had tied him to a chair and held a plastic bag over his head. Suffocated him.'

'I suppose the police suspect foul play!' said Knox.

Ian leaned over, read the article. 'Says he was a drug pusher. They're working on the theory that he tried to cross somebody, like his bosses. And this was his punishment. Sort of ritual killing.'

'Dear God!'

'And you say you knew this guy?'

'Used to.'

'Interesting circles you must have moved in!'

The rest of the day he went through the motions only, not teaching. The rows of faces might have been underwater, mouthing nonsense syllables at him. He gave out essays, reading assignments, passages for interpretation. He didn't care if they got on with it or not. He kept picturing Paki, his grotesque death, tied to a chair in some dingy kitchen, the bag over his head. The shabby horror of the image wouldn't leave him alone, kept impinging. He stared out of it at the class in front of him, saw them bored and restless, and a hopelessness overwhelmed him.

What got to him always was the specific. That cheap nylon bomber-jacket, allegiances declared in tin button-badges pinned to it – Debbie Harry, The Jam, The Clash. That hair spiked out into stiff tufts. That shaved head. That innocent swastika roughly drawn on the sleeve of a parka. That jersey a size too small, a pair of scuffed and out-of-date platform shoes. That pent-up directionless energy. The look of utter vacancy in a young face. He could teach them nothing. He had nothing to give. Every few minutes he had to yell at them to shut up for God's sake and give him peace.

After the bell had gone at the end of the day, he still sat for a while, staring at the empty desks.

As he cut down through the underpass, he saw two figures at the far end, and the scene was a rerun of something he'd seen there three years back, when Paki had handed a package to Danny Connor. But now it was Danny handing something over, and taking it from him was Sally's boy, Peter. And this time it was Peter who ran away, up towards the shopping centre, and it was Danny who stood his ground and confronted him. The day was cold, the light already dying. The boy's white face stared hard back at him, a lividness down one side where the skin was a smear of burn-scar tissue.

'Seeing plenty?' said Danny.

As a challenge it was small and pathetic, childish. Danny turned away, back through the underpass. Brian opened his mouth to call something after him, but no words came. He had nothing to say.

'So how was your day?' asked Siobhan when he got home.

'It's horrible,' she said, handing him back the newspaper. 'I can see why it upset you.'

'Execution,' he said.

'It's like one of the ways they torture people in South America. A bag over the head. Submarine they call it.'

'*Desaparecidos*.' He looked at the paper again. 'It's been some week. All this coming at me. Meeting Malcolm, and Sally. Then reading this, and seeing Danny with Sally's boy. Sometimes you actually wonder if it does all link up, if there's some kind of pattern to it. I mean, why all this now?'

'You should be writing this philosophy essay for me.'

'What one's that?'

'Teleological argument for the existence of God.'

'Argument from design.'

'My favourite argument!'

'That's because it's not an argument at all.'

'Right!'

'I remember reading an article where somebody claimed that a particular passage from Mozart was absolute proof that there is a God.'

'I'll quote that!'

'You should quote Vivekananda too.'

'Who?'

'Hindu monk. My friend Tam loaned me some of his books. Years ago. And Vivekananda said the design argument was primitive. Said if you ascribe a plan to God you limit him.'

'Or her.'

'Of course! So basically God's winging it. Improvising. Making it up as he goes along.'

'Bum notes and all!'

'That's right,' he said, quietly. 'Bum notes like cancer, and wars, and famine. Like Malcolm planning to blow folk to bits. Like Paki being suffocated. Like that white face staring at me out the underpass.'

'Can't make an omelette without breaking eggs,' she said, and made him smile.

'Putting that in your essay too?'

'Why not?'

And just for a moment he saw her clear, separate from himself, astonishing in her individuality. And he knew he had to hold on to her.

'Know what you are?' he said. 'You're a teleological argument. A one-person anti-entropic function.'

'Bet you say that to all the girls!'

He was trying to do a crossword on the blackboard, but the words kept rearranging, making no sense. Then he turned to the class, said 'Protest and Survive!' He wrote it up on the board, and they all put paper bags over their heads. At this point he knew it was a dream, even smiled as he recognized its references. 'Hundreds of us demonstrated like this in George Square,' he was saying. 'A happening.' Then Knox was standing in the doorway.

'Not exactly part of the curriculum.'

'I'm preparing them for a nuclear attack,' he said. 'Following Government instructions.'

Then he realized one boy was struggling, and his bag was plastic, clinging to his face. And suddenly it was the same with all the others. They were all dying, right in front of him, and he couldn't move, couldn't help them. Then Danny and Peter were coming up behind him, and they pinioned him to his chair, tied him down.

'An anagram,' said Knox. 'Peculiarly lifeless.'

And Paki was coming at him with a plastic bag, to kill him. He shouted as he woke out of it, sat up terrified in bed. Siobhan shooshed and soothed and calmed him. He recognized her, clung to her.

In the morning he slept through the alarm, struggled in slow motion to get himself moving. Siobhan was already up, had switched on the radio in the kitchen. The newscaster was saying something about John Lennon being shot.

3

At first George had felt nothing. His mother had phoned, her voice strange, to tell him his father had died. And he'd felt only cold and distant, listening to it. *He was fine in the morning then at dinnertime he felt a bit breathless so he didn't eat much and he just took it easy in the afternoon put his feet up then about five o'clock he seemed to be OK and he went out to the shop for his paper. Next thing was the knock at the door and it's this policeman with the bad news.*

He had never imagined this. Not-grief. Everything locked up tight inside.

That night as he tried to sleep, the same memories of his father came again and again. His father angry and skelping him and Malcolm for opening his case, clowning with his Mason's regalia. His father taking him to that first meeting, his initiation as an apprentice. His father raging at him for marrying Mary. And in amongst it was something he'd forgotten long ago. Finding a stack of dirty magazines in a box in Malcolm's room. And more than any of the other memories, it brought a resentment out of all proportion. He pushed it away, but it kept coming back with the rest. And it seemed his whole life had been one long effort to stay on the right side of his father, tensions he'd never understood and could never resolve. Now too late.

Mary lay turned away from him. He could feel the warmth from her back. From time to time she made small noises in her sleep. He felt he hadn't slept at all but knew he must have gone under. More than once he was sure his father was in the room, standing by the door, watching him. And he lay, afraid to look. But when he did there was nothing, only the dark.

At the funeral he sat beside his mother, still unable to grieve, to feel anything at all. Mary and the kids were in the row behind and she had to keep telling them to wheesht and stop fidgeting and behave. George didn't want to know, stared straight ahead.

He'd been amazed at the turn-out. Almost everyone from the Lodge was here. Old sombre men in black suits, seeing their own deaths. There were men too from the factory, and his father's two surviving brothers, George's uncles. Apart from Mary and his mother, there were almost no women.

He half expected to see Malcolm turn up, but he knew it wasn't likely. He had heard nothing from him in years. He thought he had seen him once, from a bus, but he couldn't be sure. Those two policemen had never come back, never returned the page from their album. They'd said the telegram was evidence, which seemed ridiculous. The whole business had upset his father badly.

And George suddenly realized that was the whole point. It was a thought he didn't fully understand. But somehow he saw the truth of it, that Malcolm's hatred for his father was what had made him the way he was. It had twisted into that violence, the need to destroy.

The minister was talking about the sure and certain hope of resurrection. He asked them all to stand and sing *The Lord is My Shepherd*. As they sang, the curtains opened, and with a click and a soft hum of machinery, the coffin slid through. In the furnace it would burn. His mother was crying now, deep racking sobs. He put his arm round her shaking shoulders, awkwardly because he'd never done it before. And at the same moment he knew his father was really gone. They would never see him again. And all at once it broke. He felt his face twist and grimace and the tears came. The knot inside him loosened and he let it all go.

Outside, everyone filed past, shook his hand. One old man by the name of Mackenzie said he would like to talk to him later. At the reception he came up to him. 'I hear you're out of work.'

'That's right,' said George.

'Can't have that, can we?'

He worked in insurance, and his firm were looking for new salesmen. If George was interested, he could put in a word, see what he could do.

'That would be great,' said George. 'Thanks.'

Behind him he heard his mother tell someone else her story. *He was fine in the morning then at dinnertime he felt a bit breathless.*

It had been a long day.

The firm took him on. He would have to learn how to sell. The first week they sent him to Manchester for a seminar, a three-day training course.

He had never stayed in a hotel before. He would be sharing a room with someone called Waters, from London, but Waters hadn't arrived yet and George had the room to himself. He tried both beds, bounced up and down on them. There was really nothing to choose, but he decided on the one nearest the window, put his bag on it to stake his claim. He turned on the radio, switched it through the four channels available. He did the same with the TV, but the reception was a bit fuzzy. He ran the shower, testing it. He felt the softness of the towels. He sniffed at the perfumed soap. He laughed.

Then his room-mate arrived, breezed in. He was small and chubby, his face a bit puffy, flushed.

'Hello mate!' he said, Cockney. 'George isn't it?'

'That's right.'

'Harry Waters.'

'Pleased to meet you.'

They shook hands. Grip, response.

'Like being on holiday, isn't it?'

'I was just thinking the same.'

'Couple of days away from the wife and kids. Can't beat it! You a married man yourself?'

George nodded. 'Yeah.'

'Well, there you are then!'

George didn't immediately take to him. But then he was often that way with new people he met. And at least this Harry Waters was friendly.

'Smoke?' He had flipped open his packet of Benson & Hedges, was offering him one.

'No thanks. I don't.'

'Hope you don't mind if I do. Cause if so, that's just too bad, I mean, tough!' He laughed, but he meant it.

'It's OK,' said George. 'Doesn't bother me.'

'Thank God for that! I'd hate to be sharing a room with some killjoy. I mean that's the beauty of a do like this. Come the evening you're your own man. Get out on the town. Few drinks. But of fun. You with me?'

'Sounds all right,' said George, unsure. 'Maybe not tonight but. I'm kind of tired from the journey.'

'Sure. Me too. I'll settle for a drink in the bar.'

'Suits me fine.' George was relieved. 'Been on these courses before then?'

'Something like it. A real skive. But I haven't heard this bloke.'

'American isn't he?'

'Most of them are. He'll likely be telling us about PMA and HHT and stuff like that.'

'What do they mean?'

'Ah ha! Secret formulas. You'll find out soon enough Georgie boy. First thing in the morning, all will be revealed!'

The first session was at nine, right after breakfast, in the conference room at the hotel. There were maybe thirty of them, all with pens, notepads. Harry Waters gave him a nod and a wink as he sat down beside him. Taped music was playing, not too loud, something classical but with a soft disco beat. George liked it. Then the music was turned down and the man presenting the seminar appeared. His suit was immaculate black, his shirtcollar and cuffs crisp white. His greying hair was styled, perfect. Absolutely nothing was out of place.

'Hi!' he said, addressing them in a voice that was loud and confident, assured. When nobody responded,

384

he cupped his hand to his ear. 'Sorry, I didn't quite hear you there. I said Hi!'

A few of them mumbled *Hi!* or *Hello!*

'I've heard of British reserve, but this is ridiculous! Come on! Talk to me!'

This time they all said *Hi!* a bit louder. Harry Waters shouted 'Howdydoody!'

'Hey!' said the man. 'That's more like it! I can tell we're going to get along.'

He pulled over a high seat, like a bar-stool with a backrest, perched himself on it casually. George thought he looked like a chat-show host, or one of those TV comedians, Dave Allen or somebody.

'All right. Now. I'm Doctor Norb Chester, and we're going to be covering a lot of ground in these few days. I'm going to talk you through a whole bunch of stuff. Like how to prioritize. To set your own targets and achieve them. To make your own game plan. How to evaluate the strengths and weaknesses of your customer. To use their needs, their hopes and fears, to your advantage. I'll show you how to get people to open up to you. And we'll look at some of the traps salespeople can fall into. But before we even touch any of that, I want to talk about the most important thing of all. And that's developing the correct state of mind. You've got to go at it with the right outlook from the start. You've got to have PMA.'

Harry Waters gave George a nudge, winked as much as to say *See?*

'And no, I don't mean pre-menstrual agitation.' That brought a laugh. 'Or post-marital anguish.' A bigger laugh. 'What I'm talking about is Positive Mental Attitude.' He pronounced it *additood*. 'If you want to sell, you've got to be up. You've got to be on the ball. You've got to feel *good* about yourself. You've got to be HHT.'

Waters smiled, knowing.

'And that's Happy Healthy Terrific. If I ask how you feel, you tell me *Happy!* I ask you again, you tell me

Healthy! I ask you a third time, you tell me *Terrific!* OK?'

'OK.'

'So how do you feel?'

They chorused. 'Happy!'

'I said, How do you feel?'

'Healthy!'

'Now tell me again, How do you feel?'

'Terrific!'

'That's great! Now we're really starting to get somewhere. We're cooking with gas! And if you're really up, it communicates. People like it. They trust you. And that's the bottom line. You channel that positive energy. PMA *sells*! And I'd like to share with you a little technique I use to get that energy flowing. And it's so simple it's not true!' He stood up from his seat. 'OK, so you get up in the morning and you feel anything but HHT. You know what I'm saying? Like you never even *heard* of PMA! So what do you do? Take a shower, shave, freshen up. Then what? Goddammit, you sing! And you know, a long time ago I used to do TM. That's Transcendental Meditation for those of you who don't know. And I'm not talking bells, beads and kaftans here! This was simply an efficiency-orientated technique, for business purposes. I paid my money, learned my mantra. I even became an instructor. But I want to tell you, I came up with my *own* mantra. And it's stood me in good stead. And I want to pass it on to you. So, are you ready for this initiation?'

One or two of them called out *Yes!*

'All right, repeat after me. Zipadeedooda.'

Some of them repeated it. One or two laughed.

'I'm serious! This little song is the greatest mantra ever invented! It's *pure* PMA! So how many of you know it? Let's have a show of hands. Right, so that's about half. So why don't you sing along with me, and the rest of you can pick it up and join in.'

'Name of God!' said George, as Doctor Norb Chester

sang *Zipadeedooda! Zipadeeay!* and Harry Waters sang along at the top of his voice. George looked around the room. A few others were singing out.

'Fucking hell!' he said, under his breath. Then he cleared his throat and joined in.

Harry was patting his face with aftershave, ready for a night on the town. 'What d'you think of it so far?'

George gave a Morecambe-and-Wise response, made a quacking motion with fingers and thumb. 'Rubbish!'

Harry laughed. 'Really?'

'Och no,' said George. 'It was interesting.'

'You're too much!' Harry mimicked him. *'Ock no!'*

'The singing and that was kind of strange. But once he got down to business it was good. All that psychological stuff about body language, and how to sort of manipulate the situation, how to gain the advantage and keep it. It's all things you don't really think about.'

Harry laughed. 'We'll make a salesman of you yet!'

If they wanted, they could eat in the hotel, but Harry fancied a curry. 'Feel like something a bit spicy!' he said. They found a place that didn't seem too bad. George ordered chicken biryani, the mildest dish on the menu, but even at that his mouth burned.

'That's the stuff!' said Harry. 'Cauterize the old taste buds, eh! Nothing like it for raising a sweat.' He dabbed at his forehead with his paper napkin. 'Good as a sauna!'

They swigged cold lager between mouthfuls, to douse the fire. After his third or fourth glass, George said, 'Funny how all these places have the same wallpaper. With the patterns on it.'

'Red flock.'

'Sounds funny,' said George. 'Flock!'

'Reminds me of a joke,' said Harry. George was beginning to like him. 'Remember Diana Dors?'

'Woh!' said George.

'Well, not too many people know this, but her real name was Diana Fluck.'

'Fluck!'

'Straight up, sure as I'm sitting here.'

'Fluck!'

'Well anyway, after she'd become a big star . . .'

'And you do mean *big*!'

'After she was famous, she came back to her home town. And there was this reception for her, with the Mayor and everybody. And the Mayor decides he's going to introduce her by her real name. But he knows he's on a dodgy number there. One slip and he's in big trouble!'

'Fluck.'

'So he's practising away, making sure he gets it right, you know. He keeps saying *Mustn't forget the "l". Mustn't forget the "l"*. And the big day arrives, and she's up there on the platform with all the guests of honour. And the Mayor steps up to the microphone and says *Ladies and gentlemen, I'd like to introduce Miss Diana Clunt*.'

George was still laughing out in the street. And later, in the pub, he remembered the joke and it set him off again. He even tried telling it to somebody else – a man from the seminar they'd met in the bar. But he got his Flucks and Clunts mixed up and the punchline came out *Cluck*.

'That's even funnier!' said Harry. 'Cluck!'

Outside again, at closing time, Harry waggled his elbows and strutted like a drunk cartoon chicken. 'Cluck!'

'Cluck Cluck!' said George. 'Why did the chicken cross the road?'

'Flucked if I know!'

'To see the Orange Walk. No, sorry, I've got that wrong. It was the apple.'

'To see the apple walk?' Harry was confused.

'No, stupid! Why did the apple cross the road?'

'I don't know. You tell me.'

'To get to the other side!'

'You're pissed you bastard!'

'Pot calling the kettle black!'

'In here,' said Harry, guiding him into a brightly lit doorway.

'What's this place?' said George. The glaring neon hurt his eyes as he read the sign. PLEASURE DOME. *Executive Sauna and Massage Parlour.*

'You'll enjoy it,' said Harry. 'Knock three times and ask for Joe!'

'I don't know if I fancy a sauna,' said George. 'Never had one before.'

'First time for everything.'

'Will it no sober us up?'

'Not at all. Unless you want it to.'

'Be a shame to spend all that money getting bevvied, and then just lose it all.'

'Naa! It'll get your circulation going. Send it all speeding straight to your brain. It's great! Then some doll gives you the once over. I mean, what more does a body want?'

In the sauna, George thought he was dying. It felt like being in an oven, a furnace. The heat burned, scorched his lungs. He could hardly draw breath. And Harry kept laughing like a maniac, pouring water on the hot coals, raising more steam, making things worse. 'Take it!' said Harry, laughing again. 'It's good!' But his head hurt. He was suffocating. He had to get out. Harry called after him. 'Cool off in the dip! You'll love it! Just jump right in!'

He stood at the edge of the small square pool, looking down at the clear water. He tested it with his foot, felt it icy cold. He knew he couldn't go in slowly. It had to be all at once or not at all. He dropped his towel. He sucked in a breath of air. He plunged in.

He thought the shock of it would kill him. He brought up his knees and the water closed over his head. He came up gasping, coughing. He climbed out quickly, stood dripping and shivering as he towelled himself dry.

He had left his clothes in one of the cubicles, number 6. The woman at the desk had told him to go back there when he was ready, and the attendant would be in to look after him. A couch covered with a sheet took up most of the space. There was room to walk round it and not much more. The walls were dark, wine-coloured, the lighting soft. Music played through speakers. He thought he recognized it as the tape they'd used at the seminar.

The door behind him opened and the girl came in. She was younger than he'd expected, pretty but heavily made up. She wore a red T-shirt, shorts of some shiny stuff, satin. Her hair was dyed red-brown, permed out full.

'Hi!' she said and gave him an advertising smile. Her eyes were hard, tired.

'Hello,' he said.

'Like to lie face down?' she said. 'And if you just take off that wet towel we'll replace it with this one.' She draped the fresh towel, a smaller one, neatly over his backside, and she patted it and gave a little laugh.

'I like the music,' he said, for something to say. 'I've heard it before.'

'It's called *Mozart Goes Disco*. Gives the place a bit of class.'

She was working on his shoulders, kneading deep. 'Tight,' she said. 'Tense.' She made little chopping motions down the length of his spine. 'I could help you out with that tension. Bit of quick relief if you want it. Nice little hand job. Help you relax.' As she spoke she lifted off the towel, rested her hand there.

'OK,' he said.

'Special service,' she said. 'Just a small extra charge.'

He turned over on his back.

'I see you're good and ready,' she said. And she was stroking, pulling him, and he closed his eyes, saw the first girl who'd ever, scraggy and dark on a wet night in Arran when he was fifteen, and the memory of it made him come right away.

'You really *were* tight!' she said. She wiped him with the towel, briskly, efficiently. 'You just pay on the way out.' Then she was gone.

He wanted to curl up right there and go to sleep, but he had to move. When he sat up he felt lightheaded, weak. He could smell the girl's scent, a thick sweetness that cloyed. Through it he caught a waft of his own smell. For a moment he thought he was going to be sick, but it passed. He put on his clothes. He paid at the desk. An arm and a leg. He sat and waited for his friend Harry. The room began slipsliding away. He had to get outside, out to the cold air. He only just made it out the door before he boked, honked, threw up on the pavement. Wiping his eyes, he looked up, saw Harry.

'What is man's chief end?'

'Sorry?'

'Into what estate did the fall bring mankind?'

In the morning he felt terrible.

'Happy Healthy Terrific?' said Harry, laughing at him.

George looked at his own face in the mirror. 'Zipadeefuckingdooda.'

Dr Norb Chester was looking serious this morning, solemn.

'I guess some of you probably heard the news on the radio,' he said. 'But for those of you who didn't, something very sad just happened back in my home town. The Big Apple. So good they named it twice. Sure. But it can be a bad place. And last night one of your most famous countrymen, John Lennon, was returning to his apartment in Manhattan when some madman stepped out in front of him with a handgun and blew him away. Now something like that doesn't just leave us unmoved. Because ultimately we're all part of one another. Send not to ask for whom the bell tolls, my friends.' He looked at his watch. 'Perhaps

391

before we start the day's proceedings, you'll join me in a moment's silence as a mark of respect, and to let us reflect on these things.'

After about twenty seconds, he checked his watch again. 'Right,' he said. 'On with the show.'

4

Tam had gone out to buy himself some kind of hat. The cold was getting to him, and now it had started to rain, a thin chilling drizzle. Back home he would have described the day as *dreich*. A good word. No equivalent in English. Or American. And it said how he felt inside. Dreich.

Every store he passed had a radio blasting, and every station was putting out an all-day tribute to John Lennon. He wandered through a continuous medley as one song merged into another, sometimes overlapping in strange montage. Early Beatles like *Twist and Shout* fought with bad-choice-obvious-McCartney songs like *Yesterday* or *Fool on the Hill.* The primal scream of *Mother* shouted down *Imagine. Revolution* drifted into *Give Peace a Chance.* And the broadcasts were shot through with announcements, bulletins, interviews. *Mark Chapman, arrested for the killing, claims he was an admirer of Lennon. 'I understood his words,' he says, 'but not his meaning.'* The cumulative effect on Tam was like tripping out. Acid flash memories. Freakish *déjà vu. Ticket to Ride* took him back to a party at Bird's when he was still at school. Stoned and laughing at some girl who thought he was crazy. Flying. A game of Stations. With *Strawberry Fields* he was blasting into hyperspace with Ruby that first time. *Nothing is real.*

'So do you want the hat or what?'

He had tried it on three times. A big floppy tweed cap, like an oldfashioned bunnet. He had a memory of Lennon wearing something similar. The salesman had decided to hustle.

'Hey, where you gonna get better for five dollars?'

'You're right,' he said. 'I'll take it.'

'On you it looks good,' said the man. 'Hip. Tell you what. You hear stuff like that on the news, you think, Hey, we got to start being nice to people. You know what I'm saying? Like there's enough bad stuff going down. Life's too short. So hey, forget the tax. Just give me a five-spot and it's yours.'

'Thanks,' said Tam, handing over the money.

'Sure,' said the man. 'Have a nice day.'

The ironic bit, given the way Brian had been feeling, was right after the news item on Lennon's death. A few experts had been called in to the studio to make their comments, and one of them was Bird. Spokesperson for the Sixties.

It's the end of an era he announced.

'Can you believe he actually said that?' said Brian, and the voice continued. *I don't think it's too far-fetched to compare it with the death of President Kennedy.*

'Give me a break!'

There's a sense in which both men embodied the aspirations of a generation.

'Listen to him!'

Something died last night in Manhattan. The summer of '67 is finally over.

The piano introduction to *Imagine* faded up.

'Beautiful song,' said Siobhan.

'Written by a multimillionaire capitalist,' said Brian. 'Who just got rubbed out. So what? Big deal! Why all the fuss?'

'It's really upset you, hasn't it?'

'You're right,' he said. 'And I'm fucked if I know why.'

Dr Norb Chester said he had a lot to get through. He had unfolded a chart with a list of headings, in capital letters.

LONG-TERM RELATIONSHIPS VERSUS ONE-SHOT DEALS.
GOOD WILL AND RAPPORT MEAN BUSINESS
ALL FACTS ARE NEGOTIABLE
ZEROING IN FOR THE KILL

George started copying them down.

'We'll be looking at these in a moment,' said Dr
Norb. 'But first I'd like to take time out to say a bit more
about this Lennon business. I mean let's be flexible
here. Something like this happens, you take it on
board. You with me? Now, say you were out on the
road today, trying to find new customers. Well, this
shooting's going to be on people's minds, right? One
way or another they're affected by it. So you bring it
up. Terrible thing. Tragic. Makes you think. All that.
And right away they know you're alert. You're hip to
what's going on. You've got your finger on the pulse.
Plus you're sensitive. And thoughtful. Your approach
is philosophical. People like that. It's reassuring.
You got their trust. So you steer them round
to the uncertainty of it all. Don't know what's round
the next corner. Check out their responsibilities.
What if something happened to them? Heaven forbid.
But you never know. Out of the blue. A good time to
take stock. Plan ahead. Maybe you can help. A policy
geared to their needs. So that's all I'm saying, is be
aware.'

George wrote down *Be Aware*.

'Now, before we hit *Zipadeedooda*, let's pay a little
homage here with a couple of choruses of *Yellow
Submarine*. And remember, *Nothing you can say, but
you can learn how to play the game. It's easy!* All
right, let's get those energies *up*!'

Tam pulled the cap down tight on his head, felt snug.
The Lennonfest continued. In the grocery store he
listened in to two young girls queuing just in front of
him.

'And I just had to go to the Dakota and see for
myself. And you know the whole gate was like covered

with flowers and photos and messages and stuff. It was totally beautiful.'

On the radio, Ronald Reagan was describing the shooting as a Great Tragedy. But No, he said, he would not support the banning of handguns. It was every American's inalienable right to defend himself. However, he *would* call for tougher penalities for crimes committed using firearms.

'Incredible,' said Tam.

'If you ask me,' said the man behind the counter, 'Lennon was executed. Assassinated by the CIA. They figure he's a commie and he influences too many people. So they take this nut Chapman and they brainwash him, program him to do the job. I figure he's just a patsy. Another Lee Oswald.'

'I love conspiracy theories!' said Tam.

'It's like Kennedy,' said the girl who'd been to the Dakota.

'Like Martin Luther King,' said her friend.

'More like Kennedy.'

'Where were you when John Lennon was shot?' said Tam. 'Will we be asking that in twenty years? Will we care?'

'It's taken us twenty years to get from Kennedy to Reagan,' said the man.

'From where to where!' said Tam.

'Who knows where we'll be in twenty years?'

'Quiet!' said the first girl. 'It's John!'

The radio station was playing an exclusive, a scoop. A tape of Lennon's last recorded interview. They stood and listened to the voice – the enduring accent, adenoidal Liverpool, talking to all his friends out there.

I'm saying, How's your relationship going? Did you get through it all? Wasn't the Seventies a drag, you know? Well, here we are. Let's make the Eighties great!

'Isn't that beautiful!' said the girl.

'Totally,' said Tam.

And a huge unexpected sadness welled up in him.

The radio played one of the last songs, *Starting Over*. Feels just like. And he wanted to phone Ruby, just to talk about nothing. Let's make the Eighties great. No chance.

'Did you ever actually *see* the Beatles sir? Back in the olden days?'

'As a matter of fact I did,' said Brian. 'Way back. Before you lot were even thought of. It was just before they were really big. In fact they were sharing top of the bill. With Roy Orbison.'

'Roy who?'

'Don't you know *anything*?'

'You must be dead ancient sir.'

'Feels like it sometimes.' Thirty going on fifty.

'Were they good?'

'Brilliant. I think.'

He'd been the age these kids were now. The same year Kennedy was shot. Take care in your own lives lest you murder not men but principles. He supposed that was what he was trying to say to this lot, getting them to write their own versions of Lennon's *Imagine*. How would *you* like the world to be? Imagine it. Easy if you try. Mostly they wrote about no war. And everybody in a job. And one or two imagined never growing old or having to die.

He had told them about other deaths in passing. Steve Biko. Ali Bhutto. None of it had meant much. But this one had reached them. This was their history, their sense of the times they were living in. Imagine.

At the end of the afternoon, he cleared his corner of the staffroom wall, took down the collage of cuttings he'd pinned up, put them away in his briefcase.

'Not leaving us are you?' said Knox.

'Sorry?'

'A bit like emptying your desk. Looks kind of symbolic, you know. A statement.'

'Just felt like clearing some space.'

'That's what I mean.'

Brian smiled, uncomfortable.

Harry was ready for another night on the town, but George said no.

'Too hot for you was it?'

'Something like that. Feeling rough.'

'Soon fix that,' said Harry. 'Best thing for it. Hair of the dog.'

'No. Thanks all the same.'

'Come on, live a little! I mean you're a long time dead.'

'Just feel like a quiet night.'

'Oh well. Maybe tomorrow then.'

'Maybe.'

'Be your last chance before it's back to the grind.'

'I know.'

'Well, see you later then.'

'Aye.'

'Ock aye the noo!'

When Harry had gone, George felt relieved. He lay down on top of the bed. He knew he ought to phone Mary, but he still felt bad about last night. He didn't want to think about it. He remembered being sick in the street and asking Harry questions from the catechism. Man's chief end. Into what estate. Into what a state. Happy Healthy Terrific. He really should phone.

He got up, sat at the end of the bed, switched on the TV. The news had more about John Lennon, then a warning that the IRA were planning a Christmas bomb blitz on London. A house in Glasgow had been raided, weapons found. He thought about Malcolm, the wedding telegram. All the best. He checked the other channels and there was nothing. *Crossroads. Give us a Clue.* But he didn't want to switch it off. He didn't like the silence, the room. Anything was better. He turned back to the end of the news. A story about a seal pup washed up on some shore. He might as well leave it on this channel, let it drone away. Maybe he would take a shower. Then he would phone.

Ruby called late at night, woke him.

'Funny,' said Tam, bleary. 'I was going to call you.'

'Must be telepathy.'

'Yeah,' he said. 'Oneness.'

'All those years together. Must have done something to our heads.'

'Yeah.'

There was silence, only the telephone's atmosphere, its electronic hum.

'Hello?' he said.

'Hi.' Her voice, familiar.

'Still there?' he said.

'Yeah. Still here.'

More silence.

'So how's everything?' he asked.

'OK. You know. Not good not bad.'

'Sorry I missed your show.'

'Doesn't matter. It went well enough.'

'How's your running?'

'Good. In fact I'm running a race Saturday. Ten k in Central Park.'

'Hey, racing! That's serious!'

'Not really.' She paused. 'When you going back to Scotland?'

'Couple of weeks. Just in time for Christmas.'

'Nice.'

'New Year.'

'Auld Lang Syne.'

This time in the silence he felt the vast dark of the night about them, and how their whole attention was focused down this thin link in space, this open line with its crackle and buzz, its dance of particles in emptiness.

'Listen,' she said.

'I'm listening.'

'I guess it's this Lennon thing. That's why I'm phoning.'

'I know.'

'It's got to me, and it's made me feel sad as fuck, and you're the only one it'll mean anything to.'

'The Dream is Over sort of thing.'

'That's the way it feels,' she said. 'God, it's a shitty time!'

'I bought a cap today,' he said, for no reason. 'A big tweed bunnet.'

'That's nice.'

'Because it was raining.'

'Makes sense.'

'Cost me five dollars.'

'Big spender!'

'And I heard *Starting Over*. It's a good song.'

'From *Double Fantasy*. I bought it.'

'Made me want to call you, like this, say nothing much.'

A hesitancy, intake of breath. 'Listen,' she said.

'I'm listening!'

Another silent beat, wait.

'Fuck it!' she said. 'Let's not lose touch. Maybe when you come back we can meet, talk.'

'If I come back.'

'Whatever.'

'I'd like that.'

'OK. So call.'

'I will. And take care.'

'You too.'

When she'd finally hung up, he still sat a moment or two, the receiver held to his ear, listening to that not quite silence, the hush of static, then a click and bleep, the purr of the dialling tone.

Brian took the day off school, asked Siobhan to phone in and say he was sick.

'Tell them I'm braindamaged. Say I've got an appointment for a frontal lobotomy so I can go on teaching.'

She rang and said he had gastric trouble, vomiting and diarrhoea. 'They won't argue with that,' she said. 'Won't want to know.'

'Clever.'

'Keeps your options open too. You can go back tomorrow, or stay off the rest of the week.'

'Tell you the truth,' he said, 'I don't feel like going back at all.'

'So what else is new?'

'No, but this time I mean it. It's just not what I want to do with the rest of my life.'

'So you're chucking it?'

It was hard, just to come out and say it. 'Maybe I'll stay off till the end of term. That's only a week. They'll survive without me.'

'Then what?'

'Who knows?'

When Siobhan had gone out to lectures, he footered about the house, tried to read, couldn't settle. In the afternoon he took a walk into town and wandered round the bookshops, sat in a café. But he felt disconnected, unable to relax into this unfamiliar freedom. When the pubs opened he went in for a pint, bought a carry-out to take home.

The streetlights were on, the sky dark. As he stood at a streetcorner waiting to cross, he heard, behind the noise of the traffic, the sound of a flute band from an upstairs room. The band were rehearsing, made a few false starts. Then they were up and launched into *The Old Orange Flute*. And it took him back.

'I've got an idea for something to write,' he said to Siobhan later. 'A story.'

'Write? You're going to start writing again?'

'It might not amount to much. I just want to try.'

'That's *brilliant*!' she said. 'What's it about?'

'I'll tell you when it's finished.'

'Stick!'

He made a start on it the same evening, took an hour to write the first paragraph. Siobhan went to bed and he stayed up, worked on through the night. Around six in the morning it was finished, as far as he could tell.

He would read it over again later, type it up, make it look like something.

He yawned and stretched, crossed to the window, looked down into the street. A long time since he'd been up this early, felt this silence. It wouldn't start to get light yet for another couple of hours. A thin rain fell. He watched it drift under the streetlamp, patter on to plastic rubbish bags, left out in a row for collection. A car swished past, moving slow. Then, as if cued by some offstage director, two figures entered, moving in opposite directions. From the left, maybe a workman on his way home from nightshift, bareheaded, collar up against the rain. From the right, a jogger, young man in blue tracksuit, red ski-hat, white gloves. Centrestage, they passed each other without a word. A wave of the hand. A gruff nod. Then they were gone and the street completely empty again, even more silent than before, and Brian left to his blank contemplation. Rain on wet tarmac, plastic sacks.

He turned away, put on the kettle to make tea. In a while he would make breakfast, have it ready, astonish Siobhan.

George stared out at the rain. His first day selling and he wasn't looking forward to it.

'You all right?' asked Mary, from the bed.

'Happy Healthy Terrific,' he said, his voice flat and dull.

'Eh?'

'Positive Mental Attitude.'

'What are you on about?'

'Zipadeedooda.'

'You've been *weird* since you came back from that course, you know that?'

'Aye, I know. You've told me.'

She got up, annoyance in her movements, the way she shoved back the covers. 'So what was it then?'

'What?'

'What was so bad about it?'

401

'It wasn't that. Not the course.'

'What then?'

'Nothing.'

'See? There you are!'

'What?'

She mimicked him. *'Nothing!'* She went through to the kitchen and he followed. 'You didn't even phone while you were away.'

'I meant to.'

'Just never did.' She banged plates down on the table. 'Meanwhile your mother's ringing up and she's climbing the walls because of this carry on with your brother, getting himself arrested again. I mean what am I supposed to say to her?'

'I know. I'm sorry.'

'And you still haven't called her yet.'

'I'll do it tonight.'

'Aye. Well see you do. Now, how about getting the kids up. It's time John was ready for school.'

It wasn't yet light, and he stood for a moment in the kids' room, not switching on the lamp, listening to the sound of their breathing. Above John's bed was a faint glow. He looked closer, saw it was a set of luminous stickers, tiny suns and moons, stars and planets, that shone in the dark. He had never noticed them before. When he switched on the lamp they faded, dulled. He shook the boy gently. 'Come on son. Time to get up.' He smiled at the sleepy puzzlement on the boy's face as he woke, looked out at him. 'That's it,' he said. 'That's the boy.'

In the other corner, Caroline was still sound. No need to wake her just yet. Give her a few more minutes.

'John's just coming,' he said, back in the kitchen. 'I thought the wee one could lie a bit longer.'

'I'll get her up in a minute,' said Mary. 'It's time you were getting a move on yourself.'

'First day in the new job,' he said. 'Mustn't be late for traipsing round doors in the rain. Knock three times, eh? Opportunity knocks. Knock Knock. Who's there?

Insurance man. Insurance man who? Just the insurance man.'

'There you go again.'

'I'm fine. Mister Bluebird's on my shoulder.'

'What?'

'It's the truth,' he said. 'It's actual. Everything is satisfactual.'

'What are you saying?'

'George Wilson, this is your life!'

Central Park, opposite the Dakota, was crammed – 100,000 people singing *Give Peace A Chance* – and it felt like going through a time-warp, back twelve, thirteen years. Tam hadn't intended to come, but here he was. He pushed through the crowds, tried to find his way to the start of the race. The smell of dope hung in the air. He caught a whiff of patchouli oil, and he turned, half expecting, but it was a group of heavy-metal freaks, bikers in leather jackets studded *Motorhead, AC-DC*.

Then it was all dispersing, breaking up, and he'd drifted across to another corner of the park, near Columbus Circle, and he saw a few runners warming up, followed them round to where the rest were massed for the start.

Up on a platform, Mayor Koch was making a speech, voice crackling through loudspeakers. He was there to start the race off, officially, ceremonially. But in deference to what had happened, he wouldn't use a pistol. Instead he would hit wooden clappers against each other, clack them together.

All right?

All right Ed! Way to go!

A countdown. Get set. Then the quick loud crack to start, a roar from the runners, break and surge, and the leaders charging so fast down past where Tam stood.

Somewhere far back in the bobbing pack he caught sight of Ruby in a bright red sweatshirt. He waved and called her name and she turned but didn't see him.

403

Then she was past him, carried along by the stream. He called again, kept on waving anyway. Way to go.

5

Brian's letter, a fat package, arrived as Tam was trying to get organized, ready to leave. A suitcase. His old hitch-hiking rucksack. His flute and sax packed carefully in their kitbag. He would keep that with him as handluggage. Hard cases or not, he didn't want to trust them to airport handling.

He tore open the envelope. A typescript, a few newspaper cuttings, a scribbled letter.

> *Hello there Tam!*
>
> *Hope you're still at this address – culled from a quick note you sent a couple of years back which I didn't answer, for which Sorry but you know how it goes. Mea culpa.*
>
> *Daft way to start a letter. If it's not the right address, you won't be reading this anyway, so no point – I'm simply consigning it to the void. Rule one, writing assumes reader.*
>
> *I'm gibbering already. It's been a strange time.*
>
> *Why write now? (Right now!)*
>
> *This Lennon death I suppose. Just one more killing. But what the music meant. Believed in something, didn't we? Or was it just being young? The media reruns, old black and white footage, back 20 years, looking at two decades. Our times. Hello there.*
>
> *This package is a time capsule. Where we are now. A story to take you back. Newspaper snippets. Bad about Paki. Just one more killing. I met him, couple of years ago. And Malcolm more recently. (He met the girl that blew up Eddie Logan. Small world!) George I suppose still the same normal. Rightwinging it, happy with Mrs T. (The Lodges voted unanimous* NO *in last year's*

Referendum. Made me vote YES. Meant nothing. In the end brought down Labour, let this lot in. Ironic or what?)

Hear Bird sometimes on radio/TV. Eighties man. Artspeak – Markethead. You used to think he was some kind of Sarastro. Turned out a fat old Papageno like the rest. Tying the cat to the bed.

I hope you haven't sold out. Still making music. Hope Ruby is well. I've been with the same girl, Siobhan, for 3 years now. (Hasn't seen through me yet!) No, but she's great, that's all.

Write if you feel like it, tell me how things are.

> *All the best*
> *Brian*

Tam put the letter back in its envelope with the cuttings, the story. Something to read on the flight. He stuffed it in the kitbag with his instruments, made one last check that he hadn't forgotten anything. Things he didn't need, things that belonged to Ruby, he had packed in a big cardboard box. Her father would come and collect it, take it into storage. Now the place looked just the way it had when they moved in. Not theirs. No sign they had ever been. Except for the potted plants. No point in leaving them to shrivel. He ran water into a basin, placed them in it to drink. He smiled at the thought of them humming away in the empty flat.

Now. That was everything. Make sure he had the absolute essentials. Tickets. Passport. Money. Pick up the kitbag. Everything else was extra. He took a book from Ruby's box, a paperback *Bhagavad Gita*, shoved it in his pocket. He had called a cab, would wait for it downstairs. Now. Last look round. Out the door. Go.

The kitbag sent the metal detector berserk.

'What you got there?' asked the security man.

On the X-ray the dismantled instruments, their

shadow-images overlapping, showed up like some complex and dangerous mechanism, a space-age gatling.

'A flute and a saxophone,' he explained.

Weapons. This machine kills.

'Open it up and lemme see.'

The man took out each separate bit of first the flute then the sax. He squinted along the barrels, pulled out the cleaning rods, cloths. He unscrewed the endpiece on the head of the flute, poked inside. He prodded the velvet padding in the two black cases.

'OK,' he said, grudging, and left Tam to put it all back together.

'Thanks.'

On the plane he managed to stuff the kitbag in the overhead compartment, remembering to take out the letter from Brian.

His seat was by a window and the two beside him were empty. If they stayed that way he might be able to lie out.

A taperecorded spiel came over the sound system.

At this time we would like to familiarize you with the safety and comfort features on this aircraft.

They always said *At this time.* Why not *Now*? The stewardess was miming a series of actions to the tape. *Emergency Exits. Oxygen Masks. Automatic. Life Jackets. In the Event.* The smile never wavered. She deserved applause, roses. A great performance. Then she had sat down and it was *Fasten Seat Belts Extinguish All Smoking Materials Traytables Up Seatbelts Upright Locked.* Then smooth bland muzak to comfort and reassure. All normal.

Starting to move. Look out the window. Turning, see the other planes ahead, the queue coming up behind. Then out and taxi-ing, picking up speed, silver waterdrops on the glass streaked back, and the bit Tam loved, faster and faster, the blast and roar, hurtling, then the tip up and lift off, pushed back in the seat, the sudden fairground bellyflip, the rise and soar into the night sky.

Tam laughed, a surge of sheer joy. The plane banked over the city, all of it seen from up here a great silent shimmer of light. Higher again the plane tilted, righted itself, and he saw further off another town, smaller, and another beyond that, galaxies floating in the immense night.

He woke up, groggy, when they brought round the food. But he couldn't face eating it. The smell put him off. He sat up, plugged his headphones into the socket in the armrest, read through the programme for the audio channels. Rock. Jazz. Easy Listening. The classical channel featured *The Magic Flute of James Galway,* and the two men in front of him happened to be discussing it. He had taken them for academics, English. They had their headphones on and were talking at each other in that too-loud way, oblivious.

'Not sure if I like Galway,' said one.

'Me neither,' said his friend. 'All that hot syrupy vibrato poured over lovely cool themes.'

Tam smiled. Galway should worry. A technique he could only marvel at, and something more that came from the heart. He had started out in a flute band in Belfast.

Tam suddenly remembered Brian's story, pulled the envelope out of the net pocket in front of him. He re-read the letter, then had a look at the cuttings. Willie Johnston leaving the field in Argentina. The result of the Referendum, huge banner headline reading NO. An article on arrests made in Glasgow, linked to IRA bombings. Across the top, Brian had scribbled *Malcolm?* Finally the piece about Paki's death. Tam read it, felt things shift, out of kilter. On his first trip with Ruby, they had been at a party, and someone had rammed a plastic bag over Paki's head. Tam had been terrified. Had he actually been seeing this future? Too strange to think about. He put the cuttings and the letter back in the envelope, settled to read the story.

I'm standing at this streetcorner, waiting to cross the road, and the music stops me. I hear it through a lull in the traffic noise, a flute band rehearsing in an upstairs room. And back it takes me, the best part of twenty years.

There were four of us. We all lived in the same street, were in the same class at school – the last year before we moved on to secondary and went our separate ways. Somehow word had got round that the flute band was recruiting, and that lessons were free. So we all turned up together one Wednesday night.

'Funny it's a Catholic school, eh?' said Shuggie.

'Imagine!' said Jim.

'Funny right enough,' said Bob.

'Aye,' I said. 'Mental.'

We crossed the empty playground. We could hear the thump and batter of the drums, the flutes piercing the night air with a tune we knew, The Protestant Boys.

'Ea-sy!' shouted Shuggie, and we headed for the doors.

Were there really three doors side by side, each under its own arch? Like the three doors to the temple faced by Tamino in The Magic Flute? *Or is that something I've invented, grafted on? Either way, it seems almost too neat. But no, I remember. Three doors, and above each arch a word carved in the stone. Not* WISDOM, REASON *and* NATURE, *but* GIRLS, BOYS *and* INFANTS. *The door that was open, then, was the middle one, appropriately enough, the one marked* BOYS.

We pushed it open, jostled and shoved our way in.

'Right!' said the janitor, coming out of his cubby-hole. 'Hold it right there! OK, what do yis want?'

'Flute band,' said Shuggie, gallus as you like.

'We're here for a lesson,' said Jim.

'All right well.' The janitor was grudging. 'Just keep the noise down.'

The flutes trilled. The drums thudded and rapped. A cymbal crashed.

'Right enough,' said Shuggie. 'It's that quiet here!'

'None of your cheek son!' The janitor showed them in to a classroom. 'Wait here. The man'll be down to see you shortly. And don't touch anything!'

'Crabbit auld bastard!' said Shuggie when he'd left them.

Bob had already sat down at one of the desks, was lifting the lid and peering inside. Shuggie saw me looking at a plaster Madonna and he came across and picked it up. 'She must be a Rangers supporter, eh? Wearing the right colour anyway!'

He turned it over, saw the base was chalky. He tried to use it to write something on the blackboard. But the line it made was too faint and scratchy. So he took a bit of blue chalk instead, wrote RANGERS FC on the board. 'Rangers Fuck Celtic!' he said.

'Christsake!' said Jim. 'You'll get us all hung!'

'Shut it!' said Shuggie. 'Shitebag!'

'We're here to learn music!' said Jim.

'Ach!' Shuggie used the blue chalk to write something on the base of the statue. Then he put it back in its place, but turned it to face the wall.

When he wasn't looking, I picked up the statue again. He had written RFC on it. I rubbed it off, smearing the letters. I spat on my fingers and wiped the blue dust off them. I turned the statue the right way round.

'Wish this guy would hurry up,' said Shuggie, restless.

The door opened and a big man in a dark suit came in. 'Right!' he said, and we all jumped, felt caught. He pulled over a chair and sat astride it. 'So you want to learn the flute?' He took out the parts of a small wooden flute from his inside jacket pocket, pieced it together and played a single note. 'Great wee instrument this.'

He played a tune I recognized, Lark in the Clear Air, slow and haunting, and he moved from that into something faster, a jig. Then he was playing No

Surrender, *and it lifted us up, had us stamping in time, beating out the rhythm.*

When he'd finished he laughed, said 'Who wants a shot then?'

'Me!' said Shuggie, shoving forward.

'I've heard of bluenoses,' said the man. 'And folk wi green fingers. But I see you're a bluefinger!'

Shuggie wiped his chalky hand on the seat of his denims. The man laughed again and handed him the flute. 'Nice and easy,' he said. 'Same way you blow across a bottle.'

Shuggie blew into the mouthpiece, spat spray.

'Not so hard,' said the man. 'And more across it. Make your mouth like a wee half smile.'

Shuggie tried again, made no headway, got impatient and blew harder.

'Got to take it easy,' said the man. 'Here, let somebody else try.' Shuggie handed it back, shoved it at him. 'Hey come on!' said the man. 'It's no just a dod of wood this!'

Bob tried next, was shaky and hesitant, made no sound at all.

'Remember the wee half smile,' said the man. 'The fancy name for it's embouchure. Keep the lip tight. So if I say tighten your embouchure, that means less of your lip!' He laughed at his own joke, but Bob still struggled.

'OK,' said the man. 'Good try.' And he handed the flute to Jim.

Shuggie had lost interest, stood across the room, kicking at the leg of a chair. 'Come on!' said the man. 'Behave yourself or beat it!'

Jim blew into the flute and almost had it. A bit high and breathy, but nearly a note.

'We're getting there,' said the man. Then it was my turn.

As he handed me the flute, I noticed the ring on his finger was masonic, and I wondered if he knew Bob's father who was something in the Lodge.

I raised the flute to my lips. It smelled faintly of nicotine. I tried to remember everything the man had said. The lip. The wee half smile. I blew and it came all at once, astonished me, a full clear note.

'Perfect!' said the man.

'Magic!' I said. And it was. Pure magic.

The moment comes back to me down almost twenty years, as I stand here in another city, waiting to cross the road, and listening to a flute band.

I never did learn the instrument, join the band. The way things happen.

Bob's father got him the use of the flute. But he made nothing of it. Bob too is now something-in-the-Lodge. Works as a draughtsman. Is married. Has kids.

Shuggie took up drumming. Was good at it. Marched in the band. Left school at fifteen and joined the army. Was blown to bits in Belfast in 1969.

Jim stuck with it, plays jazz. Married an American. Lives in New York.

The different directions we took.

I ended up teaching, until perhaps today, until maybe this moment as I stand and listen to the flute band rehearsing in an upstairs room. Ragged and out-of-tune but hammering it out good style.

The traffic has cleared. I could cross the road now but I stand still and listen.

Listen.

Tam had missed the inflight movie, slept through it. No great loss. Brian's story had slipped from his lap on to the floor and he picked it up, laid it on the empty seat beside him. The headphones were still hanging loose round his neck. He put them on, turned to the classical channel. Never mind those two in front, now asleep, heads drooped and nodding. He would listen to Galway. Taste that hot vibrato. Savour those cool themes. Galway had once had a dream or a vision of himself playing and a huge giant Buddha filling the whole stage.

Tam took the paperback *Gita* from his pocket. It fell open naturally where Ruby had flattened the pages, bent back the spine. There were passages she had marked, underlined in pencil. *Fire cannot burn the soul. Water cannot drench it.* And further down the same page. *Be thou an instrument.*

He rubbed his face, dry and tired. He breathed deep, the stale recirculated air. The music came through his headphones, through interference and crackling static, that flute still magic, pouring out glorious Mozart.

He pushed up the little plastic blind over his window and was startled at the sun's rays streaming in. *Die Strahlen der Sonne vertreiben die Nacht.* He pressed his head close to the glass, to see. They were flying into the sun. The great red ball was up over the Atlantic, hurrying to meet them halfway across.

ITS COLOURS THEY ARE FINE
by Alan Spence

First published to wide critical acclaim in 1977, *Its Colours They Are Fine* has since become a classic of Glaswegian fiction. Its three interlinked stories cover every aspect of life in the city, vividly evoking the slums and its inhabitants, both young and old, Catholic and Protestant, the hopeful and the disillusioned. The first section of the book has been hailed as 'the definitive recreation of a Glasgow childhood'. It describes a violent upbringing in the slums which translates in early adulthood to brawls at dance halls, the bustle and pomp of an Orange march, a Catholic Wedding and finally to the quiet and tranquillity amongst the exotic plants and statues in the Kibble Palace.

Alan Spence's writing throughout is powerful and moving, full of poetry, and with an imaginative life which transforms the book's bleak urban setting into something warm, tender and humorous.

'The finest piece of Scottish fiction of the Seventies . . . The title story, which tells of an Orange march through the city, has the sort of exuberant creativity Scott Fitzgerald displayed in stories like "May Day".'
Allan Massie, *Independent*

'Poetic, affectionate and moving stories of Glasgow street life. Deprivation, despair, casual violence and religious bigotry go hand-in-hand with pride, warmth, humour and deep humanity.'
David Sinclair, *Sunday Times*

'Beautifully observed and directly written stories of working-glass Glasgow life . . . in each story there is a shining and unforced truthfulness which is very attractive.'
Edwin Morgan, *Twentieth Century Scottish Classics*

0 552 13012 5

THAT RUBEN'S GUY
by John McGill

'A broth of wit and machismo . . . The Glasgow idiom froths and invigorates these tales.'
Independent

Number 30, a typical Glasgow slum tenement of the 1950s, is home to sixteen families. On each of its landings and behind each of its doors there are characters who, through these hilarious and sometimes poignant stories, achieve mythic status.

There's Young Jessica the dog-biter and Wee Pete, the scruffy little boy who worships Rubens. There's Sniffer O'Hara, who embarks on a quest for gold, and Big Jessie Brass whose affair with the Man with the Painted Heid goes down in legend. And there's Freddy, the pseudo-Italian fish-fryer, and Tam Burke, the legless 'war-hero' – object of fascinated pity to all the ladies on the stair. These and many more inhabit the crumbling tenement of *That Rubens Guy*, a world tinted with the magic of their spirit and strength of character.

'Considerable vitality . . . manages to turn the sixteen families into a collection of fabulous figures, each extraordinary in their own way.'
Observer

'Liberally dosed with The Patter, McGill has set out to entertain, to amaze and occasionally to shock . . . vivid and memorable.'
Scotsman

'A compelling delight . . . The Broons and Brendan Behan rolled into one'
The List

0 552 13760 X

Just You Wait and See
by Stan Barstow

'Mr Barstow's strength is in the resolute honesty of his depiction of how people feel. He is a writer you can trust'
The Scotsman

Set in a closely-knit industrial community at the beginning of the Second World War, Stan Barstow's novel tells the story of young Ella Palmer and her family. Ella wants to marry, but her affections are torn between the solid, dependable qualities of Walter, a local butcher, and the romantic enticements of Mr Strickland, a visiting tradesman with knowledge of the world beyond the village. But there are conventions to be obeyed, and with the onset of war Ella finds she cannot delay much longer.

Against this background, Ella sifts through the vagaries of her physical and emotional needs and weighs up the value of two different kinds of love. The circumstances in which Ella makes her final choice provide a poignant and fulfilling conclusion to Stan Barstow's perfectly crafted novel, which is sure to win him new readers.

'A simple tale, told with great clarity and never a wrong note struck'
Hilary Bailey, *The Guardian*

(*GIVE US THIS DAY*, the moving sequel to *JUST YOU WAIT AND SEE* is also available from Black Swan)

0 552 99341 7

BLACK SWAN

A SELECTED LIST OF NOVELS FROM
CORGI AND BLACK SWAN